# CHEAT

BY RICHARD LAWS

First published 2023 by Five Furlongs

ISBN 978-1-7397026-2-5 (Paperback)

With special thanks to trainer Ollie Pears.

Cover photography © T Fullum

# One

*Ebor Day, York, Wednesday 21st August 2002*

Jack Payne was having a perfect day. Since Hugs Dancer had won a hard-fought Ebor earlier in the afternoon, a permanent grin had graced his face. Once the fine bay gelding had been confirmed the winner, Jack spent the next twenty minutes making his way around the betting ring, visiting each of the bookmakers with whom he had backed the James Given trained five-year-old. He took his time, strolling between the bookmakers, squeezing every ounce of enjoyment from his victory over the old adversary.

Having watched Hugs Dancer win a mile and a half race at Carlisle back in June, Jack had been so impressed with the gelding's versatility he had backed him solidly throughout the next eight weeks for the Ebor, even though he knew the horse needed to win again in order to rise high enough in the handicap to qualify for York's premier handicap in August. That had meant his ante-post price for the Ebor was just what Jack liked – outrageously large!

Hugs Dancer had duly won a quality Goodwood long-distance handicap in late July, qualifying for the Ebor with a flyweight. Backing the gelding before he was qualified to run in the Ebor, Jack had managed to acquire a range of odds of between 66/1 and 100/1 about him during the countdown to one of the biggest betting races of the year.

Jack's hopes took a nosedive the day before the Ebor, once the declarations revealed Hugs Dancer was drawn in stall twenty of the twenty horses, right on the far rail. As the race got underway, his experienced jockey, Dean McKeown, confidently angled the five-year-old across from his impossible starting position to sit in a share of fourth, one horse-width off the inside rail. Over two furlongs out, Hugs Dancer loomed large on the outside of the leaders and Jack's heart had jumped in his chest. He knew the horse would see out the mile and six furlongs really well, having previously won over much further. Hugs Dancer hit the front at the furlong pole and determinedly held off every challenger to cross the finishing line three-quarters of a length ahead of the huge field. His forty-two-year-old pilot punched the air, and Jack had gone hoarse as he wildly screamed both horse and jockey home.

Depending on the bookmaker's demeanour when paying him out, sixty-year-old Jack would modify his behaviour. His yellow-toothed grin was provided to those who remained jovial. A smirk was delivered to those layers who were grumpy or complained, and dead-pan stoicism was reserved for a few who took exception to him ruining their profit margins for the day, and possibly their month. It was always sensible to know the sort of bookie you were dealing with before you approached their pitch. A self-satisfied smirk could turn into a thump at a later date if you made the wrong layer feel inadequate.

In fact, as he and his bulging Gladstone bag full of cash exited the turnstile at the back of the racecourse he was hard-pushed to think of a better day's gambling. The sun was shining, he'd won close to two-hundred-thousand pounds, and all of the bookmakers – even the tight-fisted ones - had paid up. Winning his Malton training yard in a high stakes card game had been memorable, but there was something even more fulfilling when taking a bunch of craggy old bookmakers to the cleaners.

Jack lugged his Gladstone bag stuffed full of cash up a set of concrete steps that led to the car park. Once he was dodging between the long lines of expensive cars that proudly and ostentatiously lined the Owners and Trainers Car Park, he allowed his mind to wander. He idly wondered what the collective noun for a bunch of losing bookmakers would be… perhaps a 'Grumble', or maybe a 'Brassic'… yes, he liked that... a Brassic of bookmakers.

Half-way across the grass paddock that doubled as a

car park, Jack drew to a halt, swapped his bag to his left hand and wiped the sweat from his brow. The wads of cash were heavier than he'd imagined. It would be a relief to get onto the A64 with the top down on his little convertible and stash this money safely under lock and key.

Making sure he'd got his bearings right, Jack headed downhill, dodging between several lines of cars, pleased when he spotted his old MG parked between two much larger and more modern cars that had none of the panache of his own.

His daughter, Mary, her husband Barney, and of course his little grandson, William, would be beside themselves, he told himself. The thought lit up an uncontrollably huge smile that he enjoyed for a long moment.

Whether it was the feeling of joy coursing around his body, his thoughts of his family, and how the money would make their lives easier, or simply the heat of the sun, Jack looked up, shook himself from his reverie and realised he'd just made a mistake. And it was a big one.

There were three of them. Serious men you could spot a mile away if you knew what to look for. In a car park bereft of other racegoers, they only had eyes for Jack. His smile soon faded as a second, longer glance confirmed their identities. Jolted into an instant assessment of his situation, Jack evaluated the few options available to him.

His decision made, he crouched, then darted through two lines of shiny vehicles, keeping low to the ground. After passing half a dozen car noses, he doubled back between a Jaguar and a Mercedes and fell to his knees. Quickly choosing the Jaguar because of the size of its wheel arch, he thrust the Gladstone bag between the tyre and the car's chassis, making sure it was firmly wedged. Cursing his aging, aching body Jack pushed himself up to a crouching position, took a quick glance around, then straightened and walked out into the open to face the men.

'There he is, 'Jack heard the smallest of the figures call out sarcastically, 'There's Jack. There's the little cheat.'

# Two

*Sunday, 8th May 2022*

It wasn't the first time Will had woken to the sound of fists hammering at his front door. The banging was tiresome, rather than worrying. It only became concerning when the insistent thumps resulted in the sound of heavily booted strangers climbing the stairs and two members of the local constabulary entering his bedroom unannounced.

Being a student house, it was fairly normal for him, or one of the other two lads he lived with, to have noisy callers. And being students, a thump was as good as a knock. Being bereft of a current girlfriend, Will rarely entertained callers at present, especially on a Sunday morning after a night out with his flatmates, so when the noise downstairs abated he turned over, tried to ignore his small but persistent headache, and did his best to fall back to sleep.

He was well on the way to achieving his goal when his bedroom door opened and a stern, female voice asked, 'Mr Payne? Mr William Payne?'

Shuffling up onto his elbows, and through bleary eyes Will examined a rotund, bearded policeman and an older, rather lean policewoman with heavily lined features. He frowned indignantly at them.

'What the… How did you… What do you…?' he protested, his sleepy brain failing to operate in concert with his vocal chords.

'All excellent questions, Sir,' the policewoman quipped whilst her eyes travelled over the clothes-strewn floor then up to the bedroom walls. Several large, unframed paintings jostled for position with a multitude of pencil sketches on one wall, whilst opposite, a colourful mural of a horse in full flight blocked out most of the grubby cream wallpaper. The image demanded attention and the policewoman gazed at it for several seconds. In the corner stood a group of three sizeable

5

sculptures of human torsos in white plaster. The policewoman caught herself, noting there was a distinct lack of books, posters, or games consoles – the standard contents of a male student's bedroom – although a closed laptop was just visible on a set of drawers, partly obscured by drawing pads, brushes and several half-squeezed tubes of what she assumed were paint. She returned her gaze to the long-haired boy in the single bed who was gawking at her.

'One of your housemates let us in,' she explained, 'I wonder if you could get dressed?'

Suddenly aware he'd fallen into bed naked in the early hours of the morning, Will collected his duvet around him. The policewoman sniffed disapprovingly at him as he attempted to sit up in bed without revealing any more than his bare shoulders. He noticed for the first time that behind his uninvited guests both his housemates had gathered just outside his door and were watching the proceedings with big silly grins on their faces.

'Is this a wind-up?' he ventured, flashing them a hopeful smile. The policewoman returned him a withering look that told him he should think harder.

What had he done last night? It was just a normal Saturday evening over the road at the local pub, nothing much happened, he'd not had *that* many drinks… Oh, hold on…. All three of them were celebrating passing the second year of their university courses. There was singing… and complaints, *lots* of complaint from local residents that had rained down on himself and his two student pals, Arthur and Freddie, during their flamboyant rendition of Summer Nights on their way to and from the Wallsend Indian takeaway.

'Can you confirm you are William Lester Payne, a second-year student at Newcastle University and son of Mr Barney Payne, of Malton, North Yorkshire?' the female officer inquired.

Will blinked hard, 'Errm…Yes, that's me, I'm studying Fine Art, but really, I don't think…'

'Very good, Sir,' interrupted the policewoman, 'If you could get dressed please, you need to come with...'

From behind the policemen, a deep, booming voice preceeded his friend, Freddie, entering the room, 'Oy, Winda!' he called over to Will, 'Aww, Man! Whit's the crack, like? Is this for real?'

Freddie Collier strode confidently into the room wearing a shabby, scuffed-up old silk dressing gown that only just covered his buttocks and teetered on the right side of decency when viewed from the front. Born and bred in Gateshead, Newcastle, Freddie had a strong Geordie accent and a winning smile. He was also a fiercely intelligent poet, comic, philosophy student, and earned a few quid on the side as a part-time magician and actor. At six foot four inches and built like a slab of concrete, Freddie was unmissable. Physically substantial and always vocal, he treated life as one gregarious riot. In stark contrast, Will was smaller in stature and preferred a wary, conservative approach to life. Their strong friendship bewildered some, but both men found themselves oddly better balanced when in each other's company.

Freddie also had a habit of mis-reading situations. His direct, and somewhat brash approach wasn't to everyone's taste and sometimes, he was slow to appreciate this until it was too late.

Placing both hands on his hips, Freddie inspected the policeman and woman by arching a questioning eyebrow above a dramatically bulging eye. Will stared bug-eyed at his friend and shook his head silently at him, in a desperate attempt to keep Freddie quiet, but as was so often the case, it was too late…

'Have you two come straight from a fancy dress party, like?' queried Freddie with a straight face.

The policewoman's shoulders visibly sagged.

'And you are?' she sighed resignedly.

'Frederick Johansson Collier,' smiled Freddie.

'And who is this,' the policewoman asked, pointing at Will.

'Winda. Winda Payne,' replied Freddie innocently.

The bearded policeman stared dully at Freddie, possibly having missed the joke, although Will doubted this was the case. He fervently hoped that Freddie wasn't about to explain his university nickname to his unimpressed audience. He was used to rescuing his friend from these sorts of situations, but on this occasion, Freddie got there first.

'Mmmm… Tough audience, man,' Freddie noted ruefully, tugging down at the hem of his bathrobe as if suddenly aware he was a little underdressed to be receiving guests.

'Can I ask why you need to speak with Will?' asked a very different, authoritative voice from the open door to the bedroom. It was Arthur, another good friend, also a second year student, studying accountancy and business, and the third and final occupant of their house. Will was thankful for Arthur's smooth Scottish accent, and for its serious tone. As one, the uniformed duo turned to inspect all five feet ten inches of the pale-faced student who was leaning against the doorjamb, blinking at them through round spectacles. Will took the opportunity to grab at his trousers and t-shirt from the bedroom floor and pulled them on under his duvet.

'Who…' started the male policeman.

'Arthur McClarty…' Arthur said, pre-empting the policemen's query, '… and yes. That *is* my real name. So what's Will done this time?'

'You're all students here in Newcastle?' asked the policewoman, eyeing each of them in turn.

Having received nods, affirmative murmurs, and noticing Will was now on his feet wearing jeans and t-shirt, she ordered Freddie and Arthur out of the room. Her associate herded the two students onto the landing whilst ignoring Freddie's claim that, 'I am Will's responsible adult, and have every right to stay with him!'

The policeman growled something under his breath at Freddie and closed the door behind him and Arthur with a heavy-handed finality.

The policewoman took in Will's five foot eight, lean, yet muscular figure. The only obvious clue to his student status was a shock of long curly hair that he now swept back out of his eyes, allowing it to settle onto his shoulders. He hardly towered over the lady police officer, but she found it necessary to draw herself up to her full height and adopt a softened expression.

Damn it, thought Will. It's *that* type of visit.

'Apologies for this early morning call, but I have to inform you your father has been the subject of a serious assault...'

'Oh, right,' Will responded flatly. He grimaced, but the policewoman got the impression this news irked him, rather than causing him any distress or anxiety.

'Your father is in hospital and very ill,' she pressed, keen to ensure Will was in no doubt as to the seriousness of the situation.

Will sat down on the bed, opened a bedside drawer, made a rudimentary selection, and started to pull on a pair of brightly coloured socks. As his arm muscle tensed, the policewoman noted a small tattoo on his arm; a horse rearing on its hind legs.

'Malton constabulary has been trying to contact you since Saturday morning. They even tried calling you from your father's phone.'

'Yeah, I never answer calls from numbers I don't recognise, and certainly not from my father,' Will told her matter-of-factly as he straightened the toe of his sock, 'I haven't spoken to him in almost three years.'

The policewoman's face hardened, 'He's in intensive care having been badly beaten by all accounts.'

She paused, eventually emitting a small sigh, 'You don't appear to be interested in how he's doing, Mr Payne?'

Will stared down at the worn burgundy carpet between his feet and a familiar rush of angry indignation swept from his gut, up through his windpipe and stuck at the top of his throat.

'I washed my hands of my father when I left home,' said Will, lifting his chin to stare grimly at the policewoman, 'He's a bad tempered alcoholic. Whatever he's landed himself in is entirely his own lookout and not my concern.'

The policewoman sucked on her bottom lip for a moment, watching Will pull on a pair of dirt encrusted trainers, stand in front of a wall mirror and run a brush through his knotted hair.

'I now see why I was sent here,' she murmured.

Will spun around.

'Yeah, well I'm sorry to disappoint you with my lack of empathy for my crappy father,' Will fired back.

The policewoman took a breath and her eyes settled onto the indignant Will with a dispassionate professionalism.

'Mr Payne, we are here to take you back to Yorkshire. Malton to be exact,' she said sternly, pausing to ensure Will had understood. He rolled his eyes and she continued, 'Our colleagues in Malton wish to interview you in regard to your possible involvement in your father's assault…'

Will didn't process any more of the policewoman's words, even though she seemed at pains to continue babbling about something. He became aware of his gut twisting and squeezing as a familiar pain he thought he'd conquered, was suddenly resurrected. He'd pushed his loathing deep down inside himself years ago, and buried it when he'd left the farmhouse, the Manor Stud Stables, and his father. And he'd got on with his life… without a family.

Wherever those feelings had been hiding, they were now being wrung out. Every drop of hatred for his father was coursing through him. He felt a spasm lurch upward from his gut, into his stomach, and set off a chain reaction that sent scorching bile up into the back of his throat. Will gritted his teeth and swallowed so hard his eyes began to water. This had the effect of making the policewoman fall silent. Having mistakenly assumed he was crying, her expression softened once again. If she knew the real reason for him blinking away tears, Will thought, that empathetic look would soon vanish.

'Are you okay, Mr Payne?' she asked quietly.

Will almost laughed, but managed to purse his lips and turn away. Of *course* he wasn't okay. Who would be! He was about to be forcibly dragged back to Malton. Back to his selfish, conceited, alcoholic father and a chapter of his life that held nothing but bad memories. No, he wasn't okay... he was downright angry, and sickened to his core.

He swung around to face the policewoman, studied her for a moment, and finally... shrugged to signal he had accepted his fate. Judging by the uncompromising look on the policewoman's face, there was little point in protesting. He was going to be hauled back to Malton, whether he liked it or not.

## Three

By early afternoon, Will was sitting uncomfortably on a grubby red plastic moulded chair in the foyer of Malton Police Station. During the two hour drive from Wallsend he'd employed a combination of complaining, cajoling, and eventually, pleading – without any noticeable effect on his police escort. They hadn't wavered from their task for a moment. He'd even painstakingly pointed out that Malton was the very last place he would want to be, as he detested his father and had actively sought to be hundreds of miles away from him. This hadn't had the effect he was anticipating, as the two policemen had shared a knowing glance and told him to save that information for their colleagues in Malton.

Having once been a grand old house, Malton police station boasted high ceilings, but was chilly, dusty, and surprisingly quiet, even for a Sunday. Once they'd deposited him in the care of the less than impressed Duty Sergeant, his two north-eastern chaperones departed without a word or looking back. Will had just begun to reflect on how he was going to get back up to Newcastle, assuming the authorities came to their senses, when a door opened behind him and a voice he half-recognised called out his name.

'William! It's good to see you. Come on through.'

Will turned and squinted at the squat, balding, middle-aged man dressed in jeans and a short-sleeved shirt who was smiling broadly. Despite his hairline receding another inch, and acquiring the beginnings of a double chin, Will instantly recognised Patrick, or rather, Pat, his father's best friend, or as he was referred to in this environment, DC Patrick Higgins.

'Er… Hello?' Will replied a little more cautiously than he'd intended. His uncertainty didn't appear to affect Pat's demeanour. The policeman maintained his smile and appeared genuinely happy to see him. Will followed him into a large square room dominated by two rows of cluttered desks and Pat gestured for him to take a seat beside one of them. The DC chose to half-sit, half-lean against a desk opposite him.

'It's been a long time, eh?' Pat said, smiling pleasantly, crossing his arms, and looking Will up and down, 'Three years and a few months, I guess. So how are you getting along, William?'

Pat had been a regular visitor to the Payne household during his childhood. He'd been a fair apprentice jockey in his day, but a penchant for beer and pies had cut his race riding career short in double-quick time. Luckily the police force had been less picky than the trainers looking for a light-weight apprentice to partner their racehorse. Will had no axe to grind with Pat; after all, he was his godfather. However, Pat's bond with his father was immutable, and as a result Will had kept him at arm's length during his teenage years.

'Everything was peachy until this morning,' Will replied grumpily.

Pat stroked the bristles on his chin as he contemplated how best to handle Will. He'd grown up with Barney, the lad's father, and they remained firm friends. Racehorse trainer and son-in-law of the infamous Jack Payne, Barney had… well, not to put too fine a point on it, Will's father had always been there for him. Ever since Malton junior school, they had been best friends - around fifty years. Even so, Barney's latest request had been the closest he'd ever come to a point-blank refusal. If it wasn't for the fact that Barney had looked so busted up and vulnerable…

Pat shook the image from his mind. He had to concentrate. He had to get this *right*. The lad looked tired and Pat sensed a need to be succinct. His godson clearly didn't want to be here and Pat also felt there was a restless anger about the lad, a rage that could bubble up at any moment… He decided honesty was his only way forward.

'Your father asked me to…' he started.

A flash of intense suspicion immediately rendered Will's face a mask of incredulity. Pat found himself swiftly unfolding his arms and shooting them out at Will, palms first, in order to calm and placate the lad.

'Your father's in a bad way,' he quickly added.

Pat watched as Will's anger fell away, being replaced with a heady mixture of bemusement and suspicion. He swiftly ploughed on.

'Early Saturday afternoon your father was riding alone up the Wold gallop…'

'What was he doing up there on a Saturday afternoon? It closes doesn't it?'

Pat gave his godson a disgruntled glare.

'I don't know about that. Just listen will you! He never returned to the yard. A young jockey out for a run up the gallop saw a loose horse and found Barney unconscious, lying face-down, half-way up the All-Weather gallop. Your father sustained… well, various injuries, and he's in a serious condition in York Hospital.'

Will didn't reply. Instead, he breathed in deeply and cast his eyes over to the wall where three large windows provided a view out onto a mature, and by the look of the borders, unloved garden. Pat had expected a plethora of questions, and was stumped by the lad's reaction.

He blundered on, 'He asked me to… your dad that is, asked me to get you to come back and…'

'The assault was a lie,' Will said quietly, still gazing out of the windows, 'It was just a way for my scheming father to screw with me again. In fact, the old fool fell off his horse and got himself hurt. I bet it was a two-year-old, he was always useless on them.'

Pat's mouth went dry. In a distressed tone he said, 'Your dad is in a very bad way. He is desperate to see you… I couldn't think of any other means of convincing you to come back. You don't have to visit him, but…'

Will glanced Pat's way, caught the man's eye, shook his head sorrowfully, and returned to the view through the windows.

14

'You must have risked your job to bring me down here just for him,' Will mused sadly.

'Yes I have. But your dad is my best friend. He's never let me down, and I…'

Suddenly aware that his heart was thumping against his ribs, Will clenched his fists. He'd heard enough. Pat's whiny, pleading tone was getting on his nerves and the thought of listening to any more adoration for his father was filling him with revulsion.

'Well, bully for you… Pat!' Will said sourly, spitting the policeman's name out as if saying it had left a bad taste, 'It's a shame he didn't save some of that sort of commitment for my mother and me!'

'I know you're angry about what happened with your mother, Will, but they were both to...'

Will swung around and jumped to his feet, swiftly closing the space between himself and the policeman. He grabbed a handful of Pat's jacket into a closed fist and pulled the taller policeman down to within an inch of his face.

With carefully suppressed rage, Will told the policeman, 'Don't you *dare* spread the blame for my father's actions onto my mother!'

Pat gawped at the lad, unable to respond. Will roughly let go of him and sat back down. An awkward silence descended on the room.

'Just see him,' Pat said eventually.

'What the hell, Pat! I've already told you…'

The policeman held up a hand.

'William!' he insisted loudly.

Will snorted, but remained silent.

Pat said in a soft, sad tone, 'It could be your last chance… and he's told me he has a way for you to locate your mother…'

# Four

By the time Pat brought his car to a halt on the second floor of the multi-story car park at York Hospital, it was late Sunday afternoon. Having refused several of the policeman's offers to stop and get him something to eat on the drive from Malton, Will was now regretting the monosyllabic negative replies he'd given his father's best friend. He wasn't bothered about his answers being terse; he was hungry.

Pat had been keen to understand how, on his eighteenth birthday, Will had managed to walk out of his father's farmhouse and fund a three year course in Fine Art and Sculpture at Newcastle University. Will had replied, 'The way my family always survives, on their wits.'

This was only partly true. Will's grandfather had left him five thousand pounds in his will, made available to him when he turned eighteen. Having already accepted a place on the Fine Art course at Newcastle university, Will had travelled up there knowing his student loan alone wouldn't be enough to see him through the three years of the course. Turning the remainder of his windfall into enough to sustain him for three years at university had only required a laptop, internet access, and a looped playlist of his favourite music tracks to ensure he wasn't distracted.

He'd secretly been playing online poker since he was twelve years old, after discovering he had a knack for Omaha Hold'em, played against his schoolmates during their lunch hour. He'd graduated to playing small stakes tables on websites that didn't check too robustly who was signing up – a valid debit card and ticking the terms and conditions had been the only requirement by online casino owners hungry for new players.

His ability to play the person, rather than the cards he was dealt, and remain steadfast, even when pots reached eyewatering levels, saw him consistently in profit. During his first two months at university Will spent his evenings slowly but surely converting his grandfather's five-thousand pounds gift into twenty-thousand pounds. Once he'd reached his goal of being able to cover his student outgoings for duration of his three-year course, he stopped playing. Neither Pat, nor his father needed to know anything about his skills on a poker table.

As they walked the wide, sparsely populated corridors of the hospital together, Will breathed in that strange hospital smell. It was a mixture of antiseptic, floor cleaner, and over-cooked cabbage. Despite the deplorable odour, his stomach was rumbled like a complaining old man.

Pat led him up several flights of stairs and onto a floor where the quality of the surroundings improved markedly and each door was locked, requiring the policeman to speak into a microphone and be buzzed through to the next area. Will noticed the number of nurses and ancillary staff increased as they progressed down the corridor.

'Where are we going?' Will asked in a hushed tone.

'Intensive Care,' Pat replied, 'I may have lied to get you down here from Newcastle, but I didn't sugar-coat the seriousness of your father's injuries.'

They passed through a ward filled with about a dozen beds, all occupied. It was darker in these wards and every three to four beds seemed to be overseen by a hovering nurse. Pat continued on, but after being buzzed into yet another ward, he turned to Will.

'We need to wear masks and one of these… er…smocks,' Pat told him, as a nurse busied herself around the two men.

'And prepare yourself,' he warned Will, 'He's not the man you left behind.'

Will provided the policeman with a half shrug, half nod, being uncertain of the correct reaction to such news. He was beginning to find Pat's treatment of him a little over-dramatic. Nevertheless, he followed him down the ward. The beds were much further apart here, and plastic tubes, wires, and other medical paraphernalia abounded. The nurses had their faces covered, and wore similar plastic smocks to theirs, over standard light blue uniforms. Combined with even lower lighting and the hushed efficiency provided by the staff, the ward possessed an eerie quality of suppressed alertness.

Will became aware that the ward wasn't operating to the sound of machines beeping or nurses chatter. It was filled with the sound of breathing. Every patient he inspected was pale, their pallor accentuated by the digital readouts on monitors from which shone a dim yellow glow.

'Barney's over here,' Pat said, encouraging Will to follow him on his approach to a bed three down to their right.

Before Will had reached the bedside, Pat turned, and Will noticed sweat bubbling up on the man's extensive forehead.

Pat pushed past him and approached one of the nurses. A hurried conversation resulted in a relieved Pat being led by the nurse to the end of the ward where four beds were shrouded by curtains. Will followed, arms crossed and still sceptical. Pat cast the thin blue curtain aside and plastered a smile on his face before approaching the recumbent occupant of the bed.

'He's improved today,' the nurse standing beside Will told him in a hushed tone, 'Which is why he's been moved. Mr Payne is still on twenty-four hour watch, but he's stabilized enough for us to move him here.'

Will thanked her, moved to the foot of the bed and studied the face of his unconscious father. His head was heavily bandaged and Will could make out further strapping or possibly plaster casts on his arms, chest, and legs. His nose was stitched up on one side, his lips were heavily bruised and the one ear not covered by bandages was ragged at the lobe and smeared with dried blood.

'Sheesh, Will,' Pat breathed, 'I thought he'd died when he wasn't in that bed on the ward!'

Will didn't reply, but remained at the foot of the bed

looking over the crushed remains of his father. Even in this state, Will shivered as a wave of revulsion for the monster in the bed crashed over him. What emerged from this physical reaction to being in his father's presence was a cold, steel-like certainty. It filled his mind and then shot around his nervous system, giving him strength. Standing over his broken parent, Will knew for certain they could *never* be reconciled.

'We'll wait,' Pat said encouragingly from a seat near his friend's head, 'He wakes from time to time. He'll want to know you're here.'

Again, Will remained tight-lipped, unmoved from his vigil at the foot of his father's bed. His father coughed. An eyelid fluttered, and a single, unfocussed eye peered up at Will, then to Pat. The left eye tried to open, but was unable to fully comply, remaining half-lidded.

'Wu… Will…' Barney Payne stammered.

'Yes, he's here. Just like I promised, Barney!' Pat confirmed excitedly.

Barney rolled his tongue slowly over his lips and Will noticed he had lost two teeth and another was broken, leaving a jagged edge. The movement clearly brought his father pain, as he gurgled and coughed upon his tongue reaching the worst of the bruising.

'About… time, … ss…son,' he croaked from the back of his throat, still managing to exude irritation.

Will stared at his father, thought hard about his response and eventually snapped, 'What do you want?'

'Tell him, Barney,' prompted Pat encouragingly, 'Tell Will before you need to get more rest.'

Barney's one good eye flitted from Pat to the lad standing at the foot of his bed with his hands in his pockets. His lips started to shape a word.

'R… run the… yard.'

Pat smiled and looked over at Will. He found his godson displaying a bewildered stare that immediately wiped the hopeful smile from his face.

'He needs you to keep the training yard going while he's recovering,' Pat said, uncertain whether the lad had understood his father's request.

Will shook his head, clamped his hands on his hips and said, 'Yeah, I got that.'

'Well?' Pat prompted.

'You're crazy,' Will told his father in a hiss, 'After the way you treated me and my mother, your precious training stables can crumble into dust as far as I'm concerned!'

Will's voice had increased in volume as he reached the conclusion of his reply and his words prompted an immediate scampering of feet behind him. Two nurses scurried to his father's bedside to check on him.

'And you don't deserve this sort of attention either,' Will muttered hotly under his breath.

'Hold your tongue,' Pat warned, 'No one deserves to have this happen to him, least of all your father.'

Will was about to provide a sarcastic reply, but caught the look in the eye of one of the nurses and thought better of it. Once Pat had apologised on Will's behalf both nurses nodded primly and returned to their quiet vigil further up the ward.

'Do it... do it for... Mm...Mary,' his father insisted once they were alone again. He held up an index finger that was tipped by a pulse monitor, as if to indicate there was more, 'Mary...' his father repeated, with the faintest of nods to Pat.

Pat nodded his understanding and turned to face Will once more.

'Barney's yard, or rather, Manor Stud Stables, the farmhouse and all the land is owned by your mother, Mary,' said the policeman, 'If it crumbles to dust, it's *her* business, *her* property you'd be killing off. Not your father's.'

Will stared at the broken man in the bed, 'Really?'

There was the smallest of inclinations of his father's chin. In response, Will shifted uncomfortably from foot to foot.

Pat continued, 'Your grandfather insisted his stable remained the property of his only daughter. He left it to Mary in his will. He was also instrumental in making sure you got the Payne surname and not Wilson.'

Will had known of his grandfather's belligerence where the family name was concerned. His mother had told him grandpa Payne had been adamant; Will's surname *had to be Payne*. After he died, all the horses in the yard ran in the name of Mary Payne, and ever since she'd left, as far as he was aware. Even his father went by the name Payne, something Will had never quite understood. His father's real name was Barney Wilson.

'Do it for your m… mother,' croaked Barney.

Will scowled down at his father, his words having awakened a raft of bad memories. But something stopped Will from hurling abuse and lashing his father with sharp reminders of his shortcomings. He'd not known the stables and house belonged to his mother, but when he thought about it, grandpa Payne had been a traditionalist, and had also thought the world of his daughter. It made sense.

And if the yard was still operating, there was a chance, however small, that his mother might return at some point to reclaim her inheritance…

'I'll think about it,' Will stated brusquely.

Barney stirred once more, 'Our bedroom…' he croaked, pausing to swallow and run his tongue around his mouth, 'If you want… to find… to *understand* Mary… look in the… ward…'

All tension in his father's pale face loosened and his one good eye flickered shut, the other staying weirdly half open as he drifted away. Will's initial thought was to turn and leave. And yet, he found himself rooted to his spot at the end of the bed, watching for his father's chest to rise and fall. Once Will was satisfied his father was sleeping he headed for the ward door.

# Five

The dream always started in the same way.

He was taking small steps, head bowed, inspecting his scuffed school shoes, watching transfixed as the stark shadows thrown from the green-grey slatted picket fence on his left made his shoes flash from brown to black. As he walked, the high mid-afternoon sun bore down on him, the back of his neck rippling with waves of heat.

The voice. Always the same voice. It drew his attention away from his introspection and he halted to watch as a figure within the racecourse car park on the other side of the fence hurried along, dodging between cars with their shiny glass windscreens and roofs, muttering under his breath. He was carrying a bag. Always the same bag. He knew it well. A Gladstone bag.

Whether he jumped, shinned or scrambled over the four foot fence, he didn't know. The dream was always indistinct at this point, as if fast-forwarding. But he was soon tracking the man through the car park, fascinated by his erratic movements; how he crept, fell to his knees, sidled around gleaming chrome bumpers, and peered over sun-drenched bonnets, hefting his bag along with him.

'Jack! The cheat.'

The call, made with a petulant, sarcastic, slightly amused tone, came from behind him and when he swung around three darkly clothed men with black hair that sparkled in the sun strode past his hiding place and approached the older man he'd been following for fun.

A shot of empathy tinged with fear ran through him. The old man was holding his ground, but with quick breaths and eyes full of dread, frozen in position between two lines of cars. He no longer grasped his Gladstone bag.

The bag had gone.

Crouching down onto the finely cut grass, he left the men to their conversation. Now he was searching between the rows of wheels, drive shafts and exhausts, the side of his head pushed into the warm, dry turf. Where had the old man been before he?... ah!

Squeezing under sills, rolling under dirty, oily engines and between sudden sun-rich gaps between cars, he reached his objective; the Gladstone bag, stuffed up behind the tyre of the car, but with just enough poking out to give its location away. He laid a hand on its leather handle. It sent a thrill of excitement through him. Pulling the bag towards him, he was surprised at the effort needed. It was bulky, weighty. It felt... important.

A thump, a gasp for breath, a groan... and warnings... no, *threats* from the men. He screwed his head around and with only a letterbox view, he saw the old man fall to his knees, only a few yards away from where he lay under the car. The other three sets of black shoes stayed motionless until a man's voice growled, 'We didn't get it wrong, Jack. You tried to cheat us. We know you've won big today. So get your debt paid.'

Then the three sets of shiny shoes turned and left.

He didn't move a muscle, his hand still on the Gladstone bag's handle, sweat breaking out on his forehead, fearing to make any sound. He watched the old man fight for breath, then slowly sit down and lean back onto his elbows as his breathing steadied. The old man rolled over on one side and peered under the car... their eyes met, and he... smiled.

The old man was still smiling at him when the voice spoke.

It was an angry voice. It always was. It said, 'Cheat.'

The old man started to turn his head. As the sun played upon the old man's face the first blow smacked viciously into the side of his head.

Underneath the car, he stifled a gasp.

He tried to close his eyes, but knew he couldn't. It was the second blow that was always the worst. The club smashed into the old man's face, wrecking the smile that had just been there, deforming it horribly…

He woke as he always did following this dream; in the foetal position. Cold, sticky sweat was soaking into his sheets and standing on his brow. And his right hand hurt. It always hurt. It was squeezed tight, his fingers in a closed fist, unable to release their death-like grip upon the handle of the Gladstone bag.

It took several seconds for him to unfurl his stiff, aching digits from the handful of screwed-up cotton sheet. It took another long moment to rid his mind of that word; cheat. He remained sitting on the edge of his bed for at least a minute, maybe more. It could take a while to regain his grip on reality, such was the power of the dream. Eventually, he stumbled from his bed and into his shower.

# Six

Will watched, impressed as Arthur returned to their table in the snug of their favourite local, The Black Horse, clutching three bottles of Brown Ale by their necks, a bag of pork scratchings and a trio of half pint glasses in his other hand. He pausing a moment a few yards from the table so as not to compromise Freddie's attempt to successfully flip and catch a wad of beer mats. Once the mats had, for the fourth time, been consigned to the ancient stone floor of the pub, Arthur moved in and divided the drinks up around the table.

'It's time to accept that thirteen is your limit,' Arthur suggested hopefully, as Freddie scrabbled around on the floor to retrieve his scattered drip mats.

'Never say never,' intoned Freddie from beneath the table.

'Ha'way, Freddie,' Will urged, 'I need to tell you both something.'

Arthur smiled mischievously at Will, 'Did I detect a wee bit of Geordie there, Will?'

Will grimaced. It was a running joke between Freddie and Arthur that he was slowly turning into a Newcastle local, something Will had fought at first. It didn't help that he became broader the more intoxicated he became. In truth, he was content to have the long Yorkshire vowels extracted from his language. The north-eastern accent had seemed harsh when first exposed to it upon starting university, however, it's sing-song quality had soon become easy on the ear.

'Aye,' agreed Freddie, plonking himself back down on his stool, 'We've converted him to drinking his Broon Ale out of proper glasses now. After that, his slide into full Geordie is assured!'

'I've lived in Newcastle for almost two years,' Will pointed out, 'And Lord knows why, but I've spent them in the company of the broadest accented local I've ever heard, and a Scotsman who can't even pronounce his own name without tying his tongue in a knot. I think you can cut me some slack for picking up a bit of the local lingo!'

Arthur and Freddie grinned victoriously at him, having successfully achieved the frustrated reaction they had been aiming for all along.

'Right lads, serious heads on please,' Will insisted with a resigned sigh. He stretched his neck to gaze around the pub, checking no one else was in earshot. It was unlikely; they were sitting in the Black Horse's snug, a small room well away from the bar that only tended to be used by the more elderly locals, and usually only in the evenings. At one o'clock on a Monday afternoon, the pub was dead.

Will paused and wrinkled his nose, which in turn make his lips purse. Freddie and Arthur waited expectantly, this was a sure sign Will was about to impart bad news. Will rocked uncertainly on his stool, trying to think of a way to soften the blow.

'You'd make a poor salesman,' Freddie injected into the pregnant pause, 'If you don't ask for the business, you don't get it. Come on, Will, spit it out.'

Will rolled his eyes, but got on with it.

'The doctors reckon my father will be in hospital for up to two months. I'm needed back at Malton to help run the yard… the racehorse training yard, that is. I might not… no, that's not it,' he corrected himself sadly, 'I *will not* be able to go on our holiday around Europe in July.'

Their 'Grand Tour' had been planned since the start of their second year at university. It had intended to be a month of student inter-railing, taking in the major cities in mainland Europe.

Will grimaced again adding, 'I'm going back to Malton tomorrow.'

'Is this you covering for your Dad?' asked Freddie.

Will took a gulp of his Brown Ale and contemplated his answer as the amber liquid coated the back of his throat with malty bubbles.

'It's for my mum,' Will replied thoughtfully.

Freddie and Arthur exchanged a, 'Should we say anything?' query at each other through the raising of single eyebrows.

Freddie asked, 'We know your Dad's not too well, and this has something to do with the police calling yesterday. But what's it got to do with your mother? Isn't she... um...'

'Still missing,' Will said sullenly.

Arthur and Freddie shared a knowing look and Will felt the atmosphere in the snug tighten.

To Will's surprise he had found himself sharing his mother's story with his friends within a couple of months of meeting the two of them. Up to that point, he hadn't imagined telling his story to anyone. It was far too personal, too difficult. But together, Arthur and Freddie made it easy and he'd furnished them with the full story, related to them in at the end of a pub crawl around Newcastle city centre.

As the silence in the snug lengthened, Will recalled the winter evening that had proved to be a catalyst for drawing the three of them even closer together. He'd been drunk that night... too drunk.

'My mother left me,' he'd sudden blurted sorrowfully from the lounge sofa once they'd got back to the student house, 'One moment she was there, then gone the next. No note, no reason. She just... went. She disappeared. Poof! Gone.'

What happened next, Will couldn't say for certain. It was fuzzy when he tried to recollect. Upon sharing this information, he'd apparently become a drunken idiot. A sudden burst of uncontrollable rage had consumed him. Or rather, whatever simmering anger that had resided deep inside him had bubbled up like magma and shot out of him, spewing hatred everywhere. He'd upturned furniture, smashed glasses, and all the while screaming about his mother, and mainly, his father.

Freddie and Arthur had described how they had

watched in horror as their friend became a different person before them, displaying a soul so contorted and twisted, they hardly recognised him. Being the largest, Freddie had stepped in to restrain him, but as soon as he'd wrapped his arms around Will, he'd become limp. As if his demons had been cast away, or at least sated for now, Will had halted mid-rant, turned pale, and immediately slumped into Freddies's arms, breathing heavily. Freddie had guided him onto the sofa and within moments he'd fallen asleep.

Freddie had put the outburst down to drunken babble and Will's words might have been forgotten if it wasn't for Arthur's ability to hold his drink, a quality sorely lacking in Will. Arthur also possessed a rapier-sharp memory. The next morning he'd asked one question of his friend: 'Is that why you never go home, Will?'

'Uh… Did I spout a load of insults about my father?'

Arthur had indicated he had, and repeated one or two of the more choice phrases, saving the most damning accusation until last.

'You said your father *tortured* your mother, driving her to a point of nervous exhaustion, bordered on insanity… and then she disappeared,' Arthur had related carefully, watching for signs of distress in his friend as he spoke, ready to drop the subject if necessary.

In the thoughtful silence that followed, Arthur had caught no emotion in Will's face. After considering Arthur's words in sullen silence, Will had finally replied, 'Yeah, that's about right.'

Will had become quiet, then shared his view that he was sure there was more to his mother's disappearance than her simply leaving the family home of her own accord and disappearing. He'd been fourteen years old, and left to be raised by his father alone.

Arthur had nodded his understanding and after that the subject of Will's mother and father had only rarely been revisited.

The night of Will's revelations, anger, and subsequent actions had altered the dynamics of the relationship between the teenagers. It had fostered an atmosphere of mutual trust. Slowly, all three of the young men had felt able to share, and in doing so, gained a deeper understanding of each other.

Within a few days of Will's outburst, Arthur had told his friends of how the sudden death of his elder sister had fractured his family life from the age of nine. Freddie's childhood with his single mother turned out to be nothing less than a 'train wreck', as he had described it. However, the anecdotes he chose to bring his upbringing to life were always sprinkled with humour.

'I'm amazed you're so normal!' a shocked Freddie had told Arthur upon learning that his sister had drowned in front of him, totally missing the potential for his comment to be an emotional trigger, 'It makes my childhood recollections appear serene by comparison!'

Arthur had playfully punched Freddie's arm and told him that in future, he should consider engaging his brain before he spoke upon such personal subjects. Concerning Will's extreme reaction, Arthur had made a simple suggestion.

'We should look out for you, Will,' Arthur had said levelly, 'You become maudlin after too much alcohol. Freddie and I have seen it a few times before, but never so extreme. When you drink it brings on your reaction to your past, and it's in everyone's interests that you don't tear us, or the house apart again. Total abstinence isn't the answer, as you're fun when you've had a couple. However, Freddie or I shall warn you to stop drinking if we think you're reaching that point where you're in danger of bringing on another… episode. It can be a look, a sign… something that tells you you've had enough.'

Will had agreed and Arthur's suggestion had been successful. Will had never again descended into the raging, evil-minded alter-ego they had witnessed that night in Newcastle. His drinking had always stayed on the benign side of drunk – a loss of inhibitions, and nothing more.

I'm so lucky, thought Will, I've two good friends I never expected to find, and probably don't deserve. He was still ruminating at how he'd let them down when Arthur's voice penetrated the silence around the table in the snug.

'We're not going inter-railing without you,' he said earnestly.

Freddie quickly agreed, 'We'll go next summer instead. At the end of our final year at university.'

Will nodded apologetically to his friends in turn, subsequently raising a smile when Freddie once again, tried and failed to flip and successfully catch his fourteen beer mats.

## Seven

Will trundled his suitcase out of Malton train station and after hefting his second bag over his shoulder, perused the station car park for any sign of a taxi.

He gave a heavily sigh. It was raining. His first time back in his home town in two years - if you excluded his short visit to the town's police station last week - and the weather was reflecting his mood. That was just *perfect*. It was the sort of rain that looks and feels like a light shower, but the tiny droplets were coming down in a constant sheet and he was drenched in less than a minute.

He became aware of a knot in his stomach and his shoulders dropped an inch. A cloud of gloomy doubt had grown within him the further he'd travelled south and it now coalesced with the weather and the nervousness in his gut, leaving him thoroughly miserable.

Watching a young woman take the only available taxi and drive off in a cloud of exhaust fumes served to darken his mood further and he was about to turn around and shelter back in the Grade II listed station building when he heard a whistle emanating from the small car park opposite the entrance.

The ancient Renault pulled out of its parking space and drove up to Will, the driver's window lowering in rapid hand-cranked jerks as the vehicle approached. He recognised it immediately as the yard's run-around car, and couldn't believe it was still capable of running.

'William? William Payne?' asked a bright young voice.

'Yeah, that's me.'

'Here to collect you,' the girl stated abruptly.

He'd only just realised it was a girl, as she had her hair pulled tight back on her head, her pony tail hidden under a red baseball cap that was emblazoned with the name of a horse feed manufacturer. She wore no make-up either, which meant on first look, she could pass for a young boy. He wondered whether this was the vibe she was aiming to create.

When Will didn't offer a reply, she said, 'Boot's open,' with a jerk of her head towards the back of her vehicle.

'Yeah, er… thanks,' Will managed before stowing his gear and jumping into the passenger seat.

The journey to his father's training yard only took five minutes, during which Will learned the girl was twenty, lived in a nearby village, and worked part-time at the yard as a stable lass. She rode out in the mornings, usually three lots. She was called Elizabeth, but preferred Lizzy, and had been with the yard for six months. Her most notable skill was her ability to answer every one of Will's queries in a maximum of one, or at a push, two words.

Will was sure he'd never met anyone who was quite as succinct. He decided Lizzy wasn't rude, just unerringly direct. By the time they'd turned off the main road outside Norton he was thankful the journey was so short, as he'd run out of topics of conversation.

Pulling off Beverley road, the car creaked alarmingly as it bounced over a makeshift dirt surface for a short while until reaching tarmac spotted with potholes.

Nothing's changed here, Will reflected dolefully as Lizzy tried to avoid the worst of the tyre-shredding holes in the road. With several trainers sharing access to the small cluster of yards, no one could agree on the upkeep of the private lane. And with trainers being naturally tight with their money, road renovations were usually delayed until the holes threatened to swallow up their horseboxes.

Passing under mature trees and paddocks to their right, Lizzy slowed the car to a crawl as they passed the entrances to two other racing yards before turning into the narrow lane that led to the entrance to Manor Stud Stables. Two dark, lichen encrusted redbrick columns either side of the road were topped with inelegant stone statues of horses, supposedly prancing on their back legs, marking the entrance to the property.

As it had been when he was a child, Will's attention was immediately drawn to the horses' cartoonish, sightless eyes, followed by the wildly inexact representation of the equine form. They squatted on their plinths atop the artless columns like demonic creatures. The anticipated involuntary shudder ran through Will as he passed between them. Even now, as an adult, the sight of the overly large, blank eyes of the two statues filled him with dread. He'd been told as a youngster that as long as the two prancing horses remained on their columns, success would be bestowed upon Manor Stud Stables... he'd thought it was nonsense and had fantasized about knocking the creepy equine statues off their columns with everything from a baseball bat to a JCB digger.

As the old Renault rattled into the yard proper, Roberto was waiting for him, looking disappointed. Will wasn't too surprised. A resigned look of discontent was pretty much the default setting for Roberto's Romanesque features.

'Hi, Roberto. How's it going?' Will called out as he exited the car opposite the farmhouse. He'd tried to sound as upbeat as possible, and wasn't too disappointed or surprised when all he received in return was a grudging nod.

In his mid-forties, Roberto Timpinelli was of Italian extraction and had the curly jet black hair and swarthy southern European good looks to go with his Italian accent. Once his riding career had been curtailed by a lack of decent rides upon turning professional, he'd stayed in Britain, making a living as a work rider in Newmarket before moving north and eventually taking on the role of head lad at Manor Stud Stables. He'd worked here for the last fifteen years and Will couldn't remember a time when he wasn't at either his mother's or father's side, grumpily, but expertly ensuring the yard operated smoothly.

Leaning against a stable wall with arms crossed, Roberto watched as Will hauled his case out of the boot of the car, making no move to help.

'You're back then,' remarked Roberto.

Will ignored the comment. If he'd read its underlying meaning correctly, what the head lad was really saying was, 'What on earth are you doing back here? You left without so much as a goodbye and I've not heard from you since. Now you're back and expect me to just pick up from where we left off?'

Instead, Will walked straight up to Roberto and grabbing the man's hand, shook it vigorously.

'It's so good to see you, Roberto! My father and I would like to thank you, and personally, I'd like to say sorry. Sorry for leaving so suddenly and not getting in touch... it wasn't fair. I had things to... get straight in my head,' Will said, a hopeful smile plastered on his face, determined to crack Roberto's grimace into something resembling a smile, 'And thank you for running the yard for the last four, or is it five days, on your own after my father's accident? I'm immensely grateful.'

Roberto's grimace was initially replaced with a look of bemused puzzlement and then after a submissive roll of his eyes, a generous, forgiving smile. Will continued to pump the Italian's hand up and down, whilst beaming and Roberto leaned in for a quick hug.

'I... it... was nothing,' Roberto eventually replied, a small blush of embarrassment in his cheeks.

That was Roberto. Grumpy as they came, yet honest, hard-working, loyal and committed and extremely forgiving of the Payne family's shortcomings. Will was incredibly grateful he was here, and proceeded to tell him so, embarrassing the older man further.

'How is everything? All good?' Will eventually asked, casting a quick glance into the heart of the yard.

It was a forty box yard, and on first look, Will thought little had changed since he'd stormed off the premises without looking back.

As Lizzy pulled away to park the tired old Renault at the bottom of the yard, Roberto failed to answer, preferring to suck his bottom row of teeth and regard Will with dread. Fearing the worst, Will cast his gaze over the yard once more, this time in much greater detail. On closer inspection it soon became obvious the number of horses in his father's care was worryingly low.

The brick and wood built stabling block was one of the oldest in the town, created at a time when a sense of grandeur was just as important as utility. Having originally been a stud, each box was large, built to accommodate a mare and her offspring in as close as you could get to equine luxury. A long, single line of stables ran away from the farmhouse, the red brick being offset by brilliant white painted wooden doors, window frames, and guttering. The apex of the pitched roof ran right down the line, only pausing for a moment in the centre, where a once proud clock tower sat, topped by a galloping horse weather vane.

Will studied the clock, noting it had stopped at two-forty-four. There were cracked, half-gone, or completely missing slates here and there across the roof that extended out to provide a wide, covered concrete walkway outside the stables. Supported by wooden posts every twenty yards the four yard wide walkway ran the length of the stables and meant staff, and to some extent the horses themselves, could move around and be somewhat protected from the elements.

The yard was bisected by a narrow tarmac lane that led to the turnout paddocks and a small car park tucked away out of sight at the back of the yard. On the other side of the lane, opposite the line of stables, was a good sized menage, followed by a walker, then a lunging pen, and finally a flat-roofed brick built building with only one window that acted as the tack, feed room, and store.

Originally white, the stables' yellowing paintwork was, at best, peeling, and in places completely stripped, and the yard itself looked like it could do with a proper clean. As he'd expected, his father had done little to halt the entropic nature of the weather during the last three years. It was his mother who had always insisted on the place being kept spick and span.

Will was a shade surprised to feel disappointment filling him upon discovering almost half the split stable doors were bolted closed both top and bottom, signalling they were empty and unused.

'How many have you got in at the moment?'

'Nine,' Roberto replied absently, hands on hips, 'Last season was tough. Our draft of two-year-old's were disappointing types and half a dozen of our older horses had to be retired. We've also lost five to other Malton trainers since your father's accident, which is annoying, as we've put the work in to get them fit and ready. I tried to explain he'd be out of hospital soon, but owners can be impatient...'

Roberto locked eyes with Will, a kernel of hope beginning to coalesce, 'Are you back for good?'

Will dropped his gaze, unable to maintain eye contact. Instead, he looked along the largely empty line of boxes, running a few alternate answers through his mind until he found one that would tread the line between dashing Roberto's hopes and the starkness of the truth.

'I'm here until my father...' started Will, but his voice trailed away as he heard swearing coming from one of the nearby boxes. Without waiting for an explanation from Roberto, he covered the dozen or so yards across the road in front of the stabling block and found the box from which a torrent of expletives were being angrily delivered.

Peering over the open top half of the stable door, Will watched in horror as a small, dark-haired youth lost his patience, and any last semblance of his professionalism, by aiming a violent kick at a bay filly who was lying at the back of the stable, refusing to rise to her feet. The boy's boot connected with the filly's ribs with a sickening thump. The young horse screamed and then snorted, baring her teeth, still refusing to move.

'Stop that *now*!' commanded Will in a bellow so full of

passion he was a little shocked at himself.

The stable lad spun around. A pair of wild black eyes set in a pinched white face stared incredulously at Will from the dim recesses of the stable.

'Who the hell are you?' he snorted derisively.

'I'm your new employer, *and* your ex-employer,' Will told the lad with a cold stare, 'You shouldn't be working with any sort of animals, never mind racehorses. Get out and don't come back.'

The lad sneered, 'Oh, yeah?'

For a moment Will got the impression the lad was going to take another swipe at the horse, swinging his leg back as if readying another kick. The sound of the door bolt being drawn back by Will, made the lad think better of it and he moved away from the disgruntled filly.

'I'm William Payne, my father owns this yard and according to the BHA I'm the assistant trainer, which means I can hire and fire,' Will asserted. This had once been true, but Will didn't imagine his father had kept up to the paperwork. Nevertheless, his assertion had the desired effect on the lad.

Mumbling some sort of half-baked threat under his breath, liberally sprinkled with more expletives, the lad stormed out of the stable. He pushed past Roberto at the entrance to the box, almost knocking him over in the process.

Will could hear the lad's boots as he stomped down the yard, hurling more abuse at Roberto as he went. He didn't follow. Best to let him go, rather than provoke the young hothead further. Instead, Will knelt down beside the filly and began to speak softly to her, calming her down.

Roberto returned a minute later, sighing theatrically as he entered the stable.

'Congratulations, Will,' he commented sarcastically, 'You've managed to fire the only half decent rider we had left on the yard.'

'He kicked her. He lost his temper and kicked her.'

'To be fair, this filly can be a bit of a madam.'

'That's no excuse, and you know it,' Will countered, 'What was his name?'

Roberto allowed a pause to develop. Will eventually turned his eyes on him expectantly.

'Jimmy Hearn,' Roberto sighed.

Despite being unhappy with losing a member of his staff, Roberto knew Will had been right to let the lad go. He would have done exactly the same. Even with the most belligerent of horses, bullying was never the answer.

Jimmy had started two months ago, being largely adequate to the job, but had become increasingly temperamental since the guvnor's accident, attempting to take advantage.

The teenager's departure was no great loss. He'd been a fair work rider but around the yard his cock sure belligerence, poor timekeeping, and constant grumbling had become tiresome, especially in a small team. He'd been on borrowed time until Roberto could find a suitable replacement.

'Is she okay?' the head lad asked, joining Will in running his hands softly over the filly's flank and shoulder.

'Her ribs seem fine. The kick hadn't caused any physical damage, just got her wound up. But I'm more worried about her foot,' Will replied, carefully lifting up the filly's front fore.

'Abscess?' asked Roberto assumptively, bending down to inspect the foot for signs of swelling or cracking, 'It would explain why she wasn't keen on getting to her feet.'

'Agreed. Let's get her shoe off.'

As the two of them busied themselves with the filly, Roberto found himself reacquainting himself with Will. He studying the young man's face when he spoke, examining his mannerisms as together they removed the shoe and carefully cleaned the filly's foot.

Will had been a strip of a thing, a boyish, immature teenager, when stomping angrily through the Manor Stud Stables gates with only a swiftly packed rucksack on his back, ignoring his father's ranting, and never turning back.

There were physical changes: a leaner, more muscular body, longer, much longer hair, and a few extra inches in height. But Roberto was more struck with his manner; this was a different Will. He was no longer the silent, pouting, and frankly, at times, downright annoying teenager. Will had become centred, composed, and certainly more confident. There was an air of relaxed determination about him. A couple of seasons out of racing had done him some good, Roberto decided, and it was a bonus that the lad clearly hadn't lost his touch with horses. Even so, Roberto wondered whether Will's new found composure would be maintained once his father was back around.

As they worked, Will asked, 'Who else have you got working with you?'

'Lizzy is a good rider, works hard, and is reliable enough, although her love life is a bit dicey. She goes for large, muscular types that treat her badly,' Roberto replied, 'And of course, we still have Gordy. He's in his late sixties now, so he just does a few hours here and there. The rest of the staff you'd remember from three years ago have all moved on.'

'As have eighty percent of the horses,' Will noted sourly, 'So why are you still here? My dad's results have been poor for some time and I'm guessing you'll have had plenty of offers from other yards? Don't tell me you're still here out of any sort of loyalty to him.'

Roberto regarded the younger man for a long moment. Several stinging replies came to him, but instead he eventually closed his eyes, took a breath and stated sternly, 'Your father has *always* been good to me, and my family.'

'Yeah, well,' sniffed Will, 'I suppose there has to be the odd person he hasn't got around to screaming merry hell at.'

Roberto shook his head in exasperation, but didn't reply. Perhaps the young Payne hadn't matured quite as much as he'd first thought.

They finished off poulticing the filly's foot and left her

39

sitting sphinx-like on her bed of wood shavings. Will paused to look back over the stable door and was pleased when the filly disentangled her legs from beneath her, got to her feet, and tentatively placed some weight on the bandaged leg in order to take a drink from her water fountain.

'Take me through the rest of them will you?' Will asked Roberto once they'd dropped off the abscess treatment in the tack room. He gestured at the stables with horses' heads hanging over their box doors, 'It looks like I might be here a while, so I may as well know from the start what we've got.'

'You want the grand tour now?'

'If it isn't too much trouble.'

'Sure. It's not like I've got anything else to get on with now you've sacked a third of my staff...' grumbled Roberto amiably.

'Well you've got me,' Will said levelly, 'I can still ride, and I haven't forgotten how to muck out. I would imagine an extra pair of hands to drive the horsebox and lead up at the races might come in handy too? I did this job from being seven years old, so I'm not afraid of hard work.'

Roberto knew this to be true. But wondered whether this transformation would be enough to save the ailing yard. That, he decided, would remain to be seen. However, it was a promising start... He hesitated. No, it was nothing more than a *satisfactory* start. He mustn't let the fact that a member of the Payne family was once again in situ at the Manor Stud Stables give him false hope.

The Head Lad smiled, 'Come on then,' and crossing the road and then the walkway, they approached the first occupied stable. One by one, Roberto introduced Will to each of the nine racehorses that made up the firepower that Manor Stud Stables had for the next seven months of the flat season.

## Eight

Three days after taking up residence at his father's training stables, Will stepped through the revolving doors of York Hospital again and once inside, paused to draw in a long, ragged breath. The knot of tension in his stomach combined with the dull ache of his jaw muscles from the teeth he'd been gritting throughout his car journey from Malton, were sure signs that he really didn't want to be here. Nonetheless, he set off in search of his father's ward, his face set in a disapproving grimace.

Will found Barney Payne in an improved state, transferred to a small ward with six beds and a single nurse who warily monitored each of the occupants. He was still hooked up to a bank of machines, and an oxygen line remained clamped to his upper lip. But the ghostly white pallor from a few days before had been replaced with a hopeful pinprick of colour in each of his cheeks. The memory associated with his fall was still a blank, but his father's speech was much better this time, which only served to ensure their first argument broke out within seconds of his arrival.

'The yard is a disgrace,' Will pointed out matter-of-factly after they'd both traded desultory greetings, 'So I'm going to make some changes.'

'Nowt wrong with those horses,' his father challenged.

'Not the horses,' sighed Will, failing to mask his irritation, 'Thanks to Roberto the horses get five-star treatment. That said, you've managed to whittle away at your numbers. I mean the yard itself. It's in a foul state. The buildings are a disgrace… and that farmhouse needs…'

'Which horses have gone?' Barney interrupted, suddenly rigid in his bed, 'The Clodovil filly? Has Hanover taken her?'

Will immediately knew the horse his father meant. Among the inmates, one youngster, an unraced two-year-old filly had stood out like a shining beacon when Roberto had gone down the line of boxes with him. She was a sleek and powerful grey by a classy, proven sire called Clodovil and even standing in her stable with the paint peeling and ancient cobwebs in the rafters dancing in the sunlight above her, she had shone, simply because of her physique. Roberto had told him the filly was blessed with plenty of ability and was so far ahead of the other three juveniles she was forced to work with their best horse in the yard, a five-year-old sprinter with lofty rating in the late eighties.

'Fine dad, she's fine,' Will assured his father, seeking to close the topic with a flick of his hand, 'It's the yard I'm bothered about. It's falling to pieces. And the farmhouse is a disgusting wreck. When was the last time you cleaned anything in there?'

After being introduced to all nine horses by Roberto, Will had entered the farmhouse using the spare key that was always secreted in a random hole in the mortar between two bricks in the tack room wall. Some things never change, he had thought, recalling the day his mother had first taught him how to locate the key. There had been many days when he returned from school in Malton to find the stables empty of staff, his mother and father out racing somewhere, sometimes returning home late into the evening. Starting at the base of the door, he would count five bricks along the outside of the tack room wall, and another five up, to locate a small hole in the cement from which his small fingers would rescue the keys to the tack room and the farmhouse.

However, the four-bedroomed detached farmhouse had changed in other ways, and not for the better. A combination of buddleia and weeds were infesting the guttering, and ominously dark water stains crept down the brickwork from certain points on the roof.

Once inside the house, Will had discovered a similar disregard for its upkeep. A peculiar odour that reminded him of old cabbage pervaded the house. The smell, combined with a layer of dust covering virtually every surface, gave the farmhouse an unappealing sense of decay. You could immediately determine where his father spent his time, as there were dark routes embedded into the carpet from the hallway, through to the back room where they branched off to a dining table that doubled as his work desk, his favourite armchair in front of a coal fire, or up the back stairs to the four bedrooms. Any mud, muck, or other detritus that fell onto these little thoroughfares had been ground in over time, the sight of a vacuum cleaner being a rarity in the Payne household. You could easily spot his father's meanderings by his slick, oily black tracks through the carpets.

Into the back room, the old wooden dining table Will used to eat his meals from as a boy, was now stacked high with old copies of The Racing Programme Book, along with a mixture of other racing journals and magazines. An old-fashioned telephone with a circular dial and heavy receiver lay among the literature, it's extended plastic handset wire horribly knotted. An old computer, clunky fat monitor, and dirty keyboard sat on the table. Will imagined it would be used for entries and declarations and little else; this had been his mother's job before she left, and the task had subsequently passed to Will.

The centre of his father's universe was undoubtedly the armchair in the back room of the farmhouse. It was, without doubt, the most used piece of furniture in the entire farmhouse, and took pride of place in front of an open fire and hearth that was thick with ash. A large, old-fashioned square television in a mock-wooden case faced the armchair. Two side-tables, differing radically in size and design, occupied the space alongside each arm of the chair. They were covered in half-drunk mugs of coffee, sweet wrappers, plastic takeaway bags, and even a discarded pizza box. He'd been oddly relieved when a quick hunt around hadn't uncovered any alcohol other than two empty bottles of milk stout. So far, the evidence pointed to his father drinking in moderation.

Will's relief was short-lived. Whilst trying to locate a

43

wheelie bin, he discovered a small mountain of cheap whisky, vodka, and gin bottles stacked in half a dozen large plastic bags at the back of the garden shed. It seemed his father was happy for his lack of household hygiene to go unchecked and open to public scrutiny, but he preferred evidence of his drinking problem to be squirrelled away.

'With the state it's in, I can't live in the farmhouse,' he told his father with an animated wave of his hands, 'I'm going to get it cleaned up.'

'Just look after the horses. I don't care about the house,' his father commanded grumpily, 'When I get back I want to see the horses gleaming.'

'Mum would be upset with how you've let the yard run to seed.'

His father's eyes hardened, 'Just as well she's not around to see it then,' he replied bitterly.

'I thought that was the point of me being here,' Will protested, his voice climbing higher in pitch and volume, 'Don't think for one second I'm here for you. I'm here to protect Mum's house. Mum's business. And it's pretty clear you've been running it into the ground ever since I left!'

Will couldn't help noticing that several of his father's fellow patients were now listening intently to him. He dragged the thin curtain around his father's bed in one defiant sweeping movement that made the rings attached to the top rail shriek in protest.

'That'll do no good if you keep on shouting,' his father said with a smirk.

Will rammed his lips together, bristling with barely contained rage. He could walk away. He could leave the hospital and get on a train to Newcastle and never give his father, or his dilapidated racing yard another thought. It would be so easy… And yet, there it was, nagging away in the recesses of his mind, that pinprick of hope. The hope that she would return. That his mother would arrive back at Manor Stud Stables after seven years without so much as a postcard.

Seven years, Will considered. His mother's exit from his life at the age of fourteen had been sudden and total. And she had been fastidious in her quest to be untraceable. Will had often imagined her walking past the prancing horses at the entrance to the yard, continuing down the lane, never looking back, just as he had done four years after her, and her outline eventually dissolving into the background. She had instantly become invisible and out of reach.

He'd searched for her. Informed the police. Visited her friends in Malton. There was no note, no phone call. She didn't write a letter, or give any reason… she simply left. Left him with his father, his alcoholic, ill-tempered father with whom his life had become intolerable.

And what of a potential return?

The newly discovered knowledge that grandad Payne had left the yard to his mother had given Will renewed hope. It was a vague, barely credible hope, but it was more hope than he'd ever enjoyed during the past seven long years. Besides, he'd had an idea… a way to lure his mother back to the yard. He was going to make it his own.

For his mother to return, Manor Stud Stables needed to *still be there. He* needed it to be there. And perhaps his name against the stable runners instead of her own, might bring her back. His father had always trained under his wife's name, never changing it to his own, and now he knew why – Mary Payne owned the yard!

'I'm going to clean the yard up,' he stated quietly.

'Fine,' his father offered with a shrug, 'Just make sure that filly is kept sound. She's an Ascot horse. Don't let Roberto over-work her either, she's…'

'Shut up, dad,' Will snapped, 'Roberto and I know how to train young sprinters. I was doing it from the age of eight, remember.'

His father rolled his tongue around his cheek, a mannerism he adopted when he was displeased, but unable to conjure up a sensible rebuke. Will had witnessed this almost daily during the months leading up to him leaving home. Presently Barney began again, 'Yes, but she needs…'

'Don't bother,' Will cut in angrily, 'I don't want to listen to another of your treatise on the training of racehorses!'

With eyes blazing and gesticulating wildly, he added, 'Mind you, dad, you're in the right place. You can spout your homespun wisdom to your fellow patients. They'll be perfect for you; a captive audience.'

Barney stared blankly at his son then closed his eyes. Gripping the bridge of his nose between thumb and forefinger, he began slowly rubbing the skin. Half a minute passed before he spoke again. This time, low and soft.

'So, why are you here?'

Will had remained standing to this point, but now pulled a chair over and sat down, careful to face his father.

'You're not getting out of here any time soon, and the yard is in bad shape.'

Barney shook his head, adopting a sour expression, but he didn't attempt to counter his son's assertion.

'I'll run the yard. Make it right again. Clean up that pit of a farmhouse. In return, I want the horses to race under my name.'

Will watched his father intently as he silently considered his proposition.

Presently, he said, 'You haven't passed the BHA…'

'I did the training and passed the course years ago,' Will countered,' It was the first thing I did when I left you. I used a bit of the money grandad Payne left me. My license is already approved. I can take over as the trainer at Manor Farm Stud.'

There was another long pause, during which his father stared blankly at the ceiling. When he next spoke, his voice was down to a whisper and Will could detect the faintest signs of quavering in the back of his throat.

'She won't come back y'know, son. I know that's why you've stayed. But your Mum won't come back.'

Will's eyes hardened, 'How do you know?'

Barney studied his son's face for a moment, but didn't reply. He resumed staring up at the ceiling, 'Your mother was like you. She'd never let go of things…'

'Sort the paperwork, do what you want with the yard,' Barney continued suddenly, sounding weary, 'Just make sure that filly… whatever Hanover has named her… gets to the racecourse in one piece for a maiden before the Albany. She's going to put the yard back on the map.'

A silence developed and Will searched his mind for anything else he needed to raise.

'I took that look around your bedroom.'

Barney eyed his son pensively for a moment before growling a reply.

'What's that?'

'I looked around your bedroom, in the wardrobe, like you asked,' Will replied, unable to keep from showing his irritation, 'You were talking rubbish, there's nothing there apart from mum's bits and pieces she left behind.'

'I… don't know what you mean,' Barney said uneasily, 'I must have been… out of it.'

As Will watched his father fight against his inevitable slide into sleep he pondered why his father had just lied to him. He'd had that shifty look in his eye. Perhaps his mother and father's bedroom was worth another, deeper investigation?

Just before his father's eyes flickered shut, he added, 'That filly's my meal ticket for the next ten years. Get her entered for the Albany… she's going… to…'

'Hanover has named her Catwalk,' Will said quietly, 'Roberto calls her Kitty'.

He watched his sleeping father's chest rise and fall a few times, trying to determine whether his feelings for the broken man lying before him might have altered over the last few days. He didn't loiter for long. Will couldn't locate any newfound warmth for his father.

# Nine

Getting back into the routine of living and working in a racing yard came naturally to Will. He found it surprisingly easy to rise at five o'clock, make the first check of the horses and, after consultation of the feed calendar, serve up their breakfasts. Even at university, he'd never got into the habit of sleeping into the morning unless it had been a particularly late night. Even so, he'd not seen a sunrise for some time.

There was something about rising with the sun and being alone with the horses. Will found the experience put him reassuringly at ease. He'd be accompanied by nothing more than an early morning mist, swallows diving in and out of the boxes, and that weird sense of wellbeing that comes from getting a head start on the rest of humanity. He'd missed that.

This first hour alone with the horses also allowed him to get to know them, often intimately. His first morning had seen him sustain a bite from a filly far too keen to sink her head into her food trough, another from a playful gelding who took a shine to his shoulder, and an accidental kick to his thigh from one of the more excitable young colts. None were serious, or meant to injure him, and Will took no offence – it was a standard morning in a racing stable.

By the time Roberto and Lizzy arrived at six forty-five, Will would be in the farmhouse kitchen with the kettle on and ready to get the toaster popping up several rounds of hot buttered toast, or in Lizzy's case, generously smeared with raspberry jam. He'd been pleasantly surprised to find the kitchen was relatively clean compared to the rest of the house, and soon realised this was down to Roberto, rather than his father.

The head lad kept the horse's living spaces clean and this extended to where he drank his coffee and ate his toast. The kitchen consisted of the basics, but had a wood burner that never went cold from November to March and a vast wooden kitchen table with fourteen matching chairs, a daily reminder of Manor Stud Stables' glory days. When Brigadier Walter (Wally) Wantage trained in the fifties and the yard was at its zenith, it was a big operation, boasting over a hundred racehorses on top of the thirty mares and stallions at stud, and a large staff count to ensure the smooth running of the yard. In those days the farmhouse kitchen would have been the central hub of the yard, with several sittings for each meal.

Having been split into three smaller yards in the seventies, Will had been told his grandfather, Jack Payne, had managed to fill its forty boxes, specializing in cheap, young horses and championing some of the first twenty-person syndicates, each owner having five percent. He imagined eight to ten staff would have bustled around the kitchen in his grandfather's day, making the place feel alive with a flow of people, talk, and banter. It was hard not to feel somewhat depressed when only he, Roberto, Gordy, and Lizzy sat down at a table that seated fourteen people with ease and sixteen at a push.

Will was quite sure his father's lack of business acumen, combined with his drinking, was largely responsible for the yard's dwindling horse population. His gruff, demeaning, and aggressive nature had certainly been the reason for his own exodus and he imagined contributed in a big way to a lack of owners. When Will had left Manor Stud Stables on his eighteenth birthday there had been twenty-two occupied boxes. Thirty-eight horses had been in situ before his mother had left. Will was a little surprised there were any horses at all, especially if his father dealt with his owners and suppliers in the same way he treated his immediate family.

Taking a look through his father's financial paperwork had been a painful exercise. Will had worked through a mass of receipts, invoices, and bills on his second night at the farmhouse, only to find that nothing balanced with the bank statements. A subsequent phone call to the family accountant the next day revealed that this was no big surprise. The young woman who managed the stables accounts had intimated that her quarterly balancing of his father's books was based more on leaps of faith rather than a forensic analysis of his business.

On the first Friday, his fifth day on the yard, Will rode three lots out in the morning and dismounted from the last with knees that went to jelly and almost buckled under him. If nothing else, he was going to strip a good deal fitter and stronger by the time his father returned. After thanking Roberto, Lizzy, and Gordy for bearing with him over the last few days, he made his way back to the farmhouse and settled down in the back room to assess the size of his task, and his options. Since his father's accident, the yard hadn't sent out any runners, but that had to change – they had a brace of two-year-olds ready to make their debuts and the older horses needed to have a handicapping race plan put in place.

Hunting around for the latest programme book - the publication that provided listings for every race for the next three months - Will found editions going back as much as three years scattered across the dining table and stacked around his father's armchair, but the current issue for May, June, and July was missing. Having scoured the downstairs, he extended his search, reasoning his father may have taken the latest edition upstairs to read in bed.

It was the one room in the house he had been forbidden to enter as a child. His mother had promised dire consequences would befall him, should he invade his parents' privacy. So when Will entered his mother and father's bedroom, he did so with some trepidation. Even in an empty house, and aged twenty-one, entering this hallowed ground felt very wrong. He laughed inwardly at himself upon realising he was purposefully stepping lightly to avoid making a noise.

He'd had a scout around the bedroom following his father's dazed instructions at the hospital, but found nothing of any interest beyond various small reminders that his mother had once lived and slept in this room. He'd taken a long look in the wardrobe, but again, apart from his mother and father's clothes, he'd discovered little else of interest.

Crossing the dusty purple carpet and around the bed covered in a lacy yellow bedspread, Will idly wondered why his father had allowed such a feminine touch in the room, and why it remained so, now his mother wasn't around. It did look a little faded and grubby… most likely, his father had never got around to buying anything new since his wife had left – that was certainly the case around the yard. In fact, when he hesitated for a moment and took in the scene as a whole, the entire room could have been used as a filming location for a drama set in the seventies or eighties. Apart from a couple of built-in wardrobes with Victorian styled wooden doors, the rest of the furniture and fittings screamed seventies kitsch.

Once at his father's side of the bed, Will inspected a pile of old racing magazines on his bedside table. He soon found the racing programme book he was looking for on the floor, along with the other recent missing editions. Pleased with his find, he headed for the door with thoughts of making entries at two of the local racetracks for races in a week's time, but was forced to pause at the end of the bed.

It was her smell. More accurately, it was his mother's perfume. She was suddenly inside his mind, close to him on the sofa in front of the television, leaning over him as she took his temperature when he was ill in bed, hugging him when he won the primary school sprint race on sports day. For a long moment Will closed his eyes and drank in the aroma and revelled in the memories.

Sure enough, upon closer inspection, he spied a stumpy little bottle of yellow coloured perfume standing on a thin-legged dressing table in front of the bay window, it's half-moon mirror in need of a good dusting. Will picked up the perfume bottle from its lace doily and smiled at the name written in sloping black letters: *Charlie*. However his smile faded into a quizzical frown when he realised the lemon and peach aroma wasn't coming from the bottle. A quick sniff revealed the source of the scent to be a small round piece of thick white card the bottle had been sitting upon.

Carefully replacing the bottle, Will's gaze moved down the dressing table to where a padded jewellery box covered with images of poppies was sitting proudly on another snowflake shaped doily. He reached out to open the box, hesitating to look over his shoulder at the open bedroom door, just in case his mother might suddenly enter, discover him and deliver a scolding. Once again, he laughed inwardly at how ridiculous he was being, although his amusement soon turned sour as he contemplated the grim possibility of his mother never again entering the same room as himself.

On opening the box, a range of dress jewellery was revealed. A second layer contained small square compartments where various rings and earrings were stored. Will stared wistfully at them. He was about to snap the box shut when he noticed a couple of the compartments were sitting proud. Something was causing them to lift and break their symmetry. Lifting the two compartments up between thumb and forefinger, Will peered down at an age blackened iron key.

It didn't take long to establish that the key didn't fit anything on the dressing table, so Will moved around the bedroom, searching for anything with a lock. Based on the keys' length, size, and basic shape he imagined it belonged to a drawer or chest. Having exhausted the options around the room, he inspected the three doored wardrobe built into the far wall. None of the wooden doors had keyholes, so he cautiously ventured inside them whilst experiencing the same feeling of intrusion he had with the dressing table.

Two minutes of patient searching left Will with the impression the wardrobe held nothing of significance, and no obvious keyhole. Just like his first foray into the wardrobe, he was sure his father was either toying with him, or he'd been babbling rubbish in his dazed state. Will noted this time that the area holding his mother's clothes seemed depleted, suggesting she'd taken a fair number of garments with her. The jewellery box had worried him a little, as it niggled him that so much of it had been left behind. But then she'd never been one for wearing bling, he told himself. And he wondered how much of it had been his grandmother's. At least with most of his mother's clothes gone, it pointed to the fact she may have planned her exit from his life and that she meant to start anew somewhere else. It was certainly more positive than the suicide or abduction nightmares he'd had as a teenager.

It was while he was moving the remaining dresses, skirts, and tops across the hanging rail that he noticed the back of the wardrobe. It was pitted, and marked with regular use, as if ancient hands had pushed so often against it, they had blackened an area. Will pulled out some shoe boxes, three plastic bags full of baby clothes, and a pillow case filled with old riding apparel from the bottom of the wardrobe, cleaning it out completely. Only when it was empty did Will spy the small keyhole embedded deep into the thick wooden rear of the wardrobe.

Will stared at the keyhole. With pulse elevated and his mind spinning with a mixture of fascination and excitement, he inserted the key from the jewellery box and attempted to turn it to the right. Nothing. He spun it to the left and a surprisingly solid thunk married to the movement of a mechanism from within indicated it was the correct key.

With breath held, Will stepped into the wardrobe. Brushing the hanging clothes aside he placed both his hands onto the back wall of the wardrobe, thoughts of his mother reading the Narnia stories to him as a six-year-old bringing a nervous smile to his face.

Under the least amount of pressure, the entire back wall of the wardrobe swung away into blackness. The shock of suddenly encountering an unexpected void unbalanced Will. Grabbing at the clothes rail in order to steady himself, he unwittingly unhinged the wooden pole and sent it, clothes and hangers too, along with himself, crashing to the base of the wardrobe.

Will slumped against the side of the wardrobe, and slowly picked his mother's old clothes and wire coat hangers off him. He peered into the blackness to his left. With the clothes gone from the wardrobe, more light from the bedroom was managing to penetrate the space beyond. It was a narrow, windowless room that ran the length of the external wall, behind the built-in wardrobe. Lifting a hand to brush away a nearby cobweb he noticed a protuberance on the wall; an old-fashioned, bulbous flick-switch light. Carefully pushing himself up to his feet he flipped the switch, not expecting anything to happen. A bulb flickered into life and Will gaped into the secret room.

Virtually every inch of the walls were covered in curling paper notes, photos, and string. At the far end of the room was a rickety looking chair and a desk. On the desk appeared to be a chunky laptop. Above, and dominating the small space, was a large, framed photograph of a plump, smiling man in his forties.

Entering the long, thin room, Will brushed cobwebs out of the way and peered at the photograph. Will's grandfather, Jack Payne, grinned down at him from the bare brick wall. His face held a strange expression, one of delighted surprise. It was as if Jack had been patiently waiting for his grandson to find him.

## Ten

Later that evening, Will used the farmhouse phone, spinning its heavy circular dial to call Freddie's mobile number. He'd correctly guessed both he and Arthur would be together, back at the shared house in Wallsend.

'Aye, aye, Winda!' Freddie answered.

'How did you know it was me?'

'No one else from Malton would be callin' us!'

'Ah, yes… the phone number.'

'So how's it goin' in the land of the horse?'

Will hesitated, trying to find the right words.

Freddie gave a chortle, 'That bad, huh?'

'Is Arthur there? Put your phone on speaker would you?'

Arthur's Scottish accented voice said, 'I'm here, Will. What's up?'

'You know that holiday in Europe we had planned?'

Both his friends replied with a long 'Yesss?' that anticipated his bad news.

'I just wondered whether you fancied swapping Paris, Athens, Turin, Cannes, and Rome for…'

'Malton?' cut in Arthur.

'Yeah,' admitted Will dejectedly.

There was a short pause before both his friends came back with positive replies.

'Thanks you two. I'll make it worthwhile,' Will added, a smile in his tone.

'What do you need doing?' asked Freddie.

'One of you needs to know how to handle a paint brush, climb ladders, and fix a clock, the other needs to understand accounts and operate an old computer. And both of you need to become detectives.'

There was another short pause as Freddie and Arthur conferred.

'Free bed, breakfast, and evening meal included!' Will added as the silence lengthened.

'Now yer talkin'!' Freddie cooed excitedly.

'We'll be there on Sunday,' confirmed Arthur.

**Eleven**

Will woke suddenly, threw his bedclothes back, swung his legs to the side of the bed, and stared around his childhood bedroom. It was still dark. A glance at his phone confirmed it was almost three in the morning. Something wasn't right.

A number of whinnies, snorts, and a sharp bang of a hoof slapping a box wall out in the yard brought him to his feet. Casting one half of his fading blue curtains aside, Will peered across the yard and down the long line of boxes. Each stable entrance should have been dimly lit with a night light, but with several bulbs failing to illuminate, Will was presented with a patchwork of barely visible boxes. However, his pulse quickened when he noticed over half the horses in the yard had their heads over their stable doors. That wasn't great, not at this time of night. It was most likely a prowling fox, but the thought of a horse with colic, or cast at the back of its stable, damaging itself as it desperately tried to get to its feet, thrust him into action.

Pulling on his jeans and a T-shirt, he made his way downstairs in the dark. He considered switching all the farmhouse lights on and making plenty of noise, but instead decided an investigative approach would yield more answers. He stepped into his boots at the door and ventured out into the yard armed with the torch that his father always kept on a hook in the porch for just this eventuality.

As soon as he stepped out into the yard the cool, clear night shocked his bare forearms and neck, instantly biting into his hitherto warm skin. Stars filled the sky, however; a waxing moon provided little in the way of illumination. Will shivered, and considered returning to the farmhouse for a jumper, but soon discarded this notion. The horses came first.

Working his way along the line of stables, Will flashed the beam of his torch quickly inside and around each occupant, checking for any signs of distress or injury. He was soon halfway down the long line of boxes and thankfully hadn't found anything untoward. At one time in the sixties each stable would have been home to a broodmare. Having originally been a stud, the stables were large and the way they made up the horse's beds, it was unlikely they would get cast. Nevertheless, horses, especially the youngsters were more than capable of finding novel ways in which to injure themselves.

He reached a gelding called Battle Stations and found the five-year-old in good health, staring balefully at him from his bed of wood shavings as Will's torch skimmed around the box. The gelding was lying with his head resting between his front legs and he twitched his ears as if irked by the interruption to his beauty sleep.

'Alright boy, I'll leave you alone,' Will called quietly over his stable door before moving on.

Will passed the next two stables with only a cursory inspection, as their residents had their heads over the stable doors. However, the next box was home to Catwalk, and she was nowhere to be seen. It took a few seconds to locate the filly, as she was standing tight to the right-hand corner of her stable, close to her automated water font. She snorted nervously when his torchlight flashed across her grey face with its white flash. Whether it was the location of the filly, or the way her ears were plastered back on her head, Will decided to check her over. He kicked at the bottom swing lock, pulled the top bolt back and ventured inside.

It only took a single step inside the stable for him to determine that he was sharing it with someone else. The sound of movement made him swing around, his torch momentarily flashing across a crouched figure dressed all in black. Immediately springing up from the floor with a speed that made Will gasp in shock, the black figure, its face hidden behind a mask, flew up at him. He was dimly aware of a flash of silver and then pain rushed at his temple and his knees suddenly decided standing wasn't an option. Will felt a stab of pain run across his forehead before he collapsed like a dead weight onto Catwalk's bed of straw and shavings.

***

A soft, warm spongy surface rubbed itself across his cheek. A small forest of hairs brushed his nose and the filly breathed on him.

Will gently pushed Catwalk's muzzle away and straightened to a sitting position, his legs shot straight out in front of him. He'd been asleep… no, unconscious. He took in his dark surroundings and screwed his eyes up at the oblong of sunlight once his gaze reached the open stable door.

He winced and rubbed his eyes. The morning sun's attack on his senses only served to shoot a searing pain across his forehead from left to right. Nausea and dizziness swamped him for a moment. Steadying himself on rigid arms, Will remained seated on the mat of damp shavings, leaning forward until the floor ceased its lop-sided spinning and settled back to some sort of normality.

A quick investigation with the fingers of his left hand revealed a not inconsiderable volume of congealed blood attached to his left temple. He swallowed hard and desperately tried to think straight. His night investigation came back to him, the dark figure… the blow to his head. Feeling slightly better now he knew the reason for waking with a horse breathing over him, he made to get up, but the sound of approaching footsteps and the sliding of a bolt on Catwalk's stable door sent his heart racing.

'Bloody 'ell, Guv,'

Gordy, his aged yard lad, swung the stable door wide and bore down on him. A smidgen over seventy, his official status of 'stable lad' hardly did him justice. Gordy had more experience than him and the rest of Will's employees put together. Will relaxed and tried a smile, relieved to see a friendly face.

'Morning, Gordy,' Will croaked, suddenly aware his throat was painfully dry.

'She kick you?' Gordy queried, 'Not like 'er, Guv. Kitty's usually as sweet as yer like.'

'No… it was…'

Will thought for a moment. Gordy was a decent yard man, patient with the horses, and ultra-reliable. But he was also fond of sharing his business with anyone who would listen. It wouldn't be a great advert to prospective owners, nor would this information help to attract new staff if it became common knowledge around Malton that Manor Stud Stables had been subject to a prowler only a few days into his new tenure as resident trainer.

'My fault, Gordy. Slipped up and bashed myself I guess,' Will said, refusing the yard lad's proffered hand.

Gordy manhandled the filly to the back of her box and then insisted on helping Will to his feet. He stood, eyeing the floor of the stable, thoughtfully rubbing the lengthy bristles on his chin between forefinger and thumb.

'Aye well, if you will go braining yourself with your torch, Guv,' he said, stooping to pick up what was left of a shiny steel torch. It had a significant dent running along its side and the glass lens was cracked.

'Thanks,' said Will, inspecting the torch. The flash of silver he'd experienced before being struck now made sense.

'Check the filly over, will you, Gordy. I need to get warmed up in the farmhouse.'

Gordy nodded and turned his back on Will.

'And don't mention this to anyone will you? It's a bit embarrassing… you know?'

'No problem, Guv,' Gordy answered positively as he ran his hand down the filly's tendons, 'I'll keep my mouth zipped.'

But for how long, wondered Will as he emerged into the dawn of a new day.

Inside the box, Gordy finished his inspection of

60

Catwalk, satisfied she was perfectly sound. As he set to leave his eye was drawn by something else buried among the filly's bed. He scraped away a mixture of straw, hay, and shavings, scooping up a second torch. This one was in good working order and he recognised it as the Guv's - the one that always hung in the farmhouse porch. Gordy frowned, wondering why the Guv had needed two torches on his morning round of the boxes, especially when dawn had broken over two hours ago.

## Twelve

'So what do you think?' asked Will.

The phone line went silent for a few seconds.

An unconvinced voice asked, 'You reckon she's good enough to go to Ascot?'

Will didn't hesitate. He knew he had to sound confident.

'Listen, Davy, she's that fast, I've not got anything good enough to go with her here, so I need you to come in on Saturday morning, ride her out, and tell me she's the best two-year-old you've sat on this season...'

The jockey chuckled, 'I'm just pulling your leg, Will! Of course I'll be there on Saturday morning. How could I refuse an old pal? You'll owe me a *massive* favour!'

Davy Dalton rang off, still sniggering, which in turn made Will smile. Davy was an energetic sort with an even more active sense of humour. Will was more impressed with his racing brain – the lad he'd played around Norton and Malton with as a boy and teenager was now displaying race intelligence and a real feel for pace in the saddle. This was being backed up with a steady flow of winners.

Rather like Will, Davy came from a racing family who had trained in Malton for several generations. The son of Neil Dalton, the current trainer in situ at their family stables, Davy's riding career had been brought along slowly but surely by his father, and he was still a three-pounds claiming apprentice. But having recently become attached to one of the bigger, more successful yards in Malton, rather than his father's, he was starting to make a name for himself and benefitted from sitting on some very decent horses during his working week.

Davy had just agreed to come and ride out a few of Will's two-year-olds, including Catwalk. Will was hoping this would give him some sort of handle on the quality he had among his youngsters, and specifically, whether Kitty was as talented as Will, his father, and the rest of the yard were hoping. If things worked out, Davy would also be handed the filly's debut ride.

Will replaced the phone's receiver onto its squat plastic base and regarded the large circular dial of numbers with a half-smile. The tinkle of the old-fashion bell when the handset plopped back onto the dull, grey lump brought back memories of his mother. The 1970's style phone used to sit on the windowsill and he could remember his mother speaking with agents, jockeys, and clerks of racecourses whilst leaning against the table or looking out the back window. She'd attached an extra-long cable to the receiver to allow her to walk around the table, phone clamped between her ear and her shoulder. Often, the spiral cord would twang over the chair backs as she moved around the back room, overseeing the completion of his homework to her satisfaction whilst sorting out a jockey booking.

His moment of reflection was interrupted by a knock at the front door. Will sighed. It was Friday evening, and it felt like he'd already had half of Malton beating a path to his door in the last few days. Local people asking after his father, wishing him well, jockeys looking for rides, stable staff looking for jobs… and the odd blast from the past too. With all this going on, and trying to get a handle on running the yard, he'd not had a proper chance to go through everything he found in the hidden room upstairs. He'd reluctantly accepted it would have to wait until Freddie and Arthur arrived.

To Will's surprise, two more of his old Malton school friends had pitched up at the yard over the course of the last week. Darren Blenkinsop and Suzie Tipton had popped in.

Darren had been on the fringes of his social group during his A-Levels and was a large, genial sort who spoke with a broad East Yorkshire accent. He liked his beer, football and racing, and explained he was now a salesman for an equine feed company. The suited and booted sales executive saved this snippet of information for the last few moments of their conversation. Will couldn't help feeling it explained Darren's close interest in how many horses were in the yard.

Will had quickly disposed of Darren, citing pressure of work. However, when Suzie Tipton landed on his doorstep Will found himself adopting a completely different approach.

She had been a regular member of his social group in the sixth form, a loose bunch of friends numbering between six and ten on most nights out. He and Suzie had got on well and enjoyed a laugh together, but he'd never considered her a particularly close friend, certainly not the sort he would share personal matters with, and she had never struck him as potential girlfriend material. Suzie had been a quiet, somewhat insular girl who dressed conservatively in school and out of it. At times, usually when tipsy, she had displayed an ultra-dry sense of humour that would have the group, including himself, in stiches, but Will's abiding memory of Suzie was of her being a wary type who tended to fade into the background.

The daughter of the landlord of one of the busiest pubs in Malton, Suzie had been an irregular member of Will's group of friends, her social life limited by the requirement to work for her father on busy nights, serving food, or working back of house.

She had been facing the stables, her back to him, when he opened the farmhouse door. It was fairly late on Thursday evening and he had snapped a disinterested, 'Yes?' at her.

His eyes had been on stalks when the shapely girl he'd initially mistaken for a stable lass looking for work, had swung around. Her pixie bob had danced momentarily across her cheek, a diamond nose-stud had sparkled, and she'd grinned expectantly at him.

'Never heard of email or Facebook, Will?' the girl had enquired accusingly, one hand on her hip and a sculpted dark eyebrow raised. Dressed in tight blue jeans, and with a white t-shirt under a black leather bomber jacket, Will had gaped at her for a long moment before her smile managed to bring him to his senses. The shy, rather thin streak of a girl he'd known and largely ignored as a seventeen-year-old, had become a fulsome, radiant, twenty-one-year-old woman brimming with confidence.

'Suzie! You've...'

He'd been about to say 'changed', but his mind rejected that and then cycled through 'grown' before selecting, '... come to see me!'

'Suzie had laughed generously, castigated him for such a lame greeting and they'd gone on to spend a happy forty minutes in the kitchen remembering the highlights of their A-Level years over several cups of dreadful instant coffee. Suzie had left once she'd received a promise from Will to visit her dad's pub in the centre of Malton, where she was currently working as a barmaid over summer. She too had gone off to university, but unlike Will, bothered to return home between terms to visit her parents.

To round off this memorable reunion, he had watched transfixed from his porch as Suzie had crossed the yard, pulled on a full face helmet, straddled a powerful looking Honda two-fifty motorcycle and with a small wave, departed slowly so as not to scare the horses. Upon reaching the main road, Will had heard her open her throttle and roar off into the night.

Another knock, harder and more urgent than the first, rocked Will from thoughts of Suzie. He approached the farmhouse door half hoping it would be her again, but was soon disappointed when he spotted the police uniform. Pat Higgins stared dully through the porch window at him.

The conversation didn't last long. Will made it clear he wasn't going to invite his godfather in, making a show of wearily rubbing his eyes and feigning a yawn.

'I heard there was an incident in the yard?' Pat got around to asking, 'Some sort of... argument?'

For a moment, Will's blood pressure rose and he inwardly derided Gordy for breaking his promise to keep quiet about their conversation in Catwalk's stable. He smothered his anger, knowing that Gordy probably saw Pat as a family friend.

'The young lad you sacked…' Pat continued to fill the silence when Will didn't answer, 'I heard he's been in touch with Racing Welfare. You might get a call…'

Will relaxed, cursing himself for doubting Gordy's loyalty.

'Did Jimmy Hearn mention why I sacked him?'

Pat shook his head.

'I caught him red-handed, smashing his boot into one of my horses. I'm sure he's neglected to include that snippet of information during his whinge to Welfare.'

Pat nodded, 'Fair enough. He's been round the local pubs telling anyone who'll listen that you're a… Well, you can imagine.'

The identity of his intruder in Catwalk's stable came to Will suddenly. Of course, how had he been so naïve? Jimmy had exacted his revenge for being let go by waiting, then smacking him with his torch when he'd entered the stable. Swinging a punch from out of the dark would fit perfectly with the cowardly style of a boy who could happily inflict pain on a defenceless horse.

An alternative scenario entered Will's mind and he tried hard not to allow his consternation show in his face. What if Jimmy had been about to injure Catwalk when he entered the stable? Will dismissed this notion. He reasoned that once he'd been knocked unconscious Jimmy had every opportunity to hurt the filly, but hadn't.

'You don't have to look out for me, Pat,' Will assured the policeman, 'All the same, thanks for coming around.'

Will closed the front door of the farmhouse and leaned against it, fretting. What if Jimmy had meant to hurt Catwalk, but panicked after whacking him with his torch? That would mean he could potentially return to finish the job. Will thought it unlikely. Still, it couldn't do any harm to move the filly into an alternative stable.

The steel torch caught Will's eye, its broken casing sitting on the sideboard in the hall. He picked it up and weighed it in his hand. Several heavy batteries in its broken case made it a substantial weapon. He'd been lucky to suffer nothing more than a bit of a headache. He inspected the torch with a keen eye, but no matter how many times he turned it over in his hands, it yielded no clues to its owner's identity.

Ten minutes later, Will had bedded Catwalk down in a brand new stable. Although through summer he preferred to leave the top half of his stable doors open, for the next few nights Catwalk slept soundly behind a fully closed, padlocked set of stable doors.

*** 

Next day, bright and early, Davy Dalton called round. The apprentice jockey breezed into the kitchen in the same suave, outwardly confident style he'd adopted in the last few years at school, constantly running a hand through his mop of thick, lustrous brown hair. Just like Will, he was small in stature, but Davy had a warm, positive personality, something Will had always been in awe of, and secretly, a little jealous.

The hand through the hair was an affectation Will seized upon with relish. His teasing, and Davy's friendly retaliation regarding Will's long, unkempt, and somewhat knotted head of hair soon dissolved any awkwardness the two year hiatus in their relationship might have caused. Within minutes the two of them were happily ripping good-natured strips off each other. However, on his return to the yard after working Catwalk, Davy's demeanour had altered markedly.

With cheeks blooming, Davy slid off the filly. Will waited patiently while his friend removed the tack.

'She's the best I've sat on in Malton,' Davy started, locking eyes with Will so he knew he was serious, 'She'll win a Novice, even though she's still a bit green. We only went a swinging canter, but you can feel there is plenty more in the tank. She wouldn't have blown a candle out afterwards. It was all too easy for her.'

Davy quickly made it clear he wanted to ride Kitty on her racecourse debut, already calling her by her stable name. Will jumped at the opportunity, knowing Davy's experience of riding the filly on the gallops, along with his three-pounds apprentice allowance, could prove to be invaluable. He promised to speak with the filly's owner, Louis Hanover, to clear him for the ride and suggested Davy might ride another of Hanover's filly's due to debut locally in six days' time, in order to cement him as the owner's chosen jockey. He would then ride Catwalk in her first race, a five furlong event for novices at Goodwood, the week after.

Once the talk of business was out of the way, the two of them had then spent an enjoyable thirty minutes reminiscing about their time knocking around Malton together in Davy's classic old mini as seventeen-year-olds. Davy had been fascinated to hear about Suzie, as he too hadn't seen her recently, and the two men parted with an agreement to visit Suzie's father's pub in Malton at the first opportunity.

## Thirteen

Sunday morning brought an influx of owners into the yard to chat, drink coffee, and peer at the equine athletes over their stable doors. As a rule, the horses didn't do any gallop work on a Sunday, and despite the constant interruptions, Will made a point of giving every horse their fair share of paddock time between the arrival and departure of their connections.

Will had spoken to each of the owners on the day he'd arrived in Malton, explaining the situation with his father, and how he would be taking over on an interim basis. Most of the owners were long-standing clients whom he'd already met. Their agreement had been expected, however a few new owners had sounded less than enthused with their expensive hobby being managed by a youngster they barely knew. Will had invited all of the owners to the yard on this Sunday morning in order to re-establish contact with the older clientele and try to quell any nervousness among the newer ones. The last thing he wanted, or the yard needed, was to lose any more of its nine inmates.

First to arrive was a retired schoolteacher called Henry Bigham, a long-standing owner who lived for his days at the yard and the races. He was also the last to leave, happy to stand stroking his mare, Peace Offering, for hours on end. He was followed by the 'Draw Down' syndicate, a group of four well-heeled colleagues from a financial services company in Leeds who only stayed for a short chat. They surveyed their handicapper before heading off to Ripon for an afternoon of racing, drinking, and gambling. Will was left with the impression that they ranked gambling as the highest in their order of importance.

An elderly lady called Mrs Wallace, who introduced herself as 'Jill', pumped Will for information about potential races and handicap marks for her gelding, Major Potts, and then left abruptly when she received a phone call on her mobile. Will wasn't too sure about her. She'd given him a worryingly long, appraising look up and down upon meeting him that had rattled his confidence. Will hoped the firm handshake and fixed glare she'd given him just prior to her departure were positives, but he wasn't convinced. As Mrs Wallace had turned away, he was sure she had tutted disapprovingly following one final appraisal of his long hair.

Harriet Gardener arrived in a taxi, which remained in the yard car park during her stay, the driver reading a paperback. Will guessed she was around forty-years-old, although she wore clothes that tried to suggest she was ten years younger. She flew at Will, embracing him warmly and covering his cheeks in red lipstick smudges. In his more sober moods, his father referred to her as, 'that silly rich woman'. Will knew this was a tactic his father employed around the stable staff to deflect any suggestion Harriet's advances were anything more than a middle-aged woman being over-friendly. Will believed his father was blind when it came to reading some of his owners. He'd noticed years ago that his mother treated Harriet in a rather special way, and that the likeable lady spent more time stealing sideway looks at the stable lasses, rather than the muscular lads.

Harriet produced a bag of carrots and spent most of the morning feeding pounds of veg into her two older handicappers, Battle Stations and Jumble Sail. Gradually, the yard became quiet again at around noon, with Henry and Harriet the only owners left, sharing stories of their most memorable days racing with their racehorses, current and retired.

Roberto had agreed to come in on his day off to help ease the introductions, and so when an expensive, blacked out Mercedes pulled into the yard's car park the head lad extracted himself from Harriet's latest racing story and beetled over to welcome Louis Hanover, owner of Catwalk, and two more juveniles, named Spring Ensemble, and Flared Silhouette. Roberto brought their impeccably dressed owner over and introduced him to Will.

'William Payne,' Hanover stated with a sharp, white-toothed smile, but without any offer of a handshake.

Will was immediately taken with Hanover's appearance. He was immaculately turned out. Everything about him screamed style. From his tanned, undoubtedly moisturised face, dazzlingly light blue eyes, exquisitely cropped brown hair, down to his open shirt, tartan waistcoat, and chinos topped off with a pair of expensive brogues. Will found it all a bit too much, standing there in his filthy working clothes and hair plastered to his head after having had to run around one of the turnout paddocks to catch a playful filly who had wanted more time to roam free.

Hanover looked like he'd just walked off a photo shoot for a gentleman's catalogue, which Will supposed was just as well, as he owned the 'Roar' clothing brand, currently one of the most exclusive and successful clothing retailers. According to the Roar Wikipedia page, Hanover's brand was particularly popular in the United States and was well on the way to becoming of interest to some of the larger clothing companies as a takeover target. Roar specialised in short run, exclusive designs that sold for eye-watering sums to fashion conscious twenty-somethings.

It threw up a big question to Will. Why had Hanover picked his father to train for him? What led him to choose a struggling trainer, who operated under his estranged wife's name, to train his expensive purchases at the Tattersalls Book One Yearling Sale?

Will put such thoughts out of his head and hung a smile on his face, 'Yes, Mr Hanover. We spoke on the phone. I'm delighted you managed to make it.'

Hanover beamed back at Will, but said nothing.

'Shall we take a look at your horses?' suggested Will as a way of moving things along, 'We're very excited about all three of them.'

'As am I,' Hanover agreed, never taking his eyes off his

new, young trainer.

Will guided Hanover over to the first of three boxes in the middle of the stabling block and gestured for the businessman to follow him inside. Harriet and Henry nudged each other conspiratorially as Hanover disappeared from view.

It soon became apparent that Louis Hanover was well informed when it came to horse racing. Although he didn't say a great deal, the type of questions he asked displayed a more than passable knowledge of horses, races, and the bloodstock business. By the time they had reached Catwalk's stable Will was even more confused with Hanover's choice of Manor Stud Stables as his training yard of choice. He didn't strike Will to be someone who made decisions without considering all the options open to him.

'Whilst the other two will make up into decent handicappers, Kitty could be a bit special,' Will told Hanover.

Hanover frowned, 'Kitty?'

'It's her stable name,' Will explained, smoothing out the filly's mane with a hand as he spoke, 'She will definitely win her Maiden or Novice, and I know my father thinks enough of her to be considering an entry for the Albany at Royal Ascot in June.'

'Could she be ready for the Fillies Only Novice race over six furlongs at Newmarket next Saturday?'

Will glanced up at Hanover. He stood at least half a foot taller than him and even in the dim light at the back of the stable, Will found his blue eyes somewhat distracting. There it was again, he thought, this guy does know a bit about racing.

'Mr Hanover, can I ask why you chose my father to buy and train your horses?' he blurted.

'Is it important?' replied the owner carefully after considering the question for a long moment. Hanover's face remained rigid, only his eyes made any sort of movement, a sort of faint flicker of amusement.

'I'm trying to attract more owners into the yard,'

busked Will, 'I just wondered why you chose us. I could do with another couple of owners like yourself.'

Hanover remained silent for an uncomfortably long time, but Will resisted the temptation to prick the awkward bubble of tension by speaking first.

'Jack Payne was a great trainer. He was lucky, as well as being a skilled trainer,' said Hanover eventually, 'I always told myself that when I had the money to invest in a few decent racehorses, I'd place them in yard that was, above all, lucky. Regretfully, Jack's no longer around, but your mother, and now yourself, continue his bloodline. I'm anticipating you'll have the same sort of luck with my horses.'

It was the longest speech Hanover made in the entire thirty minute visit. Will mulled over his words for a moment, becoming slightly bewildered by Hanover's assertion that his grandpa Jack had been 'lucky'. This had to be rather questionable, given he was murdered.

Will forced the memory away, snapped back, and got down to business. He informed Hanover that Catwalk was likely to start at Goodwood on the 21st of May in a five furlong fillies only Novice. Hanover reacted by nodding dutifully and telling him he would, 'Look forward to meeting you again at a racecourse in due course.'

'Catwalk will be out the week after next,' Will reiterated, 'But I intend to give Spring Ensemble her debut at Ripon this coming Thursday. Will we see you there?'

Hanover nodded again, 'Of course I'll be there, she's my favourite out of my three. Catwalk, or 'Kitty' as you call her, may be your great hope, but Spring Ensemble is mine.'

Will started to explain that each of Hanover's horses would potentially need their debut runs in order to give them much-needed race experience, and therefore expectations should initially be set low. Will continued, but Hanover soon swung around from stroking Catwalk's neck and halted Will's flow with a dismissive wave of his hand.

'Please,' he insisted in an unexpectedly strident tone, 'I

understand.'

Will was expecting him to continue, but it appeared this was all Hanover was going to offer on the subject.

A few minutes later the clothing magnate was climbing effortlessly back into his one-hundred-and fifty-thousand pounds worth of Mercedes. It was soon stealthily making its silent way down the Manor Stud Stables lane in electric mode.

Roberto joined Will to watch Hanover depart and asked nervously, 'How did it go?'

'Truthfully, I really don't know,' Will replied with an irresolute shrug, 'If anything, I'm more confused now than I was before I'd met the man.'

## Fourteen

Freddie and Arthur arrived at the yard by taxi late on Sunday evening. Will welcomed them in their usual manner, a fist bump and the quickest of embraces.

'Hey, Winda, I thought you said this was a dump?' Freddie said, taking in the yard with hands on hips, clearly impressed with its size and the stable's ornate buildings.

'It's almost dark, you can't see where it's falling apart,' Will pointed out.

'Still, it's not such a bad wee drum,' Arthur commented, 'Yer Pa must be coining it in.'

Will gave a strangled laugh, 'It's like most professional sports. The top twenty percent of clubs, or in our case, trainers, make eighty percent of the profit. The rest struggle along trying to make ends meet. You have one bad season and you can just about cope. Two bad seasons in a row and you'll be on the breadline. Three… and you're gone. My father has had two bad seasons… Come on, leave your bags and I'll give you the tour before the sun sets.'

'I'm still not convinced your family isn't made of money,' Arthur protested forty minutes later as the three of them sat around the end of the table in the farmhouse kitchen nursing cups of coffee, 'You must have close to ten acres of land here, along with the walker, stables, tack room…'

'Take a look,' Will interrupted, placing a sheet of paper between his friends containing a column of figures and a few lines of text, 'I had my dad's accountant draw it up. That's where the business stands at the moment. Don't bother trying to understand it all – just read the comments at the bottom.'

'Ah,' Arthur murmured half a minute later, 'You're dad's broke…. Oh, and this accountant reckons you're losing five and a half grand every month and will be insolvent by Christmas. Man, that's bleak.'

'And to add to my problems, I have a sickly old man in hospital, and a disgruntled ex-employee creeping around in the dark trying to knock me senseless.'

To Will's surprise, this declaration had a greater impact on his two friends than the prospect of the yard facing imminent financial ruin. Will was forced to spend the next ten minutes explaining that his father's condition was improving, but his old man was still just as annoying. He was also forced to provide a detailed description of what happened during his night time encounter with Jimmy Hearn.

'Is that the sleuthing you mentioned on the phone,' asked Arthur, 'Are we tracking this Jimmy Hearn down and pinning the dirty deed on him?'

'No, there's something else,' admitted Will with a slow shake of his head.

Arthur leaned in, his eyes seeming to enlarge through his circular spectacles as he drew closer, 'Come on then. Spill it.'

Will rolled his eyes and took the two of them upstairs. He stood impatiently as his friends did rock, paper, scissors for what both of them considered to be the 'best bedroom', and eventually showed Arthur and Freddie the secret room behind the wardrobe.

'Wow, man, this is cool,' Freddie breathed excitedly as he checked out the plethora of notes and photos on the walls.

'As far as I can make out, this was my mother's secret little study,' suggested Will, 'And I think everything in here is linked to the death of my grandfather. That's him over there.'

Freddie and Arthur bent around each other to peer at the grinning face of Jack Payne hanging on the rough brick wall above the desk. Or was he just amused, wondered Will as he took in the photo again. He still wasn't sure.

'I've found two journals on the table, one of them is Jack's and the other is my Mother's. Jack's is mainly notes about horses and recording his invoices, payments, employee stuff, and er… betting accounts. But my mother's is… well, it's about Jack's murder.'

The temperature in the ill-lit oblong room seemed to

immediately fall by several degrees.

'His murder,' repeated Arthur, his Scottish accent adding gravitas to his words.

'Yeah,' Will replied in an apologetic tone, 'You won't remember it, but it was a big deal at the time. My grandfather was the victim in the York Ebor Murder in 2002.'

There was a short silence, eventually broken by Freddie.

'You've brought us down here in the hope that we'll spend the summer trying to solve a cold case? One that, I'm guessing, your mother was unable to solve by the look of it.'

Will scrunched his face up. He said, 'That's about it,' and waited, fearing their response.

Two seconds later the small secret room erupted with the elated cries of Arthur and Freddie as they tottered around the tiny room, high-fiving each other and then Will.

'Absolutely. Bloody. Brilliant!' Arthur exclaimed breathlessly, his eyes ablaze with excitement.

It was a comment that summed up the atmosphere in the farmhouse for the rest of the evening.

## Fifteen

Arthur woke on Monday morning to the sound of voices directly beneath him in the kitchen and immediately cursed his choice of bedroom. His disgust was heightened upon inspecting his mobile phone. It was only a few minutes past six. He turned over and tried to ignore the chatter coming up through the floorboards. Just as he was dropping off again, the doorknob jangled and Freddie entered unannounced. Grabbing a fistful of Arthur's duvet Freddie whipped it clean off him and cast it onto the floor, chortling when Arthur squirmed around on the mattress and finally fell out of bed.

'Gerrup! Get dressed… come on, Arty!' insisted Freddie with an amused smirk, 'Time to embrace the racehorse training lifestyle!'

Ten minutes later, Will was holding court at one end of the kitchen table whilst coffee and teas were sipped and toast was buttered. After introducing Lizzy, Gordy, and Roberto to his new recruits, and explaining that they were here to 'make the yard's finances, the stables, and the farmhouse presentable again,' he outlined the plan for the working week.

'We're racing tomorrow at Beverley with Risky and Sponge, then Hanover's Fido will have her debut at Ripon on Thursday and we're at Thirsk on Saturday with Brian. I'll drive the horsebox to all three. Davy Dalton has agreed to ride for me this week, so he'll take the mounts tomorrow and Thursday, but I may have to book someone else for Saturday. Lizzy, Roberto needs the weekend off, are you okay to come with me to Thirsk on Saturday?'

This suggestion received a confirming nod from Lizzy and Roberto thanked her. Freddie and Arthur's look of complete befuddlement prompted Will to backtrack and try to explain.

'We have stable names for the horses. They tend to stick once a new horse comes into the yard. Besides, most are unnamed when they arrive and we can't wait for their owners to name them, so we pick stable names as soon as they pitch up. Sponge is a four-year-old gelding called Salacious Star. He always got rubbed up by his tack on the gallops as a yearling, so we had to put bits of sponge under the leather to stop him going sore, so he got called Sponge.'

Roberto added, 'Risky is a gelding called 'Risk Ebusiness'. Actually, he already had his racing name and became Risky as soon as he walked off the transport.'

'And Fido and Brian?' asked Arthur.

'Spring Ensemble's party trick is sitting down in the paddocks like a dog, hence Fido, and Brian is a handicapper called Battle Stations.'

'I thought Battle Stations looked like a 'Brian' when he first came here,' Lizzy explained with a shrug.

'Anyway, you two don't need to worry about the horses, we'll deal with them,' Will went on, 'Freddie, could you take a look at the paint around the yard, the guttering too, and possibly mend the clock on the roof?'

'No problem, Boss,' replied Freddie, grinning around the table like a Cheshire cat. Will got the impression he was amused.

'What is it?' he asked his beaming friend.

Freddie's brows lifted, 'You! I'm lovin' the no nonsense, get to work, on a mission version of you.'

Will shot him a quick 'please don't embarrass me' look and swiftly moved on.

'Arthur, could you try and make some sense of my father's accounts and business records? They're in a bunch of files in the back room. I'm guessing you'd be happier doing that, rather than getting covered in paint?'

Arthur nodded his agreement, his mouth full of a slice of buttered toast.

'And Roberto has agreed to give both of you a crash course in stable and horse management,' Will announced.

Arthur sat bolt upright in his seat, his face suddenly a mask of nervous surprise, 'We're going tae ride a horse?'

'Dear God, no!' Roberto snorted with amusement, 'I'll be teaching you how to act around the horses, the duties of a stable lad, and how to lead a horse up. If either of you take to it, you might get to lead up at the races. But for now, I'm just pleased that the stables will be getting a new lick of paint.'

The little meeting soon broke up. Arthur hung back and caught Will's arm, 'What about… the other thing?'

'Everyone finishes at one o'clock on the days we don't have any racing, and evening stables is at five, which I tend to do on my own,' explained Will, 'Between one and five in the afternoons, as long as we don't have a runner, we can sift through everything in that secret room.'

*** 

'And you did this job seven days a week from the age of fourteen through to eighteen?'

'I actually started working in the yard when I was seven, before and after school,' Will pointed out to Freddie on Monday evening. His portly friend was arching his back in front of the kitchen's wood-fired stove, displaying a white band of stomach each time his polo shirt stretched upwards.

'No wonder you're as strong as an ox, Winda,' Freddie moaned, massaging his lower back with both hands, 'One day of working around yer yard and I'm knackered. Ah man, my back! Who knew muckin' out was such a pain.'

'Hold on. You've been mucking out? I thought…'

'I've been sanding down too,' Freddie broke in, 'But that Lizzy lass needed a bit of help, like.'

Will didn't reply, but made a mental note to keep an eye on any burgeoning relationship between his stable lass and Freddie. His friend was the sort to become entranced by certain types of girls. Unfortunately, it was an interest that was rarely reciprocated. It was a real shame. Despite his XXL size and gregarious nature, Freddie could be extremely thoughtful and caring.

80

Arthur entered the kitchen and his friends both looked up at him expectantly. He had arms full of printouts and a haggard look about him, but in a different way to Freddie. His ruffled hair, pale complexion, and brow furrowed into a frown was clearly borne out of mental, rather than physical exertion.

'Think I'd rather be up a ladder sandpapering the paintwork with Freddie,' he muttered as he shambled into the kitchen and plonked himself down on a kitchen chair with a weary sigh.

'Tough day in front of your laptop, huh?' asked Freddie, smiling benignly.

Arthur didn't answer, he was busy running his forefinger down a column of figures.

'What you got there?' asked Will.

'What…? Oh, it's your grandfather's betting records. I finally got bored with your dad's accounts. By the way, if your dad bothered to charge all his owners the same daily rate as Hanover, you could immediately cancel out some of that five grand loss each month.'

'Really?' Will queried in a surprised tone, 'I always got the impression the old skinflint squeezed every penny out of his owners.'

'No, there are some really big discrepancies. In fact, if you don't get a fairly sizeable injection of capital in the next two months, the business will be officially insolvent.'

Arthur related this news in an almost disinterested, monotone voice, adding, 'But I guess you already knew that, which is why your father had that bet.'

Will leaned forward, 'What bet?'

'His bet on…' Arthur paused to search for something among his papers, '…here we are, two thousand pounds on a horse called Catwalk to win at 80/1 for something called, the 'Albany'.

He dutifully handed the betting slip over to Will.

Will didn't say anything, scrutinising the betting slip

with gritted teeth, and finally shaking his head. Freddie shot Arthur a pained look and twirled his fingers, indicating for him to get on and change the subject.

'Ten thousand pounds should keep your dad solvent for a few more months. Perhaps you should fire up your laptop and visit that poker site that funded your university education?'

Will pursed his lips tight and wondered if there was anything his friends *didn't* know about him. He silently nodded to show he understood the need for the stables to receive an injection of cash.

'Anyway, as I said,' continued Arthur, 'I got bored and decided to go through Jack Payne's betting ledger and your mother's notebook to see if I could find anything of interest.'

He produced both the tall, thin leather bound ledgers from his pocket, 'They make for fascinating reading.'

'Yeah, I've already scanned through both of them,' Will agreed, as he gave the betting slip back to Arthur and tried to concentrate on the journals. He would deal with his father's idiotic use of business funds for extravagant bets another time.

'Really?' blinked Arthur, 'You? The man who never reads *anything*?'

'Well, I tried,' Will admitted sheepishly.

Will was a skilled artist. Specifically, his sculptures and murals were the reason he had managed to secure a place on such a renowned Fine Art course at Newcastle University. However, Arthur and Freddie had soon discovered that when it came to reading and writing, Will struggled. Arthur was convinced he was dyslexic, and had told him so, but Will had done nothing about it. It made his ability to win consistently at online poker all the more astonishing.

Arthur asked, 'So what do you make of it all?'

'Grandad Jack's notebooks confirm he was a fearless punter and my mother's journal reads like a long, complicated list of conspiracy theories about his murder. I didn't know what to make of it. She seemed to jump around and throw names around like confetti. It didn't help that some of her notes made no sense at all.'

Arthur rubbed the back of his neck and shot Freddie a worried look. Freddie gave him a sad nod back and, came around the table to take a seat beside Will.

He met Will's gaze and said in a low, smooth voice, 'You know we're solid mates, don't yer?'

Will looked from Freddie to Arthur and back again. Both were wearing worryingly serious expressions.

'Yes?' he ventured nervously.

'Arty and I had a chat earlier this evening, when you were doing your evening stables,' explained Freddie, still speaking in a measured tone, 'He's the boffin who can do business accounts and make sense of those ledgers. No point me reading through it all, I'm more of a...'

'I know what you're like, Freddie,' Will advised him with a hint of impatience, 'What's the problem with the two of you?'

'We've always known you've had a problem with your Pa. And your mother... well, I don't know how it must feel to have her just disappear like that. We learned not to bring your parents up in conversation to be honest, it was just easier.'

'And I appreciate that,' Will said a little more curtly than he'd intended.

'But these journals and that wee room upstairs... Arty and I are just worried that we might be poking at a hornets nest and what we discover might not be... what you want to find.'

'You think I should let sleeping dogs lie?' Will spat back. An uncomfortable heat had suddenly flared up, spreading around the back of his neck.

'Nae, not at all,' Freddie countered, trying to soothe Will by holding up a flat palm, 'But look at yourself. You're already in a spin, and that's before we've started.'

Arthur put a hand on Will's shoulder, 'If you want our help, we're here to do that. Whether it's doing up the yard, working on your granddad's case, or if the opportunity arises, finding your mum.'

Will's eyes had shrunk to black slits and his chin was set as if he was about to scream something at the two of them.

Freddie sensed the change in his friend and reacted. Raising the volume of his voice a few notches, he lost the smoothness and snapped out his words, 'There will be consequences, Will. Arty has already found some stuff, and we need to know that you can cope with… all of it.'

'You think I'm weak?' Will asked incredulously, whipping Arthurs hand off his shoulder and pointing an accusing finger.

'No. You're one of the strongest willed people I've ever met,' Arthur answered earnestly, 'But we've been in a privileged position over the last two years. We understand you more than anyone else, perhaps even more than you do yourself!'

'Oh, right!' Will scoffed angrily, 'And how on earth did the two of you come to *that* conclusion?'

'We've both listened to your nightmares!'

Freddie squeezed his eyes shut in dismay. The words had tumbled out of him without a thought to the consequences. And now, they lay there, festering between the three of them.

Freddie and Arthur watched in terrified silence as Will's mouth fell open, he dropped his hands to the table and stared out of the kitchen window, his eyes glazing over. He didn't move a muscle. After twenty seconds the pause was becoming increasingly awkward, so Freddie spoke up.

'I think we've broken him,' he told Arthur with a hopeful grin in Will's direction.

Will went to laugh, but it caught in his throat and turned into a dry cough.

'You've *listened* to my nightmares?' he said slowly.

Arthur nodded, 'You babble, you moan, you shout, you scream. Sometimes you sleep walk and we have to put you

84

back to bed.'

'You're a bloody nuisance,' Freddie chimed in.

'You're always talking with your mum and dad.'

'What do I say?' asked Will, genuinely amazed neither of his friends had mentioned this before.

'You ask your mother questions and you generally shout abuse at your father. That… can get quite loud.'

Freddie added, 'You may have thought we were using rock, paper and scissors to determine who got the bedroom at the back of the house because of its size and view. That's not the case. It's the room the furthest away from your bedroom.'

'For heaven's sake, Freddie!' scolded Arthur.

Will stared blankly at his friends, 'Why didn't you tell me this before?'

Arthur shrugged, 'We thought it was your business and you'd tell us…'

'…when you were ready,' added Freddie when Arthur dried up.

'Which sort of brings us back to the main theme,' Arthur said with some trepidation, 'Are you ready to have your family secrets, some of them potentially… difficult to handle, erm… mentally I mean, revealed to you?'

Will thought hard, his spike of anger having quickly dissipated as he tried to cope with this new reality. Freddie and Arthur waited patiently for Will's response. The kitchen became quite still. The only sound to puncture the silence was the sporadically cawing of crows from the top branches of the large yew trees that stood on the boundary of the yard.

'Just the mention of my parents makes me lose focus,' Will said quietly, 'But if I'm ever to stop having nightmares, I guess I need to slay my demons. I think I'm ready. And I promise I won't lose focus again'

'You sure?' asked Freddie, 'We can replace these ledgers, and close up the secret room. We can help keeping the yard running until your Pa is fit, then we all go back to Newcastle and forget about your grandpa's grisly murder, your mother leaving you without saying goodbye or leaving a forwarding address, and your father's violent drunken rages.'

'Nicely put, Freddie,' Arthur said sarcastically, adding a roll of his eyes for good measure, 'That was a wonderfully delicate description of Will's family history. You really have a way with words...'

'Nae problem, Arty!' Freddie replied with a dramatic wink in the Scotsman's direction, 'I speak as I find. You can't wrap serious stuff like that up in pretty pink ribbons.'

'Pink Ribbons?' Arthur retorted aghast, 'You've just slapped Will's family life on a butchers slab and hacked at it with a meat cleaver!'

The largely enjoyable and meaningless spat between his friends continued, but Will wasn't paying any attention as they railed at each other. He noisily sucked in a breath through his nose, held it for a moment as if in contemplation, then stated loudly, 'Yes, I'm sure.'

Arthur and Freddie dropped silent and studied him.

'I'm sure. No, I'm positive. Whatever we uncover can't be any worse than what I already know. I'm tired of having dreams... well, you're right, they're nightmares. I'm *really* tired of wondering why my mother left me behind, and what caused my father to treat both of us so badly. I want to know... everything.'

## Sixteen

The following evening Arthur spread about a dozen A4 sized white pages across the kitchen table and peered down at them. Will couldn't read anything, sitting opposite his friend, but he could make out that each page was filled with Arthur's recognizable small, neat handwriting. Arthur adjusted his glasses, licked his forefinger and, rubbing it against his thumb, picked up the first page.

'The murder…' he started.

Arthur hesitated, taking a quick look at Will.

'Ha'way, Arty, spit it out, man,' Freddie insisted, 'Will says he fine about his family stuff, now get on with it.'

'Right!' agreed Arthur, 'So, the murder of Jack Payne. It's probably worth going through what was reported to have happened that day.'

Will and Freddie nodded patiently. Arthur could be a pedant at times, but unlike the two of them, he was unerringly accurate and possessed an amazing recall of both written and spoken words.

'It was the Ebor meeting at York Racecourse on August 21st 2002, which was a Wednesday,' reported Arthur.

'According to Jack's notebook, he'd wagered around three-thousand pounds in about a dozen different bets on a horse called Hugs Dancer. The horse won the Ebor, run at ten past three and he subsequently went around the on-course bookies, picking up his winnings. According to a number of people at the track that day he had a Gladstone bag with him into which all his cash was placed. There are various amounts mentioned, but it seems he picked up about one-hundred and eighty to two hundred thousand pounds.

'Who talked to these people?' Will queried.

'I should point out that it looks like Mary… that's Will's mum… did some of her own detective work. In her journal she mentions going along to York later in 2002 to speak to as many people as she could. But there's also two dozen newspaper reports and interviews by the police glued into her journal.'

'What, proper police paperwork?' Freddie asked in surprise.

'My dad's best friend works at Malton nick,' Will explained, 'I bet she got them from him.'

Arthur said, 'Mmm. That makes sense. Most of your mum's journal is dated between 2002 and 2009. But the interviews are printed copies and were added to the journal at a later date. They have a print date in the footer, and are all dated March 2007, even though the documents themselves are all from 2002 and 2003.'

Arthur continued, 'Jack watched the next race…'

'The Gimcrack,' Will murmured, 'He'd never miss that. According to my Mum, Jack loved the big juvenile races.'

Freddie eyeballed him, 'You find difficulty reading or remembering when your next lecture starts, and yet you know the name of the race after the Ebor in 2002?'

'What can I say?' Will shrugged, 'Racing's in my blood. It's all anyone talked about in my home until I was eighteen.'

'Anyway…' said Arthur, keen to continue, 'At somewhere between four o'clock and five past he left the racecourse even though there were three more races, and headed for his car in the Owners and Trainers Car Park. A steward on the exit to the racecourse remembered him leaving just after four o'clock. An emergency call was made at twenty-three minutes past four and Jack was found by an ambulance crew, lying on his back in the car park at four thirty-one with severe head and facial injuries. He'd been struck around his head by something like a baseball bat. It only took eight minutes for the rescue services to get to him because one of the on-course ambulances there for the racing was called to the scene. The emergency caller said someone had been attacked in the car park off Campleshon Road but rang off before the police could get their name.'

Arthur raised his head and stared at his friends, 'Your

mother dedicates several pages of her journal to the emergency caller. Rightly so, in my opinion. Whoever reported finding Jack may have seen what happened. They might be able to identify his attacker, or at least tell us what he said.'

'What do you mean, *what he said*? Wasn't Jack dead when he was found?' asked Freddie.

'He spoke a few words to the ambulance crew,' said Arthur, consulting his own paperwork, then thumbing through the journal, 'There's a report from one of them here in your mum's handwriting. It isn't in any of the police papers or any of the newspaper reports. I think she must have tracked this lady down.'

Arthur read out loud from Mary's journal, 'Susan Day, September 14th 2002. Nice lady. Experienced ambulance woman. She said: Jack was confused, but awake when we found him. He wasn't able to move much, and in some pain. He had sustained several blows to his head and face. The head wounds were our main priority.'

'There's more like that, but it gets interesting later on,' said Arthur, his finger moving across the page, jumping a paragraph or two. He found his place and continued.

'We asked him his name as we worked, and we eventually understood he was called 'Jack', but it was a struggle for him to form his words. As well as the injuries to his head, Jack's mouth was badly bruised, several of his teeth were smashed, his tongue was swollen, and he had a deep cut running through his upper lip, making it difficult for him to shape his words. I told him to stay awake and asked him if he knew who had attacked him. He didn't answer, but instead shook his head slightly. It was clear Jack was fading fast, so we concentrated on getting him into the back of the ambulance. As the ambulance moved off, he grabbed my arm. I remember I was surprised at the strength of his grip and he wouldn't let go until he could get a few words out. I bent down, close to his face and he spoke one word at a time. He said, 'Yellow Noise… Ed Coss…' and he lost consciousness. I think he had more to say, but he couldn't get it out. We headed to York General Hospital, running through every red light, but Jack died from his injuries before we reached accident and emergency.'

Arthur looked up from the journal, a glum expression on his face, 'According to the newspaper reports Mary included here, Jack was really badly beaten. It was one of those terrible stories the press love, especially when they manage to get a photo. A local York paper printed one of his face which is truly ghastly. Mary must have contacted the photographer and got the rest of the ambulance chaser's snaps. I don't know if you want to see them? Mary pasted them into her journal. They don't make easy viewing.'

'I've seen them,' Will said tight lipped, 'No need to see them again. It's disgusting what they did to him.'

'Let's have a look,' Freddie said brightly, and once the journal had been pushed across the table his way he pored over the two page spread of colour photographs showing a dead man's badly bruised face and neck.

'Stop being mawkish,' Arthur chastised Freddie once a minute had gone by and he was still bent over the journal, 'Come on, hand Mary's journal back.'

'So you noticed the crinkly ring?' said Freddie, his head still bowed as he continued to examine the photos.

'What?'

'Whoever hit him, I bet they wore a ring,' he said, pointing at one of the photos, 'You can see a faint outline here… and here.'

Will and Arthur moved around the table to stand over Freddie's seated shoulders. Sure enough, a faint but definite outline of a circular mark with a serrated edge took shape if you examined Jack's bruised cheek closely enough. Freddie pointed out another, less obvious example under Jack's ear on a second photo.

'Well spotted,' Arthur said, genuinely impressed, 'The

police report did say he was punched in his stomach during the attack. But the rest of the injuries were around his head and neck. But I guess they may have missed a punch to his cheek.'

Will added, 'Might be a bit difficult to find the wearer of a ring with frilly bits around it from twenty years ago, but like Arthur says, it's a good spot.'

'He shoots, he scores!' exclaimed Freddie triumphantly, punching the air with one fist and making the sound of a cheering crowd for a few seconds.

'Mind you,' said Arthur before the cheering had ceased, 'I don't want to burst your bubble, mighty detective Freddie, but the blows that killed Jack - at least two of them - came from something hard and blunt according to the police report. He had a cracked skull and… well, you can see for yourself, something made a real mess of his nose and mouth.'

'Does Mary's journal say anything about Jack's last words, or suggest anyone who might have done that to him?' asked Freddie, idly flicking through a few more pages filled with newspaper reports and notes in Mary's handwriting.

'No, I'm afraid not,' Arthur said with a quick shake of his head, 'She tried to find the other ambulance worker, but he'd left the country soon after the racecourse incident. There's a few ideas of what Jack might have meant by 'Yellow Noise and Ed Coss', but they didn't lead anywhere. I've searched for all the different versions of Bill, William, Boys, Boyes and Ed, Edward and Eddie Coss on the internet, but there's nothing that pops up from around this time in York or Malton.'

'So my mum's journal is a bust?' Will stated dejectedly.

Arthur sucked at his teeth for a moment, 'Well, it has a lot of information about Jack's death. She dated all her notes, and was still adding things seven years after he died. It went quiet for a number of years with only minor updates and then there was the police stuff with some more comments, but there's nothing in there that suggests a name. She even says at

91

one point that she isn't surprised the police gave up on the case.'

'What about the money?' asked Freddie, 'Surely the attacker was one of the bookmakers he won the money from. Two hundred grand, give or take, in a Gladstone bag. They cornered him in the car park, walloped him, and stole his winnings.'

'Mary had checked. All of the bookmakers that paid out for Jack's Hugs Dancer were still manning their boards inside the racecourse.'

Arthur continued, 'But here's the thing about the money... and Mary's journal suggests a similar thought on why Jack was targeted. Most thieves interested solely in the money would, as you put so succinctly, Freddie, knock the sixty-year-old racehorse trainer over, take the cash and flee before anyone saw them. But this one didn't. He or she stuck around. They gave Jack a proper thrashing, making sure to really bash him around.'

Arthur picked up the journal and flicked through until he reached the second last page.

'Here. Your mum says it perfectly,' he told them, starting to read once more.

'Whoever did this to dad wanted to not only take his money, but teach him a lesson. I don't think it was just about money, it was personal. Either revenge or retribution. I'm certain my dad must have recognised, or known the person who robbed him, and so they had to kill him.'

Will and Freddie sat down, Will placing his head in his hands and complained of a nagging headache. Arthur returned to his chair and he too sat down heavily. He shuddered, the kitchen suddenly feeling too large and too cold for anything further to be achieved. He closed Mary's journal and pressed its leather cover down onto the table, gazing at it disappointedly.

Presently, Freddie asked, 'What about Jack's notebook?'

'Jack Payne was a hell of a gambler,' Arthur said over the rim of his glasses, 'And a profitable one too.'

'So it's just a betting history?' asked Will in a tired voice.

'Pretty much, but he does have other yard stuff in there. But there's nothing that suggests a motive for anyone to steal from him or kill him.'

Again, the conversation stalled.

'Okay, that's enough for today. I'm racing again tomorrow,' Will said, getting up and pushing his chair beneath the table. It was getting on for ten o'clock and he was in need of his bed.

'There was one thing in Jack's notebook,' Arthur called out to him, 'Well, it's an anomaly… a dispute really…'

'Yeah?' Will said, rubbing his eyes and suddenly feeling weary as he walked around the table.

'There's a bookmaker called Lilywhites that owed him five thousand pounds, and a note beside the bet in his notebook saying they were refusing to pay. It was in…'

Will was on his way to the kitchen door again, a hand held to his mouth as he yawned, waiting for Arthur to finish leafing through his grandfather's notebook.

'…2001,' finished Arthur.

'Maybe you two can look into it?' Will suggested, stifling another yawn, 'I need to get some sleep.'

'Oh, and there's something else,' Freddie called out as Will pulled the kitchen door open, 'I think we should rent a carpet cleaning machine, invest in some heavy-duty cleaning materials and leave all the farmhouse windows open for a week. I don't know about you two, but the smell of damp in this farmhouse is getting right up my hooter.'

'Sounds like a plan,' Will agreed without really registering what Freddie had suggested, and took himself off to bed.

## Seventeen

Despite a long gap since he'd attended a race meeting, the ritual of going racing as a trainer came back to Will without him really having to think about it. Readying a brace of horses to go racing came easily to him, and by nine-thirty on Tuesday morning he was almost finished prepping Risky and Sponge for their runs that afternoon. The layout in the tack room was exactly as it had been when he'd left. The equine passports were stored in the same safe, and incredibly, his father hadn't changed the combination. It was even the same horsebox, with its dodgy second gear and braking that pulled slightly to the left. It seemed his father had allowed his business, along with his life, to trundle along the same tracks without deviation during his sons absence.

Beverley racecourse hadn't changed too much either, and Will's handicappers knew the drill and were straightforward enough, although Sponge had his customary fly-kick when he got off the transport. As he and Roberto walked the horses into the racecourse stables Will was surprised to detect a minor thrilling sensation buzzing in the pit of his stomach. Was that a little nervousness showing in his shortness of breath too? It was the first time horses from Manor Stud Stables would run under his own name – perhaps that was the reason. Or it could be that this was the first time in years that he'd been racing anywhere.

Even before they'd managed to get Salacious Star and Risk EBusiness settled in their boxes in the racecourse stables Will was accosted by a number of trainers, lads, and lasses from various Yorkshire based stables. Most were welcoming, although when his ex-employee and recent assailant, Jimmy Hearn, wandered past leading up a young horse, even Roberto stiffened.

It looked like the lad had found himself another position in quick time. Will anticipated plenty of verbal abuse from Jimmy as he passed, and wasn't disappointed. Jimmy's approach was surprisingly nonchalant and he was mute until coming up level with his two ex-employers. He then growled something under his breath and deep ridges in his face bent themselves into a unhealthy scowl, making his unintelligible speech redundant. His face said it all, thought Will. Jimmy was still out for revenge.

'Come into my yard again and I'll call the police,' Will called to him as he walked away.

Jimmy brought his gelding to a halt with a jolt on its head collar. The horse obeyed, but pulled its head upwards and away from the lad, its ears flattening.

'Better tread carefully, Payne,' warned Jimmy, bearing his upper row of teeth in a defiant grin, 'From what I hear, you'll get what you deserve soon enough.'

Jimmy yanked on the gelding's head collar once more and his charge followed reluctantly after a second, more insistent tug. Will was left so bemused by this interaction, the lad was gone before he could conjure up a reply. When he asked Roberto what he thought Jimmy meant, his head lad simply shrugged and advised him to stay well clear.

Among the trainers that came over to greet him was Joe Curran, a veteran Malton-based trainer whom Will guessed had to be in his late seventies. The small man with a walnut complexion shocked him by strolling over and after asking after his dad, wished him good luck. Will hadn't even considered he would be on Joe's radar, given he was a living legend around Yorkshire, having trained countless winners, including several top-flight Group One horses over the years. However, here he was, pumping Will's hand up and down and telling him it was good to have him back and training in his own right. Joe left, warning Will with a wry smile that his own horse, Diamond Jeff, would beat Risk Ebusiness in the sprint handicap. Will was left with the impression that Joe was a good example of what his mother had called such seasoned trainers: 'a true gent'.

Among the other trainers popping in to say hello were

Neil Dalton, his wife Bridget and their daughter Lily. They popped over to offer him the best of luck, although Will imagined it was probably more to do with the fact that he'd jocked up their son, Davy, for both rides.

Will remembered Davy's father, Neil, from the times he and Davy spent playing around his training yard as kids. Mr Dalton, or 'Davy's dad' as he'd always known him, was a consistent, if unremarkable trainer, coming from a dynasty of racehorse trainers you could trace back at least three generations. Mrs Dalton was just like her son, always a smile on her face, and Lily appeared to be going the same way, not saying a great deal, but with long blonde hair like her mother, and a ready smile on her lips. She had been a plain, racehorse obsessed sixteen-year-old when Will had left Malton, and as far as he could see, nothing much had changed now she was three years older. She had a friend called Tiffany with her, she was a dark-haired girl of a similar age who, apart from her hair colour, was remarkably similar in height and looks to Lily apart from her teeth that dazzled an unnatural bright white. She gave Will a shy nod when they were introduced.

Davy himself sauntered up just as Will and Roberto were ready to head for something to eat in the stable lads canteen, and so he joined them for lunch.

'Popular lad, aren't you, Will?' Roberto commented as the three of them sat down to enjoy a basic, but relatively cheap meal in the subsidized staff canteen, 'We must have had a dozen or more people come over to wish you well, and we're not even inside the racecourse proper yet.'

'Yeah… Can't really see why.'

'It's because they all remember you as the cute twelve-year-old who used to lead up his dad's horses,' Davy said with a grin.

'Less of the cute, thanks.'

'Oh, but you were!'

'I just hope it's not because they feel sorry for me,' Will suggested a little mournfully before biting into his tuna sandwich.

Roberto studied Will, wondering whether to speak. Will knew that look well. It told him Roberto was keen to offer his view.

'Out with it,' he ordered.

Roberto placed his half-eaten sandwich back on its plate and bent over, lowing his voice, 'At least half the people who came over to us asked after your dad's health. There's still a lot of respect for him, the yard, and its history. People around Malton still talk about your grandfather you know.'

Will took another bite from his sandwich in order to allow Roberto's words to sink in. He was a good man, a wonderful horseman, and fiercely loyal to his father, but still, the head lad's words conjured up bad memories, not good ones. Roberto hadn't witnessed all the arguments. His father's alcohol fuelled rants, the furniture being overturned, and the screams of derision as his parents argued about the horses, the yard, and always, always... his dead grandad.

'Someone down the pub mentioned Jack Payne was murd... erm, *died* twenty years ago,' said Davy awkwardly, 'Sorry, I didn't mean to...'

'It's okay, we can talk about it,' Will assured him with a forced smile, 'If there's one thing for sure, it's that we know Jack was murdered. Hopefully the twentieth anniversary won't attract too much attention. I know my mother used to hate it being brought up every August. She used to avoid the Ebor meeting like the plague, but I can understand racing people having an interest in it. I'd just rather it had been someone else's family.'

'Did the police ever find Jack's winnings won from the Ebor?'

Will shook his head, 'Nope, they disappeared, along with whoever beat him to death. About two-hundred grand. Still, it's not much for a life, is it?'

Together, Roberto and Davy grimly shook their heads.

'Actually, I've a couple of my Uni mates staying at the

moment and one of them has been reading all the old press cuttings to see if the passage of time can shed any light onto Jack's death.'

'Maybe they can solve the case!' Davy suggested positively, keen to bring smiles to the people around the table.

'You never know,' Roberto said cautiously, stealing a glance up at Will, 'But maybe the best thing is for it all to be put to bed and forgotten?'

Will didn't answer. Instead, he regarded Roberto with amused surprise. The possibility of letting sleeping dogs lie didn't even compute for Will, thought Roberto. From the look of stoic determination on the twenty-one-year-old's face, Roberto got the distinct impression that his new boss would not be deflected from his current path any time soon. Furthermore, it looked doubtful Will could be dissuaded from dropping his search at all. At best, it might fade over time.

The young trainer's mother had a lot to answer for in Roberto's opinion, but this wasn't a view he could air to the lad, or anyone else for that matter. Besides, Roberto liked Will, particularly this older version. He was a hard worker, knowledgeable, and possessed his parent's feel for the horses, and that way about him that meant people listened when he spoke. Will might be an even better trainer than both his parents, possibly as good as his grandfather. He just wished Will would buckle down and concentrate on running the yard. He knew the lad needed answers. For him, the dye had been cast at the age of fourteen, when Mary had walked out. Will had adored her. And when you form such a strong bond at such a critical age, it had to be hard to let go.

The three men finished their lunch with a discussion of the riding tactics for Davy's two rides for Will and they soon went their separate ways. Roberto returned to the stables to check on the two geldings, Davy headed for the weighing room, and Will went on a mission to meet up with Harriet Gardener, the owner of Sponge, AKA Salacious Star, due to run at three o'clock, the third race on Beverley's card.

It was one-thirty, half an hour before the first race was due off, when Will entered the owners and trainers lounge. He reckoned both Harriet and the Drawdown Syndicate, owners of Risk Ebusiness, should have arrived at the track by now. Sure enough, he came upon the four middle-aged men from the Drawdown syndicate, eating their free lunch and washing it down with copious amounts of red wine. They were intermittently laughing a little *too* loudly and Will noted the three empty wine bottles clogging up the centre of their table as he approached.

During Will's short, friendly chat with the syndicate about the four-year-old's chances later in the afternoon, which he rated as 'hopeful but not confident', he noticed Harriet Gardener standing by herself just outside the lounge, leaning against the white plastic pre-parade ring railings. Race card in hand, she was casting an inexpert eye over a dozen juveniles as they were led around the pre-parade ring. He left the syndicate to their lunch, promising to meet up with them again before their race, and hoping that by that stage they'd still be sober enough to stand. As Will made off, his father dropped into his thoughts. If he'd been here, he'd have probably joined the half-cut quartet for the rest of the afternoon. As it was, he was just about to try and correct one of his father's mistakes.

Will took a breath and approached Harriet, knowing this conversation might be a shade difficult, as he needed to broach the subject of her training fees being set far too low.

'Hello there, Harriet,' he said breezily.

Harriet looked up and smiled as he came nearer, planting a rose red lipstick mark on his cheek and making a fuss as she wiped it away with her handkerchief.

'And how is Sponge?' she enquired.

'Travelled here like the old pro he is,' Will assured her, 'He might need this run, but I think he'll show up well enough today. A few pounds off his back from the handicapper and in a couple of weeks we can take him to

99

Ripon where he's won before.'

Harriet nodded sagely, although Will wasn't too sure she'd really understood. In his opinion, Salacious Star was too highly rated to win today, and needed the handicapper to cut him some slack before he would have a proper winning opportunity. That meant a run down the field today, and hopefully, a reduction in his handicap rating once he was reassessed. As her attention had returned to her form guide once more, Will decided to soldier on.

'Actually Harriet, I do need to speak with you about the rates we're charging you for your two horses.'

'Oh, really?' she queried, her face hardening.

'Yes, I'm afraid we'll need to increase them from next month by about fifty percent. At the moment it's costing the yard more to keep the horses than you're actually paying.'

Will noticed the woman's grip on her race card was now creasing the pages. She pursed her lips before replying.

'Perhaps you should speak with Barney first.'

'I can do, but I'm afraid...'

'We had an arrangement,' she cut in airily.

With that, Harriet closed her race card and smiled at Will. It felt like her icy blue eyes were cutting him to ribbons. She stalked off toward to the parade ring without another word.

Great, thought Will. Not only have I to deal with her again once Salacious Star runs poorly, but I've now got to quiz my father about what sort of 'arrangement' he's got with her.

***

An hour later, Salacious Star entered the parade ring after his race, and to Will's relief, Roberto was able to lead the gelding in and stand him in the bay reserved for the third placed horse. He'd been a long way third, beaten by over nine lengths, but that didn't seem to matter to Harriet who fussed over the sweaty, snorting bay afterwards. There was no further mention of the training fees.

Another hour passed before the twelve runners for the five furlong handicap lined up. Although they were a little worse for wear, the Drawdown Syndicate had managed to stagger into the parade ring to speak with Will and Davy. Whilst excited, loud, and certainly tipsy, the lads conducted themselves well within the bounds of decency. Will actually enjoyed the good-natured comic banter that bounced back and forth between the four of them.

Will advised the group that at 10/1, the five-year-old was a decent each-way bet and once Risk Ebusiness left the parade ring the syndicate all rushed to the line of bookmakers for a final extra investment.

Will decided to watch the race from the grandstand. It offered a good view of the last few furlongs as the horses climbed the hill. He wanted to see how Risky saw the trip out, having had a feeling he'd made a gurgling sound on the gallops a few days ago – a sure sign of a potential breathing problem. Making his way up the huge concrete steps of the staircase into the grandstand, he noticed there was a large crowd and decided to settle on the first tier balcony. Taking up a position on the balcony gave him a good view of the last furlong and a half, and allowed him to head back down the steps straight after the horses had crossed the finishing line, thus missing the general rush to the racecourse concourse.

Risky got a good start from his middle draw and Davy was able to angle the gelding across to take up a position one off the inside rail in a share of fifth. It was as they reached the two furlong marker that Will remembered Joe Curran's words about his four-year-old, Diamond Jeff – that his horse was sure to beat his; Diamond Jeff had just hit the front and scooted a length and a half clear.

At the point where Diamond Jeff was able to assert, Risky had encountered traffic problems in behind the front rank. As the front-runners started to paddle and lose momentum, Risky was fighting for his head in behind, and two strides later Davy took a chance and dived for a small gap that had just opened up on the rail.

The furlong pole loomed ahead and Davy gave Risky a flick with his whip. The gelding rushed past the third, and then the second placed horses before setting off after Diamond Jeff, still clear. With the best part of a furlong still to run, Joe Curran's runner wasn't extending his lead. His rider was now pumping his fists up the gelding's neck.

After leaving his father and the yard on his eighteenth birthday Will had also left racing behind. He hadn't gone racing. He'd had no contact with horses. He hadn't read the Racing Post. He'd had his fill of it. His love for the sport had been slowly squeezed out of him after his mother left. So it was a surprise when he found himself screaming 'Get him up, Davy!' and pumping a fist into the air when Risky reeled Diamond Jeff back in and drew level only yards from the finishing line. That final stride confirmed the inevitable. Risky's head went down and the four-year-old went through the line a neck in front, with three lengths back to the rest of the chasing pack.

His mind in a whirl, Will headed for the grandstand staircase, still watching Risky and Davy as they disappeared around the top bend, Davy now up in his saddle, in the process of easing Risky down. Will paused momentarily a few inches from the top step to see if he could spot the lads in the syndicate anywhere in the stands, but they weren't… it was then that he felt his centre of balance alter.

A firm hand - or was it a shove from a foot? - to his lower back, on the right-hand side of his spine, propelled him forward. With hands spiralling in search of something to grasp, but finding nothing but empty space, Will lurched sickeningly beyond the point of no return knowing full well that with his momentum, he was going to crash a long way down the grandstand's tall, obtusely angled concrete steps… and Will was absolutely certain it was going to hurt.

## Eighteen

Will had been knocked off, slipped, and ejected from the saddle of enough racehorses as a youngster to know that there is an art to falling. It might seem natural to brace oneself and take the brunt of the impact with your arms and leg, but that can lead to broken bones. Jockeys learn how to manage the impact and ideally, bounce. It still leads to cuts, bruises, strains, potential dislocation and pain… lots of pain, but at least you tend to be able to walk away afterwards.

However, when parting company with a racehorse it usually meant landing on grass, woodchip, or an All-Weather surface with a bit of give in it. It rarely entailed bouncing head-first down a cascade of foot-high concrete steps until you crash into a man with a pint of lager in his hand.

Will came to rest facing the grandstand roof, his head hanging over the edge of a step and his back resting against the shins of the man who had saved him from continuing to barrel down the remaining dozen steps to the racecourse concourse below.

'…hells teeth, lad. Is thee alright?'

Will tried to open his eyes, but found that doing so only magnified an insistent, throbbing pain across his forehead. He closed them again and tried to remember what had happened. Ah, yes. He'd fallen… down the stairs… no, he'd been pushed… either way, it meant he needed to assess the damage.

The same voice, only closer to his ear, spoke again. In the deepest recesses of his mind a hazy recognition began to dawn. Will could smell beer on the man's breath. At least his olfactory system was still operating, Will muttered to himself, although this offered him little comfort.

'Take it easy, Pal. You've 'ad a bit o' a bang to yer noggin.'

It was at this point that Will realised two things. Firstly, he was wet. His chest was soaking. For one awful moment he

103

imagined blood was pumping out of… well, somewhere, and he needed to stem the flow. His eyes shot open and ignoring his complaining retinas and the thumping headache, he scrabbled up and around until he was half lying, half sitting on one of the foot-high concrete steps. The second thing was that he was pretty sure he knew the identity of his saviour.

Will took stock. His knees and elbows both sang out with pain, and his head was banging with a headache far worse than any hangover. At least he wasn't bleeding. Instead, the dampness he'd mistaken for blood was in fact beer. He'd been dowsed with the man's pint. The same man was currently leaning his legs against him and holding his shoulders in order to stop him slipping off his step and travelling further down the grandstand steps.

Will screwed his eyes up and raised his chin to peer up at the large man, meaning to say thank you. Darren Blenkinsop, his schoolmate and horse feed salesman grinned down at him and must have read his expression as he said, 'Hey, no worries, Will!' before Will could get a word out.

'Best get you off these steps though,' said Darren, indicating the logjam of people above Will with a flick of his eyes, 'Yer causin' a queue. You okay to move?'

Will nodded, an action that sent him dizzy for a second.

Without another word, a pair of big hands gripped him firmly under his arms and Will felt himself being hoisted upright, onto a shoulder, and carried down the rest of the grandstand staircase. Once on the concourse, his benevolent giant set him down softly onto his feet and a sudden rush of people swamped him. His knees wobbled a little, but he managed to stay upright, aided by Darren's giant arms. An aroma of jasmine and sweet peas suddenly filled his senses having the effect of dulling his pain. Will looked into the painted face of young Lily Dalton.

'You were so lucky,' she cooed, her eyes crinkling with concern as she noticed something, either on his face or his head. Tiffany, now at Lily's shoulder also grimaced, displaying two shiny teeth, and he thought he heard her say, 'Yuk!'

Neil and Bridget Dalton swung into view behind the two teenagers, both studying him rather strangely. Three more bystanders were doing the same. More people he half recognised stopped to stare. When he looked around again, practically everyone's eyes he met gave him the same look of worried concern.

'You've a little smut of blood on your head there Will. Come on, we'll get you cleaned up!' Darren intoned, as much to the surrounding crowd, as to Will. With that, a strong arm was wrapped around his waist and his school friend whisked him toward the gents' washroom via one of the bars. Still experiencing dizziness and the most confusing feeling of being outside his body, a glut of racegoer faces drifted by as he was half-walked, half-lifted through the post-race crowd heading for the bars.

They passed Harriet and Will caught her eye for a second. He tried to speak, but found it impossible. Instead, he gibbered at her, unable to shape his words. Her initial frown became shocked concern and then she vanished from sight as he was carried towards the washrooms. Will was sure he caught sight of the lads in the Drawdown syndicate. They looked torn between heading to the winners' enclosure and following him as he disappeared into the gents.

It turned out his guardian angel had witnessed Will tumbling down the steps towards him and being a gentle giant, Darren had simply stood in the way and caught him between his legs. They exchanged pleasantries while Will worked out that despite lots of aches and pains, and a nasty cut on the right-hand side of his head that had provided the majority of the blood, he'd come out with mostly scrapes and bruises, nothing broken. A nice set of cuts and darkening bruises on his right cheek, nose and around his lips and eye sockets were the most visible results of his fall, and Will could feel a prickly heat beginning to make his face bulge out of shape.

'You came down those steps like tumbleweed in the wind. There's nowt to yer!' Darren exclaimed happily as he watched Will dabbing a moist paper towel to one of his head wounds. He grinned, eyeing Will in the washroom mirror, 'It's a good job yer fit, you fair bounced down those steps!'

Will leaned against one of the basins and groaned inwardly as he realised his face was puffing up. An insistent, pulsing pain was making him wince.

'Look at you - bruising like a peach!' Darren noted breezily, 'You'll have some colourful bruises by the look of you. I've never seen anyone face-plant like that and get up so fast. You must be made of strong stuff!'

'I g-guess s-so,' replied Will, badly slurring his words.

His reply echoed around the vacuous, cold washroom. It took a second or two, but finally they resonated inside Will's mind and he snapped back. Turning sharply to Darren, his vision suddenly swam with weird images of taps, mirrors, and urinals. As he blinked them away, the events of the last few minutes slowly came back to him.

'My horse won that race!' he thought, 'It's my first winner as a trainer... I need to be... not here!'

'I n...nnn...eed to go,' he instructed Darren drunkenly.

It took another three minutes for Darren to escort a limping, and wincing Will into the winners enclosure. The four lads from Leeds immediately surrounded the two of them, offering their congratulations, and then commiserations, as they learned more about his tumble down the grandstand, in main, thanks to Darren's explanation of events.

Still being supported by Darren, Will pulled himself upright and told him, 'Drop into the yard. I'll try out your horse cubes.'

It came out as gibberish, but Darren seemed to understand and gave Will a delighted wink as said he'd call in soon.

Turning to Davy and Roberto, Will gave them a long-

106

winded and largely unintelligible explanation that boiled down to a request for someone else to drive the horsebox home that evening. As he continued to speak, repeating himself and confusing his audience, Will felt one knee wobble, then the other did the same. As the finely cut, lush grass of the winners enclosure rushed up to meet him, he smiled inwardly; at least this time he was landing on something soft.

Will collapsed onto the turf and promptly passed out, just as the Drawdown syndicate, along with a grinning Darren, delighted to be a part of the celebrations, were being photographed accepting the trophy for Risky winning the feature race of the day.

## Nineteen

'Man! You look like death warmed up,' Freddie remarked in a helpful voice as Will entered the farmhouse kitchen and shuffled towards the table, 'Feeling a little worse for wear this morning are we? Shouldn't go throwing yourself down grandstand steps then, should you?'

Will would have loved to reply, 'I now know what a tenderized steak feels like,' but the cuts and bruises around his lips wouldn't allow such a complex response. Instead, he rolled his eyes at Freddie and groaned as he parked himself on one of the hard wooden chairs around the kitchen table. As well as a thumping headache, it felt like every single muscle in his body had been bruised and was ready to sing with pain if called into action.

Freddie thrust a black coffee into Will's hand and he lifted it to his mouth, only to recoil once the rim of the mug touched his lips. It seemed his arms and legs weren't the only areas of his body that had borne the brunt of his journey down the grandstand steps at Beverley.

'Well done by the way. With the winner I mean,' Freddie remarked, but was soon grinning shamelessly after adding, 'It's a pity you spent all your time with an ambulance crew, rather than quaffing champagne with your winning owners.'

Will produced a watery smile that nevertheless stung his cheeks. He began tentatively rubbing at his face, trying to ease the stiffness in his muscles as Freddie busied himself with a round of toast.

'Wha.. time isss… it?' asked Will eventually, slurring his words as the throbbing in his lips maintained a steady beat.

'Quarter to twelve. You've been out for fifteen hours. It must have hit you pretty hard,' Freddie admitted, managing to keep a straight face this time.

The sound of the front door opening signalled the

arrival of Lizzy and Roberto. The look of shock on Lizzy's face was enough for Will to forget his guilt over missing morning stables. She had proved herself to be a tough, hard worker who expected the same from those around her, so if she was disturbed by his black and blue face, it had to be more than a few scratches – he hadn't bothered to inspect himself in the mirror, there was no way he was entertaining a shave today.

'It's fine, we've sorted everything that needed doing,' Roberto assured him when Will attempted to apologise for not being around, 'And I've taken the liberty of getting everything ready for Mr Hanover's first runner tomorrow at Ripon as well.'

Will tried to smile. The use of the forty-odd facial muscles gave him the feeling his skin was peeling off his face, so he gave up, aimed an appreciative nod in Roberto's direction, and managed a say, 'Ank Oow' from the back of his throat.

Arthur came through from the back room in search of coffee and winced when he caught sight of Will's face of many colours.

'That's got to sting,' he noted.

A conversation about the chances of Mr Hanover's debuting two-year-old bounced around the room, Roberto and Lizzy sparring with each other over the ability of Spring Ensemble. The arguments flowed around the kitchen table for another ten minutes without any input from Will. He slowly sipped his cooling coffee and rubbed at his jaw and cheek muscles to try and get them working again. Presently, Freddie got up with Lizzy and Roberto and the three of them made to leave, Freddie telling everyone that the stables 'Wouldn't paint themselves!', but Will indicated for him to stay.

Once alone with Arthur and Freddie, Will took a breath and managed to say, 'I wasss… pu… pushed.'

His words were mangled together and Arthur needed to guess twice, but eventually grasped their meaning.

'You're sure?' Arthur queried.

109

He watched as a look of disgust began to coalesce on Will's face, quickly adding, 'Right, Fine... So, who pushed you?'

'The stable lad you sacked... Jimmy Hearn?' Freddie suggested.

Will nodded and said 'Ee was 'ere...' and shrugged.

'But?' prompted Arthur, reading the uncertainty in Will's eyes.

Will slouched in his chair. Using his mouth was becoming easier, but speaking a whole sentence was going to need patience and probably, a certain amount of pain. Freddie came to his rescue.

'I spoke with Roberto. He was up at the top of the track, but said there were a lot of people in the grandstand. The steps you fell down are right in front of the owners and trainers viewing area aren't they?'

Will nodded.

'Besides, there must have been hundreds of people in the stands behind you, and they were all heading the same way – back down the steps after the race,' Freddie continued, 'They'd all be standing close together. Anyone could have poked a hand out and given Will a one-handed push over the edge.'

'Perhaps one of the owners or trainers might have seen who pushed you?' suggested Arthur.

'Surely, they would have said something at the time?' Freddie countered.

Will murmured something in reply but ended up shaking his head in frustration when all he received in return were blank stares.

He fell silent, trying to remember. The four members of the syndicate had been standing in the owners viewing area behind him, but so had dozens more owners of other horses. The Dalton family had been there, so they could be worth quizzing, and hadn't Harriet been around too? Jimmy Hearn had definitely been around, but he hadn't seen him in the grandstand, although that didn't mean he wasn't there, tipping him over the edge of the top step… But then there were hundreds, no, thousands of people in that stand…

'Kings Ahmss…?' Will announced. It was garbled, but his speech was definitely improving with use.

'Really, the Kings Arms pub tonight?'

Freddie's question was more of an exclamation.

'Why no…?' Will countered, still having difficulty rounding off his words.

'You look like you've been mauled by a bear, you can hardly walk, and you're slurring half your words.'

Will waved Freddie's protest away and slowly and deliberately said, 'I'll… e thine. I wanna… see a thend.'

Will was banking on Suzie. If there was any talk around town about who might be responsible for pushing him, Suzie would be the one to get to know.

Arthur suddenly held up a hand. He leant across the table and tilted his head to one side as he examined Will, his eyes narrowing.

'Say fine and friend again,' he demanded.

'Eh?'

'Say 'friend',' Arthur insisted with a roll of his eyes, 'Is it that difficult?'

Will repeated it again twice, both times, struggling to pronounce the start of the word. He did the same with the word 'fine' and then waited impatiently for Arthur to get out his mother's journal, find a specific page, and make two lines of notes.

'Now say 'about'.'

Will sighed, tiring of Arthur's game, but humouring his friend once more.

Again, the cuts and bruising on Will's lips meant he rather mangled the word.

Arthur wrote more notes alongside those he'd already made, finishing them with a large exclamation mark. He removed his spectacles and a smile graced his face.

'What you so happy about?' asked Freddie.

'Will can't pronounce his F's and R's,' he announced happily.

'Whoopie doo!' Freddie remarked sarcastically, 'He's done a swallow dive, head-first down a set of concrete steps, what do you expect?'

'So had Jack… well, not a set of steps, but he'd been badly beaten – you could see from those police photos what his attacker did to his face. And he must have been in *far* more pain than Will.'

Will rolled his eyes to indicate his sarcastic thanks for Arthur's empathy. But Arthur wasn't finished.

'Anyone who has had that sort of a bashing to their lips, teeth and cheeks, like Will, won't be able to pronounce their words properly.'

Arthur paused, waiting for the penny to drop. Will got it first but had to wait for Freddie to articulate it.

'Jack's words in the ambulance… he couldn't pronounce them properly, so if we…'

Arthur nodded and continued, 'If we can work out which letters or combinations of letters produce the words 'Yellow Noise Ed Coss' we could have the name of his killer!'

Freddie screwed his face up, adopting a deeply unconvinced expression, 'You're serious?'

'Leave it with me,' said Arthur a little huffily, collecting his papers together and getting up from the table, 'I'll work on it.'

When the door to the back room clicked shut, Freddie shot one of his, 'Yeah, right!' looks at Will and raised his eyebrows.

'Ee's umm…' Will responded, wincing as several spears of pain shot up his cheek. He swiftly gave up.

Freddie nodded and got up, 'I'm off to buy some paint. See you later. I assume you want the wood the same colour, I can't go for pink or dayglo yellow?'

Will minutely shook his head and gave a painful grin,

'Ite! Ite! Arrghh it!…' He couldn't get his lips to wrap themselves around the 'W'.

'… Sane collor!' he managed eventually.

Freddie smiled back at him from the doorway to the hallway, calling, 'Get back to bed and rest up.'

Will waved him away, knowing full well he had to check the yard, do his entries for the following week, and phone Hanover about his youngster's debut at Ripon tomorrow. Any thought of resting up had to be pushed from his mind. No one in racing stopped working after they'd had a fall. If you could pick up a broom or a rake, you could make yourself useful in a racing stable.

## Twenty

With Arthur insisting he still had work to do that evening, Will and Freddie took themselves off to the Kings Arms in Malton without him. They left Arthur in the back room, poring over lines of numbers on his laptop, piles of Barney's paperwork, and the old television burbling in the background. He admitted to being as happy as a pig in muck, and practically shooed his friends out of the farmhouse.

The pub was all oak beams and horse brasses, topped off by the gaudy sparkle of a large square bar inlaid with smoked mirrors. The same mirrors adorned the back of the bar, reflecting upon dozens of part dispensed liquors. The décor might be circa 1980's, but it somehow provided a warm, lived-in atmosphere that customers of a certain age could relax into. Will ordered two Newcastle Brown Ales and ignoring the barman's stare at the range of bruises around his face, he asked whether Suzie was working tonight and could he see her. The muscles in his face had eased off as the day had worn on, and he was at least semi understandable.

From Freddie's point of view, Suzie's entrance was both breath-taking and ultimately, frustrating. She appeared at the top of a flight of stairs set into the corner of the bar, wearing a floral silk blouse, and a cheeky smile, her pixie bob swaying with each step. Freddie was immediately smitten. She had to be half his size, but when she skipped over to Will and without hesitation or reference to his beat up face, planted a kiss on his friend's cheek, he found himself waiting for the same treatment, disappointed when it didn't happen. Freddie immediately ruled out any potential liaison; the girl only had eyes for Will. Besides, he'd quite enjoyed hanging around the yard with that stable lass today…

'So you made it…' said Suzie, biting her bottom lip as she inspected Will's cuts and bruises, 'Did you have to fight someone in the street to make it through the door?'

Will gave her a wry smile, fairly sure she must have

already heard the story of his fall down the Beverley steps. He told her it was a long, involved story, introduced Freddie, and suggested the three of them sit at a table well away from the bar and any prying ears.

'This must be serious,' Suzie said lightly as they arranged themselves around a clam-shaped booth, 'You used to be a 'stand at the bar and pontificate in a loud voice' sort of punter.'

Will took a sip of his drink. He'd not thought of himself as being loud, either now or when he was younger. He made a mental note to afford Suzie's comment further thought another time. For now, he wanted to maintain a serious tone.

'Yeah, well since I've come back to Malton I've learned to be... careful.'

Suzie smiled, 'Not careful enough! I hear you got so excited when your horse won you decided to throw yourself down the grandstand steps.'

'It wasn't quite like that,' Will said defensively.

He wondered if he should tell her the whole story. Whether it was a combination of his own personal pride, the fact she'd been a good, reliable friend for those A-level years, or the way she looked at him in that moment, he couldn't help himself.

'Actually, it wasn't my fault... I was pushed,' he blurted.

Freddie shot Will a surprised stare. This hadn't been the plan. But then Will was always a sucker for a cute girl with big brown eyes. Freddie wondered for a moment whether the two of them were old flames, but ruled it out. Will still hadn't worked out she had a thing for him - so it was unlikely he'd seen it as a teenager - and Suzie didn't seem the type to simply throw herself at him.

Suzie leaned back into the booth's velvet padded backrest, crossed her legs and waited, her expectant, and somewhat dubious gaze focused squarely on Will.

'It's true!' Will insisted, 'I've been attacked twice since I

115

arrived, and I've only been here a week!'

'Twice?' Suzie queried.

Will rubbed his forehead, then began massaging his temples. His headache was returning. He hadn't anticipated tonight would require him to defend himself, or recount both the recent instances he'd been laid out cold.

'He *was* pushed,' Freddie cut in. Will had lost the colour in his face, even his bruises seemed to have become paler, 'Someone in the crowd kicked his standing leg and he went down the concrete steps like a sack of potatoes.'

'Well, it wasn't *that* bad…' Will countered.

'It's okay, I've got this,' Freddie assured him.

'He also got brained with a torch by an ex-employee, a lad fond of kicking horses they call Jimmy Hearn,' Freddie continued, 'That's one of the reasons we called in this evening, we wondered if there had been any talk around the pubs in the town. I understand Jimmy likes a pint and a natter.'

'What's the other reason?' Suzie fired back.

Freddie grinned, remembering the way Will had reacted when this girl had started to kid him along.

'I guess Will here wanted to see you. He's off to Ripon tomorrow and there's a spare seat… that's if you fancied coming along?'

Will choked on his Brown Ale, spluttering slightly into his half-pint glass. Lost for words, and facing an expectant Suzie and a grinning Freddie he failed miserably to respond, his drink still at his lips.

Trying to swallow, some of the Brown Ale took the wrong course and caused his eyes to water, 'That's… I…'

'I'd love to come along,' Suzie said smartly, cutting him dead. She beamed at the two of them, 'I'll look forward to it.'

Suzie hesitated, uncrossing her legs and shuffling closer to Will, 'Regarding your first question. There were a group of stable lads in last night, talking about your fall. That's how I knew about it.'

She dropped her tone to a whisper, 'Jimmy Hearn was

with them, spouting off that you deserved it for sacking him. I heard a mate of his say there was talk on the racecourse that someone had pushed you. Jimmy went quiet after that.'

'I think I need to have another word with Jimmy,' said Will, 'Or maybe get Pat, my godfather to have a quiet word – he's a policeman.'

'I know who Pat is,' said Suzie, 'There's hardly a Friday or Saturday night goes by without him popping into all the pubs down the high street to make sure everything's quiet.'

Will frowned, 'Huh, I didn't have him down as the sort.'

'Oh, Pat's a decent chap,' Suzie said matter-of-factly, 'He keeps an eye on some of the young lads and lasses involved in racing, making sure they don't get into any trouble… Anyway, there was someone else in here later on last night, mentioning your name – Davy Dalton.'

'Well, Davy's okay,' said Will, touching his temples once again. His forehead was now throbbing with the sort of insistent pain that suggested it wasn't going away any time soon.

Suzie smiled, 'Yeah, Davy's fine. He was in here with his family… well, the male part of the family, his dad and grandfather. He was telling them about your two-year-old… Catwalk isn't it?'

Will nodded.

Suzie looked into his eyes and paused before saying, 'You don't look well. Perhaps I'll save this story until tomorrow?'

When Will looked Freddie's way he too was sporting a concerned grimace, but shook his head anyway.

'Finish up, and then we'll get back home if that's okay.'

Suzie told the rest of her story at a strong canter, then shooed them out of the pub, promising to be at the yard for ten thirty the next day, suitably dressed for a day at the races.

Freddie drove Will back to the yard in the old Renault, regularly checking on his friend who had gone a ghostly

117

white.

'You sure I can't take you to the doc's?' he asked for the third time, 'After all, you've had two bad knocks in the last week, you've almost certainly got concussion.'

'It's okay,' Will replied with a yawn, 'I just need an early night.'

It was true that he felt dog tired. The fall down the steps hadn't helped, but he had to admit that running the yard full time was a tough assignment. He'd taken it for granted that he'd cope, but he now understood why Roberto was so keen to get another work rider into the yard. Riding three lots a day, going racing, and having even a meagre social life was already grinding him down. They needed help in the yard, and he'd get onto it first thing tomorrow. Another jockey like Davy coming in a few days a week would help a lot.

He was reminded of the end to Suzie's story. Davy had spoken highly of Catwalk, Will's plans to debut at Goodwood in ten days' time, and his hope to be chosen for the ride. However, it was the reaction from Davy's father that had caught Suzie's attention.

'He really tried to shut Davy up,' Suzie had recalled, 'Got a bit hot under the collar too. Davy being Davy, he didn't pick up on it and soldiered on regardless. Soon enough, his grandfather joined the argument. He must be in his eighties and has trouble walking. He went really red in the face. I don't know what they ended up arguing about, but I heard your name come up a few times. When they realised I was close by, behind the bar, they all clammed up and left soon after, still not on the best of terms with Davy.'

'What did you think to what Suzie overheard at Davy's table last night?' Will asked as Freddie turned the little car into the lane leading to Manor Stud Stables.

Freddie shrugged, 'Sounds to me like a fairly normal family spat. My lot have them all the time... usually concerning me!'

Will gave a small chuckle, but groaned when his cheek

muscles tightened, sending a spasm of pain around his jaw. When they reached the farmhouse, Will called goodnight to Arthur as he went through the back room on his way to the foot of the stairs. Once in his bedroom he crumpled onto his bed and fell fast asleep, still fully clothed.

## Twenty-One

'Wake up! Come on Will, this is important!' said an urgent voice with a Scottish accent.

Will felt a slight rocking of his shoulder followed by a pang of pain that worked its way down his arm. He opened his eyes, but couldn't see anything, having remained lying on his front, where he'd landed on the bed several hours earlier. He rolled over. This movement elicited more pain from a dozen places but, when he came to rest on his back, a familiar face blinked into focus.

Lit only by the landing light through his open bedroom door, Arthur's outline loomed over him. He was clutching something under his arm and although his face was in shadow, Will could just make out that his friend was smiling.

'What is it?' he said through gritted teeth, pushing himself up to a sitting position whilst trying not to groan as a result of the pain that radiated around his stiff body. He leaned his back against the headboard and tried to even out his breathing. He doubted he would be riding out today. That made him check his bedside clock. It's luminous numbers told him it was a little after three o'clock in the morning.

'It's the middle of the night! Why have you…'

'I've found something!' Arthur interrupted. There was a boyish excitement in his voice that somehow immediately transmitted itself into Will. The time of day instantly became meaningless.

'I think I've cracked it!' Arthur continued, seating himself beside Will on the edge of the bed. He produced Jack's notebook and Will's mother's journal from under his arm and after ensuring they were open at particular pages, placed them onto Will's lap. Suddenly realising it was too dark for Will to see the pages, let alone read his own notes, Arthur grappled with the stem of the bedside lamp for a few seconds until a click cast a golden glow onto the two of them.

'Your mother had already worked it out! She had

references to someone called BB, and it was everywhere, and…'

'Arthur! Slow down,' Will moaned.

Will took a breath.

'Okay… Lilywhites bookmakers,' Arthur said slowly, 'Remember them?'

'Sure, the bookmakers Jack had a disagreement with.'

'I went through Jack's notebook, and because he reckoned he was owed four grand for an £800 credit bet at 5/1, he carried that amount forward each month. Each month from March 2001 has £4,000 set against the name of Lilywhites. Apart from one month.'

Arthur picked up Jack's notebook and opened it at a page he had marked with a yellow sticker.

'There,' Arthur indicated triumphantly, 'Instead of Lilywhites it simply says BB.'

Will squinted at where Arthur's finger was pointing and sure enough, under the heading of 'bookmaker' two B's were printed in Jack's flowery handwriting and in a column named 'owed' the amount of £4,000.

'Right,' Arthur continued, clearly not anywhere near finished, 'I checked your mother's journal for anything mentioning BB and I came across this.'

Again, he drew Will's eye to a note written by his mother. This was towards the end of her journal and simply stated, 'BB = Brillo Boys?'. It was a standalone note written in the margin and underlined twice with an arrow drawn from the note and pointing to the Lilywhite name. It was amongst a list of the bookmakers who had traded in the Tattersalls enclosure at York Racecourse on Ebor day, 2002.

'I think Lilywhites bookmakers must have had a nickname or perhaps Jack referred to them as the Brillo Boys just to wind them up,' said Arthur.

Will frowned, the words, 'So what' leaping into his mind. So Jack had pet names for his bookmakers?

Arthur pulled out a sheet of paper from under the

journal and notebook. It was covered with his own handwritten notes, all in small block capitals.

'I've also been working on what that lady on the ambulance crew reported about Jack's last words.'

Will took a sideways glance at Arthur and realised his friend was finding it hard to contain himself. He was wearing the same gleeful expression he adopted when answering an obscure quiz night question at the local pub, knowing that out of the three of them, only he knew the answer.

'The ambulance woman said Jack's last words were Yellow Noise and Ed Coss before he lost consciousness. Let's just take Yellow Noise. At first I thought it was Brillo Boys! You know, like the scouring thingy, the Brillo Pad!'

'Huh,' Will said uncertainly.

'Say it,' Arthur prompted.

'What?'

'Say Brillo Boys.'

Will sighed and said, 'Brillo Boys'. His lips and cheeks had once again become stiff as he'd slept. It seemed the effects of the pounding they'd received when he face-planted on the grandstand steps weren't going to disappear any time soon and so Brillo Boys came out as 'Ello Noys'.

Arthurs eyes lit up under the glow of the lamp.

'You can't pronounce the BR in Brillo or the B in Boys because your lips are sore. Imagine what Jack's lips must have felt like straight after his beating! You saw the photos, his face was a mess. He couldn't get the name of the people who attacked him out properly, and I imagine the ambulance woman also misheard him and tried to make sense of what he was saying and just got it wrong. But I'm sure he was saying 'Brillo Boys'. And guess what, that's what your mother guessed he was saying too!'

Arthur was becoming over-excited. He was speaking quickly and his Scottish accent was becoming thicker, so much so, Will had to concentrate hard to follow him, but he didn't interrupt. Arthur was on a roll.

'I checked with Companies House, you know, the place that lists all registered companies, and they still had a listing for Lilywhites Bookmakers Limited. They were based in York, with a betting office on the corner of one of the city centre streets. They went out of business in 2010, but I found out via Google Streetview there's a Ladbrokes there now. I reckon Lilywhites must have sold their shop to them. There were three directors, all men, all with the surname Lilywhite, and when I searched for the 'Brillo Boys' on a 'sounds like' internet search, along with 'York Racecourse' I came up with this!'

Arthur placed a printout of a photo onto Will's lap. It was a black and white image of a bookmaker's pitch in a racecourse betting ring. It was staged like a corporate photograph, and Will recognised a finishing post, racetrack and rolling grass bank in the background that confirmed to him that it was taken at York racecourse. Arthur had written three forenames underneath – John, Frank, and Clarence. Three men were standing, arms crossed, in front of their bookmakers pitch.

The bookmaker's board had a hand painted sign that read in bold black letters, picked out in white, 'Lilywhites' and underneath in smaller print were the words 'Three Ways Honest'. The men were snappily dressed, wearing matching black suits and shiny black shoes. Two of them, large, beefy sorts, sported thin black ties. The third, a smaller, younger man wearing spectacles, had a patterned bow tie. They all looked to be somewhere in their fifties.

But their attire wasn't what Will was drawn to, or even their smiling faces. Each man had a full head of black hair. Even in this grainy black and white photo printed on an ancient printer, Will could make out that each of the men had a sizeable quiff, and the rest of their hair was slicked down and shone from the over-application of styling oil, gel, or cream.

'It was then that I realised is wasn't Brillo like the scouring pad,' explained Arthur, 'It was Brylo as in

Brylcreem.'

'This is a picture of the three Lilywhite brothers and either Jack nicknamed them 'The Brylo Boys, or that's what people in racing circles must have called them,' Arthur said reverently, 'I'm sure Jack was trying to tell the ambulance woman the Brylo Boys were his attackers.'

Leaning back against his headboard, Will didn't reply immediately, he just nodded, continuing to stare down at Jack's notebook, his mother's journal, and the loose sheets of paper containing Arthur's notes. They all went a little fuzzy under the light from the bedside lamp and Will had to blink to bring them back into focus.

Whether it was the influx of so much information upon waking, or the musty smell of the notebook and journal laying on his bedclothes, Will's thoughts were carried back to his youth. He was in Jack's farmhouse. Both he, and his mother were born here. There was precious little he could remember of his grandfather, and the memories he did have were only odd snippets. And they were an eclectic assortment of memories, but still bright and colourful. For example, his grandfather's bristly face rubbing against him as Jack lifted him onto his first pony. Playing Mouse Trap at Christmas in front of the fire, and Jack's raucous laugh when the trap was finally sprung. Helping him feed the horses on a hot summers day, out in the far paddock when the grass had all been eaten away.

He'd been three years old when Jack had died, and his strongest, abiding memory was the day of the funeral; holding onto his mother's hand as she trembled, looking up to find tears streaking down her heavily made-up cheeks, and wondering why everyone else in the church, apart from her, was singing.

Will shivered. In a low voice he said, 'It's like my grandfather is speaking to me from beyond the grave.'

He'd meant to say this with foreboding. Instead his swollen lips and aching face made it into garbled nonsense that had Arthur frowning.

Perhaps it was because it was the middle of the night, or the sudden influx of childhood memories, but a wave of grief pulsed through him. If his grandfather was attempting to reach out to him, he'd achieved his goal. Will shuddered and closed his eyes tight, trying to clear his mind.

'What about Ed Coss?' he asked Arthur quietly, slurring most of his words.

Arthur shook his head, 'I don't think he's a person.'

Arthur paused, concentrating on a point way off at the other side of the bedroom. Presently, his grim stare broke into an incredulous half-smile and he turned back to Will, 'Okay, say grandfather and grave again.'

Will didn't argue, even though he was beginning to feel sleepy and light-headed once more, 'Gandather. Gave,' he spluttered.

Arthur wrote something down on his notes and held a flat hand up to Will when asked what he was doing. Half a minute of silent note-making later Arthur underlined something twice with a flourish, put his pen down, and looking up, grinned at his friend.

'You can't pronounce your R's and F's, as well as your B's!' he announced happily.

'Gate,' Will responded with a roll of his eyes, only realising after he'd spoken that the R in 'great' was missing due to his current speech impediment. Feeling weary, he said no more, instead nodding appreciatively back at Arthur.

'Ed Coss could be someone's name, or just a phrase. We've no way of knowing 'Arthur continued, referring to his recent notes, 'I suppose it could be a man called Fred Cross, but I reckon Jack was trying to say something else. There's a lot of combinations, but the one that makes the most sense is 'Red Cross.'

'Red Cross?' Will repeated with a frown, 'You mean *The* Red Cross, the charity?'

'Could be,' said Arthur, 'Or perhaps…'

'Or perhaps he was just talking gibberish because he'd been badly beaten around the head!' Will tried to say. Again, his sentence made no sense and he knew it. Not being able to pronounce half the alphabet was a pain. Jack must have thought so too, being stuck on a stretcher, his life ebbing away, blunt force trauma to his skull… A spasm of discomfort rippled cross Will's forehead and he unsuccessfully tried to stifle a yawn that had sneaked up on him.

Arthur had been watching Will, who suddenly looked pale and possibly worried. He thought about placing a hand on his friend's shoulder to reassure him, but as he began to lift his arm Will blinked and seemed to snap out of his troublesome thoughts.

'We need to find them, these Brylcreem bookies,' Will said in a more definite tone, still slurring his words and adding another yawn at the end for good measure.

'At least they are real people that we know existed,' Arthur pointed out, 'We can work on the Red Cross, or Fred Cross thing separately.'

Will nodded and murmured his agreement.

'It might be tough to find the Lilywhites after twenty-odd years,' warned Arthur as he got up from Will's bed, sensing their 3am meeting was reaching its conclusion, 'I've already searched for them online. Not surprisingly for eighty-year-olds they don't have Facebook or Instagram accounts. They could be anywhere in the world, or most probably, they're dead. We can't count on finding them.'

With Will's eyelids half-closed Arthur didn't wait for a response. He made his way out of Will's bedroom and quietly clicked the door closed behind him.

Inside his own bedroom at the back of the farmhouse Arthur got ready for bed, his mind still full of his investigations. Chances were, those three Brylo Boys in the photograph would be long gone by now. Feeling a little deflated, he cast his eye over the journal, notebook and papers he had placed on the bedside cabinet. His attention was drawn to Jack's notebook. A wafer thin, yellow triangle of paper was poking out of one of the pages. He slipped it out. It was a carbon copy of an old bet, stamped with a four digit number, a reference code, and a date.

Arthur climbed into bed, the small rectangular betting receipt filling his mind. He got to thinking about his own Grandpa, who was edging close to eighty years old. Every Saturday his Grandpa would make the half mile walk down to his local betting shop and place his bets, having no truck with internet betting via a mobile phone. Was there a slim chance that one of the Brylo Boys might still frequent their old betting shop, now it was run by Ladbrokes?

Arthur jumped back out of bed and flicked through his paperwork, consumed with a single purpose; where in York was that Lilywhites betting shop?

## Twenty-Two

'Why does Will get to go to Ripon races with the beautiful Suzie and we're spending the day in a smelly old bookmakers trying to interview ancient punters?'

Arthur shot a look of undisguised disgust at Freddie and turned to stare vacantly at the racing newspaper pinned to the wall of the betting shop.

'Keep your voice down, will you?' he pleaded, 'The manager will throw us out if you speak any louder!'

'She's not bothered about us,' Freddie scoffed, 'She's more interested in those idiots over there pumping hundreds of pounds into that fruit machine and banging their fists on it when they don't win.'

'Be quiet!' Arthur hissed, 'Haven't you wondered how three lads of their age can afford to be wearing expensive designer gear and losing that sort of money on a fruit machine at eleven o'clock on a Thursday morning?'

Freddie frowned, then spun round on his stool to take a long look at the three lads again.

'Oh right! Yeah, I get it now,' he said, meeting Arthur's gaze with eyes wide in mock shock, 'Young drug-dealing hoodlums eh?'

Arthur cringed for a moment, then took a side-long glance over his shoulder to check out the betting shop manager behind the counter. She was clearly unimpressed. As their losing run continued the teenagers' frustration was being taken out on the fruit machine, rocking it and smacking its glass facia. The manager stared grimly at the trio of boys.

Freddie and Arthur were perched on tall pedestal stools covered in dirty red plastic in a small betting office close to the centre of York. They had been there since it opened at nine-thirty in the morning, in the hope of finding someone who would know what had happened to the Brylo Boys.

The manager of the shop was a hard-faced, pleasant

128

enough lady, but she hadn't been of any help. Apparently the staff regularly moved around the shops and so she knew little of the punters. She also pointed out that being located just outside the centre of York, the shop attracted a lot of tourists, being tucked away on a side-street a stone's throw away from the Minster. As long as Arthur and Freddie didn't bother the other punters too much, and placed the odd small bet on the morning greyhound racing, she seemed happy enough to leave them be.

The shop hadn't been busy. So far they had questioned three men, none of whom had even heard of the Lilywhites. Another viable target, a chap aged around seventy had come in at ten o'clock, headed straight for the vending machine and bought a coffee. Having settled on one of the small stools in front of the bay of screens showing odds, video replays, and previews, he remained there, hunched over his copy of the Daily Mirror. And he was still there, writing out a raft of betting slips. He had given Freddie a shrug when asked if he could remember the Lilywhites and offered nothing further.

'Tell you what, I'll go get us a coffee,' Arthur offered.

'I'll have a flat white.'

Arthur eyed the vending machine more in hope, than expectation, 'It's black or white, that's the choice.'

'I'm not drinkin' that stuff!' Freddie exclaimed, 'Look, I'll stay here – get round to that Greggs we passed on the way here.'

One more glance at the vending machine and the ring of coffee stains on the vinyl floor convinced Arthur his friend was right.

He made for the betting shop door, happy to be getting some fresh air, 'I'll be back in five. If you see any pensioners come in, ask them about the Lilywhites.'

A minute after Arthur had left, one of the local lads hogging the fruit machine slammed a flat palm onto the display glass and swore. Freddie turned around in his seat and regarded the three teenagers balefully as they received a warning from the manager behind the counter. One of them caught Freddie's eye and they stared at each other for a long moment.

The boy asked, 'What you lookin' at?'

Very original, but overused thought Freddie. It had to be the top opening line for so many teenage confrontations. He shot the boy a pleasant smile, slid off his seat and crossed over to the fruit machine. He was five inches taller, and at least a foot wider than any of them, and made the most of it, rolling his shoulders as if limbering up for a fight. The three boys were all watching him carefully now, their attention diverted from the fruit machine. Freddie stopped a yard away from them and rubbed his large hands together. The boys tensed, and behind the shop counter the manager quietly took her mobile phone out of her pocket.

He nodded toward the fruit machine, and in the broadest of his Geordie accents Freddie enquired, 'I'm wonderin' why you bairns aren't using the nudge and no hold trick. Howay man, you must know that one!'

The boys looked at the machine, and then at each other.

'Howay, let me in! Divn't they teach you anything? That machine is *dyin'* tae let you win! Gan on, spin a few credits. Let's win you some cash.'

Arthur was on his approach to the betting shop when he found Freddie in the street outside, leaning against a wall, waiting for him.

'We're off to find Clarence, or rather, Clary Lilywhite,' Freddie told him before Arthur had the chance to quiz him, 'Turns out that one of the local lads on the fruit machine in there knows one of the Brylo Boys because his dad used to bet here in the nineties. He doesn't know about the other two brothers, but Clarence still lives on the outskirts of the city. He's quite a character by all accounts and well known - for the wrong reasons.'

'Really?' Arthur said incredulously as he passed Freddie his coffee, 'How on earth did you find all this out in the five minutes I was gone?'

'The result of a misspent childhood in amusement arcades over in Whitley Bay,' Freddie replied with a wry smile, 'Come on, back to the car, it's a few miles from here.'

*** 

Will always enjoyed Ripon racecourse in the spring. Every year the racecourse spent time and money ensuring their many flower beds were planted up in time for the start of the flat season. Hanging baskets were overflowing with colour and the woodwork on the hundred year-old buildings enjoyed an annual dab of touch-up paint, giving the racecourse a renewed, fresh feel. Always a springtime treat for racegoers, Ripon was a welcome change from the dour, grey surroundings generally available around the jumps tracks through winter.

From the look on Suzie's face when she and Will entered the Tattersalls area of the racecourse together, she too was suitably impressed with her surroundings. She unexpectedly linked arms with him and they headed for the Owners and Trainers lounge, Will enjoying the sensation of having Suzie on his arm.

They drew a number of stares as their walk skirted around the parade ring, most of them for Suzie. It wasn't a surprise; she oozed rebellious femininity. From her newly slicked back hair, down through her white and yellow daisy patterned dress that accentuated her curves, to her pair of classic white high-top training shoes painted with a large red heart above a skull and crossbones through which a wreath emblazoned with the words, 'love kills slowly,' were intertwined. She was the embodiment of carefree youth. And Will was loving it.

He, on the other hand, was wearing a conservative grey lounge suit and purple tie, lifted from his father's wardrobe. As a student, he had no need for a suit, and was both relieved and a little appalled to find his dimensions were so similar to his father's, the suit had easily slipped on and fitted perfectly. He'd been ready to leave in his standard shirt and jeans combo, until Freddie had caught sight of him and insisted he had to 'look the part' of a racehorse trainer. Freddie had picked this outfit for him and Will had gone along with his suggestions with little complaint. Freddie's costuming skills were apparently the talk of his fellow students on his university course, and Will had been glad of the advice once he'd laid eyes on Suzie.

With Spring Ensemble running in the opening race on the afternoon card, a five furlong fillies only Maiden due off at two o'clock, Will had set off for Ripon in good time in order to settle the filly into the racecourse stables well before race time. So he was surprised when he and Suzie climbed the stairs and spotted Louis Hanover already seated at one of the small tables on the second floor of the Owners and Trainers lounge.

'Mr Hanover,' Will announced, 'Good to see you again. Can I introduce you to my good friend, Suzie Tipton.'

Hanover swivelled in his seat. He looked Will up and down, wrinkled his nose as if his trainer's attire was an affront before transferring his attention to Suzie. He drank her in, a delighted smile gracing his perfectly tanned face.

'My dear girl!' Hanover cooed, getting to his feet, 'Loving the sixties chic and grunge mash-up. Please... sit beside me. I'm sure Will can surely spare you for a few minutes.'

Giving Will an amused glance, Suzie took the offered seat at Hanover's table and proceeded to charm the clothing retailer, engaging him in a conversation Will neither understood or wanted to understand. He nodded every now and again to feign interest, thankful Freddie had bullied him into asking her along. He studied Suzie minutely as she and Hanover discussed how linen flares would be the summer's must-have fashion statement and marvelled at how much she had altered since he'd left Malton three years ago.

As the conversation moved onto shoulder pads, Will plastered what he hoped was an endearing smile onto his face and allowed his mind to wander. He wondered how Freddie and Arthur were getting on in York.

*** 

'Here! This has got to be it!' Freddie called out, as they came upon a line of Victorian semi-detached houses on the northern edge of York. There were some grand period houses here, with large, well-kept gardens and shiny new cars in the long, pebbled drives, but Arthur noticed the house Freddie was peering at with particular interest had a small mountain of junk in the front garden and the house itself looked badly in need of some attention.

Arthur indicated left, guided the toiling little Renault to the kerbside and they drew to a shuddering halt.

'This car is jinxy,' he moaned.

'It's fine,' Freddie countered, 'It's got character.'

'Yeah, the character of an incontinent, three-legged donkey,' Arthur complained, giving the handbrake a firm little pull upwards.

An involuntary gasp forced its way from his lips as the lever came away in his hand and he was left examining the rust corroded shaft in disbelief.

'Ha! Yes, that came away a few days ago when I went to the shop for bread and milk,' Freddie told him with a grin, 'And don't open the windows, they tend to stick and then refuse to close.'

Grumbling, Arthur tossed the brake lever into the back seat, made sure to leave the car in gear, and turned to Freddie, 'So how are we going to play this?'

'Leave it with me. This should be a great test of my improv skills. I'll have whoever's in there eating out of my hand.'

'Or biting it off. Just remember, we're dealing with the

three men who beat Will's grandfather to death. It's unlikely they'll cough to killing someone, especially to two lads they hardly know.'

'Yeah, but they've got to be in their eighties now,' said Freddie, determined to stay positive, 'People change. Maybe they might have regrets. From the state of that house, maybe they...'

'Need a skip?' suggested Arthur.

'No... well, yes. But perhaps I can get them to at least admit they were there at the races that day. We can leave the rest to the police. So keep quiet and just agree with anything I say, okay?'

Arthur considered this request. Freddie was an accomplished actor, and his improvisational skills were impressive. However, he could lose himself in the moment and on occasion could get in too deep.

'O...kay,' said Arthur.

Freddie waited. He could sense a 'but' coming.

'But, if I think we're in any sort of danger, I'll say it's time to move on, and we have to leave.'

'Agreed. Come on then.'

It took a while to traipse around the lines of stacked junk that eventually beat a path to the front door through the frankly astonishing collection of items. It wasn't just the volume of rubbish, it was the variety, and the fact that every tin can, bottle, kite, plastic bottle, length of rope, bicycle wheel, and broken lock had its own designated area. Being someone who believed everything should have its place, Arthur had to admit to being a little impressed. Even within each area, the items hadn't just been thrown there, they had been carefully placed, either in order of size, or shape. Whoever was responsible for this insane collection led a cluttered life, but had the semblance of an ordered mind.

The entire front garden was laid out like some sort of maze with narrow walkways between the different types of detritus, stacked waist high in some cases. You couldn't help but admire the craziness of it all. Freddie noted that whoever was responsible for the hoarding had a penchant for Co-Op plastic bags filled with used takeaway coffee cups. Every corner they turned had its own carefully constructed pyramid of neatly tied plastic bags from the Co-Op. Inside each bag were a dozen or so cardboard cups.

'I hope he remembers to collect his divvy,' Freddie told Arthur with a thin-lipped grin, nodding towards the next Co-Op inspired pyramid.

Browning, mouldy newspapers were stacked at both sides of the porch, making the entrance to the once grand Victorian terrace house now resemble a bunker. The papers were bundled with string and stacked so high Arthur had mistaken them for concrete columns from the roadside. A knock on a large, and largely loose, fancy brass knocker brought no one to the door, so Freddie tried again, longer and louder. Growling emanated from inside the hall, then a shout. Thirty seconds later the front door creaked open six inches and the central slice of a man's bearded face appeared. He had wild silver hair and was wearing small round spectacles. Close to the bottom of the door a small tan coloured dog inspected their feet with a low, suppressed growl. It had an impressive overbite, giving it a menacing look for its size.

'What?' demanded the man.

'Mr Lilywhite?'

The grizzled pensioner eyed the two young men suspiciously from between the gap in the door, 'You from the council? Cos if you are, y'can sling yer hook.'

'No, we're not from the council,' Freddie said with a frown and a shake of his head, as if such a thought was an abomination. He'd changed his accent, his heavy Geordie had been replaced with something sounding faintly Yorkshire, but it was hard to place as it kept swinging from north to south. Arthur stared at the dirty red tiles on the porch floor and tried not to smile.

'My name is Freddie and this is my friend Arthur. We

deal in antiques and other tradeable items. We were informed you have some extremely interesting pieces. In fact, we were just admiring your collection as we came up your drive… I'm frankly astonished at the variety of *memorabilia* you have saved for the next generation!'

Lilywhite rubbed the stained yellow beard hairs on his chin as he assessed them. It made a rustling noise and Arthur was convinced he saw a cornflake crumb fall from its bushiness.

'We'd love to have a look around, Mr Lilywhite. We do make on-the-spot offers, *in cash* of course, and you do seem to have an amazing variety of collectables.'

Freddie tapped the breast pocket of his jacket meaningfully and set his gaze on the old man, pleased when he spotted Lilywhite's watery old eyes widen as his message got through.

'And I'd be very interested in your thoughts on some of your more *unconventional* items as they are often far more *valuable* than you can imagine… such as those copies of Readers Digest… I see you have an extensive collection.'

The door opened a few more inches and the dog jumped over the threshold and into the porch, sniffing inquisitively around the boys trouser legs. The growling ceased as the smell of horses from the soles of their shoes proved of more interest than their presence on his porch alone. Freddie smiled benignly down at the man and then bent down to give the dog a little tickle behind his ears. It was this that finally did the trick.

'Don't like waste… people are always tossing good stuff away,' said Lilywhite in a rumbling East Yorkshire accent as he allowed the front door to swing open, 'Got more of them magazines inside.'

He indicated the inside of his house with a swift flick of his head. And with that, Lilywhite turned his back on them and beetled off into the bowels of the house, carefully edging past a tottering pile of rusting toasters opposite a wall of cola cans. Freddie silently provided Arthur with a raised eyebrow and the two of them ventured over the threshold in pursuit of the homeowner.

***

Will was mightily relieved to be back in the racecourse stables, freed from having to make small-talk with his owner. He'd eventually left Suzie with Hanover. She'd appeared quite satisfied with his departure, telling him to get away and, 'Do whatever it is you racehorse trainers need to do!'

Suzie had proved to be an excellent distraction for his owner and more than willing to engage in a range of topics Will couldn't begin to comprehend. He also couldn't believe how chatty Hanover had been with her. The conversation had covered his clothing business, how he chose the styles for the next season, where they were sourced, and soon Suzie had moved on to investigating Hanover's childhood, his love of horses, and hopes for his three horses in training. Will had hardly spoken, but Hanover talked more in the first few minutes of meeting Suzie than he'd done for the entire hour and a half at the stables the previous weekend. Hanover had clearly been bowled over by Suzie and Will wondered for a moment whether he'd missed something and his owner was in fact romantically interested in her. He soon rejected this idea. Hanover hadn't given off that sort of vibe.

In truth, Will didn't need to be at the racecourse stables. Roberto would be leading up Hanover's youngster and was more than capable of preparing the filly for her race without his help. It was just better than being a bystander to Suzie's excellent, but bewildering performance in the Owners and Trainers lounge.

'She can go well today,' Roberto commented as they led the filly out of the stabling complex, down the chute outside the course, and to the entrance to the pre-parade ring.

'She went well for me the other day on the gallops,'

Will agreed, 'But I think she'll need the experience, she can be a bit nervous of horses too close to her when she's at full gallop. Five furlongs will be plenty sharp enough for her, but I didn't want her blowing up over six.'

Roberto nodded his agreement, 'You'll need to let Hanover know. I have a feeling he may have unrealistic expectations for this one today – she's his favourite. You might need to remind him that Catwalk runs next week and is a much better prospect.'

Meeting Suzie and Hanover in the parade ring, Will did his best to point out the filly's foibles to his owner, but got the distinct impression Hanover didn't wish to hear anything negative. Roberto had been right, for some reason Hanover had a proper soft spot for this filly. When Davy joined them in Hanover's red and white checked colours it emerged that Spring Ensemble had been his first purchase at the Doncaster Yearling Sales.

'Barney took me to the sales and when he showed me this filly I thought she was just like the rest. The stable lad walked her up and down, then stood her, and Barney ran his hands over her, just like the others we'd looked at. I gave her a pat on her neck and we were going to head off to see another, but she wouldn't move. The lad struggled with her for a minute, and Barney tried to help, but she was rooted to the spot outside her stable, standing in the sun,' Hanover related, his hands helping to animate the story.

'She was still refusing to shift when I received this call from abroad. It was great news. Confirmation that my company, Roar, had won a huge contract in South America! And would you believe it, as soon as I finished the call, the filly snorted, and walked as calmly as you like into her stable,' Hanover said, his eyebrows now high on his forehead.

'I'm a great believer in luck,' he continued, 'And I try to surround myself with lucky people and, in this case, lucky horses. Believe me, you have to look out for the signs of good luck and not ignore them. That phone call and how she reacted afterwards was a sure sign that this filly is surrounded by positivity – so Barney bought her for me!'

Davy and Suzie smiled appreciatively. Will tried very hard not to roll his eyes.

'Are we going to watch the race with Louis?' asked Suzie innocently once Davy had mounted the filly and was headed for the racetrack. They joined the torrent of racegoers snaking their way towards the grandstand and in answer to her query, Will took Suzie's hand, guiding her along a different route to Hanover.

Will pulled a wary face once they had settled on the concourse opposite the winning post and the large television screen, 'I have a feeling we'll be better off meeting up with Han... er, Louis, again after the race. He seems to think his filly will win on debut, but I'm doubtful. Mr Hanover may be a little, um... *irked* straight after the run.'

'Hmm... irked, eh?' Suzie mused, 'I might have to turn on some more charm then.'

'Yeah, and thanks for everything you've already done with him. I really appreciate it. I don't remember you ever being so talkative when we were at school, but you've...'

He caught a dangerous glint in Suzie's eye that made his next word catch in his throat.

'I've what?' she pressed as Will found himself searching desperately for the right words but coming up blank.

'Um.. well, *flowered*, I guess,' he said self-consciously.

Suzie didn't say anything. Instead, she looked towards the finishing post, thirty yards distant, her bottom lip stuck out, as if she was contemplating the notion of having 'flowered'.

'Both socially, and as a... woman,' Will added lamely, immediately wishing he'd remained silent.

A few seconds later an announcement over the public address system said the last horse was being loaded into the stalls. Suzie was still standing, staring into the distance, rocking slightly.

'And.. they're off…' barked the commentator.

A couple of fingers touched, and then squirrelled their way into Will's hand and he looked at Suzie, taking her hand fully in his. She was smiling. It wasn't a beaming, false smile, this was a smile with her eyes, and when they met his a delicious shiver of delight ran down his spine and into the pit of his stomach.

'Watch your race,' she called above the sound of the commentary.

Will shook himself mentally, and tried to concentrate on where the filly was positioned. The huge television screen in the centre of the course showed Hanover's colours bobbing along behind the front rank. Davy had managed to get her out cleanly and travelling one off the rails in a share of fourth, a length behind a line of three horses jostling for the lead. The trio included the hot favourite.

Already impressed that the filly could lay up with the speed over the first three furlongs, Will was waiting for her to start labouring, but was shocked to see her move into third, and then challenge between the two leaders, contrary to her preference to challenge wide, and his instructions to his jockey. However, the filly ran right through the gap and she and the favourite were neck and neck with half a furlong to run. Spring Ensemble put her nose into the lead, stretched out… and went wrong.

There was a disquieting gasp from the crowd that blanketed the enclosures with a numbness for the next few seconds. Spring Ensemble had lost her action in her back right leg. Where there had once been perfect balance and a fluid stride pattern, there was now an awkward, crab-like jerkiness. The filly began throwing her head around in confusion, and possibly, in pain. The favourite pulled away and Spring Ensemble stopped quickly. Davy angling his distressed mount across the track to the inside rail to avoid the rest of the field, and as their competitors thundered past he brought Spring

Ensemble to a standing stop.

Will and Suzie were at the entrance to the racecourse chute by the time Davy had jumped off the filly and were soon running across the track. Davy held onto her, looking Will's way with a grimace on his face. An air of sadness hung heavily over the racecourse as Spring Ensemble stood motionless, holding her right back leg awkwardly, bent at the knee, her hoof suspended six inches from the turf.

***

Arthur sat on a crusty old armchair, surrounded by piles of magazines, books, and, inexplicably, polystyrene blocks on his right and to his left, cereal boxes, crisp packets, and sweet wrappers, along with other miscellaneous rubbish. He found himself wishing he'd gone to Ripon races instead of trying to track down Jack Payne's murderer. Will had to be having a much better day than he was.

The house had once been grand. In amongst the rooms filled to their high ceilings with the hoarder's spoils were half-covered paintings, decorative cornices, and ornate fireplaces. There was also a peculiar odour. A mixture of rotting cabbage and eye-wateringly strong bleach pervaded each room.

The tour of his house consisted of Lilywhite proudly leading the two of them around each room, during which Freddie would wax lyrical about the contents. Rather like the front garden, every room was its own little maze, with a designated area for every kind of detritus you could imagine.

The smells were explained when they came across a set of eight stinking composting bins in what served as the old man's kitchen. Even Freddie had a job finding a suitably upbeat comment for them. Lilywhite sniffed and told them the contents of the bins were for growing giant marrows.

'Can't keep 'em outside,' the bespectacled hoarder told them, 'Valuable stuff, that is. Full o' goodness. Specialist growers nick 'em. I've lost a couple that way.'

Freddie nodded sagely in agreement, secretly doubting the loss of a bin or two was down to jealous gardeners. It was more likely that a neighbour, fed up with the smell, had whipped the bins away to the recycling centre.

The smell of bleach turned out to be Lilywhite's liberal spraying of the substance onto his skirting boards, in the places where they weren't covered by his collection of rubbish.

'Keeps 'em away,' Lilywhite had informed them, tapping the side of his nose, and without going into any further detail. Freddie had assured the old man that he agreed with him, and commending him on such a novel and inspired solution. Arthur wasn't so sure. Clarence Lilywhite's mental wellbeing was clearly on a downward spiral and Arthur couldn't help feeling a shade guilty at the lies Freddie was spinning in order to win him over.

Freddie was currently admiring Lilywhite's pile of broken record players that were stacked one on top of another against the back wall of the living room. To be fair, Lilywhite appeared to be thoroughly enjoying sharing his 'collection' with someone who, like him, recognised the importance and value of each item.

'I have to admire your attention to detail,' Freddie told the old man, making a point of turning to Lilywhite and giving him an appreciative nod. The old man was seated in an armchair held off the floor by a dozen beermats under each leg that meant his feet were almost on top of an ancient two-bar electric fire, his eyes wide with pleasure.

'There's every sort of record player here going back to the fifties. You must treasure them. And I see you have the records to go with them...' Freddie commented, running his finger along several columns of miscellaneous LP's flat stacked to the ceiling.

'All in order,' stated Lilywhite.

Arthur couldn't help himself. He started to speak before he realised what he was doing.

'What order is that, Mr Lilywhite?'

'Can't you see?' he barked, flicking a wrist in the direction of the back wall, 'By colour of course!'

'And a wonderful rainbow effect they do make,' Freddie interjected before his friend could offer a follow up. Arthur idly wondered whether it was the colour of the sleeve artwork, the record, or the musician's colour that mattered most to the old man, but remained silent.

'Gorgeous... absolutely... Oh my! Mr Lilywhite, what wonderful photos,' Freddie said quickly, moving across the room. This was quite a feat, as the piles of books, golfing magazines, and a pyramid of saucepans, took some navigating.

Lilywhite watched Freddie cross to his fireplace, lean over an old wooden dresser and remove several boxes filled with beer can ring pulls in order to examine a series of framed photographs that had been pushed to the back. He inspected them, asking who the 'wonderful men' were.

Arthur stiffened, suddenly realising what Freddie was doing. The photos were of Lilywhite's brothers.

'Brothers. Both gone now. Weak hearts,' Lilywhite replied bluntly and without passion.

'And I see you were... Am I right? Were you bookmakers Mr Lilywhite? Do I see you there holding your betting clipboard?'

Freddie's query was filled with what Arthur considered over-dramatised awe. He studied the old man carefully for any sign of suspicion and was relieved when Lilywhite answered with a touch of pride in his voice.

'Forty-three years. Was a grand business until they started charging for the pitches,' Lilywhite complained.

'So did you have a pitch at York?' Freddie enquired.

'Of course, best racecourse in the country.'

'I hear you.'

Lilywhite's eyes screwed up, 'What? Can't you hear me? I said York was the best.'

143

Freddie smiled beatifically, 'I agree. It's a wonderful racecourse.'

This seemed to satisfy Lilywhite, but Freddie took it as a warning that he could easily lose the man's confidence if he used inappropriate language.

'Plenty of tourists,' the eighty-four year-old ruminated, 'Ebor crowds will back anything. Was easy pickings.'

'A bookmaker at the Ebor!' Freddie reiterated, his attention drawn to one photo in particular, 'I suppose you'll have some stories to tell! Punters who lost a fortune, others that won... and I bet there were those who didn't pay as well, but I'd not want to get on the wrong side of your family – you were all big lads!'

Lilywhite actually laughed as he agreed with Freddie.

'Came across some right clever little buggers,' the old man chortled, 'But you didn't mess with me and my brothers.'

Freddie bent over Lilywhite's armchair to show him the photo he'd picked out from the back of the dresser. It showed the three brothers at the finishing post at York, each of them with wads of money in both hands and cigars hanging from their mouths.

'Aye, that's us,' Lilywhite confirmed happily, 'Had a good meeting so we had that taken.'

'This was taken in 2002 I see... twenty years ago,' murmured Freddie, 'Wasn't that the year of the Ebor murder? I think he was called... Jack... Jack....'

'Payne,' grunted Lilywhite, shifting uncomfortably in his armchair, 'He was a rum 'un.'

'Really?' Freddie queried innocently, 'What was he like?'

Lilywhite didn't answer straight away. He went a little glassy-eyed and seemed to drift off, his mind elsewhere.

'Poor sod,' he said finally, 'Saw him that day. Had to give him a thump because he wouldn't pay us what he owed, the cheating little git, but he understood it was just something we had to do. Jack understood.'

'You thumped him?' Arthur asked.

'Yeah, just a tap,' Lilywhite confirmed, still immersed in the memory, 'You know, to keep up appearances. All part of the job in those days. Half an hour later we found out some nasty bugger had whacked him around the head and killed him. Bad do, that was. Jack was a rum 'un, but he could train a sprinter.'

Freddie swallowed hard and asked his next question, knowing it could blow his cover, but he had to ask.

'So, you didn't see anyone else around when you left Jack that day?'

Lilywhite thought for a moment, then sighed.

'We saw nowt out of the ordinary. Would have passed it onto the police if we had, y'know through a third party. Couldn't say we were there. Policemen jump to conclusions! All I remember is that there were kids walking though the car park as we went back to the racecourse entrance. Bloody school kids. Who puts a school beside a racecourse and makes 'em go to school in August?'

Freddie immediately thought of the summer school activity weeks he attended when the holidays were beginning to drag.

The old man ran two dirty fingers and thumb through his greasy white and yellow flecked beard, and looked up at Freddie suspiciously, 'Anyway, lad. You going to make me an offer on those magazines or what?'

***

'We won't know the extent of the injury until we can get her x-rayed,' Will told Hanover, 'It could be a pull, strain, sprain or the worst scenario is a tendon injury or a fracture. There's too much swelling at the moment for us to say for certain. She's been sedated and is comfortable, but she's not placing any weight on that leg. I'm taking her home, and I'll report back in the morning. Once again Mr Hanover, I'm

145

terribly…'

'That young jockey, Dalton…'

'Yes, Davy.'

'He shouldn't have pushed her when he did,' Hanover said with barely concealed anger, 'That's what caused her to take a wrong step and hurt herself.'

'The course has undulations, the filly just got unbalanced. I'm terribly sorry, but…'

Hanover's cheeks flushed red.

'I know, you've said you're *terribly sorry* several times! We'll speak again tomorrow. Call me immediately if there is any change in the filly.'

Hanover made to leave Will and Suzie, but stopped after a couple of steps, and turned back to lock eyes with Will.

'This isn't the experience I'm looking for from my involvement in horseracing. Something, or someone, has stopped the luck from flowing.'

Hanover flicked his gaze towards Suzie and managed a weak smile for her before turning on his heel and stumping off towards the racecourse exit.

Drained with the stress of having to look after the injured filly and a distressed owner for the past hour, Will sucked in a deep breath. He let it out slowly, watching the most important owner in his yard flounce out of the racecourse.

'Did he seem to be angry with me, or am I reading too much into what just happened?'

'Nope, I'm afraid you've got it spot on,' Suzie confirmed with a shrug, 'I don't think he knew where to direct his anger and frustration, so you copped for the lot.'

'Great,' Will grumbled, 'Just brilliant. My dad is going to love this.'

Suzie didn't reply. He caught her eye and could see she was tired too.

'Super fun date eh?' he said wearily.

She managed to twitch a sardonic smile onto her lips.

'Oh! Is that what this was?' she said, playfully punching Will's arm.

He desperately wanted to step forward, take her in his arms and hug and kiss her, but didn't. She was an old friend. Her friendship was more important to him at that moment. The last thing he needed was to ruin it with a silly, misplaced pass.

'Come on, let's get ourselves home,' Will told Suzie after consulting his text messages on his phone, 'Roberto has managed to load her up. Let's get the filly back home and pray she can put weight on that injured leg tomorrow.'

Will couldn't help wondering whether he shouldn't also pray that Hanover didn't over-react... and take his horses, including Catwalk, elsewhere.

## Twenty-Three

Arthur completed his synopsis of the encounter with Lilywhite by placing both his hands onto the kitchen table, palms down, and concluding, 'The Brylcreem boys didn't kill Jack.'

'But how can you be certain? Clarence Lilywhite admitted they beat Jack up, didn't he?'

As their story had unfolded, Will had become convinced Freddie and Arthur were about to announce they had struck gold by eliciting a confession from the one remaining Lilywhite. Consequently, Arthur's final statement had been somewhat deflating.

When all Will received from his first set of questions was a pair of shrugs from the amateur detectives, he concentrated on Freddie and asked, 'What do you think?'

'Sorry, Will. He isn't our man,' Freddie replied with a shake of his head, 'He was one crazy guy for sure, and I think he and his brothers weren't the sort of people you wanted to owe money to, but there was a sort of warped professionalism about them. It was a sort of code of ethics... if you didn't pay your debts you got a thump to make sure you paid in a few weeks. Murdering people for five-hundred quid doesn't fit with their style, or their business model... they actually thought your grandfather was a decent sort.'

'So we're no further forward,' Will griped.

'Not true,' Arthur with a wag of his index finger, 'We've ruled them out, and we know there were other people around in the car park.'

Will gave a resigned sigh, 'I seriously doubt a schoolkid bludgeoned my grandfather to death.'

This brought a silence to the table. It did seem they had reached a dead end.

'I'm still considering the Red Cross angle,' said Arthur brightly, trying to inject some positivity into the room, 'St John's Ambulance used to send people to the racecourse back in 2002. It's not much to go on, but I'm still investigating.'

'And I'm really grateful,' Will told him, 'You too Freddie, you both did a grand job to track Lilywhite down.'

'Perhaps we should concentrate on finding out who is trying to hurt you. What about this Jimmy Hearn, your fired stable lad?' Freddie offered.

'Isn't it more like scare tactics?' suggested Arthur.

He received perplexed looks from both his friends.

'I mean… if he or she *really* wanted to hurt you, they could have done anything when you were unconscious in Catwalk's stable. But they didn't, they just left. And pushing you down the stairs meant you got bruised, but you're young and fitter than most twenty-one year olds. It was hardly going to cause any lasting injury.'

'I'm sure that as Will face-planted on the grandstand steps, he was content knowing that any injury he sustained wouldn't be long lasting!' Freddie observed.

Arthur produced a short sarcastically comic smile for Freddie but soon continued, 'Why don't we go down to Malton and ask around about this Jimmy Hearn?'

'Aye, go on,' agreed Freddie, 'I could do with a pint.'

\*\*\*

The Black Horse was the busiest of the three public houses they'd tried when they walked in at half-past nine in the evening. Freddie led the way, swaggering, then turning to the other two, 'I feel like a gun-slinger. I'm busy cleaning up the lawless streets of Malton, one saloon at a time!'

'Keep your pistols in your pocket, Sundance,' warned Arthur, 'This is a reconnaissance mission, not a shootout.'

Noticing Suzie was serving behind the bar, Will quickly offered to buy a round, leaving Freddie and Arthur to wander around the pub to see if they could find anyone they could quiz about Jimmy. Will never reached the bar and his friends were quickly back at his side. Jimmy was advertising his presence loud and clear.

He was with a small group of stable lads at the far end of the bar. By the look of them, they were well into their drinking session, loudly mocking each other and slopping their pints onto the bare floorboards. Suzie was speaking with them, trying to calm them down, but to little effect.

'I don't know if confronting him at this moment will be sensible,' Arthur suggested.

Will was about to agree, but anything he might have said was soon rendered irrelevant, as Freddie was already on his way over.

'Good evening, gentlemen,' Freddie said over the sound of the four lads teasing Suzie. They turned as one to regard him. A good foot and a half taller than all of them, Freddie grinned at the group. He'd discovered that a well-practised, sweet smile was much more effective at holding people's attention. It was unexpected, and therefore far more sinister than a sneer or grimace. Singling Jimmy out with a pointed index finger, Freddie announced, 'I require a moment of your time, Mr Hearn.'

Jimmy froze, and Freddie's smile broadened.

Behind him a voice said, 'I hope we're all going to have a good time here tonight, boys. I'd hate to have to go to work while I'm not on shift.'

Freddie whipped around and found a rotund, middle-aged man with a serious face staring up at him.

'This is Pat, Freddie,' said Will from just behind his godfather.

Will noticed one corner of Freddie's mouth curl upwards and reading his friends thoughts he quickly added,

'Before you ask, he's a policeman, not a postman.'

\*\*\*

'We learned one thing tonight,' said Arthur as the three of them crossed the road in the centre of Malton.

'What's that then?' asked Freddie.

'Manor Stud Stables is far better off without that foul-mouthed degenerate around.'

'Agreed,' said Will as they bundled into the little Renault, 'But more importantly, we learned that he can't be the one who attacked me in Catwalk's stable, or sent me down the steps at Beverley.'

'Yep, Pat was very clear on that score,' Freddie chipped in, 'Being held at the local police station for being drunk and disorderly that night sure makes it difficult for him to be in your yard in the wee hours.'

'He looked scared to death when Pat asked him which trainer he'd been working for at Beverley races,' noted Arthur, 'He was relieved when Pat changed the subject. But you could tell he knew nothing about pushing you.'

'He must have been doing some leading up work for someone and used his old stable pass from Manor Stud Stables to get access,' Will explained.

'Which means it's another bust,' said Freddie, staring forlornly out of the window as Will pulled away from the kerb.

'At least we can rule Jimmy out,' Will pointed out as he aimed the Renault's nose towards Norton. The little car whined and complained as it picked up speed.

'Oh, and by the way,' Arthur announced from the passenger seat, 'I've been digging deeper into the stable's accounts and I can't find any evidence that your father has taxed, tested, or insured this car for the last ten years.'

Will took a horrified sideways glance at his friend, slowly applied the brakes so as not to pull too violently to the left, and spent the rest of the journey anxiously checking his mirrors for flashing blue lights.

## Twenty-Four

It took Will two days after the Ripon race for him to pluck up the courage to face his father. He chose a Sunday evening, and found Barney sitting up, arguing with the chap in the bed beside him. Will wasn't too surprised. His father had an uncanny knack of annoying anyone who remained within a ten yard radius of him for more than a few minutes. This argument concerned, of all things, a lost piece of a jigsaw puzzle, with his father insisting his fellow patient had stolen it to ensure he couldn't complete the snowy scene of a church in winter.

Will had wondered why the male nurse had rolled his eyes when he'd asked where he could find Mr Payne. The bickering between the two men was no doubt part of an ongoing feud. His father was now in an open ward, sharing a medium-sized room with seven other poor souls who'd had the misfortune to become sick at the same time as Barney Payne.

Will gave the man in the next bed a short apology and drew the curtain around his father's bed, standing over him and shaking his head.

'Even when you're ill, you're a blummin' liability,' Will told him crossly, 'You can't help yourself, can you?'

'What happened to you?' his father asked, ignoring his son's question, the argument with his fellow patient immediately forgotten, at least for the moment.

Will crossed his arms and stared down, deciding how to respond. It had been six days since he'd been pushed down the grandstand steps at Beverley and his lips and nose had pretty much healed, but there was still plenty of bruising stubbornly refusing to fade.

'What happened?' demanded his father again.

'Never mind that, I need answers to a few of my own questions,' Will said brusquely.

'Did someone do that to you? Who was it?'

152

His father had certainly improved from the last time Will had visited just over a week ago. There was a sparkle back in his eye, and the fact he was able to find the strength to argue with his fellow patients told Will his father was on the mend.

'I was pushed down some steps,' replied Will, slightly embarrassed, 'It was nothing.'

His father closed his eyes and pursed his lips, 'I need to tell you about my accident,' he said.

'Yeah, later, Dad,' Will cut in tersely, 'First, why didn't you tell me the yard was in financial trouble?'

Barney gaped at his son before slowly clearing his throat.

'The fortunes of a small yard like ours ebbs and flows. You know that! It'll be fine,' Barney said dismissively.

'What? Define *fine* for me, Dad! *Fine* like when Catwalk wins the Albany and the business collects on that stupid bet you've had?'

'As long as you train her right, then yeah, we'll be fine!' Barney countered, a dangerous edge entering his voice.

Will paused to take a calming breath, determined to keep his cool, 'Okay, and what about the training fees, eh? How come Harriet Gardener pays half of what the others are charged? Is that for services rendered, eh, Dad? Is that why mum left you and me?'

Will spat the last accusation at his father, his words filled with venom. Barney glared up at Will from his bed, an uncontrollable rage bubbling up within him. The almost complete jigsaw and the tray it lay on suddenly became airborne as Barney hurled it at his son. Will didn't move. He'd been well aware that his father was about to lose control. He closed his eyes, allowing the pieces of jigsaw to rain down on him, remaining steadfastly rigid beside his father's bed. Once the tray had clattered to the floor he blinked his eyes open.

Barney was bent double, grasping forward at his son's midriff, but the pain from his ribs halted his progress and drowned his rage in pain. His head began to spin and his eyes rolled in their sockets. He felt a pair of hands roughly push him back into his pillows.

'You're days of giving me a cuff around the ear are over,' Will hissed quietly into his father's face, then stood back, watching him breathe heavily.

After thirty seconds Barney spoke. His voice was much gruffer and he held a hand to his chest, as if breathing and speaking at the same time was causing him pain.

'Harriet Gardener is a great owner you ungrateful little sod. Check her daughter's invoices. Jo Gardener. She's my back-man, and a damn fine one too. I deduct her charges from Harriet's fees. It's an arrangement that works well for both of us you bloody idiot.'

A bad taste circulated slowly around Will's mouth. This explanation made perfect sense – Jo Gardener was the yards equine chiropractor. Arthur hadn't known about it, if he had, he'd have realised Barney was getting the better deal out of the arrangement. His father was undoubtedly charging on the costs to other owners at a vastly inflated rate.

'I've had enough of you,' Will said, angry and embarrassed. He brushed a portion of the thin cloth curtain aside in order to make his exit.

'No,' groaned Barney, holding out a hand towards Will, 'Listen to me, William… my accident wasn't… it wasn't an accident...'

Will looked back over his shoulder. His father had turned pale, his recent exertions having taken a toll on his energy levels. Yet he still felt so little compassion for him.

'You said you were pushed?' asked Barney.

Will allowed the curtain to fall back into position, 'Yes?'

'Has anything else happened, to you, or the horses, or maybe the yard?'

'Someone took a swing at me in Catwalk's stable...'

Barney waved a hand awkwardly, 'The gelding I was riding on the All-Weather gallop tried to jump a ribbon, or something like it… maybe a rope… It had been hung between…'

Will watched his father's eyes flutter and inexplicably found himself moving to be at his side.

'It's okay,' Barney assured his son,' It comes and goes. They're scanning me tomorrow, trying to get to the bottom of it… But I didn't fall off Battle Stations, he saw the ribbon and ended up going through the rails to avoid it. Thank God they're made of plastic these days… But the ribbon, or rope… was gone when they found me… I was thrown… someone wanted me to fall…'

Will stared down at his father, desperately trying to make sense of this new information. His father's eyes were half closed and Will could sense he was having trouble fighting the urge to close them completely and doze off.

'Wake up dad!' Will said, shaking his father's arm. 'Why would anyone want to hurt us?'

A puzzled look came over his father, but that was swiftly swept away by an earnest need to impart more information to his son.

'Your mother…' Barney muttered, 'She knew… She knew why Jack was killed. I'm sure of it. I tried to work it out… It could be why she left… Did you look?…'

Will shook him again, but this time his father had fallen into a deep sleep and wasn't about to be woken up. Barney wouldn't be answering his questions any time soon.

Will sighed inwardly. He hadn't had the chance to tell him that Spring Ensemble had recovered, that she had simply received a dead leg, or that Catwalk would be running later that week at Goodwood. And he hadn't been able to ask him how he should play Hanover when he went to meet him tomorrow in order to convince him not to remove his horses from the yard. Then there was the progress Freddie and Arthur had made on tracking down who Jack had met before he died… or that his mother had been right about the Brylo Boys…

It was the same. Ever since mum left. The two of them managed to conjure up an argument within moments. They could never just *talk*.

A middle-aged nurse bustled in, whisking the curtain along its rails. She took a long look at the jumble of jigsaw pieces on the floor and made a harassed sighing noise and gave Will an unimpressed glare. Bending until she was on her haunches, she started retrieving the nine-hundred and ninety nine pieces of the thousand piece puzzle. Without a word, Will joined her.

'He's improving, but he is still a long way from being well you know,' she said curtly, once the mess was cleared up, 'Unnecessary stress from petty arguments won't do him any good.'

Will nodded his understanding, but his mind was elsewhere. His mother knew. His mother *knew*. His father's words rattled around his head. Unfortunately, they were creating more questions than answers.

## Twenty-Five

'Are we going to Goodwood with her for that fillies' novice over five this Thursday then?'

Davy was calling his question down to Will from the saddle of Catwalk, having just returned to the yard after her final workout gallop, three days before the race, and only a day before the declarations needed to be made.

Will tried not to appear as sheepish as he felt inside, and called back, 'Yeah, come into the kitchen and get a coffee. Gordy will wash her down and put her on the walker.'

'She's got a ton of speed, Will,' remarked Davy as he entered the farmhouse kitchen, hanging his helmet and whip on the rack of hooks, 'She's as ready as she'll ever be and might easily win that Goodwood Novice if there isn't something as special as her in the race. I know there are some big southern yards with entries, but they'll have to go some to match her ability. She's got a proper decent forward attitude and I reckon she's far better than any of the youngsters my boss or my dad has for this season.'

'Yeah, about that race at Goodwood,' Will said with a grimace, 'I want you to ride her…'

'I sense a 'but' coming…' Davy said with a hangdog expression, 'My father and my grandfather warned me about this.'

'Is that what the three of you were arguing about in the Black Horse last week?' Will asked.

Davy frowned, taken aback for a moment, 'Ah!' he exclaimed, the frown quickly melting away, 'Suzie must have told you?'

Will nodded.

'Yeah,' Davy moaned, 'Dad was proper weird about me riding for you. He's got a filly he's sending down for the same race at Goodwood, and said I should be riding it, but it's nowhere near as good as yours. Dad's only entered it because the owner paid a ton of money for it at Tattersalls Book One sales and expects it to be decent. I told him he was being daft. He even got grandad involved. I reckon he might be a bit jealous of your filly. It's my own fault, I've been shouting about how good Catwalk is to anyone who would listen ever since I first got on her back.'

Will recalled Suzie's rendering of the argument, which matched perfectly with Davy's version. Trainers from the same training centre tended to support each other on the whole, but when it came to winning races, they could get overly petty about their rider being stolen, especially in a high profile race. Will supposed having his own son choose to ride for a young, inexperienced trainer instead of his family's yard might be a little hard for Neil Dalton to accept.

'I really want you to take the ride on Catwalk, but after that issue with Spring Ensemble, the owner, Mr Hanover needs to be… won over. I'm having a video chat with him this afternoon.'

'I thought the filly was okay when she got home?' Davy queried.

'Yes, thank goodness. It looks like she was struck into when you went past the third and fourth horses and it caught a nerve and made her lose feeling in her leg a few strides later. I reckon she stopped quickly because she knew something was wrong, but was right as rain the day after.'

'She'd showed a bit of quality up until then,' Davy pointed out, taking a seat at the end of the table, 'She'll win races, might even win a Novice if you can find the right one for her. She was reaching the end of her tether when we challenged the favourite the other day and needed the experience. I had to go through that gap two out, but she did it well enough.'

Will nodded his agreement. If Davy hadn't forced the filly through the gap, and instead, pulled her out, he'd have lost a length or more on the favourite. He'd made the right decision. Will found himself once again reflecting on the fact that Davy had matured into a very decent apprentice. He had the ability and confidence. Importantly, he possessed the intelligence and humility to be successful as a pro rider.

They continued to discuss Spring Ensemble and Catwalk for a few minutes. Their conversation convinced Will that Davy was the right jockey to be partnering the filly at Goodwood.

Toying with the ceramic handle on his mug of coffee, Will adopted his serious face, the one he liked to think was appropriate when playing poker. He even used it when playing online where it couldn't be seen – it helped to make him concentrate.

'Thing is Davy, it turns out that Louis Hanover is a bit of a superstitious sort. Suzie was talking with him at length before the race at Ripon and he's into all sorts of weird stuff, you know the sort of thing; astrology, biorhythms, and all that malarkey. I think he's got it into his head that the two of us are unlucky.'

'So my Catwalk ride isn't certain?'

Will took a sip of his coffee and after a pause, slowly shook his head, 'I'm not even sure whether Catwalk will run with me as her trainer. We'll know tonight, after the video call.'

'Owners!' Davy complained, 'It would be a straightforward sport if we didn't have to deal with them. I hope you're getting Suzie in on this call with him?'

Will smiled, 'Yeah, she's my secret weapon. I called her earlier and she's promised to bob over and try to sweet talk Hanover. She certainly made an impression on him the other day.'

Davy grinned, 'She's changed a bit since school, hasn't she...'

'Hmm... Really?'

'Not that you would have noticed, eh, Will?'

Will kept his gaze concentrated on his coffee mug, mumbling, 'I don't know what you mean.'

'No, I guess not,' Davy said with a knowing smile, 'But

you must have known she used to have a thing for you.'

Will choked on his mouthful of coffee.

'Blind as a bat you are, mate,' Davy laughed, 'You're telling me you never knew?'

*** 

Suzie drew up on her motorbike late evening and Freddie, who had been peering through the kitchen window in anticipation of her arrival, rushed to the door to let her in.

'Your prom date is here, darling!' he called up the stairs to Will. His high-pitched, Australian accented voice was a perfect impression of Dame Edna Everage.

'Come on in, Soooz!' Freddie said to Suzie invitingly, swinging the farmhouse door open, 'He's upstairs getting ready!'

'Enough!' Will insisted as he entered the kitchen, 'Stop mucking around, Freddie.'

'Ow, come on Winda…'

Suzie snorted with laughter.

'You see! Freddie exclaimed, 'Winda *is* funny!'

Beaming as she was introduced to Freddie and Arthur, Suzie also waved a quick hello in Davy's direction.

'So we all know what we're going to say?' Will asked his friends as they prepared to make the video call to Louis Hanover, 'I can't stress enough how important this call is going to be. Catwalk is the best horse we've had in the yard for years, if not decades, and Hanover's other two youngsters are pretty decent too. We can't afford to lose any of them.'

Will paused, fixing his gaze on each of them, employing his poker face. When he reached Freddie he loitered for a moment longer.

'No joking or laughing in the background!'

Freddie grinned and them mimed a zip closing across his mouth.

'Good,' said Will firmly, then lifted his chin to peer

through the kitchen window and out into the yard. He signalled with a thumbs up and turned his attention to Arthur's laptop that was sitting open and ready to initiate the call.

Suzie, Davy, Arthur, and Freddie waited in nervous silence for the clock on the laptop to reach six-thirty, at which time Arthur asked if everyone was ready. After receiving a swift round of nods he leaned forward and tapped the keyboard. There was another pause as the call connected and suddenly Louis Hanover's face filled the entire screen. He leaned back, and the rest of his room came into focus.

Hanover was sitting at his desk in what looked like a study or library. It must be a large room, thought Will, as the wall behind him, filled with framed certificates, photographs, and a display cabinet containing trophies, was a good three yards behind him.

'Hello, Mr Hanover,' Will started, shifting awkwardly in his seat. Hanover cleared his throat and rumbled a greeting back.

'This can't take long,' Hanover said, 'I have other calls.'

'Yes. I understand. It's just I wanted to…'

'I've heard your apologies before, Mr Payne, and I've invested the required amount and given your yard every chance, but I see no alternative but to remove…'

Will's heart sank. This conversation was only going to reach one conclusion; he was about to lose all three horses. His knack of being able to read people from their actions, expression and mannerisms had already told him he'd lost his owner. He'd planned an introduction of Suzie and Davy, but Hanover wasn't giving him the chance to even get a word in.

Will knew racehorse owners could be fickle creatures. Eighteen years of listening to his mother and father speaking with them had taught him that. He knew Hanover's reason for leaving the yard was nothing to do with his own ability as a trainer, it was just down to the multi-millionaire's jaundiced view of the world. Hanover believed in the supernatural and that luck was something that some people possessed and others didn't. It was hard to argue a case against something like that! Will caught Suzie's eye, and as Hanover's diatribe began to peter out he gave her a dejected look of defeat.

'Hiya, Louis,' Suzie said quickly, plonking herself onto the edge of Will's seat. She shuffled him across with her backside and waved a hand at the screen whilst smiling.

'Oh! Hello, Suzie,' Hanover said, surprise registering on his face. His hard tone with Will immediately softened, 'I didn't know you were there.'

'There's actually quite a few of us here,' Suzie said, and we're all hoping that you'll allow William to prove he is the right trainer for you, and that his aura is perfect for the job.'

'I understand you think highly of him, but…'

While Hanover continued to speak Suzie was on the move. She leaned over the table and picked up the laptop, holding it at arm's length and angling the camera so that Hanover could see her in the corner of the shot.

'I understand Louis, but perhaps you don't realise that the is a team effort, and I have to say that since William has been here I've sensed a really positive vibe. It's actually why I was drawn to the yard when he first returned.'

By slowly turning, she introduced Will, Davy, Arthur and Freddie.

'I know the race at Ripon didn't work out, Louis, ' Suzie said sweetly, 'It was awful. But it looked much worse than it was…'

'Yes, let me show you,' Will said, popping back up beside Suzie. He met her questioning look and directed his eyes towards the kitchen door. It only took her a split second for her to understand.

Still speaking with Hanover about karma, wellbeing, and how important luck figured in success, Suzie followed Will, carrying the laptop outside. The others filed out after her. Outside, Roberto was standing with Spring Ensemble, Hanover's injured filly by his side, but she appeared to be in excellent health. She wasn't injured, just splendidly turned out. Credit to Roberto, thought Davy as he inspected the two-year-old whilst running a hand down her flank, the youngster was a good-looking individual – and her leg looked perfect. The small gathering agreed. Standing still in the late evening sunshine with her head raised, mane without a hair out of place, Spring Ensemble looked stunning.

'I know I reported that your filly was fine, I just wanted you to see her for yourself,' said Will, going to stand beside the filly, 'You've met Roberto, my head lad. He was at Ripon the other day and he was instrumental in identifying that Spring Ensemble's injury wasn't life-threatening and in fact, was nothing more than a minor knock with no lasting effects.'

Roberto waved a slightly embarrassed hand at Suzie and the laptop. Suzie studied Roberto with interest and an idea popped into her head.

Will raised his eyebrows at Davy and he responded by entering what he hoped was the laptop's camera shot. He said hello, and added, 'I've been around horses all my life, Mr Hanover. Both my great grandfather and grandfather were trainers in the sixties through to the nineties. My father is currently a trainer in Malton. Will and I are the latest in a long line of successful…'

Once again, Hanover interrupted. He was no longer smiling. Will guessed it was because Suzie had disappeared from the camera's viewfinder.

'I don't doubt you all mean well, and as individuals you will each be successful in your chosen sport,' said Hanover curtly, 'However some relationships are just not… fruitful. I've always found that being guided by my own beliefs has always worked for me, whether it's choosing my staff, a new range of clothes for my Roar brand, or the companies I employ to make them. There has to be a spiritual synergy between us. When it's not there, as it wasn't at Ripon the other day, I have to move on.'

Whilst Hanover had been delivering his final nail in the

coffin, Suzie had handed the laptop to Arthur. She was now standing directly in front of Hanover, blocking out the filly, Davy, Will and Roberto.

'Louis, Suzie here again. What if I was to tell you that we have a member of one of the oldest Romany gypsy communities looking after your racehorse. This person is deeply spiritual. I believe that his attendance at Ripon may have been instrumental in ensuring that Spring Ensemble didn't come to any lasting harm.'

Hanover didn't answer. For the first time during the call, he was looking thoughtful.

'I think you've already spotted his aura,' Suzie continued with a knowing nod, 'Now, just imagine how the afternoon of racing at Ripon might have panned out if he wasn't there? You might have lost the filly. I really think you need to consider the possibility that rather than the events last week being a negative omen, you may have escaped an even greater catastrophe.'

Hanover leaned back in his chair and stroked his jawline, 'I suppose it's possible. You're talking about that chap Roberto are you, He's the Romany Gypsy? I did sense there was something about him...'

Suzie took the laptop back from Arthur. Before facing the screen again she turned, gave all the men a big wink and wandered into the farmhouse. She was still deep in conversation with Hanover when she kicked the front door closed behind her. Outside, the five men looked at each other in disbelief.

'Are all your owners as fickle and cuckoo as that one?' Freddie asked.

'And since when am I related to Romany gypsies?' Roberto asked with a shrug.

Will decided to refrain from attempting an answer to either question.

Three minutes later, Suzie emerged from the farmhouse, her eyes sparkling and a spring in her step.

164

## Twenty-Six

It was a bright, yet brisk May morning on the Sussex Downs, thanks to a minor overnight frost. Having spent a restless night in the racecourse's stable staff lodgings, Will had risen early, keen to check on Catwalk on the day of her racing debut.

He was pleased to find the filly bright-eyed and keen to be tucking into her feed. She gave a little whinny of anticipation as he approached with the feed bucket, poking her head over the stable door, then withdrawing to complete a little spring-heeled trot around her box before returning to the door to see where Will had gone with her breakfast.

The six hour road journey down from Malton the previous afternoon had been tortuous. Catwalk had been stiff, tired, and with her patience wearing thin when she eventually walked off the transport. Will had forgotten how long and boring the two-hundred and seventy-five mile trek to Goodwood could be when travelling at a steady fifty-five miles an hour - the maximum speed his father's fourteen-year-old horsebox could manage without complaint. He'd been glad of Lizzy's company, even though the stable lass wasn't the sort to indulge in deep, meaningful conversation.

Seeing the filly with a spring in her step after a night in strange surroundings was both a relief and a good sign that she would be able to cope with the rigours of travelling to racecourses in the future. He'd considered waiting another week and running her at Redcar in a lesser race, but that would have been getting dangerously close to Ascot, and Will wanted the filly to have a three week break between races to ensure she was at her peak when she went for the Albany. This five furlong Goodwood race fitted in perfectly, both in terms of timing and its grade.

Will opened up the stable, gently pushing the filly backwards, and once inside, checked her over and gave her a pre-race feed under the light of a single sixty watt bulb. She was running at ten past one in the afternoon, so this was her last bucket of grub before she would race. Will leaned against the brick wall just inside the box and divided his time between looking out over the top half of the stable door and watching the filly eat.

Ten minutes later, footsteps approached and the sound of tack being deposited onto the concrete floor outside the stable door told Will his jockey had arrived.

'Are we ready to stretch her legs?' Davy called into the box.

'Aye,' Will returned amiably, 'As much as we ever can be. It's up to you and her now. I've done my job.'

Davy grinned as Will swung the stable door open for him, 'No pressure then!'

'When's your entourage arriving?' Davy asked as he helped Will place a saddle cloth onto Catwalk, aiming another cheeky grin at Will to check his reaction.

'My *mates* are pitching up at about half ten,' Will replied, 'They're travelling down this morning.'

'They're decent lads,' Davy continued, pulling at a strap and buckling it tight, 'Spent some time with them the other night down at the Black Horse. They're good fun. That Freddie is a right laugh. Had me in stiches when he was doing the barman. He's brilliant mimic.'

'He's a lot of things,' Will agreed with a friendly roll of his eyes.

Lizzy poked her head over the stable door.

'What's that? Is something wrong with Freddie?'

Will looked up. If he wasn't mistaken, Lizzy had been showing a significant interest in Freddie in recent days. He'd had to break up a couple of conversations between the two of them so that work could get done. Freddie hadn't said anything to him, but that didn't mean nothing was going on.

'Nothing's wrong with him,' Will replied, aiming to shift the conversation away from Freddie and Arthur, 'I thought you were having a lie in?'

166

'Can't sleep on soft beds,' she responded with a dismissive sniff and toss of her head, 'And I wanted to see Kitty this morning.'

A minute later Will led Catwalk out of her box and she stood looking down the line of horseboxes, her neck and shoulder muscles rippling in the morning sunshine.

All three of them stood admiring the filly. Kitty had a deeper chest than most, but her incredibly powerful neck and overall size meant she carried it well. Her backend was her crowning glory; large, muscular, and tight, exactly what you wanted from a sprinter.

'A dozen times around the menage at a trot and then an easy canter,' Will told Davy as he gave him a leg up onto the filly.

As Davy poked his toes into his stirrups a small group approached. It was the rest of the Dalton family, led by Davy's father, Neil Dalton.

'So, this is Kitty, the wonder horse I've heard so much about from my son,' remarked Neil.

It was probably meant as a throwaway comment, but Will noticed a sardonic overtone. Davy must have felt it too, as he gave his father an irritated frown from the saddle.

'I've chosen the right filly, Dad,' Davy stated firmly, turning Catwalk so she was side-on to him, showing off her impressive physique, 'This filly could take me to Royal Ascot with a proper chance of winning the Albany.'

Will watched Neil's eyes widen as he took in Catwalk's full dimensions for the first time. He wasn't surprised with Neil's reaction. Any experienced horseman would know with one look that Catwalk was a forward filly for her age. Will was particularly pleased with how she'd recently gained confidence on the gallops, and would have mentioned this to a suitably interested fellow trainer from Malton, but Neil seemed reticent to engage.

Davy noticed this too, shaking his head and giving his father a bitterly disappointed look. His mother, acting as a

167

peace-maker, said something Will couldn't catch but which spurred Neil into eventually muttering, 'Alright Bridget! Yes, David… well, you've made your choice.'

Bridget forced a smile, and asked Will whether he was fully recovered from his fall at Beverley. He provided a short, but courteous reply to assure her he was fine.

Throughout this exchange, Davy's grandfather, Ernie Dalton looked on, leaning heavily on his walking stick. Ernie assessed Will's filly with an impenetrable stare and passed no comment. Similarly, Davy's sister, Lily, remained mute and failed to make eye contact with anyone, preferring to stare at the filly.

As Davy made to set off to the menage with Kitty, there was the sound of approaching hooves and Tiffany appeared on top of Neil's filly, Crackerjill. Competing in the same race as Catwalk, the two of them were greeted enthusiastically by Lily. Will was unsure whether Lily's effusive welcome was for the filly, or for Tiffany. He rather thought it was for the girl and not the horse.

Thin boned and rather slight, to Will's eye, the filly looked to be on the weak side. As Tiffany brought Crackerjill alongside Davy on Catwalk the difference in size and scope became pronounced.

Will took the opportunity to break up the encounter with the Dalton's and instructed Davy to walk the filly on and made his excuses.

'The best of luck,' Davy's mother called after them.

Will thanked her, wishing Neil the same, and they moved off to watch Kitty do her warm-up.

*** 

As Louis Hanover entered the Goodwood parade ring he dabbed at his brow and stretched his neck to the right in order to ease the discomfort he was feeling from the heavily starched collar of his wing-tipped shirt. The journey down to

Goodwood by car from his city-centre apartment in Leeds had taken longer than expected, and he'd arrived late. He hated having to rush anything.

A traffic jam getting into the racecourse had necessitated a jog to the Owner and Trainers' entrance across an immense field full of cars. Why did they always run two-year-old races first on the card?

His mood darkened further as he stepped out into the open parade ring grass, in front of a huge crowd, and realised perspiration was making his shirt stick to his neck. He winced, fearing that the beads of sweat running freely down his back might work through his shirt and stain his velvet jacket. He should have known better, it was far too warm to be wearing velvet… but then again, he did look extraordinarily dashing in this outfit.

Will and Davy waited for Hanover and went to shake his hand when he arrived at their side. Louis would have preferred not to offer his sweaty palm to his trainer and jockey but did so anyway. He'd calculated he was in front of an audience numbering over two thousand surrounding the parade ring, and possibly millions more if the television crew caught him on camera, so on balance, a handshake was required. There would be customers of his clothing brand watching, and possibly his investors as well. Keeping up appearances was all part of the job of an international entrepreneur, especially one selling exorbitantly expensive designer clothing.

Once the small-talk was done with, Louis gave his trainer and jockey the short speech he'd learned by heart for this moment. Bowing his head, he regarded the finely cut turf and delivered his ultimatum.

'I know I am demanding and perhaps, unorthodox. My belief that the aura a person possesses defines the luck and success they experience in their lives, is for some, difficult to swallow. However, this is who I am. Against my better judgement I was convinced to grant you both another chance to prove yourselves. Suzie has an inner radiance and a very positive aura. In contrast, I sense both your auras are cloudy and indistinct at present. Perhaps this race will settle my quandary.'

With that, Louis left the parade ring.

He took up a position in the March Grandstand in the Richmond Enclosure, his preferred pitch because it granted him a view directly down to the winning post. Eventually, the runners started to make their way to the start. When Catwalk was announced by the racecourse commentator, he felt his stomach buzz a little and his heart quicken for a few beats. It hadn't done that at Ripon. He watched his horse canter powerfully past the furlong pole and wondered whether absolution was at hand.

Ten minutes later, the stalls at the five furlong start opened. Louis watched from his seat, the huge television screen in the centre of the course giving him a visual description, while the racecourse public address system delivered the audio version of the race. Against all expectation, Louis felt his heart lurch when Catwalk immediately powered into a two length lead. She swiftly extended this lead in a matter of strides. After only one furlong she was three lengths up on the rest of the field, Davy Dalton sitting motionless as the filly whipped over the emerald surface, darkened by the overnight spring rain.

It struck Louis that the positions of the horses didn't appear to alter for the next two furlongs. So as Davy and Catwalk left the two furlong pole behind them, the rest of the field remained several lengths in their wake. Davy remained as he had throughout, unmoved and unconcerned by anything occurring behind him. In contrast, the other nine jockeys began to push their mounts, whips were flicked, and energetic urging suddenly replaced tight reins as they realised the leader wasn't coming back to them.

Louis wasn't aware of how he'd got to his feet, or the fact that he was shouting Kitty's name. For a split second, he caught himself and took a breath, before allowing the excitement to fill his mind and body completely once again. He screamed as Davy gave his filly a single push at the furlong pole and immediately pulled well away from the rest of the fillies.

With Catwalk's name being bellowed in his ears by the race commentator and referred to with superlatives, Louis Hanover joined the rest of the grandstand in a round of applause. As the clapping subsided, he suddenly felt weak. Heart racing and excitement still pulsing around his nervous system, Louis fell back in his seat.

'Jack Payne's luck is as strong as ever,' he said to himself gleefully.

## Twenty-Seven

A week after Catwalk had shaved an eighth of a second off the Goodwood track record for a five furlong juvenile race, Will stepped out of the farmhouse, breathed in the sweet evening air full of the scent of brand new hawthorn blossom, and surveyed his line of newly painted boxes housing a total of fourteen horses.

As well as a breeder switching his three older horses into the yard, another couple of owners had chanced sending their unraced juveniles for Will to train. The Racing Post had reported on the Goodwood race at length, and being an unknown young trainer, and the grandson of the famously murdered Jack Payne, Will had been featured in several articles over the weekend. Kitty's impressive win also spawned a couple of television interviews. Over ten days later his filly's run continued to be discussed at length by the racing media. Kitty's expected run at Royal Ascot in the Albany in just over a week's time was now hotly anticipated, and her odds for the race had contracted, making her second favourite in most ante-post betting lists.

The hype surrounding Catwalk had run to even higher levels when Louis Hanover had made himself available for interview. Already well known in business circles, Hanover's involvement had been seized upon by the newspapers. Overnight, he'd become a prominent owner worthy of filling a few column inches because of his flamboyance, confidence in his racehorse, and, of course, his 'Roar' brand of outrageously costly clothing.

Catwalk's debut win didn't go unnoticed by his father either. Will hadn't visited him in hospital since he'd come away two weeks ago with his head spinning from the confusing conversation they'd shared. With so much going on in the yard, he'd consigned his father's garbled words to the back of his mind. However, Pat was providing updates on his father, calling into the yard every few days to relate Barney's progress towards a full recovery.

Pat had dropped in the night before, reporting that Barney was improving. Apparently his father had been placed in a private room due to him arguing too much with his fellow patients. His father had also watched a replay of Catwalk's win at Goodwood and a rather embarrassed Pat reported that Barney had insisted he reprimand Will for the filly having been allowed to show off too much of her ability. Will had replied rather pointedly that his father no longer trained Kitty.

Progress with his mother's journal and Jack's betting records, and last words, 'Red Cross', had somewhat ground to a halt. In frustration, Arthur had spent more time on the business accounts and helped Freddie around the yard, including getting on the stables roof to fix the yard clock.

The stables had been repainted, and the gutters, roof slates and other bits of cleaning up were complete and so Freddie was now attending to the interior of the farmhouse. Whilst feeling increasingly guilty about their unpaid work, Will was both pleased and bewildered by the fact that both his friends were clearly enjoying their time in Malton. Freddie always had a smile on his face and a joke to tell, whilst Arthur had unexpectedly become quite attached to a number of the horses, regularly wandering out to spend time with them in the paddocks during the long summer evenings.

Tonight was a chance for Will to show his gratitude for the work both his friends were doing, as well as a small reward for his stable staff. He was taking them to the charity event of the year for the racing fraternity in Malton, the annual Casino Night. That was why he was wearing a hired suit, a bow tie, and a pair of dress shoes that made his feet shine – a new experience for Will.

It was an opportunity for everyone in racing around Yorkshire to descend on Malton and enjoy an evening around horsemen, lads, lasses, owners and trainers, whilst raising money for a racing charity. For a few hours Will could push worries about the yard finances, whether Catwalk would be okay for the Albany, and his very different issues with both his parents, all to one side. Suzie, Lizzy, and Roberto, were joining himself, Freddie and Arthur. Gordy had agreed to stay and look after the yard; they were all set!

Will noticed a taxi had turned into the lane leading to the farmhouse and was trundling lazily towards him. This had to be Suzie and Lizzy, and Roberto, as Arthur and Freddie were enjoying a pre-night out drink in the kitchen. Will's smile faded when the car pulled up beside him. Someone with a hood pulled over their head, effectively obscuring their face, was sitting in the back seat. The figure was remonstrating with the driver, who in turn was arguing back.

Will waited, not quite sure whether to intervene. As the argument inside the car became heated, Will was joined by Freddie and Arthur.

'What's going on?' Freddie asked, smiling as he heard some ripe language emanate from inside the car. He took a swig from his bottle of beer, craned his neck to look into the back seat and added, 'Never mind, looks like I haven't missed the best bit.'

Before Will could respond, the driver's door burst open and a red-faced chap stomped around the car and flung the back door open. He screamed, 'Get out of my car you stingy old git!', and turned to face the small crowd of onlookers.

'Who's going to pay the extra thirty quid he owes me?'

'Don't pay him a penny!' exclaimed a determined voice from inside the car.

Will's whole body sagged. He'd immediately recognised the voice.

'Dad! What the hell are you doing?' he called into the car.

'Hand!' bellowed his father, 'You can't swing a cat in here, give me your hand!'

Will did as he was told and helped a bent over, groaning Barney Payne exit the car. As he straightened, he

174

winced and gave a couple throat-shredding coughs.

Another taxi now drew up to the bumper of the first and Barney glared as Lizzy, Roberto, and finally, another young woman jumped out. Then he squinted at Arthur and Freddie, who were staring at him. He scrunched his face into a disbelieving frown. Their clothes looked outrageously out of context for a racing yard.

'Going somewhere are we?'

'Never mind that, what are you doing here!' demanded Will, who was trying to concentrate on his father while his eyes were being drawn to the outfit Suzie was wearing. She looked worryingly incredible, putting his rented tuxedo to shame.

'Sort this idiot out,' Barney instructed his son, waving a desultory hand at the taxi driver, 'Bloody rip-off merchant,' he grumbled under his breath as he made for the farmhouse door.

Will watched open-mouthed as his father half-limped and stumbled into the farmhouse. After giving his friends an exasperated look Will shot after his father.

'I'll sort the driver,' Arthur called after him.

'Better give him a tip too!' Suzie remarked under her breath, 'The poor chap looks ready to explode.'

Will scurried through the kitchen and checked in the kitchen before finding Barney, already lounging in his favourite armchair in the back room. Gordy was standing over him, a look of wide-eyed shock on his face.

'He's not right, Guv. He needs to rest,' Gordy told Will.

'Rubbish! And don't call him Guv. I'm the Guv,' Barney barked, 'I'd had enough of that hospital. Full of sick old men! Was feeling fine, so I checked myself out. I'll be right as rain now I'm back here.'

Barney warmed his hands on the open fire for a few seconds, then leaned back and closed his eyes. Will watched his father suck in a large breath and exhale contentedly. Barney sank gratefully into his favourite chair, as if being consumed by it. Will studied his father for a long moment. His father was thin, frail even. Not a bit like he remembered him. Trying to decide what was for the best, Will reasoned that the inevitable car journey back to York Hospital with Barney would have to wait until the morning.

'He's fallen straight  to sleep,' Gordy said in a hushed tone, 'Go on, get going. I'll keep an eye on him.'

Will went to find a blanket and draped it over his sleeping father. He made sure Gordy had his mobile phone number and left the two pensioners in the back room with a promise that he'd return before midnight.

Outside, Will faced a barrage of questions from his friends and work colleagues, but answered them all with a single reply.

'My father's resting. He's going nowhere tonight, so we may as well go and have some fun.'

## Twenty-Eight

The annual Malton Charity Casino Night had started as a toy roulette wheel in a nearby church hall, a stack of lager, and a few plates of sausage rolls and sandwiches, northern racehorse trainers being notoriously easy to please. However, with the passage of time it had morphed into a huge upmarket event attended by owners, trainers, jockeys, selected stable staff, and the racing media. Increasingly, a smattering of celebrities were invited to add a degree of exclusivity to the evening. Tickets for the event were eye-wateringly expensive, however 'Casino Night' had become the social event of the northern flat season, being staged at the start of June, the weekend before Royal Ascot week.

Just to receive an invite was an achievement. Will was pretty certain no-one from Manor Stud Stables had attended in the past and when the invitation had arrived in the post, Will had jumped at the opportunity to bag six tickets for himself and his team.

Entering the five-star Tagora Hotel at eight-thirty in the evening down a forty foot long red carpet onto which were projected glinting spiralling stars and crescents, did bring a smile to Will's face. By the time they'd all begun sipping at their welcome champagne, among the masses of flowers and incredible bunches of metallic coloured balloons in the reception area, Will had forgotten about his father's unexpected arrival.

Once directed into the ballroom by the charity's welcoming committee, the six of them entered an unexpectedly spacious room called the Emperor's Ballroom and stood clutching their glasses, drinking in the scene.

'This is... spectacular,' said Arthur as he marvelled at the stone columns and vaulted ceiling that made the ballroom feel like a Roman temple.

There was a murmur of agreement from the others as they took in the roulette and blackjack tables, already busy with hundreds of immaculately dressed gamblers, and manned by male and female croupiers wearing bright red waistcoats. The standard gambling tables were augmented by various games of skill, and in the centre of the ballroom a large, colourful upright wheel spun periodically with a loud clicking sound that bounced off the walls.

At the far end of the room, on a slightly raised plinth, six musicians were playing a lilting blues melody. They soon transitioned into a boogie-woogie beat that immediately had Freddie tapping his toe and moving his hips in time to the music. Lizzy noticed him jigging around and made her move, grabbed hold of his waist and ushering him towards the open expanse of dancefloor before the musicians. Freddie was a willing accomplice. The two of them started to dance in front of the band on their own, but within seconds were joined by another four or five couples spurred into action by Lizzy and Freddie's energetic gyrations.

'You wouldn't think to look at him he could move like that, would you?' Suzie commented, her lips set in a smile as she watched Freddie spin Lizzy from one hand to the other and move around the dancefloor with an enviable fluidity. Despite his size, he was incredibly light on his feet, and because of this, Freddie was all the more mesmerising.

'I don't think I've ever seen Lizzy smile like that,' Will commented, 'The two of them are well-matched.'

'Seems like it,' agreed Suzie.

Will took a sidelong look at her. Suzie really did look fabulous. He steeled himself with a couple of large breaths before he spoke.

'By the way. I didn't get chance to tell you, what with my dad turning up like that… but you look fantastic tonight.'

She turned to him, initially unable to meet his eye.

'Thanks,' she said self-consciously, eventually looking up. He was fascinated to find her brown eyes somehow twinkling, even though the lights in the ballroom were purposefully low to be as close as possible to the atmosphere in a real casino.

Will locked eyes with Suzie for what felt like far too long, and silently gulped inside. It felt like his heart had heaved to one side.

'You going to register, Will?'

Will hesitated, not sure whether it was Suzie who had spoken. However, the question was repeated by Arthur and his moment with Suzie was lost.

'What do you mean?' Suzie asked Arthur, still smiling and starting to move her own hips in time to the music.

'There's a poker tournament. Our Will is a good player, according to himself that is! Fifty pounds to enter, and it's a Speed Hold 'Em tournament... right up his street.'

She turned to Will again, 'Really? A poker player eh?'

'I... um... dabble,' he replied.

'So do I.'

'Oh, well, I don't know if I should...'

Just for an instant, a strangely alluring expression graced Suzie's features.

'I'd *love* to see your poker face,' she said, raising her eyebrows, 'I reckon I could read you like a book.'

***

At a few minutes to ten o'clock Will found himself sitting at one of several circular card tables, each with ten chairs. Only five seats were currently occupied and the dealer, complete with red waistcoat, bow tie, and white gloves, was waiting patiently for his table to fill. He was in another low-lit, stylish room, situated just off the main ballroom, waiting for the poker tournament to begin. There was a warm, friendly atmosphere in the wood-panelled room, and he watched with interest as his and the other seven tables filled with largely excited, good-natured, and in some cases, slightly tipsy people from the racing industry, speaking louder than was necessary.

Will looked over at the next table, to where Freddie

was sitting, chatting with an older man. Beyond him, Suzie's allocated table was almost complete. He nodded to them both separately, and received a grin and thumbs-up in return. Arthur, Roberto, and Lizzy were standing together behind a roped off area, looking on.

The preceding hour had been filled with a little bit of fun on the roulette table, more dancing, a couple of drinks, and an awful lot of meeting and greeting. To Will's surprise, several of his owners had come up and said hello, including Louis Hanover.

Louis had been in his element, apparently enjoying his racing celebrity status following Catwalk's arrival on the Royal Ascot scene. Immaculately turned out, complete with a tweed morning suit and cane, he told Will's group how he'd been approached by the charity organisers to replace one of the evening's sponsors at the last minute, and had been happy to do so.

However, Hanover had proved to be in a distracted mood and once he'd told his sponsorship story, quickly moved on to intercept one of the charity bigwigs. This was in contrast to his owners Harriet Gardener and Henry Bigham, who were in high spirits and thanked Will loudly, and profusely for introducing them to each other on that Sunday he'd returned to Malton. They'd apparently arrived at the hotel together and seemed to be thoroughly enjoying each other's company. Will had never thought of himself as a match-maker, but enjoyed an unexpected warm glow of pride when Harriet eventually departed for the blackjack tables attached to Henry's arm.

Davy Dalton popped up with a smile on his face once he caught sight of Will and Suzie, and as expected, his entire family were there too, even his eighty-year-old grandfather.

'I can't shake them off,' Davy had complained to Will once his family were out of earshot, 'You would think they'd be happy I'm riding a fancied horse at Royal Ascot next week, but no... they still think I'm a blummin' traitor for not riding their filly. I wouldn't mind so much if Crackerjill was a contender, but Catwalk beat her sixteen lengths at Goodwood! They've gone on so much about it, I've been sleeping on a friend's sofa for the last two days.'

'You're not going to switch are you?' Will had asked, hoping his question didn't betray his sudden nervousness.

His concern must have struck a chord with Davy, as his reply was immediate and definite.

'What? After all that convincing we had to do with Hanover and the trust you've placed in me? No way. They can do one. I'm riding Kitty and that's that!'

The conversation had quickly moved on to how Catwalk was doing ahead of the Albany and Davy disappeared into the crowd knowing the filly was in great shape and a definite runner for the big race the following Friday.

Will was still ruminating upon how racing was so capable of dividing families and splitting allegiances when Pat took a seat beside him.

'What are you doing here?' Will asked the policeman.

Pat regarded him stoney faced, 'Should it be such a surprise?'

'Sorry, Pat. It was a shock when you were suddenly just... there beside me. I wouldn't have imagined this was your sort of night out given...'

The policeman eyes narrowed but he remained silent, patiently waiting for Will to continue. Will's head bowed and he leaned in so their heads were almost touching.

'You're gambling problem...' Will whispered.

'That's all in the past,' Pat said quickly, 'Besides, this is for charity. The only winners tonight will be the staff that work around the yards.'

Pat studied Will for a moment. The lad was clearly uncomfortable with him around. Perhaps he thought Barney had put him up to this. In fact, it was pure luck that they'd been allocated the same poker table, but given his own loyalty to Barney, maybe Will had a right to feel uncomfortable.

'I'm here every year,' sniffed Pat, 'The organisers like the idea of having a policeman around on a night like this… you know - just in case.'

Will provided him with a half-smile.

'You seen Barney lately?' Pat ventured.

Will turned to minutely examine Pat's expression and watch the policeman's smile evaporate, 'You *knew* he was going to land back at Manor Stud tonight, didn't you?'

Pat scrunched his face up in a sort of non-committal grimace.

'Come to think of it, Barney did mention something about leaving hospital when I visited him on Thursday. I… er, never thought he'd actually go through with it,' he said with a shrug, diverting his eyes to the one-hundred starting chips that lay before him on the table.

'So your father's back at Manor Stud Stables?' said a female voice from across the table, 'You must be pleased!'

Will looked up to find an eighteen or nineteen-year-old girl smiling sweetly at him, her long blonde hair sweeping around her bare shoulders. He tried to return the smile, but found all he could manage was to force the corners of his mouth upwards a few degrees. Her oval face was covered in too much make-up and the small strapless dress she was almost wearing made him feel cold on her behalf. Perhaps it was the way she was systematically rubbing her hands up her arms, one after another. He half recognised her, and then it struck him: it was Lily Dalton's friend, Tiffany. She had been transformed with the aid of make-up, party clothes, and not having her long hair scraped back into a ponytail. The fact she wasn't leading up a horse, or riding one, had also contributed to Will's confusion.

'Yes, I'm delighted,' Will found himself declaring in an unintentionally sarcastic voice, 'It means I can leave the yard to him and get out of here.'

'When you say here, you mean Malton?' Tiffany asked

in surprise.

'As soon as I can.'

Pat bowed his head towards him and whispered, 'Barney won't be up to running the yard yet, Will.'

Will stared open-mouthed at him for a moment, 'I said I'd run the yard while he was away, that's all. I won't nurse him, or listen to him criticising everything I do. Now he's back, I'll be going.'

Feeling uncomfortable, the policeman proceeded to rub his hands together as if he were also cold. He was eventually released from Will's glare by one of the tournament organisers ringing a bell and asking for silence.

Within five minutes Pat was on his feet and heading for the sanctuary of a position hidden within the audience after Will had challenged him by going all-in post-flop and easily beating his failed attempt at catching a flush.

Will didn't watch Pat leave the table, preferring to order his second whisky and ginger.

*** 

It had been some time since Will had played face-to-face poker, rather than the online variety, however he soon found his groove. His tactics for tournament Speed Poker was to start conservatively and slowly become more aggressive. A relatively new variant of Texas Hold 'Em, Speed Poker required the players to act on their cards (bet, fold, or check) within fifteen seconds, or their hand would be considered 'dead' by the dealer. Will was quite partial to these rules, as it did away with ponderous players spending several minutes contemplating every decision, and it tended to force less capable players into catastrophic mistakes.

He made an exception with Pat, taking an early chance that his suited King-Queen would see off his father's sycophantic friend. Will matched another king on the flop and was relieved when Pat didn't catch his fifth heart. Being knocked out so early would have been embarrassing, especially with so many of his friends keen to follow his progress. Tiffany followed Pat in quick order, the girl exhibiting a suicidal approach to the game by going 'all-in' at every opportunity. She smiled, bounced up to her feet and said her goodbyes with a wave as she left the table, seemingly pleased with her performance.

Players started to drop out quickly once the blinds started to increase and after about twenty minutes Will was moved to another table. He had been chip leader on his original table, but joined Freddie and another five players, two of whom boasted almost double his stack. Freddie had groaned when Will sat down opposite him, and sure enough, his friend was heading for the other side of the ropes within a few minutes. Knowing Freddie as he did, Will was well aware of a number of his 'tells', and he made short work of whittling away at his last few hundred chips.

Looking around while the next hand was dealt, Will saw that Suzie was still seated a couple of tables away. She grinned over at him as he watched her over his shoulder. He inexplicably grinned back, once again, feeling a warm glow fill his chest and stomach.

By a quarter to eleven the tables were consolidated once more, so only three tables of seven players remained in the room. News from the second room was that they were down to two tables of eight. Will had increased the intensity of his play and was pleased when this new arrangement of tables still saw Suzie playing elsewhere. He didn't know why, but he fervently hoped that someone else would knock him or her out before they had to face each other.

Within fifteen minutes Will realised the poker gods were messing with him. Three tables had become two, and he was ranked as the third highest chip count. However, Lily Dalton and Suzie had just joined his table to top it back up to a total of ten players.

Suzie gave him a big wink as she sat down and Lily

184

smiled sweetly. In contrast to Suzie's tasteful gown, Lily had opted for bare shoulders and an eye-popping sugar pink ribbed tubular top with cut-out diamonds down one side. It stopped a few inches before her navel to show off her tight young stomach. A matching pair of skin tight bottoms left precious little to the imagination. Will smiled inwardly as he sipped at his whisky. All eyes were on Lily, as she intended, which would mean he could play his game with little or no scrutiny.

As the players had been systematically whittled down, so had the tables, and the roped off audience was now spread into a rough semi-circle on one side of the room. Their numbers had swelled considerably, with interest being generated by regular announcements piped into the ballroom of who was leading, and those well-known players who had been knocked out.

Within a few hands of the restart, Suzie and Lily were locked in an intense battle with a third player, a southern-based professional male jockey, and the three of them ended up going all-in. To Will's relief, both Lily and Suzie lost out on an unlucky final river card that delivered the pro rider with a wildly improbable full house.

Suzie sniffed, rolled her eyes, gave Will a small smile that he read as meaning 'make sure you get him for me,' and quietly left her seat to a smattering of applause. Lily took longer to accept defeat, staring hard at the table with pursed lips and eventually bending her pretty face into a scowl. Her mother, Bridget, called something soothing from the front row of the watchers, but it landed with little effect. Lily eventually pushed back on her seat, standing to run a petulant hand through her hair and fix her glare onto the jockey. He squirmed in his seat and tried not to catch her eye. She left at a slouch, but only after the croupier had pointed out to her that the next hand was ready to be played.

\*\*\*

At the back of the crowd, Arthur looked on, but the cut and thrust of the poker tournament was no longer holding his attention. He was gazing up at the wall where a large board was being constantly updated with the progress of the top players. The statistics were being updated every few minutes as the chip counts altered and players were knocked out. Arthur had become beguiled by what he realised was nothing more than an active spreadsheet. As the chip numbers changed he couldn't help but begin to commit the highs and lows of certain players to memory.

For the first forty-five minutes the see-sawing of certain players' chip counts had fascinated Arthur. Specifically, a set of players who emerged with similar traits. Brendan Murphy, whom Roberto had helpfully informed him made a living as a bloodstock agent, was a perfect example of someone with ever-changing fortunes. He had been an early leader, consecutively knocking out a number of players. Arthur had assumed the defeated players had to be inexperienced, but soon discovered there was more to it. Then two hands later, Murphy's chip count had dived, losing eighty percent of its value in less than three minutes. Yet it bounced back ten minutes later. Arthur saw similar patterns in several players, including Louis Hanover, a local trainer called Liam Paige and Ernie Dalton, Davy's grandfather. All of these players were up against each other in the second room. He'd come to realise that these were the biggest risk-takers. Players willing to push all their chips in on a regular basis, happy to risk everything for instant, high rewards.

In contrast, Will and a small number of his competitors played a different, more measured game. Their statistics showed steady chip growth, rather than the all-or-nothing tactics. He and Freddie had always taken Will's claim that he'd paid for his stint at university via several months of poker playing with a pinch of salt, but given his progress this evening, Arthur was slowly becoming more inclined to believe him.

Arthur rarely gambled, and considered the whole concept of a charity raising money via a night of casino games a touch distasteful. On Will's advice, he'd kept this view to himself this evening, and realised it probably had more to do with his love of risk-averse accounting and a tendency towards the conservative, rather than an aversion to gambling. As Will was quick to point out at every opportunity, his worldview also fitted perfectly with the myth that every Scottish male over eighteen was a penny-pinching miser. Although in Arthur's case, it was worryingly accurate.

Admittedly, the evening's entertainment seemed mostly harmless, and Arthur reminded himself that it was the stable lads and lasses in the racing industry benefitting from the losses racked up on the gambling tables, rather than a faceless gaming corporation. As the poker tournament had developed, he had to concede that people were, on the face of it, enjoying themselves. With his original fifty pounds worth of chips still rattling contentedly in his pocket, Arthur consoled himself with the thought that this just wasn't his scene.

Which was why for the last fifteen minutes his concentration had wandered from the poker tournament leader board. Instead, his mind was full of Jack Payne's last words, the state of Will's training business, and the various mishaps that had befallen Will since taking over the stewardship of Manor Stud Stables.

The more he thought about the Lilywhites, the more convinced he'd become that they were not Jack's killers. It just didn't fit their modus operandi. They had wanted to extract money from Jack, not leave him incapable of paying. No, they may have been present that afternoon in the York racecourse carpark, but Arthur had ruled them out. Which meant there had been someone else in the carpark that day, someone with a greater, more pressing need to land that killer blow.

Jack's 'Red Cross' had kept Arthur awake. He'd tossed

and turned for several nights after meeting Clarence Lilywhite, trying to tease out any meaning from those two words. Clarence himself had stared at him blankly when he'd mentioned Red Cross to him. He'd scoured Mary Payne's journal, and although she too had noted the possibility that Jack had been saying 'Red Cross', if she had determined its meaning, she'd left no written explanation. It was frustrating, and in Arthur's world, that meant he'd failed. Failed to find an answer... and he believed there were always answers if you looked hard enough.

Just at that moment Arthur was staring at the poker tournament leader board, but wasn't really *looking* at it. As more versions of what a Red Cross could mean to a dying man in the back of an ambulance flitted across Arthur's mind, a whistle blew. He was only dimly aware of the shrill noise, or of the announcement that the tournament was now down to its last ten players, and the final table would be transferred into the main ballroom.

As people bustled past him, keen to take up positions around the final table in the ballroom, Arthur remained stock still, his chin tilted upwards, maintaining his gaze on the leader board. But it wasn't the player names or the chip counts that were causing his eyes to narrow and a frown to wrinkle his forehead. It was the corporate logo of the tournament sponsor.

It was a Red Cross. It was stylised, for sure, but he'd been looking at it all evening and only now saw it for what it was... and yet it also made no sense... and the link was so... so... *tenuous*. Beside the two red painted strokes that made up the logo, was the brand name, 'Roar'. It was Louis Hanover's company logo for his clothing brand. The same clothing company whose products were currently successfully sweeping the world. Whether it was emblazoned across the chest of a t-shirt, on a label or sown into a pair of jeans, that slightly off-centre red cross logo adorned every single item his company sold. It signified brand style, sophistication, and quality.

Soon left alone in the room, Arthur retrieved his smartphone from his suit pocket and began to tap out the Roar brand name into a search engine.

***

The poker tournament final table was given pride of place in the centre of the ballroom. In replacing the huge gambling wheel, the last ten players brought all other activity in the ballroom to a halt. The band took a break, the roulette wheels stopped spinning and due to a number of spotlights, the focus of the evening quite literally became the round table occupied by the final ten players. One of the leader boards was wheeled in, the lights dimmed, and one by one, the players were introduced to a mixture of cheers and heckles from the good-natured, and by now, well-oiled crowd.

Will was the fifth player to be called by the announcer, making him middle-ranked in terms of chips. Of the other players he knew, Louis Hanover was ranked ninth, Ben Stiles, the southern jockey was in second place, and the Dalton family had managed to be doubly represented with Neil in sixth and Ernie Dalton, Davy's grandfather, in a surprising eighth position. Ernie had experienced difficulty taking his seat, requiring his son to help guide him into position. Once seated, he treated his opponents to a doughy-faced grimace.

Will knew Ernie was somewhere in his eighties, whilst he imagined the chip leader was the youngest at the table. Jason Taylor, a pinched-faced eighteen-year-old amateur jockey was the exact opposite of Ernie, as his resting face was a Cheshire cat-like grin. As the youngster took his seat and accepted the small cheer from the crowd with a nonchalant wave, Will was left with a feeling that his grin held a hint of arrogance.

Will's bunch of supporters from Manor Stud Stables had massed opposite him, at the front of the thick, ceremonial rope hooked onto brass columns that ran right around the circular table. This cordon kept onlookers five yards away from the players. As the table settled and the croupier reminded everyone of the rules, Will and Freddie's eyes met and he immediately received the silent 'stop drinking' sign from his friend. Will nodded back and picking up his glass, mouthed the words, 'Ginger ale.'

Will didn't mind the reminder, he was glad of it. He actually marvelled at the fact that both his friends went out of their way to look after him. And he certainly didn't want to become a replica of his father.

Will watched Arthur arrive beside Freddie as the cards for first hands were dealt. He looked concerned and Will noticed him poke a finger into Freddie's midriff. They exchanged a few short words and Freddie nodded and aimed a thumbs-up at Will. However, as the hand started to develop, Will was slightly perturbed to notice his friend's conversation continuing and becoming more animated. When Arthur started to show Freddie something on his phone their discussion became a silent staring match, as if Freddie was being allowed time to mull something over. The next thing Will knew was that he was almost timed out of calling pre-flop and after concentrating on the game for a few seconds, looked back up to find Freddie and Arthur's backs retreating through the crowd.

*** 

Louis Hanover was enjoying himself. Being a wealthy clothing magnate ensured he enjoyed first class service, the best rooms at top class hotels, and meant he was treated like a minor god by many of the suppliers that actually made his clothing. However, it didn't win him friends. Or at least, not the sort of friends he could trust. It had been a lonely climb to the top, and it was even lonelier at the summit. However, the convivial crowd, and the friendly group of poker players, very few of whom actually knew who he was, had made him feel welcome and part of their racing fraternity.

He'd not played tournament poker too many times. He preferred to gamble incognito, and on racehorses, rather than sitting around a table where your fellow players could eyeball you. But with the stakes being low, combined with the players taking things less seriously because of the game's charitable status, he'd allowed his normal defences to drop. It had resulted in a number of enjoyable conversations, and Louis was feeling a sense of belonging flowing through him.

That was, until he sat down at the final table. He'd seated himself with the obligatory wave at the crowd surrounding the table and looked around at his competitors feeling happy and confident, but by the time the first hand had concluded all his goodwill had drained away. Louis felt sick to his core.

As the third hand developed, he and Will were the only two players left playing after the flop. With a grimace, Louis pushed all his chips into the middle of the table and waited as his trainer made the right decision, matched his bet, and won the hand. He nodded to Will, thanked the croupier, and keeping his eyes set firmly on the ground, grabbed his cane and after a short call on his mobile phone, made straight for the exit. His car was delivered to him at the end of the red carpet by the valet and he soon put distance between himself and Malton.

***

As Louis Hanover's blacked out SUV melted into the night, he was unaware that two sets of eyes had watched his departure. Freddie turned to Arthur, with a sceptical eyebrow raised.

'You're saying Hanover based his company logo on the cross of St George... because it featured on the crest of his school blazer?'

'That's what his Roar corporate website says in its background section about its founder, the wonderful Mr Hanover. Apparently he loved his boyhood school. It talks about an art teacher who inspired him to start designing clothes.'

Freddie was confused. Peering down on his substantially shorter friend he asked, 'So what are you suggesting, Arty?'

'I think that's what Jack saw before he died. The crest on the blazer of a pupil from Hanover's school!' Arthur said, holding up his phone to display a school website.

Freddie looked unconvinced, so Arthur continued.

'When Lilywhite said there were lots of schoolkids around the day they met Jack in the carpark, I assumed the kids were from the primary school that's only a stone's throw away, on the same road as the racecourse. I didn't realise there was another school, a comprehensive with children between eleven and sixteen, only a short walk away.'

Freddie remained quiet for a moment, then asked, 'So you reckon the red cross Jack told the ambulance crew about might be this crest?'

'Yes.'

'And you think that some kid from that school murdered Jack?'

'No!' Arthur fired back in rebuke, 'I think Jack used what few words he was able to get out to try and tell the ambulance crew who *witnessed* his assault. For weeks now I've been assuming Jack was trying to tell them his attackers name, but he was cleverer than that.'

Freddie screwed his face into yet another sceptical position, 'Wouldn't telling the ambulance crew his attackers names be clever enough?'

Arthur grinned, 'Not if he didn't know his attacker, or didn't see them! Maybe a kid came along and found Jack after he'd been attacked.'

'I suppose it was around four in the afternoon when it

happened,' Freddie reasoned, 'The schools would be finishing and releasing the kids to go home. But how does Hanover fit into all of this?'

'He doesn't. Not really. His company logo was the prompt I needed to work out what 'Red Cross' meant. I suppose it's a bit of a coincidence that Hanover attended that school, but Hanover had already left years before Jack's murder happened.'

A ripple of applause coming from the ballroom caught Arthur's attention, 'Come on, we'd best get back.'

Together, and in silence, the two friends wandered back through the reception rooms and into the ballroom. The poker tournament was down to eight seats, but with several players nursing small stacks and blinds increasing every few minutes, the game would soon be reaching its conclusion. Freddie was pleased to see that Will was still holding a strong position, being third in the chip count, albeit Jason Taylor and Ben Stiles were well out in front.

'Does knowing… or at least, *presuming* to know there was a kid present in the car park when Jack was being beaten to a pulp, actually help us?' Freddie asked once they came to a natural halt at the edge of the poker crowd.

'Not really,' Arthur sighed, 'They'd have to be… what, between thirty-three and thirty-eight years old by now. If they were going to come forward with information, you'd imagine they'd have done so by now.'

They watched the next hand result in a small win for Neil Dalton.

'Of course, they never recovered the money.'

Arthur looked up at Freddie and found him unfocussed, arms crossed, staring over the heads of the people in front.

'What do you mean?'

'Jack's winnings. Two hundred thousand quid,' Freddie stated in a faraway voice, 'It was never found. I'm just saying… that's a lot of reasons not to tell the police.'

***

Will was troubled. Why had Hanover gifted him all his chips? And where had Arthur and Freddie disappeared off to?

He mulled this over for the next two hands, during which he opted to fold early and give this conundrum all of his attention. It didn't make any sense. It was as if Hanover had *waited* for the opportunity to hand his stack to him. It hadn't gone unnoticed around the table. As Hanover had left, both Neil Dalton and Brendan Murphy, the bloodstock agent, had made barbed comments, questioning Hanover's actions. His soft exit had not only been bewildering, it had also meant Will now occupied third position on the leader board.

Unable to reach a satisfactory conclusion, Will tried to push all thoughts of Hanover to the back of his mind. However, he found himself being strangely pleased that Hanover had chosen to gift his remaining chips to himself, rather than anyone else around the table. Will further consoled himself with the thought that Hanover might believe him to be a little luckier than the average trainer if he finished in the first few tonight.

***

So far, Will had found the final table nothing less than fascinating. This was a truly eclectic group of racing people. A feisty young stable lass living on a minimum wage was trading racing stories with the millionaire owner sitting next door to her, meanwhile across the table a corpulent, red-faced northern bookmaker was busy berating the clerk of a midlands-based racecourse about pitch fees by wagging his pudgy index finger in his face. Neil and Ernie Dalton sat like Will, silently waiting for the poker game to restart, and further around the table, the bloodstock agent and another trainer, female this time, and beside her sat an almost bald, middle-aged man described as an 'auctioneer' by the announcer. He was similar to the Dalton's; seemingly incapable of cracking a smile.

Will stole a quick glance over at Ben Stiles, the young southern-based jockey, and the current chip leader. He'd been impressed with his opponent's play and recognised a similar ability at the poker table to his own. The youngster had a knack for escaping from costly confrontations, especially those when he held strong, but not necessarily winning cards. Will had been deeply impressed with his ability to spot when his hand had been beaten, even when he had been gifted a strong, potentially pot winning hand. Where most players would play through, convinced their cards were strong enough to win, the teenager was confident enough to lay down good cards and wait for a better opportunity. Will had watched with interest as the young jockey folded an ace-high straight, saving himself the loss of several thousand chips when his opponent revealed a flush. Age really was no barrier to success as a poker player.

His attention shifted to the audience standing in a circle behind the thick purple rope, and to Suzie, who was standing with Roberto and Lizzy, sipping at a champagne flute. Freddie and Arthur's continuing absence probably meant they were busy at the bar. He smiled over at Suzie and not for the first time in the last few days, wondered why he'd not noticed her during their time together at secondary school. She mouthed 'good luck' to him and raised her glass in salute, her eyes wide with a mixture of excitement and… something else. Will wasn't sure at first, but after mouthing 'thank you!' back to her a memory popped into his head. It was Barney, his father, catching his eye and smiling as he sat nervously on the back of a strapping gelding. His dad was checking over his tack at the bottom of the Malton All-Weather gallop, ahead of his first canter at the age of… he can't have been more than eleven years old. Suzie had given him that same look his father had that day, the one that had prompted a heart-warming feeling inside him. It had been a look of... *pride.*

Before this thought managed to manifest itself any further, the croupier spoke, 'Ladies and gentlemen, we are ready...' and within another few seconds, all of Will's attention was back on the game.

***

As the blinds grew into the thousands, a couple of players with small stacks started to play loose in order to try and force a few lucky pot wins. Neil Dalton and his father Ernie bossed the next few hands with aggressive play and in doing so the table lost another three players, including the bloodstock agent, the female trainer, and the brash bookmaker. The latter took his beating badly, chuntering about bad beats and co-operative playing. Will didn't look up as he left, but felt the bookmaker had a point. Neil and Ernie Dalton were definitely protecting each other, playing to some sort of team tactics. They never contested the same pot, and there were far too many knowing glances between the two of them. In fact, their presence was beginning to sour the mood around the table.

Will put paid to Ernie's involvement twenty-five minutes into the game. With two Jacks and a King communal cards showing on the flop, the eighty-year-old made a two thousand chip bet and then looked up to measure the response from the other five players. And that was his mistake. Will had noticed the old man rolled the end of his long eyebrow hairs between his thumb and index finger when waiting for a response to his bets. A soft roll indicated confidence, and a harder, more vigorous rub denoted anxiety.

As far as Will could ascertain, Ernie hadn't played a single hand to a complete bluff, and as the octogenarian man-handled his long, bushy brows (far too long in Will's opinion), the pressure he applied resulted in a few of the silvery hairs dropping to the green baize.

As expected, Neil folded, as did everyone else to Will's right. Noting Ernie's stack only contained another six thousand chips, Will made a bet of eight thousand. This was met with a scowl from Ernie. He pushed his entire stack into the pot and turned over an unsuited Jack and Two, giving him three of a kind. Will responded by showing his suited King, and Ace of clubs, giving him the possibility of a flush as well as building upon his pair of Kings. He waited for the final two communal cards, knowing he was currently beaten, but with the odds very much in his favour.

The turn provided a third King, and Ernie's face darkened. Will watched fascinated as the retired trainer pursed his lips to such an extent, they turned a disturbing off-white colour. Already beaten, Ernie didn't wait for the river card and instead, began struggling to his feet, pushing away his son's offer of help. He left the table to a respectful smattering of applause, and fire in his eyes.

Only three minutes later, Will was also leaving the table.

***

Freddie sidled up to Lizzy, placed a hand around her waist and gave it a gentle squeeze.

'Ay 'up Lizzy.'

'Jesus! You're cold!' she complained, grabbing Freddie's dinnerplate sized hand and rubbing both her own, far more petite hands, over his to transfer some heat into them. She smiled at Arthur, who came up and was now standing beside Freddie.

'Went for a breath of fresh air,' Freddie told her, 'Never mind my hands, how's Winda doing?'

'They're down to the last four,' she whispered.

'Will's been whittling away at the leader in the last few hands and has gone into second,' Roberto informed the newcomers, 'But that Neil Dalton is a wily sort. He's been gunning for Will since the final table started.'

A few seconds later, Will was pulling another sizeable pot towards himself and the auctioneer was looking frustratedly down at his remaining few chips.

'That should be it for him,' Roberto observed.

As the croupier began to collect the cards and prepare for the next hand, the burble of conversation among the crowd altered to reflect the fact that someone was pushing authoritatively through the forest of people, demanding they step back. Arthur and Roberto were summarily pushed aside as Pat Higgins reached the roped off area, straddled it, and made his way around the playing table to where Will was sitting.

Arthur managed to fight his way to the front row and frowned as Pat bent down and said a few words into Will's ear. Pat straightened and waited by Will's side. Will had frozen in his seat, staring blankly at the three community cards the croupier had just revealed in the centre of the table.

'I'm afraid I must retire,' Will told the croupier quietly, suddenly rising from the table.

He grabbed his jacket from the back of his seat, and as if remembering his manners, turned to the remaining three players and apologised.

'I have to leave,' he said, his voice a little croaky, 'It seems there has been an accident... and I need to go.'

Will looked over to where his friends had been standing and saw Freddie and Arthur were already pushing their way out of the crowd, closely pursued by Lizzy and Roberto. Suzie was where she had been throughout the final table; in the front row. She had her arms tightly wrapped around her chest and looked scared.

As their eyes met, she knew. She knew something dreadful had happened.

## Twenty-Nine

Barney was lying at the bottom of the stairs, his torso crumpled, one arm, presumably broken, was twisted unnaturally back on itself and lay over the back of his neck. His head lolled over the final step as if he was inspecting the carpet. Will approached him quietly, thankful that the police and various other people who had been milling around the farmhouse taking photos and measurements, had turned their backs long enough for him to slip inside the farmhouse to be alone with his father. It didn't matter that he couldn't touch anything, Will had no wish to do so.

He had seen a number of dead horses in his time. It was an inevitable consequence of living in a racing yard. Even so, he wasn't prepared for the unworldliness of the scene.

Pat had been serious in tone and direct in the words he chose to relay to him at the poker table. It had helped. He'd known straight from that first moment that he was unlikely to find his father alive when he got home. He supposed that was what twenty-five years as a policeman gave you; the ability to be succinct, accurate, and emotionless with a person when you had to deliver news that would rock their world. And yet, Will wasn't rocked.

Sure, the sight of his father lying head-first at the foot of his stairs wasn't pretty, but Will wasn't choked with grief. Far from it, his thoughts centred around how stupid his father had been to leave hospital when clearly, he wasn't fully recovered. To then climb the stairs, presumably to visit the bathroom, and lose his balance at the top of the stairs as he returned was reckless, and directly contrary to the orders he'd issued to him before he'd left that evening. To round off his father's ill-fated journey back down the stairs, he'd managed to smash his head into the balustrade as he'd fallen down the nineteen steps that led to the back room. And he'd done all of this when Gordy wasn't around to offer him any help.

Will slowly lowered himself to his knees, looked into

his father's face and tried to ignore the matted, bloody area just above his hairline. His eyes were closed. He actually looked serene, which was rare for his father. Will spent a moment trying to commit this expression to memory. It was better than the angry version he usually visualised when recalling a mental picture of his father.

Will didn't loiter. With a small shake of his head he got up and quietly left the room.

***

Gordy looked up across the crowded kitchen as Will re-entered. Tears were streaming down his face, giving it an unusually rosy glow. Will immediately caught his haunted expression and held up a hand to halt the stream of heartfelt apologies he'd already heard from his yard man.

'It wasn't your fault,' Will assured him quickly.

The entire Manor Stud team was camped around Gordy at the far end of the huge kitchen table. Lizzy was holding his hand and providing him with a steady supply of tissues.

'I had to go catch the filly, Nancy. She's a bugger for pulling her box bolt out. I wish I'd never taught her to do it to my whistle. It was just a bit of fun. I… I must have left the bottom latch undone… Took me ten minutes to catch her, fetch her back and… he… your dad was…' said Gordy, his voice trailing away and his eyes filling with tears once more.

Suzie and Lizzy soothed him with quiet, confident words while Roberto, Arthur, and Freddie looked on. A couple of policemen in their garish bright yellow jackets were sipping at cups of tea whilst leaning up against the kitchen units and Pat was with them, still dressed in his casino night outfit but now adorned with a police waistcoat and cap.

'It was his own, stupid fault,' Will said abruptly, 'He shouldn't have been here in the first place.'

This received an immediate disapproving glare from

Suzie. Arthur wouldn't meet his eye. Freddie did so, but only to give him a sad shake of his head that told his friend he was treading a sensitive and dangerous line.

Roberto cleared his throat, 'It's late,' he stated, meeting Will's angry stare with a warning look of his own, 'Freddie, Arthur, with me. You can stay over at mine. The rest of you go home and try to get some sleep.'

He looked over at Will, 'Guv'nor, can I suggest you do the early morning feed and Lizzy and I will take over at ten and ride out the three running next week?'

Will gave him a nod and slumped into a kitchen chair.

No one argued and the group quickly broke up and everyone filed out of the farmhouse apart from Pat and the two policemen.

Once they were alone, Pat started to explain that Barney's body would soon be moved, giving Will the freedom of the farmhouse once more, but he stopped mid-sentence. The lad's eyes were almost closed and his head was slowly dipping forward. Helping him to his feet, Pat took Will by the arm and guided him into Barney's old armchair in the back room. The chair felt warm and seemed to embrace him. By the time Pat had located and then draped a blanket over him, Will was fast asleep.

## Thirty

Will woke, as he had for the past few months, at six twenty-nine, one minute before his alarm was due to go off. It took him a long moment to get his bearings and realise it was Saturday morning and he was in his father's favourite armchair, covered by a blanket. He started to recall the events of only a few hours before, then heard his alarm beeping its digital wake-up call from upstairs. Relief flushed through him when he took a side-long glance at the foot of the stairs; his father's lifeless, mangled body had been removed.

Working on auto-pilot, Will was showered, changed, and into the yard within ten minutes, setting about the first morning feed. By nine o'clock all the horses had been checked over, fed, and he'd mucked out four boxes. He'd been pleased when Catwalk's head was one of the first to poke out over her stable door; the filly was in great shape and ate up every scrap of her food.

He kept busy, trying to concentrate on the job. At nine thirty he went to take a closer look at the filly who had broken out of her box, necessitating Gordy to chase her down in the dark the night before. Nancy was in the box furthest from the farmhouse, the last in the line. He could have sworn the four-year-old smirked at him as he approached her box.

Nancy bent her head over the half-door and deftly removed the top bolt with a combination of her lips and teeth, sliding it from its broken housing and tossing it high into the air. The filly blew out a triumphant breath that made her nose vibrate, delighting in the jangling metallic sound the bolt made as it bounced several times across the concrete walkway, coming to rest at the edge of the lane running through the centre of the yard. She pushed at the box door, however, the foot operated metal sneck at the bottom of the door was safely engaged, so she was going nowhere this time.

Will grinned appreciatively and told the filly she was far too clever for her own good, and proceeded to bend down to inspect the foot operated latch, opening and closing it with his hands several times. It worked perfectly. As Gordy had said, it must have been human error. Someone had forgotten to kick the metal latch to lock it yesterday evening. It could have been anyone. As he turned to leave the filly's box he realised he'd kicked the foot latch shut automatically, without thinking. He stopped to consider each member of his staff, all of them did the same as he had... it was an automatic action on leaving any stable, you didn't even think about it. Will looked back at the box. The cheeky Nancy had her head out again and was already trying to curl her tongue around the top bolt... He really had to get that fixed, maybe Freddie would... and as the bolt pinged onto the concrete once again, he wondered why the filly had waited four hours after her evening feed last night to complete her party trick and discover she was free to roam around outside her box.

Just before ten o'clock Roberto arrived with Lizzy, Arthur, and Freddie. The head lad waved away Will's apology to everyone for his outburst the previous night and ordered him back to bed. Will didn't need convincing. At twelve thirty he was woken by a sharp knock at his bedroom door. Pat's voice came through.

'I'll be downstairs,' he called, 'I need to close off a few things with you.'

Will croaked out an affirmative response and after shaking himself awake, shambled downstairs. Pat had opened the back room patio doors and Will found him standing on the aging brick patio with his back to the farmhouse. He seemed listless, hands by his side, and as Will joined him he realised the policeman was taking in the view down the overgrown patch of rough grass behind the farmhouse. The garden, if you could call it that, was mainly wild grass dotted with gnarled old fruit trees that were somehow managing to break into flower. His father's large shed, once his grandfather's shed, stood to one side in the shade of an old apple tree that had been allowed to grow to such a height that picking it's fruit was impossible. Any apples that managed to grow eventually clattered onto the shed roof through the autumn months. The lumpy grass eventually led to a substantial fence and a well-worn grass paddock beyond.

Will, hands in pockets, stole a quick glance at Pat's face and was a little shocked to find there were large, fat tears running down the man's cheeks. He was making no attempt to wipe them away, apparently preferring to allow them to slide down the contours of his newly shaven face and be sucked beneath his shirt collar.

'There will be a post-mortem,' Pat told him, still staring into the distance, 'There always is with these sort of accidental deaths. You'll have to wait for the coroner to release the body before you can organise the funeral. If you want, I can let you know when that happens.'

Will swallowed hard and managed an, 'Okay'. He'd never attended a funeral, never mind actually organising one.

'Also, there's this,' Pat said, pulling a thin manilla envelope from his inside pocket and handing it to Will, 'It's the deeds to the stud. They were in your father's hand, the one that was under his body. It must have been the reason he went upstairs.'

Will nodded, thanked Pat, and shoved the envelope into his back pocket.

Pat sucked in a deep draft of the cool, spring air. He needed to get this next bit right. He let out a sigh and said, 'There's also… something else.'

He paused enigmatically, blinking away another surge of emotion, 'Funny really,' Pat said, finally submitting to the urge to wipe a palm across his cheeks and eyes, 'I never cried until I was in my fifties, and now I can't stop, even at the smallest thing.'

Will didn't answer, he didn't see how he could. This was a version of Pat he'd never come across before. He said nothing and continued to stare into the distance where the green grass of the paddock met a wood, and above, where grey clouds slowly melted into blue sky.

'Your father…' Pat said, his voice breaking slightly, '…was a good man. And you should know why.'

Will frowned, and felt a familiar tightening in his shoulder blades, followed by a shiver of resentment travelling down his spine. He hunched slightly, crossing his arms and balling his hands into fists.

'Look Pat, if you're going to try and place a rosy glow around my father's memory now he's gone, then don't bother. I don't want to hear it.'

Ignoring Will, Pat continued, 'Barney wouldn't allow me to speak with you when he was alive, and he would never have told you himself. That's the sort of man he was. So tell me, Will, what do you remember of your mother?'

Perturbed by the question, Will agitatedly shook his head in disbelief. He studied Pat standing rigid, like a statue forever gazing in the one direction. He considered simply leaving him standing there. Pat had no right to question him about his mother. Yet Will remained, unable to leave his godfather like that. Pat's handling of the situation the night before was still seared into his mind, especially the way in which he'd passed on the news. However pompous and deluded he was about his father, Will reckoned Pat had earned the right to have his views aired, however wrong they were. Perhaps by allowing him to have his say might allow the policeman to move on. There was no doubt that for whatever twisted reason, Pat had held his father in high regard. Will decided he may as well find out why.

Making an effort to relax his shoulders, Will straightened, and after a calming breath, told himself he would see out the next few minutes of their conversation without losing his temper. He joined Pat in resetting his gaze onto the horizon. The sun was slowly lifting itself from behind a bank of low cloud and weak shards of light began to play on the men's faces.

'Okay, Pat,' he said, 'Tell me. Tell me why my father

was so great.'

Pat gave an unexpected crackle of laughter, 'Oh, he was no saint! He could be a tough man to please and even if you achieved what he wanted, he didn't shower those around him with praise or affection. You'd know that more than most, after all, he always expected the most from you. But where your dad made up for his shortcomings was in his loyalty.'

'What?' spat Will, spinning around to regard Pat with scepticism, 'Who the hell was he loyal to? ' It certainly wasn't my mother.'

So much for keeping my temper, Will thought. I've managed to fall at the first hurdle.

'My father was an overbearing, controlling bully who was too fond of the whisky bottle,' Will blustered, 'He drove my mother out of my life and never even apologised. Then he spent the next five years finding fault in every little thing I...'

'Your mother was an alcoholic,' Pat interrupted in a loud, steady voice, switching his gaze onto Will. They locked eyes for a moment, but Will broke the contact. The earnestness in Pat's eyes was troubling him.

'Your father didn't want you to know because he knew how much you loved your mum... and she loved you.'

'You're joking, aren't you?' Will scoffed, 'You can't believe that can you? He was a bloody animal! He used to lock me in my room for hours as a kid, and then trash the house in a rage, picking fault with my mother. He was always falling off the horses when he was riding out and having to be taken to A&E because he was riding drunk. For Christ's sake, take a look at all the empty bottles in that shed! He had that much alcohol running through his veins, I'm surprised he didn't kill himself years ago!'

Pat waited, making sure Will's tirade had finished. Seeing the lad's chest heave from a lack of oxygen, he began to speak slowly, careful to adopt a level tone.

'There were two sides to your mother's drinking. She was a high-functioning alcoholic most of the time, keeping most of the signs hidden from view. But from time to time, she would slip. That's when the blackouts, the sudden rages, and the... well, she would become dangerous, to herself and people around her.'

Pat could sense Will wasn't accepting this, and immediately changed tack.

'Remember being picked up from school and Mary... your mother... taking you to the river. You'd be about nine?'

'Of course, it was awful, she tripped...'

'She was drunk, Will. She fell into the river because she'd been drinking all day. Those falls off horses – it was your father taking Mary to hospital, not the other way around. Can you count the number of times your mum didn't turn up at school to pick you up? Do you remember who arrived to rescue you from the headmaster's office? I did it sometimes, or Barney would rush to the school after getting back from an afternoon racing after finding Mary sleeping off a drinking binge in the farmhouse.'

'That wasn't my mum, that was him forgetting about me,' Will retorted.

'So he told you. Those times he locked you in your room... it was to protect you. It was when your mother was in such a state he needed to make sure she didn't throw something at you or accidentally attack you. Ever wondered why your Mum was always asleep on the sofa in the afternoons, or why she got so many headaches? And can you remember any times when you saw your father actually drinking anything other than...'

'Milk stout,' Will said blankly.

'Milk Stout,' echoed Pat, 'Hardly the choice of a hardened drinker.'

Pat rubbed both sides of his temples, as if imparting this information was causing him pain.

'Those bags of empty bottles down there in the shed,' Pat said, throwing a couple of his fingers in that direction, 'Your dad collected all your mother's empties for about a year.

He kept them in those see-through plastic sacks because he wanted to confront her and shock her into stopping. Check the dates on the bottles if you want, they're all from ten years ago. He tried everything with Mary; Alcoholics Anonymous, replacement drugs, cold turkey, retreats… the lot. But your mum didn't want to stop, not really. She eased off for a little when she became obsessed with finding her father's murderer, but when that went nowhere, she started again, and was worse than ever. But during the six years she drank, Barney didn't once give up on his wife. She took Jack's death badly. That's when it started, in a small way, and over the next ten years it grew to consume her. But Barney was loyal, he even allowed you to believe he was the one with the drinking problem, to protect your relationship with your mum and to save his relationship with his wife. Then there was the day Projector died.'

Will suddenly felt cold. He knew about this horse. It had been the best racehorse his father ever trained, winning several high quality sprint races back in 2013 and 2014, when he'd been twelve and thirteen. The horse had died in its box on a Sunday afternoon. Will knew the exact day and date Projector died, because that was the day his mother left and never came back. It was almost seven years ago.

'She'd been drinking in the morning. Your father didn't realise she'd refilled her water bottle with neat vodka. By early afternoon she was asleep on the sofa in your back room. He thought she'd be out for a few hours, but instead, your mum must have woken. Mary went out into the yard in a drunken stupor, with the idea that the horses had missed their noon feed, even though it was two in the afternoon. She picked up the wrong bag from the tack room and fed Projector rat poison. He died of colic within eight hours. As you can imagine, your dad was livid.'

Will's memories of that day were still hot and angry. He remembered discovering his father berating his mother in the yard outside the farmhouse. She was lying on the concrete, laughing, while his father was angrier than he'd ever seen him. Will had tried to come between them and caught a slap in the face from... his mother's ring had caught his cheek and gouged an inch-long bloody slit that wasn't deep, but had bled like a fountain... His father had stuck a plaster on his face, then locked him in his room all evening and all night, and when he'd been released from his cell the following morning, his mother was gone.

'According to your dad, when Mary sobered up and realised what she'd done, both to you and the horse, she was so distraught, she packed a rucksack and left that night. Barney thought she'd be back... but the days turned into weeks...'

Pat studied Will, who was now standing, hands in pockets, inspecting the grass beneath his feet, poker-faced. He couldn't read whether his godson was taking his news well, or even whether he believed him.

'I don't get any joy from telling you this, you know!' Pat exclaimed, 'But you needed to know what sort of father Barney tried to be.'

'I *needed* to know?' Will shrieked indignantly, 'This is nothing more than my father's final set of lies, being played out from beyond the grave. You must be mad if you think I believe any of this. My father is *using you*, just as he used you throughout his entire life!'

Pat's shoulders dropped, and he lowered his voice, 'He didn't use me, he was a good friend. Is it so hard to believe that your father loved you and was protecting you? Also, with the deepest respect Will, you weren't the easiest of teenagers... Christ, you're not the easiest of adults either!'

When Will didn't react, Pat continued, 'You needed someone to blame for your mother abandoning you. Your father enabled this because he blamed himself for his wife leaving and it allowed him to wallow in self-pity. Between the two of you, you managed to cook up a poisonous relationship that suited both of you, but was completely fabricated and

209

untrue. The two of you are… *were* so alike.'

An awkward silence developed, until Will felt compelled to be alone.

'You know the way out, Pat,' Will stated sullenly.

Will stepped back into the farmhouse. He closed, and then locked the patio doors.

Pat watched Will retreat into the farmhouse, sighed, and picked his way around the side of the house.

From his bedroom window, Will followed Pat's progress down the yard. The policeman's car was soon crawling along the line of stables before turning at the farmhouse and disappearing down the lane. He stopped watching once Pat's car passed the two prancing horses on their brick columns.

Sitting on his bed, head in hands, Will tried to shake off all the questions now swamping his mind. He managed to clear his head, but one thought remained. If Pat was telling the truth, his father deserved an apology… an apology Will was now unable to offer him.

## Thirty-One

During the rest of Sunday and much of Monday, Will went through the motions around the yard, constantly replaying that ten minute conversation with Pat over and over in his head. It had taken a good sleep and the absence of alcohol in his system for him to properly consider and then, much to his annoyance, begrudgingly accept that certain elements of his godfather's story made sense.

When the yard staff departed on Monday afternoon a troubled Will wandered down the road that bisected the yard, still trying to work through the memories of his teenage years.

It was cool for late May. Due to a grey, cloudy sky and lack of direct sunlight, a thick fog had hung around until late morning, and small pockets of mist were still stubbornly loitering in the bottom of the valley. Will shivered as he passed the menage, lunging pen, walker, and tack room to his left, the long line of stables and walkway to his right. He didn't mind the chill, it was helping him concentrate. Beyond the tack room he glanced right. The horsebox and little Renault were parked under a stand of trees.

Drawing to a halt, Will studied the group of eight mature trees a moment, remembering how he used to climb each of them regularly when he was younger, more often than not, to escape his father. He'd been able to look out over the entire yard from the branches of the biggest tree, a gnarly old sycamore. He walked on. Everything was in its rightful place, but his inventory of the yard was, in truth, only occupying a small piece of his thoughts.

The concrete road finished abruptly, but a few more strides on Will was at the three-bar gate to the paddocks. He leaned over the top bar, resting his chin on his hands, and stared across the trio of ten acre grass paddocks that completed Manor Stud Stables.

The trouble was, Pat's revelations *hadn't* been that revelatory, and Will was regretting how he'd turned on his godfather. Rather like the mist that was still settling in the low-lying areas of the paddocks, Will had always had a nagging feeling that there were hidden pockets of his parents relationship he'd not been privy to as a child and teenager. Like the sun appearing in a break in the clouds, the mist had evaporated and Pat had exposed the true nature of his parents deception.

Will closed his eyes and gave a long, low sigh. He was an artist, a sculptor, and now, a racehorse trainer. All of these activities required deep thought, but not this sort of soul searching. He found it exhausting. And yet, he kept returning to the same basic question. Had he contributed to his parent's messy relationship, his mother's problems, his father's deception. In short, had it all been his fault?

Opening his eyes, Will stared at the bare, hard earth around paddock gate, the ground having been pounded by the constant equine traffic. He should really get some grass seed onto that.

As his mind queried where in the tack room his father might have squirrelled a box of seed away, a solution to the question of his guilt presented itself. He would ask the people who knew him best. He would seek confirmation from his friends.

***

Freddie and Arthur listened attentively for a few minutes, looked at each other for no more than a second or two when he'd finished speaking, then with almost gleeful zeal, spent the next thirty minutes agreeing with Pat.

However, it was Suzie who really brought Will some sort of closure. During a telephone conversation she described what it had been like to be around him at the age of sixteen to eighteen. At the end of the call, Will was in no doubt he had been, in Suzie's words, 'a bit of an arse ' for much of the sixth form, brought on by the loss of his mother, and the fact that he had been in a sort of 'constant rebellious stupor' that became worse when he'd had one too many drinks.

'I'm not *that* difficult to get on with, am I?' he'd moaned to her.

Suzie had sighed, 'You spent most of the lower sixth glowering at everyone and picking petty fights. Then you spent the upper sixth telling anyone who would listen how you hated Malton, everyone in it, and couldn't wait to get out.'

'Right. But apart from that, I was a good friend?'

Suzie had ignored the question and gone on to say, 'You had moments where your softer side came through. But look at your first few days back here. You managed to sack someone, upset your sick dad, are clobbered in your own stable, get pushed down a set of concrete steps, and alienate your most important owner, Mr Hanover.'

There had been a long moment of silence on the line.

'Will? Are you there?'

'I've been a jerk for seven years, haven't I?'

Suzie had given a small snigger and her voice, softer this time, came back on the line, 'Oh, I wouldn't say that. You do have a few redeeming qualities.'

Will hadn't fished for what those qualities might be. Instead, he thanked Suzie profusely for her honesty and rang off with the impression the call had confirmed what Freddie and Arthur had told him; that he was lucky to have all three of them as friends.

He'd tried twice to call Pat, but each time, the opening words he played in his mind ahead of tapping the call button hadn't seem right.

It was now Wednesday afternoon, and he was on his way down to Royal Ascot with Catwalk. Roberto was with him in the small, two-horse box, their valuable cargo snorting impatiently behind them and occasionally aiming a kick at the sides of the box. They were still on the long slog down the M1 when Will's phone vibrated in his handsfree holster. The

213

mobile started to play Will's, 'Flight of the Valkyries', ringtone and Pat's name flashed up.

'You going to speak with him?' Roberto asked as the Valkyries headed closer to Valhalla and the final apocalyptic battle.

Will tapped the accept button in apprehensive mood.

'Hi, Pat.'

'You sound like you're driving.'

'Yeah, we're on our way to Ascot.'

'Of course... the Albany. You got someone with you?'

Will hesitated. Pat sounded like he was in policeman mode. His direct manner was tinged with a serious edge that indicated this was no precursor to a reconciliation speech.

'Roberto's with me.'

'Okay. So it's just Roberto?'

'Unless you count Catwalk.'

There was a few seconds of silence on the line. Will considered explaining his flippant comment, but Pat let him off the hook by posing another question.

'Okay, Will. Have you been aware of anyone watching you recently? Or have you been involved in any arguments or altercations?'

Will glanced over at Roberto in the passenger seat. His head lad raised both eyebrows expectantly.

'I wouldn't call them altercations.'

'What *would* you call them?'

'Someone took a swing at me a few weeks ago.'

'Right, and you thought it was Jimmy Hearn.'

'Yes, but it wasn't. You had him in the cells that night. I couldn't be sure who it was. I didn't get a proper look before I was hit with a torch.'

This was greeted with silence and Will imagined Pat was writing something down.

'Anything else? What about when I saw you with those cuts and bruises to your face?'

'I fell... Well, I was sort of pushed down the

214

grandstand steps at Beverley races.'

Pat seemed more interested in this, and went on to quiz him for a further few minutes and seemed disgruntled that the number of potential culprits included most of the trainers and stable staff in Malton, as well as a few thousand members of the general public.

'What's all this about?' Will eventually ventured.

'The results of the post-mortem on your father came back today,' Pat said levelly, 'According to the paperwork that's just hit my desk, there is a wound to his head that is unexplained. Blunt force trauma that can't be ascribed to the stairs or banister. We're therefore treating his death as suspicious.'

An image of his father's hair matted with his blood curdling into a sticky mess filled Will's mind, the indentation on his scull... and someone causing that horrific aberration with a killing blow...

'Will! Road!' shouted Roberto, grabbing the sides of his seat with both hands.

Will snapped awake from his bloody daydream and managed to reduce Roberto's consternation by re-directing the horsebox back into the left-hand lane of the motorway, having allowed it to drift into the hard shoulder.

'What's happened? Are you two okay?' Pat called out loudly.

'We're fine,' Will replied, trying not to allow the sudden jump in his pulse rate and hammering of his heart show in his voice, 'We've just discovered it's time for Roberto to take over the driving.'

'Yeah, the faster the better,' Roberto agreed quietly, still holding the sides of his seat like a scared kid on a rollercoaster.

'You need to be careful, Will. Do you hear me?' Pat interjected, a new note of seriousness in his voice, 'Whatever you think of me, you *must* understand this... your own safety could be at risk.'

## Thirty-Two

The dream was sharper, more vivid than it had ever been. The light when he crawled out from beneath the Jaguar had burned his retinas, the second blow inflicted on the poor, defenceless old man had made a whistling sound as it cut through the air. It had never done that before.

Then there were the sounds. The horrifying noise as the attacker grunted as he wielded the long, club-shaped weapon. And the disgusting, nausea inducing crunch of teeth, bone, and flesh as it struck eyes, nose, and mouth.

But most shocking, for the first time in hundreds, perhaps thousands of times he'd had to endure this dream, he had heard the old man. He'd heard him plead for his life. It was the first time since that day in 2002 that he'd reached this far in the dream. He usually woke as the assailant raised his wooden club way above his head for a third time, so far over his shoulder, the shaft hung there, hovering in front of his nose.

Usually, he would wake in a cold sweat, half imagining, half recalling the swing of the club. Not tonight. He sat on the edge of his bed with cold beads of sweat all over his body, seeping through his hair, making him shiver at first, then the muscles in his back spasmed as he recoiled in shock and disgust, recalling the moment the heavy end of the walking stick struck home.

And yet, even as he wiped the sticky sweat from the back of his neck, he drew hope from his dream. To hear the old man beg for his life for the first time... he was closing in, drawing closer. The dream was a reflection of his own journey, it had to be. And with what he had planned, he might end that journey. Then the nightmare would surely reach its conclusion... and the old man would die.

## Thirty-Three

Catwalk was throwing her head upwards and snorting loudly, a sure sign she wanted more exercise than Davy had been prepared to give her this morning. It was to be expected. The filly would be running in the Albany in seven hours, and Will didn't want her leaving her best work on the exercise gallop. Davy had cantered the filly for four furlongs and then returned to the Ascot stables to allow the two-year-old to spend the next twenty minutes on the walker, warming down.

'She feels like an express train when you're on her,' Davy told Will as they watched Roberto removing Catwalk from the walker, 'And when you ask her to gallop, it's like she's a mass of dynamite that keeps exploding all the way.'

Will forced a smile, 'Hopefully she won't blow up. Today's the important one... for all sorts of reasons.'

Davy gave Will a sidelong glance, then returned to watching Roberto, 'Yeah. I know.'

He considered saying more, but refrained. Will had been his friend, on and off, since childhood. They knew each other, and racing, well enough for further words to be unnecessary.

They followed behind as Roberto led the filly to her temporary stable for the day. It took a little encouragement from Will's flapping hands to encourage the filly to enter the dark recess of her box, but once inside Catwalk stood attentively and both Will and Roberto checked her legs over one more time.

'You still sleeping on your mate's sofa?' Will asked Davy.

He nodded, 'I don't know what it is with my family. I knew they were miffed because I wanted to ride Catwalk instead of Crackerjill, but they all seem to have closed ranks on me, like I'm consorting with the enemy. Even my mum was funny with me when I popped into the yard the other day. She said I was better off staying well away from everyone.'

'I'm sorry if I've caused a rift,' Will said as the three of them re-emerged into the cool morning air.

'It's not you,' said Davy, 'My sister, my dad, and my grandfather have all been acting weird. Even after my dad won that poker tournament last weekend, he's been in a really bad mood ever since.'

Will nodded. He'd heard Neil Dalton had won the tournament after he'd left the hotel the night his father died, but hadn't given it much thought.

'Your dad must have played well to beat that jockey with the big lead.'

Davy shrugged, 'I guess so. I thought he might thaw a bit after he'd won, but instead he seemed even angrier with me when I saw him up the gallops the following Monday.'

'I'm sure he'll come round,' Will said, then dug into his jeans pocket for his phone, 'Sorry, Davy. It's Arthur. I better take it. It must be important because I only spoke with him last night.'

Davy nodded, shot Will a quick smile, and headed off to get changed out of his riding gear.

'Arthur, everything okay?'

'Horses-wise, all's good. Gordy and I have just been doing the first feed of the day.'

'So what's up?' pressed Will.

'Just a couple of things. The first is that I happened to start reading through the deeds to this place over breakfast – you'd left the paperwork on the kitchen counter. By the way, it's not a great place to keep documents as important as that…'

'Yeah, okay, thanks Arthur. Get them filed will you?'

'Sure, but have you read them?'

Will sighed, 'What do you think?

Arthur crackled with a half-laugh, 'Yeah, thought so. Well you need to know that the farmhouse and the Manor Stud Stables and all the land is held in the Payne name on a leasehold basis with a single provision.'

'Which means?'

'Which... means...' Arthur repeated in a ponderous tone, 'Your father, or rather Jack Payne, who was the original tenant... or I suppose now *you*... don't actually *own* the stud.'

Will closed his eyes and tried to make sense of this jumble of words.

'I checked the accounts. As far as I'm aware, neither Jack, or your father have ever paid any sort of rent. The reason is in this deed – it has a provision...'

'Please, Arthur,' Will interrupted. 'What's a *provision*?'

'Sorry, Will. It's just a rule. In this case, you have to abide by the one rule in order to not have to pay anything for the lease on the yard.'

'Okay. Got that. What's the rule?'

Arthur cleared his throat and when he started to speak it sounded like he was reading.

'Mr Jack William Payne or any of his blood relatives are granted in perpetuity free, uninterrupted, and undisturbed use of the buildings and land that form Manor Stud Stables. This provision will remain in place until the day the active training of racehorses by Mr Jack William Payne or a blood relative of Mr Jack William Payne ceases at the premises of Manor Stud Stables.'

Will allowed this to settle on him, and he almost immediately came over light-headed. Sitting down before he toppled over, he chose a patch of rough grass beside the stabling block, sat down heavily and pressed his back against the wooden slats of Catwalk's box.

'Are you still there, Will?' asked Arthur cautiously.

'I'm here.'

'Does any of this make sense to you?'

Will could feel a tension headache coming on, and started rubbing the tips of two fingers to the bridge of his nose, 'Sort of. My mother told me that grandfather, Jack Payne, had won the stud in a card game.'

'Aah!' Arthur purred, 'That explains the next bit.'

Will stopped himself from asking, 'Which next bit!' and bit his lip instead. Arthur must have taken the hint, as he swiftly continued.

'It says, upon a blood relative of Mr Jack William Payne not being in situ at Manor Farm Stud, the buildings and land shall revert to Red Estates. I've searched for Red Estates, but can't find anything about them at Companies House or on the internet. It could be a holding company of some sort.'

'I'm the only blood relative Jack's got left,' Will murmured.

'To be accurate, you're the only blood relative he's had for the last seven years,' Arthur pointed out, 'Your dad wasn't a blood relative, even though he had the Payne name.'

'Yeah, Jack insisted he change it. He was originally called Barney Wilson.'

'Yep, I've seen the paperwork in your dad's things. It's probably why he trained racehorses under your mum's name, with him as the assistant trainer. Anyway, that's it for that. Want me to do anything?'

'Let Pat know, will you?' instructed Will, 'He asked me to tell him if anything out of the ordinary turned up, and this seems to tick that box.'

'No problem. You should also know that I've discovered that Louis Hanover is forty-five years old. That means that he couldn't have been involved in Jack's death. He'd have been twenty-five, so far too old to still be at secondary school.'

'Yep, okay. Understood,' Will responded.

Ever since Freddie and Arthur had told him about the red cross of Hanover's brand and the likelihood Jack was trying to tell the ambulance crew that a boy or girl in a blazer had been around when he was attacked, he'd doubted Hanover's involvement, and this proved it.

Arthur rang off after wishing Will the best of luck with Catwalk in the afternoon. Will thanked him, feeling a little guilty that he'd had to leave his friend back at the yard.

For the next half a minute he tried to determine what effect the deeds might have on his future plans, but soon became lost. With his forehead beginning to throb, he decided to just clear his mind, and deal with the consequences of this latest discovery once he was back in Malton.

With Catwalk's box being located in the last stabling block, Will had a view of one of the tarmac and grass carparks. Cars were already trundling across the empty field and being lined up against the far fence. An unbidden smile crept over his face as he was reminded that Freddie, Lizzy, and Suzie were all due to arrive in a couple of hours.

An image of his father smiling at him from the back of a horse came to him - and the smile remained on Will's face. There had been so many messages of condolence in the last few days, and people had been coming up to him at Ascot last night and already today, all of them expressing their sadness… always with a few words along the lines of 'What a grand chap, a decent man.'

Hardly the ogre of a man I made him out to be, thought Will.

'All done and ready for the two-thirty,' stated Roberto confidently, closing Catwalk's stable door, and kicking the bottom lock shut.

Will hadn't even noticed him return. He got to his feet and clapped Roberto on his back.

'The Albany, Group 3, Class 1,' said Will, 'Win it and we get to meet royalty. You ready to rub shoulders with the great and good, Roberto?'

## Thirty-Four

There were no two ways about it, Will moaned inwardly, not only was he nervous to the point of feeling nauseous, he was so self-conscious he could hardly walk straight. The morning suit Suzie had insisted he hire for the occasion was uncomfortable, and the top hat he'd acquired, at outrageous expense, ensured there was a halo of sweat bubbling under its rim. He walked across the clipped grass of the Ascot parade ring, certain in his bones that the crowd packed into the graduated steps around the oval amphitheatre would, to a man and woman, be pointing and laughing at him before too long.

Having helped Roberto tack up the filly, Will was at the stabling entrance to the parade ring. Even though it was barely two o'clock, and the race wasn't due off for another thirty minutes, the ring was busy with connections. He dodged around several loose groups of owners and trainers, trying to locate either Louis Hanover or his friends, but wasn't able to find anyone he knew. He assumed they hadn't found their way in yet, or were running late. A camera crew was scuttling around in the wake of a long haired lady with a microphone that only added to Will's nervousness, and so he decided to stay put, on the opposite side of the ring.

Removing a race card from his inside pocket, Will turned to the page listing the runners for the Albany. He'd spent hours looking through the form of the eighteen other contenders, although with everything that had been going on in Malton, what with the aftermath from his father's death, and Pat's revelations, he doubted his time had been well spent. His concentration levels had dipped severely in the last week. He'd also not had chance to really study the betting, so it came as something of a surprise to learn Catwalk was quoted as co-favourite of three horses at 9/2, even though she had been given a less than perfect draw on the far rail.

Will sucked at his front teeth as he perused the race

card comment attached to Catwalk, that read, 'Surprise winner of fair novice race over five furlongs at Goodwood when breaking the 2YO sprint record on good to firm ground under the apprentice who rides again today. Hailing from a small northern yard not noted for juveniles and trained by young, inexperienced handler. May struggle to replicate that first run now over a furlong further and against classy opposition.'

The comment for Neil Dalton' Crackerjill was even more stark, 'Beaten nine lengths in Goodwood Novice won by Catwalk who re-opposes. Needs major improvement to figure today.'

With his head still bowed, studying the race card, Will suddenly felt another presence close to him. He flinched as a voice spoke to him only inches from his ear.

'Aye, aye, Winda. You lost?' Freddie whispered.

'Blimey, Freddie,' Will choked out, catching his breath, 'You scared the heck out of me!'

Freddie grinned maniacally and took him by the arm, starting to guide him across the parade ring that had now become a forest of people.

'You've been standing on your own for the last two minutes, you twit,' said Freddie, dodging around a group of tall, swarthy men Will recognised as members of the Saudi royal family, 'We've been waiting for you over here.'

Lizzy and Suzie, dressed in summer frocks, turned to greet the two of them as they approached. Smiling and giggling at each other, the two of them were acting like excited schoolgirls enjoying their first school trip abroad. They both looked stunning, and for the first time, Will was pleased he'd been bullied into wearing his penguin outfit.

It was as they were trading compliments with the girls, and drinking in the atmosphere of the occasion, that Louis Hanover made his entrance. Heads turned, conversations were halted mid-flow. It was like Hanover cast a spell over the parade ring.

Louis seemed to float over the lawn, a wan smile on his lips, covering the ground from the paddock gate to where his trainer was standing, seemingly in a single fluid, graceful movement. He was wearing a morning suit, but describing it as such was difficult, it being so far removed from an ordinary morning suit. His jacket was dark, yet seemed to sparkle, or possibly shimmer at certain angles when the afternoon sun caught it. Worn at a rakish angle, his top hat was black, but a thick band of the same shimmering material gave it a magical quality.

His waistcoat was a delicate pink, however a tie had been replaced with a cravat that was fashioned to represent his Roar brand logo, an stylised red cross. Somehow, the material of the cravat managed to ebb and flow as its wearer perambulated across the parade ring. Will had to hand it to Hanover, it was as if he was on a catwalk.

'Now *that* is how to make an entrance,' Freddie said to Will with a nudge and an impressed chuckle.

Will scanned the other sets of connections around them and then the crowd beyond the white railings. If Hanover's intention had been to become the centre of attention for the fifteen seconds it took him to cross the parade ring, he'd succeeded. Even the stable lads and lasses leading up their runners were craning their necks to get a glimpse of the shimmering man.

The only element of Hanover's attire that didn't surprise Will as he approached, was his cane, or rather, his walking stick. As expected, it was being confidently gripped and expertly handled, but Hanover's usual ornately carved black, gold topped cane had been replaced with a walking stick that appeared to be made of a single piece of highly polished wood that twisted from its thin brass toe, up to its sleek, palm-sized, somewhat bulky spherical grip.

'Good afternoon, everyone!' Hanover said with a well-practised tip of his hat as he reached the small group of young people associated with his racehorse. He was pleased Will had filled up his unused allocation of owners badges, and especially that two, rather pretty young ladies were there to meet him.

'Ladies, you look amazing, and gentlemen, I can say with confidence that I've never seen you looking as good. I trust I find you all well?' he asked, skimming his gaze around his mostly wide-eyed  audience.

'Crackin' man,' Freddie replied with a big, silly grin.

'Good, good,' Hanover responded, 'I do hope I haven't overdone it, but I do run a clothing business. It would have been churlish for me to arrive at an event like this and be dressed like everyone else. Too good an opportunity, and beside, my investors would *expect* it.'

Suzie had held her tongue up until now, but couldn't hold herself in any longer.

'Your… that cloth… its incredible!' she said, holding back from stroking Hanover's morning suit, 'What is it that makes it shimmer like that?'

Hanover's face crinkled into a delighted smile.

'Do you like it? It's fabulous isn't it? Brand new, and going to be a sure fire hit at the shows this season. I could bore you with the process, but basically they *grow* the cloth and the shimmering effect happens when incredibly small reflective cells align as you move.'

Hanover traced the toe of his cane through the grass as he explained, 'I knew the 'shimcells', as we call them, were going to be a hit and bought the rights as soon as I came across the boffins who invented them.'

With most of the initial hubbub surrounding Hanover's entrance subsiding, and some of the jockeys appearing, Will noticed that most of the islands of owners were thankfully turning their backs on him and concentrating on their own conversations regarding the impending race. Davy was now on his way towards them in Hanover's familiar red and white crossed colours, but had to walk past his own family, who somehow had managed to amass a group of a dozen or more people to support their filly, Crackerjill.

To a man, the group studiously ignored Davy as he passed them. Will watched as Davy sadly shook his head. Only his mother, Bridget, turned to mouth a silent 'Good luck!' and flash him a fleeting smile. He smiled back, and seemed happier as he travelled the final few yards to meet Will's party.

'Still giving you the cold shoulder, eh', Will said apologetically, meeting Davy's eye as his jockey took up the standard riders' stance when meeting an owner; legs apart, a determined smile, and whip tucked under his arm as the cap is tipped and hands shaken.

Hanover beamed down at Davy, standing at least a foot and a half above him, and opened his mouth, as if to speak. Silenced reigned for a long moment as Hanover's attention had been drawn over the jockey's shoulder. He smiled, and with his eyes still way beyond Davy, Louis muttered a quick apology to his jockey and strode off towards the Dalton family.

Davy and Will watched bewildered as Hanover reached the Dalton clan and began to speak with them. Neil seemed to be the main recipient of Hanover's attention, however Bridget, Lily, and her friend, Tiffany all seemed to be nodding and smiling. Will watched Hanover tip his hat to them, no doubt ensuring it sparkles, he thought. Then Hanover said a last few words, thrust his walking stick into the ground theatrically, and seemed pleased when his words elicited a polite smattering of laughter. He spun around and re-joined his own group in a few short strides.

'Best to keep your friends close and your enemies even closer!' he stated in a low and enigmatic tone when he returned.

Davy gave Will a questioning look to which he could only purse his lips and get on with giving him his riding instructions.

'You're drawn over on the far side, so, as we've

discussed, try to jump well and get a good position in the leading rank,' Will began, 'Don't be frightened to lead if you can. She loved it out front last time. They will go much quicker than they did at Goodwood, so be careful not to do too much too early. I think she'll stay, but you might need to save some petrol for the final furlong. Otherwise, just keep out of trouble, she needs an even gallop and will hate being stuck behind other horses when she's motoring.'

Davy looked like he was nodding his agreement, but in fact, he'd heard all this before, in much greater detail, but kept the fantasy going, knowing that it was for the benefit of Will's friends, and mainly, Louis Hanover.

'I'd like to thank you for the ride, Mr Hanover,' said Davy, 'I really do appreciate the faith you've placed in me and I'll give your filly every chance to prove she's the best.'

'I think you're a lucky lad and she's a lucky filly,' said Hanover nodding towards Catwalk as she was led past them by Roberto to do another circuit of the parade ring.

'Sir?' Davy ventured, 'Can I ask what you said to my family?'

Hanover gave a little snort, 'I apologised for stealing their lucky charm… and told them that I was surprised you weren't scared to death to be riding for me!'

Davy gave a half smile and was relieved to hear the bell ringing to tell jockeys to mount. Hanover was beginning to make him nervous. As Will and Davy headed to the walkway in order to intercept Roberto, Suzie suddenly remembered the one thing Will had asked her to do for him.

'Louis?'

Hanover turned to regard her with an expectant gaze.

'Can I be awfully cheeky… and ask how old you are? It's just your website says you're forty-five, and yet you look much, much younger. I'd say you can't be more than thirty-one or two?'

She married a hopeful smile to her query, and wrung her hands slightly, as if she was embarrassing herself.

'Hmm...' Hanover pondered, 'It's not a date I like to advertise, as people place such importance on age, when really, it's meaningless. The Roar website is there to do only one thing: to impress investors. For some reason the money men prefer their CEO's to be in their forties, so that's what I am. But... just for your ears only, I'm actually thirty-six.'

## Thirty-Five

Davy Dalton turned Catwalk around once they reached the two sets of starting stalls at the six furlong start and looked back down the straight track. It was slightly downhill for a furlong or two before bottoming out, and then it was a gradual rise all the way to the finishing line in front of the magnificent Ascot grandstand, rising six levels and dominating the skyline.

Davy had only ridden at Ascot twice before, and one of those was in a pony race at the age of fifteen. Being located in Malton meant the bulk of his rides were on the northern circuit, and now, staring up the Ascot straight course, he felt a tingle of fear mingling with the excitement that had been building in him for the last few days.

The filly joined the growing number of competitors, pooling around, waiting to be called behind the stalls. Kitty was the best two-year-old he'd ever sat on. Davy was in no doubt about that. He'd been sitting on young fillies like her for the last fifteen years of his life, hundreds every season, and yet none of them had felt like Catwalk. As soon as he got on her there was something purposeful, powerful, and electric that coursed through her and transmitted itself into him. He'd never experienced anything like it. And when she went from walk to trot, from canter to gallop, and from gallop to a serious racing speed, it was like the thrill of changing gear in a monstrously overpowered sports car, the transition was effortless, and the thump of raw speed at each gear change took his breath away. This was a racehorse and a race that might help define the rest of his riding career.

Catwalk threw her head up unexpectedly and snorted, demanding attention and breaking his train of thought. Davy wondered whether the filly could read minds as well as project her abundance of ability into him. She seemed to be telling him to calm down and concentrate.

The strangest thing, he thought as they went behind the

stalls, was the way his family, all of them, had treated him. It meant he wanted this more than anything he'd wanted before.

Another thought struck him; could that be why they were being so mean and resentful? Again the filly threw her head around and jinked slightly to her right, ensuring all thoughts of his family left him.

A few seconds later he was led into stall seventeen and after a heart thumping wait of another minute, nineteen stalls clanged open in unison and he and Catwalk leapt forward and accelerated.

The familiar thrust of power from behind took Davy forward as he expected, but he was shocked to find himself in a length lead after three strides and a two length lead after five strides. He stole a glance to his left. As he and Will anticipated, the field had already split into two groups. Davy was leading a group of seven, maybe eight fillies, and away towards the stands side, a bigger group was being spearheaded by two juveniles who were matching each other stride for stride, but perhaps a little behind him.

Resting his hands onto the filly's withers, Davy checked her speed, concerned she might be using too much energy, too early, but the filly was working well within herself, eating the ground up... two furlongs had already flashed by and he was holding her together, balancing her, hardly moving in fact. Catwalk was cruising... if they didn't come to her soon...

The two lengths margin back to his nearest rival became three. Davy looked across the heath again. They were closer to him on the far side, and the challengers were in greater abundance, but with ten, maybe twelve horse-widths between them, he could only guess at the real distances. No, he was convinced he had at least a length, if not more over them...

'Concentrate on your own race, not the race of others,' had been Will's final words before he'd seen him off at the racecourse gate.

Davy saw no need to begin riding Catwalk aggressively at the three pole. At the two pole he could sense the urgency of his fellow riders behind him, whips landing blows, the growls of encouragement. Yet he didn't ask the filly for anything more than she was already giving him. Her cruising speed was speed enough, even if she had edged slightly towards the middle of the course. A sly look to his right told Davy he was unlikely to see any sort of challenge from his own side of the track. And he was convinced he was still a length up on the far side group.

Davy waited with Catwalk, keen not to ask her too early for that final effort. Becoming aware of the grandstand to his left he thought it strange that he wasn't able to hear the roar of the crowd and sharp, tinny echoes of the race caller's commentary bouncing around the stand. The only noise he could hear was the filly's breathing, the thump of his heart in his chest and her hooves, slapping the ground like a great mechanical beast, focussed on pulling him towards the finishing post.

'Come on, girl,' Davy said between gritted teeth, and he pushed his hands down the filly's neck for the first time.

Catwalk gave a small squeal of excitement, put her head down, and surged forward. A shiver of pure joy thrilled through Davy's body, making his toes in his boots and his fingertips tingle. Further intervention by himself was pointless. Catwalk was giving him everything, and he was a mere spectator from now on.

***

Will had known from two furlongs out. There was no way his filly could maintain her current speed. Davy had got it wrong. No, he corrected himself, *he* had got it wrong by expecting a three pounds claiming apprentice with no experience of race riding at this level would be able to judge the pace in a Group race.

The nearside group were closing, ready to pounce on her… to embarrass his filly.

Why hadn't he moved on her? Why didn't Davy ask her to at least make…

When Catwalk hit the furlong pole, the complexion of the race altered so radically, so memorably, even Will joined in. As one, the Royal Ascot crowd, numbering seventy thousand people, collectively took a sharp intake of breath and experienced that warm, fuzzy feeling that signifies you have just witnessed something special, and possibly historic.

\*\*\*

Now in the centre of the racecourse, Davy pushed, careful to retain the rhythm of the animal beneath him, allowing her to power to the line. He knew he'd beaten his eighteen rivals… simply because he couldn't see them. And as they crossed the line, he caught himself laughing, as the filly wanted to keep running. He took his time pulling her up; Davy didn't have the heart to disappoint her.

## Thirty-Six

'Nine lengths!' Roberto screamed, drumming his hands on the huge plastic dashboard in the passenger seat of the horsebox as they headed north, 'Nine, bloody lengths she won by!'

Will took a sidelong glance at his head lad and let out a raucous laugh. Roberto had just finished recounting Catwalk's win in the Albany for the upteenth time, and each time the curse words in his commentary had increased. This was probably due to his description of her fabulous win becoming extended with each retelling, or more likely, it was as a result of his gradual consumption of an entire bottle of champagne that had been gifted to him for leading up the winning horse.

'Only a fraction of a second off the course record for a juvenile filly too. She's a hell of a horse!' Roberto bellowed happily.

'She's pretty special,' Will agreed.

'And that ride! I thought… well, we all thought Davy had got it wrong, but he must have known, he must have been *sure* she had that finish in her.'

The Ascot crowd's immediate reaction to the Albany result had been nothing short of euphoric. Close to Will, some onlookers had been cheering throughout the two minutes it took to pull Kitty up after she went through the finishing line.

In keeping with his parade ring entrance, Hanover wasn't going to miss an opportunity to place himself in the centre of things. Within seconds of Catwalk crossing the finishing line he had run onto the racecourse, brandishing his cane above his head, and waved it around like a demented pensioner. He was literally jumping, or rather, *leaping* for joy as he rushed over to the returning Davy and the filly like an excited child running into the sea, vaulting the waves. The television correspondent had quickly curtailed her interview with Davy, instead spending a minute with a breathless Hanover who extolled the virtues of being lucky, and owning such a wonderful animal whilst hugging and stroking Catwalk's neck. Within moments, the sixty seconds of footage of him running over and providing an extraordinarily gushing interview was already trending across the social media platforms under the headline of 'Deliriously Happy Hanover – Clothing Mogul Goes Crazy For Catwalk'.

There had been chaotic scenes when Davy and Catwalk had returned to the winner's enclosure. Horse and jockey had entered a rarefied atmosphere, with a rapturous welcome from the crowd that started with applause as soon as they stepped off the racecourse, and only subsided when Davy, waving at the throng around the parade ring, slid off the filly three minutes later.

Will unknowingly smiled as he concentrated on maintaining the horsebox at a steady sixty miles an hour in the left-hand lane of the M1. His interview with ITV had been short, and hopefully, memorable. Surrounded by a dozen or more journalists holding recording devices or phones, he had spoken to the ITV anchor in something of a haze. He'd heaped praise on Catwalk and Davy, and explained how blessed he was to have such an understanding, and indeed, *lucky* owner. He'd tried to emphasise that last point. And to his surprise, and subsequent shock, Will found himself dedicating Catwalk's incredible performance to his father's memory.

He hadn't planned to. The words just came to him. And they'd simply spilled out. Something had told him it was the right thing to do. He hadn't cried, his voice hadn't cracked. As far as he was aware, he'd remained unemotional and concentrated on how, from the start, his father had believed this filly had been an Albany horse.

Once the cameras had moved on, and the press were satisfied with their soundbites, Will had turned back to Louis, Freddie, Suzie and Lizzy. Louis was beaming. Freddie gaping at him, whilst both the girls were dabbing their eyes.

'I… may have given my dad a rougher ride than he deserved,' he'd said with an embarrassed shrug, 'It's taken a few days since Pat called, but some of the things he told me about my dad… have started to fall into place. It was only fair that I let everyone know it was dad who deserved the praise…'

Will had trailed off, then shuddered. The manner of his father's death returning to swamp his thoughts for a moment.

He hadn't quite understood why at the time, but his short explanatory speech was enough for the two ladies to both immediately grab him and hug him tightly for the next thirty seconds.

Since the horsebox had joined the bottom of the M1 motorway, Will had tried to keep concentrated on his driving. Whilst he and Roberto had enjoyed the aftermath of the Albany and the presentation afterwards, they still had a job to do. They'd managed to get Catwalk washed off, cooled down, walked back to her stabling box and by four o'clock she was ready to travel home. Looking at his phone clamped to the dashboard, Will anticipated they should be reaching Manor Stud Stables at about ten o'clock that evening, perhaps a little later, if the anticipated fog arrived in Yorkshire.

In a rare period of silence brought about by Roberto checking the many messages of congratulations on his phone, the smile on Will's face began to straighten as the image of his father lying crumpled and lifeless at the bottom of the backroom stairs filled his thoughts. Since Pat's phone call, he'd tried not to dwell on the circumstances of his father's death, preferring to concentrate on the Albany. Now the race was over, he no longer had an excuse. Only Roberto's horsebox celebrations had stopped him devoting some serious thought to the possibility that his father had been murdered.

Will spent the next ten minutes of driving mulling over the circumstances surrounding his father's fall on the gallops, and the importance of his father's unexplained fatal blow to the head. Finally, he wondered what role the puzzling contents of the deeds to Manor Stud Stables might have, and why his father would be holding them when he fell.

Will could feel a headache coming on. When he added in him being knocked unconscious in Catwalk's box, and pushed down the grandstand steps at Beverley, not to mention the evidence Arthur had uncovered regarding his grandfather's murder, it was all one big bewildering mess. He consoled himself with the knowledge that Arthur and Pat were far better at picking through this sort of confusion than he was.

It was almost relief when his mobile phone juddered into life and Will saw Freddie's name pop up on the small screen slotted into a holster on the dashboard. He leaned forward and tapped the phone to accept the call.

'Yeah, what is it? You set off for Malton yet or are you still drinking champagne?' Will joked.

There was a few seconds pause before Freddie replied. When he did, it wasn't in the happy, comedic tone Will had been expecting. Freddie's voice was low and serious.

'We're in the car park, Will. At Ascot,' Freddie told him, 'There's been an… I don't know what there's been…'

Roberto looked over at Will.

'Is that shouting and screaming I can hear in the background?'

Will nodded, remaining silent.

Freddie continued, 'I'm looking at a Mercedes that was on its way out of the racecourse car park. It's… well, it used to be dark green and I think it has blacked out windows at the back. It's on fire. I mean, *really*, properly on fire, Will. The heat is…'

Freddie fell silent again. The sounds of instructions being shouted or screamed in the distance and snatches of worried talking close by filled the cab of the horsebox.

'Will, what colour was Hanover's Mercedes?' Freddie asked.

Before Will could reply there was a huge whumping sound, accompanied by the noise made by dozens of car alarms going off, then more shouting.

'Freddie?' Roberto and Will called out, almost in unison, 'Freddie!'

A scuffling sound, as if the phone was being scraped against something, came and went as they continued to call Freddie's name whilst swapping worried looks. Will pulled the horsebox over onto the hard shoulder and brought it to a stop. He and Roberto sat like statues, gaping at the phone and desperately calling out Freddie's name every few seconds, willing him to reply.

A hoarse, trembling voice answered, 'It's okay. We're all okay.'

Freddie sounded scared, his breathing laboured as he tried to talk above the wailing of alarms and distant sirens.

'It was filled with fire and then it exploded! The car just exploded! there's nothing left except a mess of metal and the burning chassis. Hanover's car... it *has* to be his car, Will... and I can't see him anywhere.'

'Call him!' Will instructed Roberto, 'Call Hanover. Now!'

## Thirty-Seven

Will pulled over in front of Roberto's house in Norton and parked the horsebox haphazardly, leaving the engine running, knowing he'd soon be leaving again for the final three miles drive back to the stables.

Roberto went to open the cab door, but was made to wait by Will.

'I'll let you know if I hear anything from Hanover.'

Roberto grimaced. They'd not been able to raise Hanover on his mobile phone for the last four hours. No one had.

'He always reminded everyone how lucky he was,' Roberto moaned, 'It sounds like his luck ran out.'

They both remained motionless, staring through the windscreen. It was dark outside, but it felt claustrophobic as what should have been a bright moon was incapable of cutting into the dense fog that was lying in clumps in the bottom of the Derwent valley. They had driven through patches since by-passing York, but the fog seemed particularly dense now they were back in Malton. Fog or mist was a regular nuisance, especially to those located in low-lying areas around Norton.

The horsebox tilted slightly as Catwalk adjusted her stance behind them. A snort from her prompted Roberto to grab the door handle. Once again, he was halted by Will.

'When I first came back, you said that my father was a good man,' Will stated, still gazing into the murky grey fog.

'That's right.'

'You worked with him for years. And you've known me since I was thirteen… I was wrong about him wasn't I?'

Roberto considered this for a long moment. The effects of the champagne had long since worn off, and presently he answered, careful to maintain a level tone.

'Your father was a good, but complicated man. He didn't suffer fools and was strict, but fair. People around here like that. I know you two butted heads from time to time, but from where I'm sitting it's because you were too similar.'

Roberto went for the car door, opened it, and stepped out. He turned to regard Will, and their eyes met.

'Your father also had a proper eye for a racehorse. I reckon you have the same thing,' Roberto added, and then his face fell and he shot a horrified look at Will.

'I'm so sorry.'

'What for?' Will said, genuinely surprised at Roberto's sudden apology, 'You're right. I agree! He was a good horseman.'

Will frowned, as he realised Roberto now had tears streaming down both cheeks and the forty-five year old's shoulders were convulsing.

'He should have been with us,' Roberto managed between sniffs and more apologies, 'Thanks for today, Will.'

The door slammed shut and Will watched his head lad cross the front of the horsebox and hurry towards the driveway that led to his end terrace. Will couldn't see him enter his house, the fog consumed Roberto a matter of yards from the horsebox.

Will made a quick call to the farmhouse and told Arthur he'd be home with Catwalk in a few minutes, although with the fog closing in, he thought it could be longer. Mentioning he hadn't eaten since lunchtime, Arthur promised to have something hot waiting for him.

Tapping his phone to end the call, a wave of exhaustion came over Will, as if it had been waiting until he was alone before swamping his senses. He yawned twice, blinking away weary tears, and told himself the day was almost done. Then the image of those last few strides in the Albany returned to him. Catwalk's perfect isolation when she and Davy passed the post. A smile spread across his face.

Will pointed the horsebox in the direction of home, squinting into the ever-thickening fog, his smile never quite leaving him.

## Thirty-Eight

Manor Stud Stables nestled in the bottom of a shallow valley, so the fog was even worse once Will turned off the main road from Norton. He edged the horsebox along the single-track lane in second gear, flicking his headlights between dip and full beam, cursing when neither of them were capable of penetrating the grey wall of fog he was pushing through. Grumbling as he passed the two awful prancing horse statues on their brick columns, Will pacified himself with the knowledge that they at least acted as a marker in the fog. Besides, he couldn't actually see their sightless eyes because the fog was so dense.

He stopped the horsebox close to the farmhouse door, expecting to be greeted by Arthur. However, there was no sign of Arthur. Will got out and found the farmhouse locked. Several knocks didn't raise anyone. So much for him preparing me a meal, Will thought ruefully.

Jumping back in the horsebox Will continued to creep along the lane dividing the yard in two, driving right down the line of stables until he was opposite Catwalk's box. He pulled the handbrake on, but left the headlights shining into the grey cloud that surrounded the vehicle. It was a handy feature of the yard that you could drive a horsebox to within a few yards of a stable. In this case, Will reckoned the headlights might help the filly recognise her surroundings, as even the new lights Freddie had installed over every stable door were unable to make any significant inroads into the thick fog.

Curious horse's heads would have undoubtedly poked out as he made his way down the stables, but there was no way to tell, they were all lost in the grey gloom. Once out of the cab, the fog felt oppressive, pushing in on Will, and he found himself working quickly to lower the back of the horsebox and see to Catwalk.

The filly trotted amiably down the ramp and once back standing on level ground gave herself a shake and snorted twice, as if to say, 'About time too. I've been in there almost six hours!'

Will smiled, giving her neck a pat, and whispering a few calming words to her. He led her around the front of the horsebox and paused so the filly could see a little of where she was headed. He was pleased when, without any fuss, she followed him into her stable and immediately made for her water trough. His usual check of the filly's legs and back done, he bolted the stable door and was careful to ensure he kicked the bottom lock shut.

The thought of driving the horsebox down the line of stables and then pulling into the tight, tree-filled car park filled him with dread. He was tired and didn't fancy taking his chances in the fog, so he decided against it; he could move the vehicle in the morning, by which time this fog would hopefully have lifted. Besides, he was keen to get inside the farmhouse and catch up with Arthur.

He'd asked both his friends to contact him as soon as either of them had more news on Louis, but apart from confirmation from Freddie that the burnt out car was definitely Hanover's, he'd received no further texts or calls. Freddie, Lizzy, and Suzie would be another hour or two at least, as they'd been unable to leave Ascot until long after the last race. The car fire had caused significant delays for anyone wishing to leave the Owners and Trainers Car Park.

Will was crossing the beam of the first headlight when he heard a sharp, tinny click. He froze. Whatever had made the noise had to be close to the stables, only yards away. It wasn't a sound you would associate with a horse, or any other animal. Another click, closer this time, and the creak of material rubbing together meant it was human. Will took a breath, ready to fend off whoever was approaching. If it was Arthur mucking around, Will was going to give him…

'It's alright son. Take is easy, it's just me,' said a man's voice in a guttural Yorkshire drawl that cut through the fog. It wasn't even close to Arthur's smooth Scottish accent.

There was another, similar, but louder click, and a figure, slightly hunched, and head bent, stepped into the weak arc of light thrown downwards by the bulb above Catwalk's stable door. A hooded jacket meant only the tip of a bulbous nose could be made out, and the man was leaning heavily on a walking stick Will half recognised... Wasn't that Hanover's walking stick? His mind suddenly registered to whom the voice belonged.

'Is that...? er, Mr Dalton?'

The figure lifted a liver-spotted hand and drew back the hood that had been hiding his face. Straightening his back slightly to the sound of a soft groan, the sharp and craggy features of Ernie Dalton revealed themselves.

Realising he was still standing in the relatively perfect light of the horsebox headlights, Will crossed over and joined Ernie beside Catwalk's stable door.

'Are you okay, Mr Dalton? You look...'

'I'm good,' Ernie snapped, 'I just wondered what your plans are, now you've... lost your father.'

Will gave Ernie a quizzical look and crossed his arms, trying to work out what the old man was after.

'With my dad out of hospital, I was going to leave. But now... I'm considering staying.'

'Really,' Ernie sighed sarcastically, 'I bet you are!'

Confusingly, the pensioner had aimed his comment at the stable wall.

He's frustrated thought Will. Upset about something. He thought about Davy's success today and eyed the old man's substantial walking stick, manufacturing a small step backwards, just in case.

'You know why I'm here, son?' Ernie asked, his saggy blue eyes meeting the younger man with an earnestness that made Will blink.

Will shrugged, 'Davy?'

The old man's eyes narrowed, squeezing a drop of water from one of them so large, it fell straight to the walkway like a fat raindrop. Ernie slowly shook his head, adopting an expression that poured silent scorn onto Will.

'You don't know, do you? It's been seven years. Seven bloody years I've had to wait, and then you turn up... and you don't even know what you've got,' Ernie spat.

Will felt a kernel of anger spark in his chest, but forced himself to pause for a second, trying to give the old man the benefit of the doubt. But he was dog tired, and the fog was settling on him, cold pinching at his toes, nose, and fingertips.

'Spit it out Ernie, it's been a long day.'

'Huh! I told your father. I told him, but he ignored me. I told him I would claim it back after seven years.'

'What about this seven years, Ernie?' Will demanded, lifting both shoulders in an agitated shrug.

Ernie slammed the butt of his walking stick down, the steel tip cracking loudly as it made contact with the concrete walkway.

'I own Manor Stud Stables,' Ernie hissed, spittle dancing on his greying teeth, 'And now your mother has been gone for seven years, she is legally dead. That means this yard is about to become mine, once you leave. What I want to know is... What will it take...? What will it take to make you go?'

It took a moment, but once he had processed Ernie's words, Will understood.

'You lost the yard to my grandfather in that card game. You are Red Estates,' Will asserted.

Ernie barked out a short mirthlessly laugh.

'You're a student. You don't want to be stuck here,' said Ernie drawing closer to Will, 'How about ten grand? That will help pay off your loans. Leave tonight, and I'll throw in another five thousand.'

'Why come straight here from Ascot to ask me this?' Will asked, sensing a kernel of desperation entering Ernie's words.

'Okay, okay,' Ernie twittered, shuffling closer to Will, 'Twenty grand, and you can have the weekend to get your stuff out of the farmhouse.'

'Ernie!' Will exclaimed loudly, his hands held out, fingers splayed to hold the old man back, 'I'm not going anywhere!'

Will watched, fascinated, as the yearning in Ernie's eyes gradually transformed into anger. The old man began fiddling with his walking stick, slapping its bulbous, gnarly top into his hand so it made is thwapping sound. Will frowned.

'Isn't that Mr Hanover's walking stick?' he challenged.

Ernie's lips peeled back to reveal a grey-toothed smirk as he flipped the stick end over end, gripping close to the steel butt with both hands. He let out a groan as he raised the thick, hooked end above his head, his mouth now curled into a snarl. Will now understood Ernie's intentions.

The walking stick had become a club. Albeit being wielded by an old man, it's slightly hooked end looked thick and weighty. Will anticipated whatever the bulbous end came into contact with would either break or shatter, especially if the band of in-laid silver around top managed to catch him right. Ready to fend off the fall of the stick, but too late to back away, Will tensed, eyes almost shut, holding up one arm. However, his thrashing never came.

Will opened one eye and was fascinated once again. The anger inside Ernie had soon ebbed, to be replaced with exasperation, and then shock. He was frozen in time, both his hands white at the knuckles, trying to bring his stick down. Something was holding the base of the walking stick in place over his shoulder, refusing to allow it to whip viciously through the fog.

'You really should find an alternative weapon,' said an amused voice from behind Ernie, 'This is the second time you've been foiled like this. And the first time was by a fifteen year old boy.'

Louis Hanover stepped from behind Ernie Dalton and yanked hard on the end of his walking stick, pulling the wide-eyed pensioner off balance and sending him crashing to the ground with a shriek and a sudden expelling of air that left him gasping and red-faced.

'Hello, Will,' Louis said with a grin, running the shaft of the walking stick through his hand, 'It appears our run of excellent luck continues unabated!'

'You weren't in your car in the car park? And you knew about... him?'

Louis' grin faded slightly, 'I'm afraid we're due an awkward conversation, Will. One that I should have had with your father a long time ago. Perhaps we can scoop up Mr Dalton and you will allow me to explain further in your farmhouse? It's getting nippy out here in this...'

Hanover's gaze had lifted over Will's right shoulder, and his eyes had become black slits. Satisfied that Ernie Dalton was no longer any threat, Will whipped around to discover what had caught Louis' attention. At first, he couldn't see anything. The horsebox headlights were still on, but their round beams only penetrated the fog for a couple of yards. It was only when you peered beyond the two tunnels of light that a ghostly figure could just be made out.

'Who is it?' Will called.

The figure stepped forward, the silhouette picked out by the headlights revealing it was a woman. It was definitely a woman. She was shapely, and moved forwards towards the three men with grace, stirring a memory in Will. Cutting through the bands of fog, her approach was measured. An image of his mother flashed before him and he compared it to the emerging figure, his heart immediately thumping wildly in his breast.

'Is that you, William?' remarked the woman in a light voice not dissimilar to his memories of his mother's, as the figure slowly but steadily closed in on the horsebox.

Will wanted to call out to her, to demand answers, but a quirk, a slight inflection in how she'd called his name forced him to hesitate.

245

'Oh, yes! It's William!' said the female ghost, finally stepping into the full glare of the horsebox's headlights.

Behind him, Will heard a dull thud and a sigh as air escaped from lungs. Swinging around, Will saw Hanover was no longer standing beside him. He had crumpled onto the concrete walkway and was lying awkwardly across Ernie.

## Thirty-Nine

For the second time that night, an angry Ernie Dalton gasped for air. It had taken all his strength to push the unconscious Hanover off him and now he was sitting splay-legged on the walkway with his back to the stable wall, complaining bitterly about pains in his legs, arms, and neck, between short panting breaths.

Where a moment ago, Hanover had been confidently controlling the situation, there now stood a second, far more intimidating woman. She wore a hoodie that threw shadow across her eyes and nose. Will could only make out her mouth and a pointed chin. This second woman was grinning down at the inert Hanover, her teeth so bright they shone through the fog. She was apparently enjoying the litany of foul-mouthed complaints coming from Ernie, and nodding encouragingly at the old man as he kicked out at Hanover's unresponsive body.

Will thought about making a sudden bolt for the safety of the fog, but soon realised Hanover's hooded attacker was holding a short baton. It was gripped tightly in a raised right hand, ready to inflict another blow, this time on him.

Sensing movement behind him from the ghostly woman in the headlights, Will chanced a quick check back over his shoulder. The first woman was now approaching them, crossing between the beams. He swung his gaze back and peered closer at the woman with the cosh and the unnaturally white teeth. She feigned a strike at him and he flinched. Her grin gave her away, recognition rushing at Will. It was Tiffany, which meant the first woman had to be...

'Lily?'

Will called his question out quickly whilst keeping his attention focussed on Tiffany and the weapon in her right hand, 'Why has your friend just hit my best owner over the head?'

He knew this sounded lame, but by the look of Tiffany, she'd thoroughly enjoyed coshing Hanover. She also appeared to have a knife sheath hanging from her belt. By keeping his query neutral he hoped Lily might favour a chat and dissuade her friend from further violence. As he waited for a reply, something dropped over his head, struck his nose, before landing roughly on his collar bone.

Before he could turn around, the noose drew tight around his throat and he was yanked backwards. His fingers went straight to his neck, clawing at the rope, trying everything to loosen its grip. Made of rough nylon, the rope immediately cut into his neck and pushed in on his windpipe, and he reflexively gagged.

Lily Dalton emerged grinning from the fog, marching up to Will halting just out of swiping distance. She tugged on the rope, ensuring it tightened around Will's increasingly reddening neck. He was treated to a waft of perfume and spearmint.

'Hello, William!'

'What the hell…?' Will croaked, trying to push his fingers beneath the coarse nylon rope to loosen its grip on his neck. It was already biting into his skin.

Lily giggled, once again tugging at the rope, pleased with her level of control over Will. That set off Tiffany giggling, the two of them enjoying the sight of Will, now on his knees, as he tore desperately at the rope with his fingertips whilst trying to reason with Lily in a rasping voice.

He soon gave up trying to speak normally. It was impossible. Will choked out single words, gasping hoarsely for breath between each plea for more air. He found sucking in air through his nose was slightly preferable until Tiffany landed a booted kick into his back that sent him sprawling forward to join Hanover and Ernie on the concrete walkway outside Catwalk's stable door.

'That'll do us,' Lily advised Tiffany, indicating one of the horizontal wooden beams supporting the porch that projected out over the walkway. While Lily placed a foot on the squirming Will, Tiffany took the end of the rope from Lily and on her third attempt, managed to toss it over one of Freddie's newly painted walkway beams. Will was hauled to his feet, the fingers of both hands still desperately clawing at the unforgiving rope as Tiffany pulled it taut against the beam.

Having scrabbled ungainly to his feet, Ernie eyed the girls pensively as he steadied himself against the stable wall. Breathing heavily, he flashed his two female accomplices a grim smile. They appeared to have a grip on the situation, but he wasn't too sure how they'd managed it, having spent the last minute straining to extricate himself from under Hanover. Ernie sneered down his nose at Hanover, still lying face down on the cold concrete. He aimed a weak kick at the prone owner and almost fell over again when his foot lodged under the man's shoulder.

'Careful grandpa!' Lily scolded him.

Ernie steadied himself and tried to make sense of the situation. He'd expected to make a few threats, pay off the young trainer if he needed to, and after having had to wait twenty years, finally regain control of his yard, but… he examined Will, who was on his toes, struggling for breath… with Hanover pitching up when he should have been a pile of ash in Ascot car park, and the girls arriving all tooled up, the situation, and his place in it, currently had him flummoxed. They were supposed to wait for him in the car.

It was Tiffany who read the bewildered look on Ernie's face and offered him an explanation.

'Me and Lil' saw Hanover arrive in a taxi,' she told the old man gently, 'So we kinda thought you'd need some help.'

'Good, good. You did well. Both of you,' Ernie rumbled earnestly, 'So, what would you suggest we to do with him?' Ernie asked, indicating Will with an expectant nod.

Will, inhaling short, sharp breaths through his nose, stared bug-eyed at the old man. Ernie's query had been delivered to the two girls as if he was their mentor, seeking the correct response from his young apprentices.

'We thought we might hang him for you?' Lily replied gleefully, 'It'll look like suicide. You know, young son can't face life after sad death of his father sort of thing. Would that do, Grandpa?'

Upon hearing this, Will reflexively screamed, but only managed to emit a hoarse whine that developed into a dry stuttering cough. Tiffany gave him an amused grin as she pulled a little more on the rope, tittering as Will was forced to balance even more precariously on the tips of his toes in an effort to keep breathing. As he tottered on the concrete, Lily busied herself, dragging a bale of unopened wood shavings towards him. He realised with growing dread that she was expecting him to stand on it. The girls' hangman's gibbet was almost complete.

Ernie produced a throaty chortle, 'You're thinking like intelligent, powerful women…. I like it.'

Basking in the old man's admiration, and grinning from ear to ear, Lily continued, 'We did for his old man too, just like you suggested – well, Tiff did that for us – and now we'll get rid of this last Payne for you!'

Tiffany gave a little chuckle, 'I copied you, Mr Dalton! I whacked him on the head with one of your walking sticks. He fell down the stairs like a sack of potatoes.'

Ernie's eyes popped, 'You… you killed Barney Payne… for me?'

'Sure. How else would we get the yard back?' Lily queried, giving the old man a quizzical look. She smiled beatifically then stooped to pull out his walking stick from under Hanover. Giving him a little hug and peck on the cheek, she placed the walking stick in his hand. Before she could pull back, Ernie gently took hold of his granddaughters wrist with his free hand, pulling her closer to him in order to lock eyes with his favourite grandchild.

'Lily, I've promised this yard to you and Tiffany, and we've often talked about when you'll get it. But Barney Payne… well, he wasn't a *real* Payne. Don't you remember? I told you and Tiffany about the seven years I've had to wait because of his wife, Mary Payne? And why Barney trained under his wife's name...' he told her quietly, looking for a spark of understanding in Lily's eyes.

Lily's smile didn't waver. She flicked her eyes around the old man's sagging, tired face until finally her sculpted eyebrows inverted and her mouth turned down into a bewildered pout.

'He wasn't a blood relative of Jack Payne,' Ernie continued gently, 'It was his wife, Mary, who was the Payne. Mary Payne. There was no need to kill *anyone* my darling child. I just meant for you to try and force Will here to leave the yard when the seven years was finally up. *He's* the blood relative.'

Lily's pout had become a deep frown.

'But you've always said the only way we'd get the stud was to drive the thieving Payne's out, and Barney was a Payne!' she whined, tears beginning to form in her eyes, 'Tiff and I were *so* looking forward to taking over this yard. We thought we'd sorted Barney for you when we made him fall off that useless handicapper he always rides out on Saturday afternoon. All it took was a bit of ribbon.'

Lily pulled back from Ernie, giving the walkway a childish stamp of her foot, 'And we *have* been making sure Will won't stay. We've done all sorts of things... I came to have a look at that Catwalk filly Davy was so in love with and managed to knock Will out! But that did no good, he just blamed some stable lad. Tiff even pushed Will down the steps at the races! He would have got really hurt if it wasn't for some big lout getting in the way.'

'I know my darling,' Ernie said sorrowfully, 'But I didn't ask you to *kill* anyone!'

Lily crossed her arms petulantly, 'Oh, but it's alright for you to kill someone isn't it! Will told me he wasn't staying, and his father was in hospital, which would have been perfect for us to take over the yard. Tiff and I were properly upset

251

when we found out at the poker tournament that Barney Payne had come back home from hospital. So we decided to *do a Jack Payne* on him.'

Ernie winced, then glanced over at Will. The next-in-line Payne had his hands to his throat, being forced onto his tiptoes each time Tiffany pulled the end of the rope tight. The young man's eyes were bulging, his nose contracting and flaring every few seconds as he took in small gasps of air.

Tiffany said, 'Will's slobby friend, Eddie… or Freddie I think, was telling this story at the tournament about a filly called Nancy that could unlock her stable door. He said she was in the last box in the line. So I left the charity night, came here and let her out.'

'The old bloke they have here came out of the farmhouse and started chasing the filly,' Tiffany sneered, 'I walked straight into the house. After that, it was easy to force the old idiot up the stairs, give him a whack, and make it look like an accident.'

Ernie sighed and slowly shook his head at Tiffany.

'I was going to offer Will money to leave,' he said with a tinge of regret, 'But… I have to admire your dedication.'

Lily's frown vanished, replaced with a childlike toothsome grin. She threw her arms around her grandfather and placed a kiss on his cheek.

'Best get on…' said Lily, still gazing soulfully at her grandfather, 'Will's not going to hang himself, and his awful friends will be back soon.'

From the floor, Hanover groaned.

Lily tilted her head down towards Hanover's body, 'He refuses to die,' she complained, 'That's the second time Tiff has coshed him unconscious today! He must have got out of his fancy car…'

'That's okay, my darling child,' Ernie said soothingly, hushing her with a flat index finger on her lips, 'It would have been nice to see Mr Hanover burn, especially after his little display of my old walking stick in the parade ring at Ascot this afternoon. But I was thinking. When he ran off with my stick all those years ago at York, he was also dragging a heavy case. That was Jack's Gladstone case, I'd recognise it anywhere, and it had his winnings in it. It was one of the reasons I did for Jack... he didn't *deserve* to be winning again, after he cheated me out of this yard. He was nothing but a big cheat. The thing is... his money was never recovered.'

Ernie smirked, 'That kid is a man now, and it's time for payback. I think a bit of blackmail could be in order. Starting with the filly that won the Albany staying right here to be trained by you and Tiff!'

Lily noiselessly and repeatedly clapped her hands together, bouncing the base of her fingers together like a six-year-old being told she could have another slice of cake.

Will chanced a look at Tiffany, still holding the rope. She'd been watching the interchange between Lily and the old man and Will noticed her eyes were glazed over. She's actually *touched* by Ernie and Lily's sick conversation, Will realised. Whatever she was feeling, the rope had sagged slightly and without the constriction around his neck he managed to loosen the noose slightly and take a few deep breaths.

Lily added happily, 'I'm just like you, aren't I grandpa?'

Ernie smiled and slowly nodded, 'You're just like me, Lily. We're winners. It's in the blood. We don't cheat like the Paynes.'

Tiffany released one hand from the rope, dabbing at the corner of her eyes, then made a meal of clearing her throat in order to demand attention.

'Can't I just hit Hanover again and be done with it?' she asked, then indicated Will, his hands still at his throat, 'Wouldn't it look like this one hit Hanover after an argument, realised he'd killed him and then hung himself out of...'

Tiffany's face blanked for a long moment as she searched for a suitable emotion or condition.

'Grief, pity… self-loathing!' Ernie offered, 'Yes… Actually, you're right Tiffany, that's… very clever. Very clever indeed.'

Lily's smile grew so unnaturally large, Will felt it took on a ghoulish quality. Tiffany too, was glowing with pride. Again, Will was left with the impression that Ernie had an unnatural hold over the two teenagers.

As the trio continued to wallow in self-adoration, Will worked on his noose. In a few seconds he'd managed to wriggle a couple of fingers underneath the unyielding twists of the nylon rope as Tiffany lost concentration. He took a couple more deep breaths and was amazed at how the increase in oxygen helped to clear his fogged mind and sharpen his resolve.

Lily was now centring the bale of shavings under the beam. He had seconds. Soon the two of them would pull on the rope, or tie the end off, kick the bale away and… He considered shouting out, but who would hear him?

Will shot a desperate look around. If anything, the fog had thickened. The three of them were now within a small arc of light thrown by Catwalk's stable light, and then the horsebox's headlights were still piercing the fog about ten yards away, but their distant glow was of little use to him. He was relieved to see that Hanover was no longer face down on the walkway below him. Now on his side, his chest was rising and falling sporadically, his eyelids flickering every few seconds. But he was in no fit shape to be lending Will any assistance.

Tiffany now had both hands back on the rope, but he saw she held it in a basic grip. Like all careful stable hands, you learned on day one not to wrap a lead rein around your hand. If a horse spooked and reared, or set flight, the last thing you wanted was to be dragged along behind. If the rope tightened around your wrist, you risked being thrashed around behind a galloping horse. You maintained a good grip, but made sure you could let go of the animal when your own safety was at risk.

As Lily ordered him onto the bale, Will refused, backing away a little, but keeping his two fingers underneath the rope, even though he could feel the nylon cutting into both his neck and his fingers. He was sure he could feel blood dripping down his neck and a crazy thought concerning his fancy, hired shirt getting blood stained momentarily clogged his brain.

Annoyingly, these few seconds of frivolous thought had given Lily and Ernie, aided by Tiffany at the end of the rope, the chance to bundle him onto the bale. Now she pulled on it to force him to stand straight, the bale rocking under his weight. He had moments before the rope would be tied off and the bale kicked from beneath him.

Will studied Tiffany again. Whilst she was small, she was strong from riding and mucking out every day. Her muscles hardened as she ensured the noose remained taut. Gripping the rope with both hands, there was no way he could simply pull on the rope and wrench it from her grasp. He needed someone to suddenly arrive. He needed her brain to get clogged with a frivolous thought, just like his had done. He desperately needed a diversion.

'Tie it off over there,' Ernie instructed Tiffany, 'Let's get this done before his friends get back from Ascot. Then we can deal with Hanover.'

Ernie pointed to one of the large metal rings that adorned the external wall of every stable and Tiffany edged towards it, pulling so hard against the beam that Will's toes were dancing on the bale's plastic coating

Of course. A diversion.

Will pulled his fingers from under the rope, inhaled deeply and licked his lips. Then, he produced a short, sharp whistle.

## Forty

All three of his captors, froze.

'What the hell,' Ernie urgently whispered, 'Get him strung up. Now!'

Will waited, slowly lifting his hands above his head and taking as firm a grip on the rope as his chaffed and bloodied hands could manage. Inwardly, he prayed for Nancy. He willed for the filly at the end of the row of stables to not be half asleep, or in a bad mood. He needed her to have heard his whistle and be up for some high jinks in the dead of night!

Tiffany was straining with the rope and had almost reached the metal ring when behind her, there was a rattling in the fog. Will's heart lifted in his chest and he readied himself. The two girls froze again, but Ernie, who perhaps hadn't heard the noise, urged Tiffany on to finish her job.

Just as the two girls made to move again, a loud, jangling, metallic sound rang through the fog. It continued for several seconds as Nancy's stable bolt tumbled around on the concrete. Will watched Tiffany, the noose now making his breathing almost impossible. She turned towards the foggy blackness behind her and asked in a scared tone, 'What was that?'

As she cocked her head over her shoulder, one of her hands left the rope.

Will pulled. He yanked on the rope above him, stretching every sinew to place as much force into what would be his first, and most probably, his only almighty tug.

Tiffany screamed in shock and pain, as a yard of the nylon rope ran through her hand, causing a friction burn. She dropped the rope and fell to her knees, cursing and shaking her hand as if to cool it, no longer concerned with the rope or the person that should have been hanging off the end of it.

Will was careful to step swiftly down from the bale, ensuring it acted as a barrier between him, Lily and Ernie. The noose was still around his neck, although the newly slack rope allowed him to loosen it with alacrity. As he tackled the noose, he kicked out at Lily and Ernie. They had rounded the bale, each taking one side and looked ready to pounce. He managed to open the noose enough to wrench it over his head, still kicking out as the two members of the Dalton family converged on him, rage burning in their eyes.

Lily was scratching at him from the left, desperately trying to get a hold of his arm, clothes, anything. But Ernie was a bigger threat. From the right-hand side of the bale Will saw the old man raise his walking stick with murderous intent. Ernie's stick arm lifted high to the right of his head and he brought it down with an evil malice in his eyes. The heavy wooden staff swooped across, aiming to land a killing blow to the side of Will's head.

Will jerked backward, eyes closed, waiting for the pain, and felt nothing more than a draft as the stick swished past the tip of his nose... and slammed into Lily's neck.

He didn't wait to discover her fate. Free of her clawing fingers, Will took off, darting behind the horsebox, then set off running blindly into the fog. Seconds later he realised he was practically invisible. If he made no noise, the fog was his friend. Then it struck him that he'd made two miscalculations. He was heading away from the farmhouse, and more worryingly, he'd left Hanover lying defenceless on the walkway floor with a murderous pensioner and the two ghoulish girls.

Veering to his left, he dropped to a walk, in search of the horse walker. When the walker suddenly loomed up in front of him without warning Will took a much needed calming breath. He'd never been so happy to lay his eyes on its bituminous clad roof. Another two steps revealed the wired screens and lines of wooden boards rising five feet from its base. The same ones his father had insisted he paint with creosote every summer. He placed his back to the walker and slid down so he was on his haunches, hopefully making him difficult to locate, but ready to spring to his feet should the need arise. In front of him, a small cloud of fog flashed a shade lighter and he almost bolted. Torches, he told himself, but they had to be at least ten yards away. The girl's pencil torches or phone flashlights wouldn't penetrate far into this fog. A safe distance in this sea-souper. His phone! Will's muscle memory had him touch his trouser pockets just in case, but he already knew his mobile phone was still clamped to the dashboard of the horsebox.

'Lily, Tiffany, come back here!' called a voice in a low, urgent whisper.

It was Ernie. There was another split second flash of light in the fog, dangerously close to Will, then no further light and the sound of slowly retreating footsteps. Will let out the breath he'd been holding and tried to steady his heartbeat.

'Payne! If you're out there, listen up,' Ernie called out in the same, strange, stage whisper, 'I've got Hanover here. He's still alive. We can talk. Reach an agreement and we'll leave you and your owner alone.'

There was a short pause, where it sounded like there was a whispered conversation going on between the three of them but Will was unable to pick out any words or phrases.

Desperately trying to ignore the pain in his fingers and all around his neck, Will emptied his mind of everything causing him physical pain and forced himself to concentrate. His shirt, damp front and back with sweat and blood, was sticking to his skin, so he could feel the grain of the wooden boards biting into his shoulder blades. Dry and dusty, he thought. In his time at the yard these boards would have smelled of the creosote all year long and stayed tacky to the touch for months. They'd probably not been treated since he'd left four years ago. Smiling inwardly, Will got to his feet and walked away from the Dalton's and into the fog. He reached where he imagined the tack room should be, several yards to his right, before turning to face the direction of his father's and grandfather's murderers.

'I'm coming back to talk,' he called into the fog, 'But I need a minute to get my breath.'

Ernie's voice came back through the thick grey cloud, 'That's sensible Mr Payne. I'm sure we can reach an amicable arrangement.'

Immediately, Will was on the move again.

The fog held no fears or secrets from him; he knew this yard intimately. He reached the tack room in a matter of seconds, felt along the brickwork, located the key and went inside. He hunted around and soon found what he was looking for.

\*\*\*

Will was thankful for the horsebox pointing up the yard, its headlights still attempting to penetrate the fog. It at least allowed him to get some sort of bearing on where Ernie and his two acolytes had to be waiting for him.

Rather like Lily had done minutes earlier, Will stepped into the edge of the horsebox light, hoping he would provide them with his hazy outline.

'Okay, Dalton. First, I want to know Hanover is alive,' Will called quietly into the dense fog.'

'Will-i-am!' Ernie replied slowly, extending each syllable of his name, 'Thank you for seeing sense. We can sort this… misunderstanding out.'

His senses on high alert, Will peered in the direction Ernie's reply had come from and picked out his hunched figure beneath Catwalk's stable light. He heard a small squeak of a training shoe to his left and fought the urge to swing his head around to look. They had to come to him.

Ernie made a movement and Will instinctively stepped back, out of the direct shafts of light provided by the headlights, effectively making himself invisible again.

'Come on, Hanover,' Ernie growled, 'Speak for the man. He wants to know you haven't died yet!'

A groan and the scraping of a shoe on concrete was followed by a quiet, 'Will? Are you... there?'

The voice trailed off. It had to be Hanover, thought Will. He sounded confused, but at least he was talking. He didn't reply, it wasn't the time to be giving away his position in the fog.

Will stepped forward again, purposefully standing directly in the full beam of the left-hand headlight. It would make him an easy target. His hands were balled by his sides, but otherwise he was the same, unarmed young man wearing a bloodied and damp grey shirt, dress trousers and shiny black shoes.

'I hope you heard Mr Hanover,' Ernie said in a stage whisper.

Will could imagine the smirk on the old man's face.

'He's conscious now, but... a little worse for wear.'

Will tensed a little, and braced himself.

'What will it take to keep Hanover conscious and for you to hand him over?' Will asked in a loud, demanding tone that broke the spell of the whispers.

To the sound of two squeaks of her trainers , Lily appeared in the left-hand headlight beam. She lunged forward, her hands grabbing at Will. He'd gambled that they wouldn't risk attacking him with their knives. For their sickly scheme to work, he had to appear to have committed suicide. Being peppered with stabs would test that outcome. Still, he was relieved when there were no flashes of steel in Lily's hands.

Will waited until she was almost upon him. In that instant he opened his hand wide and pushed it into Lily's face.

Lily blinked, uncertain what had happened. As soon as she did, the screaming started, followed by the clawing at her face.

'What did he do, Lil?' asked Tiffany desperately, suddenly appearing to Will's right. Ignoring the screams, he stepped towards her and threw his right fist out, opening it an inch from Tiffany's nose and allowing the second rag he'd dowsed with creosote to slap wetly into the girl's face. Some of the strong, oily liquid missed her wide-eyed grimace, but it only took a few drops of the nasty substance to find a home in her eye for the effect to be immensely painful.

A significant pang of guilt speared Will as Tiffany spun away into the darkness, her howls of pain even louder than Lily's. His first victim of the wet creosote cloths was now on her knees, fingers tugging desperately at her eyelids. He didn't feel good about that, not at all. He couldn't forget the day he'd been creosoting the stables and a large drip of creosote had run down his knuckle and splashed into his eye socket… it was excruciatingly painful, but faced with limited options, and a man's life to save... Even so, the guilt weighed heavy on Will and he winced as both girls continued to yell, cry, and swear.'

'What have you done to Lily?' Ernie shouted angrily from under Catwalk's stable light. He was only ten yards away from her, yet Will knew the old man would only be able to imagine what had caused his granddaughter to scream with such venom. Very slowly, Ernie moved blindly in the direction of her pitiful hollers, slashing the air with his walking stick so it made a whooshing sound as it cut through the fog.

'Think yourself lucky,' Will called out from the safety of the fog, 'If I'd used neat creosote it would have burned the skin off your faces and blinded both of you. This stuff got banned a couple of years ago, and quite right too – it's properly nasty! – which is why I diluted it.'

There was more moaning from the two girls and a weary sigh from Ernie.

'You'll get your sight back, but it's going to hurt like hell for the next few hours,' Will called out to the three of them amiably, carefully peeling the set of plastic gloves from his hands, 'It's excruciating for half an hour, but improves from then on. There will be no long lasting effects. By the way, I've saved some for you, Ernie. That's if you try to come near me. Drop your walking stick below the light of the stable *now*! Or you get a face full!'

This had an immediate effect. Will was pleased with his bluff. Ernie stopped swishing his stick around, and almost immediately there was the sound of wood rattling on concrete. The old man headed in the direction of his granddaughter's anguished cries, ignoring the calls for help from Tiffany on the other side of the horsebox.

Will was able to stand close to Lily. The selfish child had become oblivious to anyone other than herself. Will waited until Ernie arrived by his granddaughter's side then strode in the direction of the horsebox headlights, and then Catwalk's stable light.

He found Hanover slumped against the stable wall, eyes shut. He was shivering, teeth chattering. Will paused to listen out, just in case any of the Dalton gang fancied a second go at him. The whimpering from Lily and ripe language from Tiffany at the other side of the horsebox on the road, told him his window of opportunity was still open. He bent down.

Hanover was in a bad way, his breaths coming in short, sharp gasps and he was unable to get to his feet. Instead, Will took hold of his owner under his arms, took a deep breath, and began to drag him along the stables' walkway into the fog. He knew he couldn't pull him too far, his owner was twice Will's size, but within fog this thick, he could hide him.

'In here,' Will told Hanover between gritted teeth, as they reached the third stable along from Catwalk's. Jumble Sail's head poked out and he eyed the heavily breathing trainer and dead-weight owner on the concrete floor beneath his stable door.

Will undid both the locks as quietly as he could and after pushing the inquisitive gelding back, dragged a moaning Hanover inside the stable, covering his Ascot clothes in dust, muck, and wood shavings in the process. Jumble Sail gave a contemptuous snort and whipped his tail around once in the dark recesses of his personal space, showing his disgust at having to share his home.

'Be quiet and they won't find you,' he whispered to his owner before leaving him propped up against the stable wall. Hanover cast a glazed eye up at his equine roommate and shuddered.

Will added, 'Don't worry, he's a licker, not a biter.'

Outside, Will silently pushed the stable bolt home, looked around into the darkness and listened. Complaints and urgent speaking between what sounded like Ernie and Lily and Tiffany were coming from his right-hand side.

'Mobile phone', he muttered under his breath, 'That will end this.'

Jogging about twenty paces into the darkness, Will then stopped, turned ninety degrees and strode forward, hoping to see the red rear lights of the horsebox within a few seconds. It took longer than expected. He'd over-shot the horsebox by a good few yards but eventually found the red night lights shining off to his right. Making his way around the box, he reached the passenger door, opened it as quietly as possible and standing on the footplate, leaned over and plucked his phone from its dashboard holster.

Wasting no time, Will called Pat's number, holding the phone to his ear and turned around to face in the direction of Lily's moaning, just in case Ernie tried anything stupid. Having already experienced the searing pain creosote was capable of inducing, Will couldn't believe either girl would be in a fit state to be worrying about his actions at the moment.

It struck him that there was an eery glow as he waited for the policeman to answer his call, and cursed when he realised his phone was displaying its bright orange calling screen as he held it to his ear. It provided a near-perfect target.

Tiffany jumped from the fog, and was on him in a flash, her nose's touching his for a split second, her hand raised. She plunged a knife into him, close up to her prey, pushing down as hard as she could, until she could push no more.

Will was numb. Unable to move. He found himself nose to nose with Tiffany, marvelling at the whites of her eyes. They were no longer white, but a swollen, bright, fire engine red, surrounding a tiny, wholly black iris. It seemed those eyes were burning, and the irritation extended onto the girl's rouge cheeks and even her lips. She grunted, her face still only a couple of inches from his, her rage twisting her features into a crazed caricature of the smiling stable lass he'd encountered earlier today at Ascot.

He'd managed a jerk of his head to the right as Tiffany's knife hand slammed down onto him, but for what seemed an age, he was unable to react. It was surreal. Shock made him feel no pain as the knife's handle buried itself to its hilt, just above his collar bone.

He watched Tiffany as she pushed herself off him, then slowly stepped back into the fog, leaving her knife in him, each pace backwards allowing more tendrils of the fog to envelope her until she was just a shadowy outline. As she moved away, she gazed at Will, a manic grin on her face, squinting proudly at her handiwork.

Tiffany frowned, stopped, and stepped one pace forward again. Will was still holding his mobile to his ear.

As the phone continued to ring out unanswered, Will risked taking his eyes off Tiffany to turn his head and once again regard the hilt of the knife protruding from his shoulder. This inspection somehow flicked a switch in his brain, releasing him from the numbing effect of the shock. A sudden surge of pain screamed down the left-hand side of his torso, then down his right leg. Just like horses, he thought miserably, if it's a pain in the front left leg, look for a muscle pull on the right-hand side of their back. More pain shot down his leg and it began to wobble. Will compensated by transferring his weight to his left side.

Tiffany sneered. She'd been watching in blurry amusement as Will fought off the pain. With teeth clenched he'd resurrected himself to stand cock-eyed on one leg. She eyed Will's phone greedily. The garish orange light was pinned to his right-hand ear. The automated lady's voice had ceased and now a long digital tone sounded from the phone.

It was Pat's voice mail. Will could hardly keep his hand to his ear, his whole body was now beseeching him to give up, relax, close his eyes, curl up, and go to sleep. It was over. If he didn't bleed to death, then the Dalton's would string him up. Either way, he'd never wake up and Hanover would be found and killed. A recorded message just wasn't good enough, Tiffany needed to know someone was coming immediately.

Pain flowered across his chest as he used his thumb to drop the call and tap the redial button. Tiffany made to move toward him again, ready to relieve him of the device that could save two lives. Will tried to summon the last of his strength. He kept his eyes open and remained standing crookedly as Tiffany, bearing her teeth in a rictus grin, set herself to rush at him for a second time.

There was a dull thump and a screech. Will had been tensed, awaiting Tiffany's onslaught. But she was no longer moving through the fog towards him. Tiffany was cartwheeling over the bonnet of an ancient Renault.

The little car hit Tiffany side on, sweeping her legs from under her and propelling her over the bonnet. Momentum did the rest. Elbow, shoulder and one side of her head crashed into the windscreen, which immediately shattered into thousands of small hexagonal pieces. That Renault really was *old*, thought Will. He'd never seen a windscreen do that before.

Will breathed out, then sucked in a calming breath. His nose and throat filled with the smell of burning rubber and his eyes began to water. Blinking away the tears he tried to make sense of what lay before him. Tiffany was splayed, partly inside and partly across the little car, resembling an injured little bird. From inside the car, someone was chuntering in a Scottish accent.

Arthur got out. Tiffany was screaming abuse and threats at Will, but unable to extract her arm and shoulder from the mangled windscreen. Her legs looked… very wrong, making Will feel a little nauseous.

'I was only going slowly… I didn't see you in the fog…'

Incandescent with rage, Tiffany switched to ranting at Arthur.

Horrified, Arthur murmured apologies as he inspected Tiffany. He winced when her red eyes locked on him. She had at least one broken leg and was holding the shoulder that had smashed through the windscreen. Lying on her back against what was left of the Renault's mangled windscreen wipers she resembled an upturned crab, thanks to a combination of injuries and where she'd come to rest. Becoming increasingly frustrated, Tiffany waved her one good leg and one arm around, desperately trying to get up but screamed in frustration when ultimately unable to lift herself off the bonnet.

'I'm so… sorry,' Arthur told Tiffany again.

She responded with a low moan. Her head lolled and her arm and leg stopped thrashing about.

'Don't be sorry. And you can leave her there, please. She was going to kill me,' Will called out gruffly.

Arthur wrenched his gaze from Tiffany to peer over at Will, seeing him properly for the first time. He swiftly concluded that Will was in just as bad a way as the girl he'd just run over. His friend was sitting on the horsebox footplate, holding his mobile to his ear.

Arthur winced when he saw the burns, cuts, and smears of blood around Will's neck. Then he noticed the knife embedded into his friend's shoulder, and gawked at the steady dark ooze that was soaking into Will's shirt. He rushed over, but was immediately instructed to, 'Leave the knife! For pity's sake, don't pull it out!'

A chime emanated from Will's phone. He tapped it, and over the combined moans of Tiffany and Lily, Arthur could just hear Pat's tinny male voice demanding why Will was calling him at this god-awful time of the night.

Arthur took a moment to take in everything he'd seen in the last few seconds. Will looked awful, and the blood… He swallowed and tried to think of the most relaxing and positive thing he could say to Will.

Blinked through his spectacles, Arthur conjured up his most soothing of Scottish accents and said, 'Sorry I'm late, Will. There was a queue at the fish and chip shop.'

## Forty-One

THREE MONTHS LATER

'So they've left for Newcastle?'

'Went this morning. Last year of their university courses start this week. They'd stayed a lot longer than they should have, anyway,' explained Will, 'Arthur won't be back until Christmas, but I'm expecting Freddie will be a regular visitor.'

Pat crossed his arms and gave a knowing smile. He was soon crinkling his eyes into slits as the late afternoon sun burst from behind a cloud being carried along on the light breeze. The bottom of the yard was bathed in sunshine and Pat lowered the brim of his hat and continued watching Will as he systematically slapped creosote onto the horse walker's wooden slats with a large paintbrush. The dry, sun-bleached wood was soaking up the pungent brown liquid like a sponge hungry for water. Pat got a whiff of the creosote, wrinkled his nose and took a step back.

'Ah, I imagine his liking for Lizzy may have some bearing on the regularity of Freddie's visits?'

'It may have,' Will responded airily, dipping his brush back into a large plastic bucket, 'I prefer to think it's because Freddie loves fixing my fences, stripping my wallpaper and cutting the grass on a lawn that hasn't seen a mower for seven years. But you're probably right.'

He lifted the dripping brush and grimaced, dropping it back into the bucket and began massaging his shoulder with eyes closed.

'That knife went in deep, eh?' Pat ruminated.

Will nodded grumpily, 'I rode out the other day and Jumble Sail almost ran me off the top of the gallop. The rascal seems to know my right arm is still weak. He almost pulled it off. But it's improving and the doctor says I'll be fine eventually, although there will always be some weakness there.'

Pat paused, watching his godson struggle to complete level brush strokes with his left hand.

'You're not going back to University?'

'No, but… actually Pat, I've had enough of this for now,' said Will, dropping the brush back in the bucket once more. He grinned, 'Come on, I've something to show you.'

A few minutes later Will and Pat were stepping out into the farmhouse's back garden. Pat was impressed.

'When did *this* happen?' he asked, taking in the newly mown grass beneath the half a dozen recently hard pruned fruit trees, new fences, and most noticeably, what appeared to be a replacement for the old shed. Only, it wasn't a straight replacement. This was a shed on the grandest of scales. It had also been relocated.

'I wanted to finish the last year of my university course, but remotely, so I can still keep the lease on Manor Stud Stables going and keep training,' Will announced.

'The university is allowing me to do my third year from here, as long as I have the facilities. What do you think?'

'Impressive,' Pat admitted, upgrading this judgement to, 'Very, very, impressive,' once they'd reached the bottom of the garden.

The front of the wooden construction was dominated by a long glass facia and a high pitched roof. The building had water and electricity and was built at an angle to allow the best possible uninterrupted view over the paddocks and to the foot of the Yorkshire Wolds in the distance. Clever planting of a number of mature bushes softened the edges of the hexagonal construction and Pat noticed honeysuckle and clematis were already winding their way up colour co-ordinated trellises.

'Can I ask how you paid for all of this?' Pat queried.

'My dad,' Will replied happily, 'I'd forgotten all about it, but he'd struck a bet months ago, with one of the national bookmakers, on Catwalk winning the Albany. Arthur dug out the betting slip and we collected a hundred and sixty thousand.'

'This didn't cost…' Pat started worriedly.

Will chuckled, 'No, I got Arthur on the job. In return for using my name and Catwalk's in their advertising, we got it at a knock down price. Kitty's wins and the exposure she's got helped, of course. Don't worry, eighty percent of my dad's winnings are going into the business. Arthur has the finances all sorted out.'

Pat nodded his approval.

A generous deck, complete with outdoor furniture looked out over the paddocks beyond the garden fence. Will scampered over the deck and pushed at one of the large panes of glass at the front of the pavilion. The glass slid soundlessly across tracks embedded into the wooden floor.

Nice, thought Pat. Nothing on the floor to trip over. He considered his own back garden with its moss covered lawn, overgrown hedges he irritably hacked back once a year, the patio doors that always stuck and in particular, the bottom sill that he always tripped over, whether going in or out, and gave a little regretful sigh.

'The company I got in to build it called it a 'Garden Pavilion', but it's really my art studio,' Will called over his shoulder, heading for a coffee machine tucked away in the corner beside what appeared to be a massive steel oven. Pat detected a mixture of pride and barely concealed delight in his godson.

Standing at the entrance to the studio, Pat viewed the large, hexagonal room and its contents in more detail. It seemed to him to be a mishmash of artistic equipment; large bags of clay, stone blocks, several spools of industrial wire, and a few devices he couldn't name. He now realised the steel oven had to be a kiln. The walls were covered with sketches, randomly arranged, most of them unfinished. At the centre of the airy room, in an area where the floor was covered with several layers of plastic sheeting and cloth, two plinths were draped with white sheets.

Will finished off in the kitchen area, walked over with two steaming cups and pointed Pat to a large table outside and they sat down opposite each other.

'So, is this a social or professional call?' Will asked, taking a sip of his coffee. Pat did the same, enjoying being out in the open, with the sound of the breeze rustling the leaves of a nearby pear tree.

'A bit of both,' he admitted, 'So I may as well get the police stuff over with first.'

Pat took a gulp of his coffee and in the time it took him to replace his cup on the table and settle back into his seat; he'd studied Will across the table and come to a satisfying conclusion. There had been a definite change in his godson since the day of the Albany. He was more relaxed, not necessarily happier – no, that wasn't it. But there was an inner peace about him that hadn't been there before. Pat didn't know if his blossoming relationship with Suzie had any bearing on this, the success of the yard, with Catwalk having gone on to win a further Group 2, or simply the fact Will was no longer wasting energy despising his father. Whatever the reason, that restlessness that had always placed an edge on his godson, had vanished.

Pat cleared his throat, 'Tiffany and Lily are to be charged with a variety of offences, but… the Crown Prosecution Service can't pin a murder charge on either of them. The best we can do is your attempted murder.'

Will buried his bottom lip into his upper and remained silent. It wasn't a huge surprise.

'The hard evidence just wasn't there. We have your statement on what Tiffany claimed to have done on the night of the poker tournament, but we can't place her here at the farmhouse that night. The good news is that we have both girls for GBH on the night of the Albany and thanks to CCTV in the Ascot car park, we've got them in the vicinity of Hanover's car, and the cosh Tiffany used will help us push for another attempted murder charge.'

'I thought Ernie did that?'

Pat shook his head, his face suddenly turned sour.

'Richard Earnest Dalton has to be one of the most manipulative, sly, and downright evil old men I've ever had the misfortune to interview,' Pat said with such venom, Will was unable to take his eyes off him, 'He's been grooming those two girls to do his dirty work since… Well, we reckon he started to poison Lily from a young age, but when Tiffany, an easily manipulated, bi-polar stable lass with questionable morals came to work at the Dalton's yard, he had the perfect, evil little crew.'

'The two girls became smitten with each other. Can you believe they both refused to give any evidence against Ernie for the entire first month we had them in custody? They maintained it was just the two of them that planned and executed everything,' added Pat.

Will was now staring wide-eyed at Pat, 'Does that mean Ernie's not being charged with *anything*?'

'No. We'd got him for your Grandfather's murder,' Pat assured him, 'And it was in no small measure thanks to your Scottish mate, Mr McClarty.'

Will's frown deepened, 'Arthur? What on earth did *he* do?'

'It was Ernie Dalton's walking stick. We took it in as evidence the night we found all of you strewn around the yard in the fog. Arthur helped us link it to Jack's murder.'

Will was reminded of how Hanover had insisted upon swapping his fancy walking stick with Ernie's before the police arrived that night. Will tried to stifle a smile, now understanding why. Hanover had been planting evidence from a murder he'd witnessed twenty years previously.

Hanover had come to visit Will in hospital a few days after the Albany and explained at his bedside how pleased he'd been with Catwalk, how grateful he was for Will coming back for him at the yard that night, and finally, that he had witnessed the attack on Will's grandfather, Jack Payne, over twenty years ago. His rendition of how, as a fifteen-year-old he'd watched from under a car as Jack was being struck senseless by an unknown man in his fifties had been a tough listen.

Will didn't know how to react to Louis' confession. With his head bowed in very un-Hanover style, Louis had detailed three heavy blows to his grandfather, and how he had intervened by grabbing the walking stick-cum club from Ernie's grasp, then run away. He delivered his story in a faltering, low voice; nothing like the man Will had pigeon-holed as a successful, luck obsessed clothing magnate.

'I was just a child on my way home from school,' Hanover had impressed upon Will, 'I reacted to the situation and then fled. I doubt Jack even knew it was Ernie who hit him, it was all so sudden. I ran across to the wood on the far side of the Knavesmire, climbed a tree and didn't stop shaking for hours. I kept remembering what the killer had screamed after me: 'Speak to anyone and I'll kill you too!'

Hanover had gone on to explain that to his dismay, despite the passing of twenty years, he'd recognised Ernie as Jack's killer across the final poker tournament table. It had been one of Ernie's looks. A specific expression had sent a shiver of recollection down Hanover's spine. Ernie had scowled. Losing a hand with a bad-beat had led Ernie to bend his face into a shape that bordered on malevolence. Hanover had seen that exact scowl in his nightmares for over twenty years.

'But I wasn't sure,' Hanover had told Will, 'I had to be *sure.*'

Royal Ascot had been Hanover's chosen event at which to satisfy himself he was correct – that Ernie Dalton had been the murderer he'd come face to face with in the York racecourse car park on Ebor day in 2002. By ostentatiously displaying the walking stick to the Dalton party in the parade ring Hanover had hoped to force a response from Ernie that would confirm his suspicions.

Ernie had watched in slack-jawed horror as Hanover had twirled his murder weapon around in front of his family, and Hanover had been immediately convinced. Once his owner's prize had been collected, he'd headed back to the car park, intending to drive straight to the Malton police station. If he'd needed any further confirmation, it came only minutes later. Whilst hanging his show-stopping suit carefully inside the back of his car, Hanover was knocked unconscious by an unseen assailant. He woke to the smell of petrol, smoke, and flames licking around his ankles. Grabbing a few things close to hand, he'd scrambled out, in the process noting that the walking stick had been stolen. Fearing his assailant might be watching, Hanover had hidden under a car, just as he'd done twenty years ago. The irony hadn't been lost on him.

'I felt like a fifteen-year-old all over again,' he'd told Will, 'Lying under a car, feeling vulnerable, witnessing another tragic event. Only this time, it wasn't me who had run off with the murder weapon, it was the murderer.'

As his expensive car was being consumed by flames he'd realised that without the walking stick he had no evidence to present to the police. So Hanover had found an Uber driver willing to take him north and headed straight to Malton, intending to come clean to Will about his involvement in Jack's death and to plan what to do next. He'd been amazed to hear Ernie's voice through the fog when he'd arrived at Manor Stud Stables and walked along the walkway to listen.

Pat put paid to Will's daydreaming by rattling his coffee cup and continued, 'The walking stick was a fancy, heavy topped thing with a ring of braided silver inset into the wood around the top in a very specific pattern. That Arthur lad told us in his interview to check whether it was a possible murder weapon, as he thought he recognised the pattern imprinted on Jack Payne's face in the twenty-year-old police photos. Sure enough, the same pattern was on his walking stick and forensics found a trace of Jack's dried blood under the silver braiding.'

'Well done, Arthur. He saves my life and sends my grandfather's killer down,' said Will, prompted by Pat's encouraging smile, 'I'll let him know. He'll love the idea that all the work he did on my grandfather's murder file was worth it in the end. And I suppose I have you to thank for supplying my mother with a copy of Jack's file. I hope that hasn't got you in trouble?'

Pat shook his head.

'Ernie eventually admitted to Jack's killing, but it's taken a couple of months on remand for Lily to confirm everything about his Ebor day confrontation with Jack in the York car park. The scales are slowly starting to fall from Lily's eyes regarding her grandfather, so we're hoping to get more from her and make sure Ernie gets convicted of all his crimes. Lily seems to have been carried along with Ernie's warped plans, although it worries me that she was quite happy to watch you hang. However, it's becoming clear that it's Tiffany who had the stomach for hurting people.'

'Tell me about it,' Will stated dreamily, unconsciously rubbing his shoulder, 'So, your propensity to commit murder *is* in the blood. Makes you wonder what else is.'

Pat shot him a questioning frown.

'Just something Ernie said to Lily as they prepared to watch me hang,' Will explained, 'Presumably he thinks the same about cheating. He reckoned Jack cheated him, so that meant I was a cheat.'

The policeman didn't reply, preferring to lean back in his chair and adopt a sage expression, whilst surveying the hills in the distance. They both polished off their coffee in a comfortable silence.

Making sure not to catch Pat's eye, Will asked, 'I don't suppose Ernie said anything about what happened to Jack's winnings?'

Pat shook his head sorrowfully, 'He claims he never saw any winnings. We're assuming he took it, although he made up this fantastical story that Louis Hanover had stolen it! We spoke with Louis and of course he knew nothing about it – he was just a schoolkid at the time.'

Will didn't reply, still studiously avoiding Pat's gaze.

Presently, Pat made an excuse and got up from the table, thanking Will for the coffee. He was about to leave when Will reminded him that he'd said there were police matters, but also a personal matter he needed to address. Pat sighed heavily and sat back down.

'Now, I don't want you to feel deflated in any way,' started Pat.

He was treated to a roll of Will's eyes and, preferring to rip the plaster straight off rather than pick around the edges, he blurted, 'You shouldn't believe you're an unbeatable poker player!'

Keen to get this over with, Pat ignored Will's deeply furrowed brow and battled on, 'Your father knew you played online poker. You may not believe me, but your father could find his way around a computer. He knew how to get into your laptop and being a busybody parent, made sure you were safe, and found the details of your online poker account. When you left, a friend of yours, Davy, I think, let it slip that you were trying to raise your living costs and pay yourself through university by playing poker. So, for several months he and I set up alerts and 'friended' your poker username. So whenever you logged on we made sure we were sitting at the same tables.'

Will had become bug-eyed, his mouth open.

'Your father knew you'd never accept money from him. So, using numerous accounts and usernames, he and I systematically lost about twenty thousand pounds of your father's money to you.'

Will became aware his mouth had dropped open. He closed it, swallowing hard. He was intending to challenge Pat, but as he thought harder about that three month spell of online poker, many of his questions were swiftly rendered redundant. It had been too easy. Far too easy.

'Whenever Barney had runners at Newcastle races, he would set off early, get dropped off at Four Lane Ends Metro station and travel to wherever you were living at the time and check up on you.'

Pat rose to his feet once more, 'Don't worry, Will, there aren't any more revelations. That's my lot. But I thought you ought to know. I don't want you gambling away everything thinking you're a poker god. Your progress at the charity poker event was more by good luck than judgement!'

Will, experiencing a strong wave of emotion, managed a sad smile, but remained mute until he thought he could speak without his voice catching.

'Pat?'

'Yep?'

'Did Jack cheat at cards in order to win the free lease to this place?'

'I really don't know,' he replied with a shake of his head.

'Didn't my father discuss it with you? He knew about the lease, didn't he? He knew he had to keep my mum as the named trainer or he'd lose the yard. Did he or she know what happened at that game of cards with Ernie Dalton?

Pat didn't reply, his face crumpled with indecision.

'Come on, Pat, you must have talked about it with dad. Did Jack cheat? Was Ernie duped out of this yard?'

Pat considered his reply, choosing his words carefully. He eventually looked up, locking eyes with Will.

'Your father thought Jack was a cheat,' said Pat without emotion, 'But your mother believed there was no way her father could have cheated. There were rumours, of course... But personally, I believe Jack was clever enough to beat Ernie Dalton at cards without needing to cheat.'

Pat screwed the side of his mouth up, regarding Will once more. He seemed to reach a decision, giving a little nod, and began to speak again.

'During the investigation we went to see one of Ernie and Jack's old poker pals. The story goes that in the early-seventies, the landlord of the Black Horse in Malton held a poker game every Friday night. Jack and Ernie were of a similar age, I guess around their late twenties. Growing up in Malton, there was never any love lost between Jack and Ernie and the story goes that one night there was a poker hand where neither of them would back down. Ernie's father had just bought Manor Stud Stables and installed Ernie as the trainer in order to kickstart his training career. They reckon Ernie tossed the keys to his new yard into the pot, convinced he had a winning hand, expecting Jack to back down.'

Pat paused, glancing at Will unhappily.

'Remember, this is all hearsay, based on one chap's recollections,' he told him, 'And he was in his nineties.'

Will nodded, gesturing his keenness for Pat to continue.

'Well, Jack didn't have anything like that sort of value to cover the bet, but Ernie is supposed to have suggested something else....'

Pat paused to take a breath and his wrinkles deepened across his forehead. He regarded Will dolefully, not sure whether he should continue.

'What I'm telling you came from one of the other poker players that night. Neither Jack nor Barney ever mentioned it to me. So don't read too much into...'

Will's exasperated expression halted Pat's flow. He sighed and resumed, wishing he'd never mentioned the poker game.

'Ernie Dalton apparently had a thing for your grandmother, Lois. She'd gone through school with him and they'd dated on and off until Jack had arrived on the scene. Jack had just proposed to Lois and she'd accepted. Ernie offered Jack the opportunity to cover his bet. He said he'd accept a promissory note. The note would state that should Jack lose, he'd promise to break off his marriage to Lois and leave Malton. If he won, he'd get a free lease on Manor Stud Stables.'

Will's mouth fell open and he stared wide-eyed at Pat.

Pat added, 'Ernie was confident his hand would win. There were another five people around the table, all of them horsemen who counter-signed the promissory note once Jack had agreed to the stakes. Then they showed their cards. Ernie turned over four aces, and your grandfather revealed a running flush… and took up residence at Manor Stud Stables the following week. Meanwhile, Ernie…'

'…became bitter and twisted,' finished Will.

Pat ignored the interruption.

'…Ernie was forced to wait fifteen more years until his father died in order to take charge of the family training business. His own father was livid. He hardly spoke to Ernie for several years and never trusted him again. Didn't even make him his assistant. If this story is true, then I think it was his father's rejection of him that made him a man capable of murder.'

An uneasy blanket of silence fell upon the two men. Presently, Will cleared his throat.

'It doesn't paint a pretty picture of either of them,' he admitted, 'I never met my grandmother, she died before I was born. Do you think she knew Jack used her as a stake in a poker game?'

Pat thought for a moment, then shrugged, declaring, 'I really hope not.'

Pat took a breath before continuing.

'No-one was sure who owned Manor Stud Stables when the original yard was sold off. Jack agreed to keep the owner's identity secret, so saving them any embarrassment. Even your mother and father didn't know who they were. Your mother was adamant her father was an honourable, honest man who wasn't capable of cheating.'

'I choose to side with mum,' Will said quietly, 'And you.'

Pat gave a single, affirmative nod.

'She's not coming back, is she,' Will said unexpectedly, 'My mother... I thought Lily was her, just for one moment, in the fog. I thought she'd come back to...'

Will swallowed hard.

'Save you?' Pat asked with eyebrows raised, 'You didn't need her, you saved yourself... and Hanover. Both Mary and Barney would have been proud of what you've become.'

Will broke eye contact with his godfather and gazed beyond him, towards the Wolds. It didn't stop him missing her... and being riddled with regret over his father.

They sat in silence for a minute. Unannounced, Pat got to his feet and clapped his godson on his arm, immediately apologising when Will winced in pain. He said goodbye and wished Will the best of luck with his next few runners. As he made his way back up the garden towards the farmhouse, Pat called out that he'd look in again soon. Will fervently hoped he would. Pat was all the family he had left.

Davy, Hanover, and Suzie stepped out onto the patio just after Pat entered the house. Will heard them trade a few words with Pat through the double doors and then the three of them headed down the garden with Will in their sights.

Davy was the first to join Will, 'Look who I found feeding carrots to Catwalk?' he remarked loud enough for Hanover to hear him, 'Our favourite owner!'

'How's the shoulder, Will?' inquired Hanover, seating himself at the table.

'Getting there. How's the head?'

'Hanover chuckled, 'Tiffany didn't knock the self-confidence out of me, that's for sure. And I hear congratulations are in order for you two?'

He indicated Davy and Will with a flick of his eyes between the two men.

'Ah hah! The marriage,' Suzie joked.

'Well, that's not so far from the truth,' Davy agreed.

Will smiled, 'We're going to run Manor Stud Stables together as named trainers. Now the BHA allow joint names on the license, we're both going to be the official trainer here. Davy will continue riding, and I'll do my sculpting and we'll share the running of the yard.

'Davy was looking for somewhere to live, given the problems with his family. The Dalton family name is a bit toxic these days,' Will added.

'I was bowled over with Will's generosity,' said Davy 'Given the lease of this place caused all the mess with my family in the first place, I thought it was a great idea to co-train from here. It's a proper partnership and allows us both to pursue our chosen careers as well as manage a yard. And… it will allow me a fresh start.'

The three of them shared some small talk for a few minutes, during which Suzie drew closer to Will, squeezing his knee and nodding at him.

'Suzie wants me to tell you both that I've been teetotal for the past two months. She reckons that's why I'm less…'

'Grumpy!' Suzie concluded.

'I did wonder,' said Davy, 'Your two mates went away saying you were a changed man, but I put it down to Catwalk winning again at Glorious Goodwood!'

The conversation turned to the yard, the race plans for Hanover's horses, and Davy boasted happily about the new owners that Catwalk's winning streak had attracted into the yard. Their stable now numbered twenty-five horses. Presently, Hanover took something from his inside pocket and slid it across the table to Will. It was a cheque.

Will stared at the small oblong of paper that was in danger of being swept away in the breeze, pinning it down with his index finger. It was made out to 'Mr William Payne' for the sum of six hundred thousand pounds.

'What's this for?' he gasped, picking the cheque up and holding it reverently in both hands.

Hanover grinned, 'Call it a long overdue loan

repayment to the Payne family.'

'Yes, but this is…'

Hanover held up a hand to silence him.

'Twenty years ago I ran away with a walking stick and a Gladstone bag full of Jack Payne's winnings. I didn't know what to do with the money; I was fifteen and I was frightened that if I took it to the police they'd want a description of the attacker, and he'd threatened to come after me and kill me if I talked. I couldn't do anything with it, not until I was eighteen.'

Hanover paused and gave Suzie a wink, 'I always intended to somehow give it back, and after twenty years I reckoned if I bought some nice horses with Barney and stuck with him for a few years, that would be the best way to pay the Payne family back. You see, I hit eighteen and used Jack's money to start Roar. Although I only got to see his last moments, meeting Jack was the luckiest moment in my life. There would be no clothing brand called Roar without him. But then, my plan took an unexpected turn the night of the poker tournament when I discovered whose walking stick I'd pinched…'

'But this is a personal cheque. It's got my name on it. You're giving it to me?'

'Like I said,' Hanover said with a shrug, 'I'm just repaying a family debt. The police don't believe I was involved on Ebor day back in 2002, and I'm grateful you didn't raise the question of the missing winnings.'

'I can't accept this,' Will complained, pushing the cheque at Hanover, who point blank refused to take it back.

'You must be the luckiest man I have ever come across,' Hanover told him gravely, 'And very much like Napoleon, I prefer to have *lucky* generals rather than skilled ones. Only thing is, you're not just a lucky trainer you're a skilled trainer. That's rare. Look upon this money as my *retainer* for your luck and you're skill as a trainer.'

Hanover refused to break eye contact with Will,

watching as his trainer contemplated his words. Waiting until Will took a breath and started to shape a reply, Hanover continued with what he hoped would be his coup de grace.

'And it's also an upfront payment for the first of your sculptures I'm going to commission. So it's all above board.'

Somewhat pacified, and knowing any further rejection of the money might offend, Will folded the cheque and popped it into his pocket. He thanked Hanover profusely, who waved his words away as if it was nothing. Then Will's face lit up.

'Speaking of sculptures, I'd like your opinion of these two,' Will said, jumping to his feet and disappearing into his studio. When he didn't re-emerge, Davy, Suzie and Hanover left the table and followed him in. He was waiting beside the two sheeted sculptures in his central work area, whipping the white cloth from both once his friends were ready.

Will revealed two identical stone sculptures, each a racehorse, caught perfectly standing erect on their hind legs, their front legs pawing the sky. Their unveiling was met with an awed silence.

'I so want to touch them,' Suzie whispered, stepping forward. She looked to Will for permission and then ran a hand down one of the horse's backs, around its rump and down to its stifle, 'They're so lifelike, and the way their manes are being caught in the breeze... they're *wonderful*, Will.'

Davy and Hanover soon chimed in, with Hanover insisting Will produce something similar for himself.

Grinning, Will disappeared into the back of his studio, shocking his friends by bringing back a huge, long-handled lump hammer.

'I've been wanting to do this for years,' he told them, amused by their open mouths.

He passed between the two statues and set off back to the farmhouse, creating a furrow as he dragged the hammer behind him over the lawn, whilst encouraging Davy, Suzie and Hanover to follow.

Through the farmhouse, out into the yard, past the end stables and down the lane Will went, his giant hammer's head trailing behind him. When he reached the entrance to Manor Stud Stables he stopped and eyed the two sightless, anatomically incorrect prancing horses atop their dreadful columns, then handed the hammer to Davy.

'A new generation of Paynes and Daltons are starting over, and a new start demands a decent pair of prancing horses welcoming our owners into Manor Stud Stables,' announced Will.

Davy didn't hesitate to swing the hammer.

**Enjoyed this story?**

I do hope you have enjoyed reading this horseracing story. If you have, I'd *really* appreciate it if you would visit the Amazon website and leave a rating and perhaps a short review. Your ratings and reviews help readers find my books, which in turn means I can dedicate more time to writing.

Simply visit **www.amazon.co.uk** and search for 'Richard Laws'.

You can also register for my book alert emails and learn about the stories I'm currently working on at **www.thesyndicatemanager.co.uk**

Many thanks,

Richard Laws
May 2023


**Other Racing novels by Richard Laws**
(In order of publication)

The Syndicate Manager
Gimcrack
An Old-Fashioned Coup
A Run For Your Money
The Race Caller
Causing Interference
Cheat

**Racing and Betting Short Stories**

A Stable Full Of Winners (Collection)

Printed in Great Britain
by Amazon

24291632R00162